M

LE COLONIAL

Le Colonial

A NOVEL

Kien Nguyen

LITTLE, BROWN AND COMPANY NEW YORK • BOSTON

Little, Brown and Company

Time Warner Book Group

1271 Avenue of the Americas, New York, NY 10020

Visit our Web site at www.twbookmark.com

FIRST EDITION

The characters and events in this book are fictitious. Any similarity to real
persons, living or dead, is coincidental and not intended by the author.

Library of Congress Cataloging-in-Publication Data
Nguyen, Kien.
   Le colonial : a novel / Kien Nguyen. — 1st ed.
     p. cm.
   ISBN 0-316-28501-3
   1. Vietnam — Fiction.   I. Title.

PS3614.G89C65 2004
813'.54 — dc22   2004001416

10 9 8 7 6 5 4 3 2 1

Q-FF

Designed by Iris Weinstein

PRINTED IN THE UNITED STATES OF AMERICA

TO MY WIFE, KATHLEEN,

AND

TO MY CHILDREN, DANNY AND AMORY

LE COLONIAL

PART ONE

Faith

Empty shells, filled by many hands.
Such labor only for a glimpse of glory.
The louder you burst, the more tattered you become.
All you can ever leave behind is an echo.

— "Firecracker," NGUYEN HUU CHINH (?–1787)

CHAPTER ONE

Avignon, France, 1771

The brush was a hickory twig, its end hammered into a soft, pointed fringe. The painter drew it across the canvas, tracing a long stroke of cobalt blue — the light of predawn. Another dash, a smear, a twist of the bristles, and a cluster of areca palms silhouetted the horizon. The only movement was a blur of wind across a colony of stars.

It was the first day of winter. The inside of the church was so cold that he could see his breath in the candlelight. The painting was a rectangle of oils on sheepskin, stretched on a wooden frame. Its image resembled nothing of the splendor and immensity of the surrounding medieval architecture but was cast in the bold colors of his imagination. Hanging by cords over his wool coat was a collection of curios — fragments of broken clay pots, pinecones, a metal goblet, clumps of feathers, a bird's wing. The rest of his belongings were leaning against the wall — five rolls of unfinished paintings, sketches, and a bundle of soiled clothes.

A deep voice echoed outside the realm of his concentration. Across the room, a priest was reading from his notes to an assemblage of novices.

These tall palms, with trunks as straight and smooth as masts on a ship, have simple crowns of large fan-shaped leaves. They grow in the deep shadows of the ancient forest, surrounding picturesque rivers, mountains, and villages. I have traveled through the mysterious lands of ancient Tsiampa, visited the ruins of Angkor in Cambodia, and witnessed the vast grace and wealth of the coastal cities of Cochin China . . .

The artist stepped back and examined his work. Its balance pleased him, but it needed detail. He cleaned his brushes, fumbling through his pockets for another color, a light green with a touch of blue. He imagined a bed of vegetation carpeting the forest floor, as if anticipating the sun in the lush landscape.

Around him in the cathedral, sumptuous paintings, tapestries, and fresco murals depicted the lives of saints and angels, their faces serene under golden halos. Although it was his first time in Avignon, he knew its history. At the beginning of the fourteenth century, the Palace of the Popes had been erected as the new home for Pope Clement V after the authority of the Holy See was shifted from Rome to Avignon. Now more than four hundred and fifty years later, the palace complex was still one of the most impressive Gothic castles in Europe, an imposing fortress made up of towers linked by stone galleries. But to him, the wealth and the beauty lay in the artwork.

There in the exotic lands of Asia, the voice was reading, *I beheld the wide variety of human types, communities, and political regimes, which are unknown to the Western world . . .*

The cathedral he had chosen to work in was housed in the Tower of Saint John — the quarter that was reserved for the resident scholars. As the first pale gleam of sunlight glanced over a row of gray stone corridors, the young man shivered. His eyes were burning, his stomach grumbling, his body aching. It had been days since he had eaten a good meal or enjoyed a restful sleep. The bustling city of Avignon had little hospitality for drifters, vagabonds, and artists.

Ahead of him, a long narrow passage led to the nave. Beneath a series of tapestries depicting the martyrdom of Saint Sebastian, seminarians from many orders huddled on pews facing a black-robed priest. It was his voice the painter was listening to. Above the altar, Christ hung on a cross, carved from wood — his head bowed, his face hidden beneath a tangle of hair. It was an image that the artist had copied over and over, trying to invoke Jesus' essence.

The priest put down his notes and leaned forward, addressing his audience more personally. "You are all preparing to be ordained." His voice struck a low pitch, and its vibration rumbled in the cavernous hall. "With the conquest of heathen lands all over the world comes an opportunity for the expansion of Christianity. To novices of any order who have strong faith, I offer a chance to serve in a foreign place, along with the guaranteed reward of immortality in heaven. There will be a series of planned voyages and explorations of Southeast Asia, a pagan civilization open to conversion to the true faith. We need physicians, scientists, botanists, engineers, and artists to effect and record the dawn of the Christian era . . ."

The artist paused in the midst of his brushstroke. Those last words seemed to speak directly to him, and he saw that his intuition had served him well when he had decided to come to this place.

The ghostly dawn poured in through rows of stained-glass windows and bathed the statues. Along the walls, the fresco murals absorbed the light, and the figures within their panels seemed to breathe. The artist coughed. The seminarians turned their heads and whispered in one another's ears. A round-faced youth wearing the brown robe of the Benedictine order looked him up and down. The lecturer rapped his knuckles on the dais to regain their attention.

In contrast to his impressive voice, the priest's body was slight. His thin dark hair, combed back from a high forehead, failed to cover his balding crown. From within two gaunt sockets, his eyes captured the sunlight's golden hue yet reflected none of its warmth. As he spoke, his lower jaw revealed a row of uneven, yellow teeth. Everything about him, from his features to the simplicity of his cassock, reminded the artist of portraits of suffering saints from a bygone era.

A hand from the audience rose. The priest acknowledged a young man in the second pew.

"I pray of you, Monsignor de Béhaine," said the novice. Most of his face was hidden under the hood of his robe. His clear voice suggested that he was in his early twenties, slightly older than the artist. "Please tell us more about the geography of these places that you are talking about. I've never heard of them."

The priest tilted his chin forward and addressed the student. "Very well. Brother João, have you heard of China?" he asked.

"Yes, sir. It is a country east of India."

"Excellent. Now, imagine, just below China, along the edge of the South China Sea, which is part of the Pacific Ocean, a land three thousand kilometers in length. We call this land Annam, and the people who live there are the Annamites or Annamese. Theirs is a primitive but ancient society. For the last few hundred years, a civil war has divided this country into two separate kingdoms. The North is called Tonkin, while the South is Cochin China. Both of the kings were anointed when they were mere children, and so the two countries are ruled by high-ranking nobles, who are known as vice-kings."

He paused, allowing the seminarians to digest the information. "It took me some time to understand the many ways in which their culture differs from ours. If you decide to accompany me on my next voyage, I promise that you will gain more knowledge about the world than you could ever read in a book — that is, if you could ever find one that is written about these undiscovered lands. Who among you has the hunger for adventure and the dedication to faith required of a missionary?"

The room fell silent. Even the saints on the walls seemed to avert their eyes.

The monsignor chuckled. "Here in Europe we have been blessed with true religion. A priest must be above reproach because he represents God, and also because others on Earth are so lost in their paths that they need guidance. It is now our obligation to rescue the savages. Nothing must be allowed to stop us from carrying out our mission."

Another silence followed his remarks. The same novice stood, pulling back his hood. He was a handsome man with dark features. "What dangers should we expect to face if we join you in your mission of glory?"

De Béhaine squared his shoulders. "The East is a strange and mysterious place," he said. "Starvation is prevalent. Natural disasters are frequent. And death is commonplace. The natives do not believe in our God. Doubtless, you will be embarking on a very dangerous assignment."

Brother João mused, "Then, dear sir, should we risk our lives?"

"You should, and you must," the priest replied. "Because it is your duty as a priest to serve God's kingdom and the Mother Church. Your life is not yours to keep. It belongs to our Heavenly Father."

He adjusted the pin on his right shoulder, which held his ankle-length silk cassock together. A large crucifix was suspended by a thong from his neck and tucked into the folds of his sash. He looked out again at the audience and saw that the painter had disappeared down one of the many corridors. All that was left where he had stood was the canvas he had been working on, placed on a bench next to a flickering candle.

The assembled crowd followed the monsignor's look. Decorum forgotten, the novices murmured at the image before them. The monsignor rapped his knuckles on the dais again, but the sound was lost.

De Béhaine stepped down from the altar and marched toward the painting. He forgot about his sermon as he lifted the sheepskin by its frame. The paint was still wet.

The monsignor took in the scene of mountains and palm jungles. The strength of the young man's brush had turned the silent landscape into successions of broken curves and angular turns. The river's pale blue water foamed where it passed through cliffs and emptied into a grassy ravine.

The monsignor laughed out loud in satisfaction. The artist, with his perceptive skills, had created a distant world with amazing accuracy.

"Silence!" he commanded. "Does anyone know the painter who left behind this canvas?" He held the picture above his head so everyone could see.

"The Church allows strangers to come and go as they wish," answered Brother João. "We do not know who that was. He could have been a vagrant, coming here to seek alms and refuge in the church's sanctuary."

"No, the technique is much too sophisticated for a vagabond," replied de Béhaine. He lowered his voice. "Whoever he might be, he is certainly an educated man. This painting is not a gift. I have no doubt that I will meet that painter again."

CHAPTER TWO

Monsignor Pierre Pigneau de Béhaine retired to his room after supper. A copper urn, hanging from the wall on an iron armature, glowed with red coals. The evening was harsh, with a bitter wind. Gray shafts of light wafted over the Rhône River like faint smoke. Looking from his small lead-glassed window, he saw a monk striding across an open meadow toward the cobblestone roads of Avignon. The lantern in the man's hand sliced the night like a golden blade.

The Tower of Saint John was steeped in frosty stillness. The Benedictine priory where Pierre was lodging was a low, dark fourteenth-century structure with a church on one side and a cloister on the other. With the sanction of Pope Clement XIV, he, along with other pioneers, had traveled to the major cities to recruit missionaries from various orders for journeys to the Far East. Now, for the final stage of his mission before returning to Annam, the monsignor had come to Avignon.

For three days his efforts had yielded few results. All over France, his arrival was preceded by stories about the persecutions of missionaries in the Far East and, in some cases, their martyrdom. The newly consecrated priests listened to his sermons with fear and skepticism. He did not understand their reservations. After all, another Jesuit, Alexander de Rhodes, who was a native of Avignon, had brought the Gospel to Annam a hundred and fifty years ago. And the Portuguese mission to these uncharted territories had been in place for two centuries. *Why are these novices so ignorant and afraid?* In the early days of his priesthood, the monsignor had been driven by his thirst for adventure and a total devotion to his faith, a devotion that seemed to be lacking in younger priests. Their unresponsiveness frustrated him.

Across the monsignor's throat ran a scar, purplish and embossed like the tattoo of some primitive tribe. In an absentminded gesture, he touched its rough surface. He often explained to his audiences that it was the seal of God, inflicted by an Annamite lord — an indelible testament to his Christian convictions. Unlike the Mother Church, Pierre did not believe in assigning priests to the missions, even though he himself had been chosen for the Far East at the seminary where he studied. He would rather accept a body of explorers who volunteered. In his experience, those with courage and tenacity had the best chance of success.

He listened to the murmurs of the night — the seminarians' snores through the thin walls of their cells, the opening and closing of the front entrance, and the scratching of rats on the wooden beams — all reassuring sounds to him. He liked the solitude and calm confinement that allowed him to be alone with his books. He was compiling notes for an Annamese-Latin dictionary for the next generation of missionaries.

Few suspected the truth: the monsignor harbored little affection for Annam. His expeditions were to fulfill a higher purpose and responsibility, first to Louis XV, king of France, who was in desperate need of new colonies to augment his wealth. France had already lost India to the English, and China was too ambitious an undertaking for the monsignor to contemplate. Annam, with its modest size yet immense assets, weakened by its prolonged civil war, promised to be a vulnerable target. If Pierre could establish a lucrative outpost in Annam, the country's riches would help restore the status of the Society of Jesus, which had lost favor with the king and Parliament in recent years.

His secondary devotion was to the Church of Rome. It was a central tenet of Catholic doctrine to spread the words of Jesus Christ and baptize heathens. Europe, as Pierre saw it, had been tainted by Protestantism, which had been incited by the devil himself, Martin Luther. The monsignor felt that he had been chosen to sow God's truth in the new territories of the Far East. There were many difficulties and hardships, but Pierre took comfort in knowing that he had been among the first explorers. Salvation, like all things of value, could only come at a high price, and this alien land would be no exception. No other Western beliefs would compete with his master plan.

A knock on the door pulled him from his thoughts. He lit another candle and neatened a few stacks of books on the floor before opening the door. A gray-haired Benedictine monk was waiting on the other side. The monsignor squinted into the dim hallway as the monk raised his lantern to expose his face.

"Monsignor de Béhaine, you have a visitor," he grumbled. Before the priest could reply, he leaned closer and whispered, "This one insists I announce to you that he is an artist. Be careful, Father. You know they are all thieves."

Pierre lit a knowing smile. "It's all right, Brother Angus. I'm expecting him. Let him in."

The monk shuffled away, irritated at being disturbed from his sleep.

A figure stepped from the darkness — the painter from the morning sermon. He was about twenty, with thick eyebrows and deep-set eyes that receded into the shadows. He shifted his belongings from one shoulder to the other. Looking beyond the monsignor, the artist caught sight of his painting, which Pierre had propped on his desk. A faint smile appeared on his flushed face.

"You came to retrieve the art piece, I presume," said the monsignor.

The artist shook his head and attempted to say something, but stopped. He rubbed his hands together, and Pierre noticed that his fingertips were discolored with paint pigments and dirt. The monsignor opened the door wider and stood back. The presence of another person made him aware of how small his cell was. He beckoned.

"Enter!" he said. "You will be more comfortable inside."

The copper urn emitted a steady glow under a thick layer of ash. Its light fell on the boxes of books he carried with him on his travels. The room's heat had made the pages curl at the corners. The artist let out a groan of pleasure, thawing out his muscles in the warmth of the coal brazier. His cheeks were crimson. He covered his mouth to stifle a cough. Pierre offered the only chair to his guest and settled himself upon a wooden crate.

"In this cold," he muttered, "staying close to the hot coals can help protect the lungs against pneumonia. Do you feel better?"

The young man nodded, still clutching his bundles.

"I am Monsignor Pierre Pigneau de Béhaine," he said. "And, sir, what is your name and title?" He leaned back, studying his guest.

The artist regarded him steadily. "My name is François Gervaise. As you can see, I am just a humble painter with no title."

Pierre watched the artist scratch his head. The thick chestnut hair was pulled back in a braid.

"Remove your coat," he said. "Put down your possessions. Be comfortable!"

François glanced at him from under his eyebrows and unbuttoned his coat. "I am sorry for choosing such a late hour to visit. If you wish, I can return at another time."

"Don't be ridiculous!" the priest said. "You're already here. I have been studying the painting you have left behind. That is what you wanted me to do, is it not?"

"What I want is to get out of France," blurted François.

Pierre barked a laugh of astonishment. "And you think I can help you? Monsieur Gervaise, I don't know how you came to that conclusion. How did you learn about me, or my lectures, or my planned voyages?"

The artist looked back at him with blue eyes full of expectation. "At the Carthusian monastery of Val-de-Bénédiction."

"Oh, the charterhouse. Is it located across the river, in the town of Villeneuve lès Avignon?" asked the priest with a vague recognition.

"Yes, sir. There were three monks who worked as almoners, feeding the hungry in one of the cloisters every afternoon. Your adventures have made you a man of legend. I overheard their conversation about you two days ago."

Again the monsignor laughed, rising from his seat. "Listen to me; I am a missionary, not a sea captain. I only recruit priests." He reached for the door handle.

"Please, let me explain," François persisted. "You need an artist to capture the beauty of the lands you travel in and to chronicle your work. Remember the reaction of your students when they saw the painting? My art can help them experience the same excitement you once had. For that, you'll need my assistance."

"Ah!" said the monsignor, narrowing his eyes. "So you have thought of everything to your advantage, even the response from my students. But have you thought about the dangers of these missions? The natives often react violently to intruders. You could be shunned, tortured, or even murdered."

"Every day I confront the same risks here in France."

The priest lowered his voice. "Monsieur Gervaise, you don't act like an ordinary vagabond. In fact, you seem intelligent and calculating. Tell me, why is it so important for you to abandon this country? What are you running away from?"

François slumped in his chair, looking down and tapping his foot against the stone floor. "We have just met," he said. "I would rather not speak in detail of my past. All you need to know about me is my talent, and that I am a good and honest person. I can be of use."

Pierre turned his gaze to the nothingness outside his window.

Even though he was just thirty years old, he knew how to use his poise to seem older. He enjoyed intimidating others and taking control of conversations. "Then why should I believe in your goodness? So far you have shown me only that you are a troubled soul."

The guest coughed as he traced a crack in the wall with his fingernail.

"Are these your drawings?" the priest asked, reaching for the artist's sketchbook.

Without asking permission, he turned the pages, going through them with the tips of his fingers, discarding each sheet of paper on his bed as if he were sorting through a deck of cards. The room was silent except for the rustling of the pages and the crackling of the coals.

"These are the work of a talented artist," he said after a moment. "Where did you learn such technique? Who was your teacher?"

"My skill has been largely self-taught."

The priest responded with a look of doubt.

"At the age of sixteen," added François, "I was introduced to Monsieur Jean-Baptiste-Siméon Chardin in his apartment at the Louvre and was fortunate enough to be invited to attend his master class."

Pierre was taken aback. Chardin was, in his opinion, one of the finest painters of his day, although unappreciated by the Royal Academy because of his simple subjects. He remembered seeing one of the artist's early works, a painting of a youth playing with cards.

He cleared his throat. "Monsieur Chardin has the support of many wealthy patrons, including His Majesty King Louis XV. How can you, a drifter, claim the company of such an illustrious individual?"

François's only answer was to continue tracing the invisible pattern on the wall. Pierre's patience was fleeing.

"I have a strict policy," he said. "Because you cannot answer my simplest questions, I will not be able to accept you. What kind of missionary would you be if you cannot be forthright with your superiors?"

"In due time, sir, I will."

"Time is something I have very little of. Soon I will be leaving this seminary. If you have anything to say, tell me now. As a priest I am bound by God to keep my silence when it involves a confession. Are you a Catholic, my son?"

"Yes, I am," replied François.

"Then tell me who you are, where you came from, if you want to join me."

The artist gathered his drawings from the bed and stacked them back in the sketchbook, saying nothing.

Pierre dismissed his guest with a wave. "You are a fool!" he said. "I can no longer be bothered with your nonsense."

François's face darkened with defeat. Leaning forward, he muttered in dismay, "Please, wait." With downcast eyes, he said, "Bless me, Father, for I have sinned. It has been two years, four-and-twenty days since my last confession. I was born in Villaume on the thirty-first of October. The year was 1751."

Under the flickering light of the candles, a smile tugged at the corners of the monsignor's mouth. He reached under his pillow for the wooden box that held his Bible.

As François uttered the words that led to his past, shame flooded his soul. The artist had come to visit the priest with one hope in mind — escape. He had believed that his talent would be enough to impress the monsignor. But now, although the priest was expressing interest in his sketches, he realized that to achieve his goal, he must give up a part of himself.

François was in despair. Before he arrived in Avignon, he had been struggling to find the barest necessities of life. All the changes he had made seemed to lead him in a downward spiral. He was elated to be inside a warm room and hated the prospect of returning to the bitter cold outside.

"Villaume," said the priest. "Where is it?"

"Sir . . ."

"Don't tell me," interrupted de Béhaine. "I've heard this name before. Is it between the towns of Saint Gilles and Beaucaire, in Nîmes?"

François nodded. The sound of his village's name coming from the mouth of a stranger made him realize how unprepared he was to confront his past.

"I was born in Villaume," he repeated. "As an infant of about a week, I was abandoned in the stable of Saint Mary Magdalene Priory and was discovered by one of the priests. That was the only home I knew in all my twenty years. There in the church I was fed, clothed by the parishioners, and educated by Father Dominique, who was both my guardian and teacher."

An expression of pain gripped his face. He grabbed his coat in one hand and his possessions in the other, strapping them over his shoulder. "I have told you enough," he said, rising to his feet. "I can't say any more. What kind of priest are you if you turn away a needy soul like me?" He flung open the door.

Before the monsignor could recover from his accusing words, François disappeared into the dimness of the hallway. The whooping sound of his cough lingered.

CHAPTER THREE

*T*ime began its torment once his guest departed. Alone and dreading the next six hours of darkness, Pierre tossed on his cot. He knew the routine of insomnia so well. It had first troubled him in his old bedroom when he was ten, the evening his mother had died, and it had returned to disturb him every night since. Here in another unfamiliar room, when the light faded into obscurity, he again became that bereft ten-year-old.

His cell was warm, and the night, through his half-closed eyelids, was an undulating indigo in which he was sinking. In this viscous space burned the red shadow of the urn, so dim he seemed to be staring at the sun from deep within a pit.

He had gone to the Far East at the age of twenty-four, and had lived in India, Siam, Kampuchea, and Annam. Six years ago, under a cluster of bamboo by the edge of a rice paddy, he had built his first mission, a bunch of mud-drenched, thatch-covered huts. The image of the Annam that he knew merged into that of the painting created by the drifter. He marveled at how accurate it was for someone who had never set foot in a tropical terrain. Could some intuitive bond between them have provided the artist with such keen vision?

Soon Pierre would be traveling to the Far East again, leaving the winter behind.

He turned to one side, his eyes squinting shut as he tried to trick his mind into drowsiness. If he achieved two hours of sleep tonight, he would consider himself fortunate. Often, he masked his frustration by conducting predawn sermons, seizing the opportunity to ridicule any monks or novices who were unable to keep awake. He regarded those who overindulged in sleep as grave sinners. He knew his suffering showed clearly in the dark rings under his eyes and in the lethargic way he moved.

Pierre ran his fingers under his pillow to search for a crude wooden box. The unvarnished texture was familiar to his touch. On the lid he felt the metal crucifix fastened next to a faded inscription. In the box he kept a small Bible, a rosary made from olive pits, and a few unopened letters from his brother Joseph. These were the only possessions that remained from his past.

Home was a comforting word that soothed his mind with tranquil images. Many a spring day he had sat on the doorstep of his house on the outskirts of Origny watching his brothers and sisters play in the meadow. Once, behind the rows of apple trees, he had spotted a pair of young lovers, their colorful garments showing through the green leaves like ripened fruits. Curious, he observed them. Their passion made him wonder about his own sexual apathy. For as long as he could remember, he had felt no interest in women nor courted any from them. Something inside him seemed radically wrong; he believed it was his heart. Instead of love, it harbored only resentment, and most of it was directed toward his father, Doctor Abraham Pigneau de Béhaine. His mother's body was not even cold in the grave before there was a new bride in the house.

When Pierre decided to leave home at the age of seventeen, his family's governess, Mademoiselle Émilie Tournelle, had already been Madame Pigneau de Béhaine for more than seven years and had borne five more offspring for his father, including a set of twins. Pierre needed a change in his life. Enrolling in L'université théologique de Paris was his way to escape the infirmary, a household full of noisy children, the country life, and a woman who every day attempted to erase his mother's presence with her own offensive traits. He knew that if he allowed the memory of his mother to dissipate, he would retain nothing of his spirit. He would become an empty shell, a walking corpse among the living. With all his will, he kept alive his belief in the heavenly world where his mother was now dwelling.

As the day for his journey to the seminary drew near, the atmosphere in his family had quieted to a deceptive calm. Dr. de Béhaine, still tending his duties in the somber, rustic hospital, hoped his eldest son would come to his senses and accept his rightful place as the heir to his father's profession. But no miracle intervened. The doctor accepted his son's decision with ambivalence. He did not hold the Church in the same esteem as Pierre did. But what was happening to his son was now a private matter between the boy and God, and even a father could not enter that realm.

Pierre remembered the galloping of horses on the cobblestone pavement, the fresh scent of a spring morning, and three of his siblings — Theresa, Mary, and Joseph — pressing their faces against the kitchen window. He also recalled the way he had forced himself to be polite and not give in to his feelings as he bade Godspeed to his father and stepmother.

In Paris, Pierre used his newfound freedom to submerge himself in his studies. Slowly, like the winter in Origny, he grew icy.

The next dawn, he conducted his sermon in the Tower of Saint John. Pierre paused in the middle of a sentence and squinted above the students' heads. There was an empty space in the dark opening of the corridor where the artist had stood the day before.

François Gervaise and his painting weighed on the monsignor's mind. He could not deny the impression the drifter had made on him, and on the novices. Why couldn't he captivate his audience the way a simple painting had? The artist added a new element of turmoil to his already restless mind.

His words flowed as he sped through the lecture. Phrases leaped from his mouth as if to catch up with the time he had wasted. He was preaching with such fervor, he wondered if he had gone mad. In his excitement, he raised his voice and stretched out his arms. Over the last bench, where the air still seemed heady with the odor of wet paint, all that he looked at became bright and colorful, full of promise.

He must find François Gervaise and confront him. Talent alone would not be enough to stir the heart of Monsignor de Béhaine.

Pierre decided to start his search at Villeneuve. The city's reputation for generosity, unlike that of Avignon, attracted the poor. Most of them would congregate at the charterhouse of du Val-de-Bénédiction for a free noonday meal. François, with his distinctive bundles of canvases, wouldn't be difficult to spot in a crowd.

It took the monsignor a half hour to cross the river by ferryboat. He could see his destination at the foot of Fort Saint André, behind the Tower of Philippe le Bel. Back across the Rhône, Avignon was a cluster of Gothic castles wrapped in an amber bed of foliage, unfurling like an exaggerated sunflower. The winter in the south of France, although milder than the season in Origny, was still bone-chilling. The long stroll in the blustery wind tightened Pierre's legs and cramped his muscles, but he refused to rest. He walked faster, until he came to the entrance of the charterhouse.

The structure was one of the largest Carthusian monasteries Pierre had ever seen. It comprised a church and three cloisters as well as forty monks' cells, or so he had been told. Every building within the compound was constructed of limestone, with a tile roof. In addition to the resident priests in their simple black cassocks, at least a hundred people scurried about. Lay brothers in brown robes mingled with servants and workers in coarse breeches and layers of sleeved vests. He felt conspicuous in his Jesuit uniform, which often drew negative reactions because of the order's poor reputation.

When Pierre entered the chapel, the Carthusians' wealth was evident in the gold, marble, and paintings that lined the walls. Most of the frescoes depicted the life of Saint John the Baptist, as did the painted wood panels covering the windows — those that had escaped the damage of time. The luxurious vision lifted Pierre's spirit. Looking farther into the sanctuary, he marveled at artistic renderings of the miracles of Christ, the feast of Hérade, and the decapitation of Saint John. He roamed through the building, projecting an air of confidence that discouraged others from approaching him.

After passing through several manicured gardens, he exited the vestibule of the monastery where the public gathered, and strode into the sacred cloisters and living quarters of the monks. No one was in sight. His footsteps echoed down the stone galleries. He regretted not having asked the way to the kitchen. After he went through a series of colonnaded hallways, he detected the pungent aroma of grilled meat. Somewhere in this maze, the monks were preparing the only meal of the day.

At last he found the kitchen, a small square building attached to the north walk of the cloister, with smoke rising from a shaft in its roof. The morning was approaching midday. The rusting iron latch on the kitchen door was within his reach, but he hesitated to open it. The Carthusians were a strict order of contemplative monks, and Pierre was not sure how he would be received. In a clearing to his left, he spotted a group of more than fifty people, mostly women and children. They, too, were lured by the scent of stew.

Look at those faces. He had seen so many like them at the Saint Roch hospital where his father had worked. Despair glazed their eyes and dimmed their spirits. Hunger draped them like a blanket. Any acts of mercy showered upon them would wash away unseen, for they would never be able to change. He remembered helping his mother distribute food to the sick when he was a boy, but pride and duty were stronger in him then because of her presence. As time passed, he could no longer summon that sense of pure kindness, and he relied instead on his commitment.

The artist was not among this group. But it was still early, and more people were coming. Pierre decided to wait. The wind chilled his fingers and the tips of his ears. He put on his white gloves, pulled the rounded crown of his hat past his ears, and sat on a patch of grass under a leafless tree. A few paces away, four little girls picked tiny yellow flowers off the ground with their dirt-stained hands. He watched them fasten the blossoms in the folds of their clothes, a gesture that was more mechanical than playful. No laughter came from their lips.

He wondered whether these children had been baptized.

He caught a flower between his gloved thumb and forefinger. A milky juice oozed from the broken stem, creating a brown stain on his glove. The withered yellow petals fell to pieces under his touch, releasing a smell of fresh mud. The girls looked up in surprise, and one of them offered him another blossom. In the community of beggars, he felt out of place. All his life, he had been an outsider: his family, the whole world — everyone — seemed to be standing on one side of the road and he on the other.

No one spoke. The adults stared at Pierre.

"Go on, take it," the little girl said, thrusting the flower forward. She brushed a lock of brown hair from her eyes. She wore a stained dress made of rough gray fabric, and she was shoeless despite the chill. He saw that her face, like every exposed part of her body, was filthy. He received her gift, using both hands and carefully avoiding touching her.

"What kind of flower is it?" she asked.

"*Dent-de-lion*," he answered. "See how the petals resemble a lion's tooth?"

The girl said, "If you are waiting for food, you must get in line like everybody else. And don't ask the monks for meat in your stew unless you have money to pay for it."

Her mother pulled her away. Pierre started. He suddenly understood why everyone was staring at him. *Not because I am a Jesuit. They all think I am trying to get ahead of the queue.*

"I am here to look for someone," he said. Rising from his sitting position, he addressed the adults. "Does anyone among you know a man — a young artist around twenty years of age? His name is François Gervaise."

Only silence ensued. Pierre spoke louder and added a more commanding tone to his voice. "Anybody know a wandering artist named François Gervaise?"

A woman spoke up. "I know who he is. For two sous, I'll take you to him."

CHAPTER FOUR

After leaving Monsignor de Béhaine's room at the Tower of Saint John, François returned to the street. The city was asleep, submerged in blackness. A torch crackled in his hand, emitting only a small circle of light to guide him. In the distance, a dog bayed at the moonless sky.

François staggered and trembled. His teeth were chattering, but he could do nothing to stop them, for the shivering came from deep within his bones. The road seemed to stretch endlessly ahead, weaving between the pine trees that grew at its sides.

He missed the warmth of the monsignor's cell, the stacks of books and papers, and the wet, sweating stone walls. How he had wanted to collapse on the wooden bed, to battle his illness under the heavy woolen blankets. He had hoped the monsignor would offer to let him stay. But to earn the comfort of the charcoal brazier, he would have had to surrender the secrets that he had buried so carefully. Even through confession, he was not ready to relinquish them.

A few miles from the Rhône River, François found the only shelter he could afford: a deserted stable in the wooded area outside Villeneuve. Such enclosures were common — huts of twigs and thatch, with mounds of straw on the floor. As the city and its churches grew in size, new facilities had been built closer to the monasteries, leaving the old structures to decay with the weather. They became the homes of cripples and beggars, or sometimes served as secret hideaways for outlaws. François chose a cabin that was nearly hidden by a stand of tall firs. The roof had caved in, so he rested in a corner under the hayloft.

Among the dry leaves and hay, he sprawled on his back, then realized he was not alone. A rhythmic panting in the next stall indicated that a whore was plying her trade in the same makeshift shelter. A drunkard slurred encouragement to her moans. All François could do was clutch his head and allow himself to melt into the chilly debris.

His fever persisted, intensifying through the night. His head was throbbing, his eyes blurry, his tongue encrusted. On his cheeks he could feel two burning patches of flame. The attacks came in waves, flooding through him. His strength ebbed until nothing was left but a constant burden of self-pity.

He had no way of escaping the guilt of his misdeeds. Only he was to blame for the troubles that had torn him away from the paradise that once was his life in Villaume. His past haunted him, from the bittersweet childhood incidents to the most recent hapless event. How sublime his former ignorance had been! The most blessed thing of all was to have an identity and a station in life. It brought tears to his eyes to think how he had lost everything. If only he had shown more strength of character.

The moaning of the whore blended with the wind. He noted that a curtain hung from the spindles of her stall; this was why he had not realized her presence when he'd first stumbled in. He wished he could block out her pretense of ecstasy. But unlike his fever, her throes of feigned pleasure followed no pattern or frequency, and he believed that when her heavy breathing faltered, it was to disguise a yawn.

The whore's insincerity was obvious. But he remembered a woman who was far, far more deceitful. He dared not think of her. But it was too late! The sound of her name was already bouncing inside his skull like an echo. *Helene! Helene!* He remembered the branches of an oak tree reaching to her bedroom window, forming a natural ladder that he had climbed many times. On the last occasion, he had seen the orange glow from the flickering candles that lit her room, through a curtain of leaves, through a layer of lashing rain . . .

The grunting quickened.

"Damn you, she-devil!" he roared, feeling the veins jut from his temples. "For heaven's sake, cease your beastly noise!"

"Now, be good, my pet," coaxed the whore from across the stable. "Pay heed and you may learn something."

Her companion guffawed.

Again her voice screeched through the night. "Oh, God, oh, God, oh, God, please take pity on me."

The gale howled, and the prostitute's curtain whipped against the stall's outer wall. François closed his eyes, and the image he carried in the depth of his soul rematerialized. He grew rigid at the scene being replayed in his mind. Through the beckoning window of Helene's bedroom, the candles danced to the rhythm of the wind. Two naked bodies entwined in her bed, their skin rosy in the fire's glow. She was lying on her back, looking straight at François. The expression of bliss on her face turned his stomach sour . . .

Above him, the trees murmured. The frosty stars that pricked the black sky winked at him. He reminded himself that he must rise above his suffering and make his heart devoid of feelings. He dozed fitfully, drifting in and out of consciousness until a blaze of light penetrated his eyelids and made him wince.

He awoke. His body was shivering. It was early afternoon. A few black crows were flying high in the sky. From where he was lying, they looked like floating crosses. Around him the forest was silent, and he had no way of knowing if the whore and her customer had left or were merely sleeping.

He rolled to one side and propped himself up on an elbow. Dizziness made him nauseous. He swallowed a bitter taste rising to the back of his throat. A violent heaving twisted his innards, and François vomited until he felt he was drowning.

Oh, God, oh, God, oh, God, please take pity on me! his mind cried, mimicking the prostitute's wail. The blue air above him faded.

As he slipped into the gray abyss of nothingness, he heard the voice of the same woman. "Is this the artist you are looking for, Father?"

He was melting. His body was a river of paint. Where its current took him, there was no concept of time. But the fright was overwhelming — choking him, spreading until he was nothing but a tiny particle in a vastness of pure terror. For each drop of water that was dribbled on his tongue, for every gentle touch of a wet cloth over his lips, his stomach would expel bursts of bitter bile in response. A hand was massaging his back. Its heat was like fire, scorching him.

A flash of lightning illuminated an image. He saw Helene's heart-shaped face, the thick waves of light brown hair that cascaded down her shoulders, her high cheekbones — he gasped. In his fevered consciousness, she represented everything that was lost. The lightning had revealed her entwined with her lover in her bed. They turned to look at him through the open window of her bedroom, through the gushing rain that blurred his vision. He was unable to move. The man on top of Helene ceased his rocking motion. In utter panic, she clutched her limbs around his glistening body. And then something struck the side of François's head. Hot wax sprayed his face, but he could barely feel the heat. He saw her reach for another candle.

I gave you all my love. Why are you doing this to me?

Go away! Her shout drummed against his face, the language dripping with poison. *This is how it has to end. My love for you is over. I am no longer amused by a boy's inexperience.*

Soon his ears were filled with the whispers of strangers. It seemed other people were coming and going, talking to him and about him. He tried to listen to their words. The voices coalesced and dispersed until all became one, belonging to the Jesuit monsignor. It sounded far away, distorted, and strangely elongated. *François* . . . He heard the hissing repetitions of his name, full of entreaty and despair. *Pray, pray! François! We beg mercy in His glory, forever.*

The blur in his mind abated, and his delirium took physical form. The whispers became dark shadows of people moving swiftly against a wall. Of his whereabouts he was uncertain, but he could see that he was lying on a simple bed in a dimly lit, high-vaulted, cavernous tower. A black curtain shielded him from the rest of the hall. His body seemed light. *François* . . . The whisper returned; then the voice materialized.

"Very glad to see you are recovering, François Gervaise."

He turned and beheld the face of Monsignor de Béhaine, like parchment suspended in a wan halo of light. Behind the priest, the window was curtained, but through a small opening, a few sunbeams poured forth a sliver of radiance. The monsignor towered over him. François burst into tears.

"Where am I?" he asked between sobs. His thin shoulders shook like the wings of a chick. He realized that he was without clothes. From under the bedspread, he caught the odor of his own excrement.

The monsignor seated himself on the windowsill. He removed his white gloves and pressed them neatly across his knee. Then he rolled up his long sleeves. François could not see the expression on his face. His voice, however, was gentle.

"We are inside the charterhouse of Val-de-Bénédiction. The city is suffering an outbreak of cholera. You are being quarantined for observation." He scanned the room and added, "And so are they. For many of them, death is very near."

"How long have I been here, Father?" asked François.

"Three days! I did my best to stay by your side."

François wept into his hands, overwhelmed by the attention the priest had reserved for him. "Dear sir, you should not have risked your life to save mine. I am not worthy of your concern," he said.

The priest leaned forward and rummaged through a casket that was set against the wall next to him. From it he drew forth a glass bottle of colorless liquid and poured some of its contents over his arms and hands. The smell of vinegar exploded in the air.

"Through these hands of mine," the priest said, "God has performed many miracles. Your survival is just one of many. Since childhood I have been blessed with the power to heal. With the angels in heaven watching over me, I fear nothing. You would not believe, sir, what deep solace it gives me to see you well. But you must be exhausted. I shall leave you alone to rest, as there are many others in this hall who need my services. We can talk more when I return for a visit this evening. One of the monks will bring you a basin of water so you can wash yourself. I have retrieved your belongings and placed everything on the floor next to you. The clothes you were wearing had to be burned, so you will need to put on fresh garments.

"In your delirium many times you shouted out a name in great distress. Helene!" A twinkle of malice crept into de Béhaine's eyes as he leaned forward and read François's expression. "She must be someone important. Who is she, Monsieur Gervaise? A ghost of your unruly past, perhaps?"

Without waiting for François to answer, he put on a wide, stiff-brimmed hat and walked away.

The hall was silent except for an occasional moan. No doubt the others were also lost in frightful dreams.

He cursed his vulnerable condition. How much of himself had he revealed during his delirium? How much of his shame was made public? François rested his head and again felt himself drifting away. The images materialized in spite of his effort to repress them. He could see the tile rooftop of a roadside inn, shimmering under a summer sun. He approached the stone structure, noticing the tall gables and ornate details that blended against the bright sky . . .

Stop it . . .

François could not stop.

The laughter and music drifting through the inn's thick walls stirred in him a longing that felt almost like homesickness. It was a harmless memory. It did not make his heart ache when he decided to enter the building through the back door near the kitchen. He knew he would find her there, an attractive woman a few years older than he. A large loaf of bread nestled against her bosom. The crust, honey-colored, emitted a scent of baked yeast that made his mouth water. He stared at the bread and the girl. His mind was vacant, but his stomach rumbled out loud.

I am Helene, daughter of the innkeeper . . . She lowered the bread, and he could see more of her chest. He had never seen skin so beautiful so close. He looked away and caught her stare. She had large, sky-blue eyes capped by neatly shaped brows. Her gaze seemed to penetrate his mind and expose his thoughts . . .

François moaned. The memory he knew so well faded, losing its sharpness. It was like watching his life reflected in a lake. One touch and everything that had once been real was swept away in the ripples. When the calm returned, another scene rose to the surface.

What must I do in order to escape her bewitching stare? He could live a thousand years and would never know the answer. He fought the urge to cling to her feet like her shadow. She reached for a sheet to cover her nakedness. A few paces away stood his rival. François turned his head to stare directly at him.

Get out! Her voice was devoid of sympathy.

I can't! Tell me what I have done to cause the loss of your affection.

The sound of her laughter made François furious. He looked up as the other man stepped forward, brazen in his state of undress. His flaming red hair and dark umber eyes matched the fire behind them. The stranger reached into the pile of his discarded clothing and grabbed an iron dagger, which he shifted back and forth from one thick hand to the other. François could tell he was an experienced fighter. Even his grin was intimidating.

Are you brave enough to challenge me? said his rival.

Helene quivered with laughter. Her hand pressed against his chest, forcing him to retreat. He could feel the open window and the rain against his back. She looked at him. Both her hands were on his body as the sheet slipped, forgotten, to the floor. The black circles of her irises dilated. And without a word she pushed with all of her strength.

Caught off guard, he fell out the window. The tree's branches embraced him, breaking his fall . . .

François sat up. His body was bathed in sweat. The monsignor, like a statue, stood in front of him. His black robe was invisible against the dark curtain.

"Why are you here?" he asked the ghostlike vision.

The monsignor looked at François. "The monks have always considered this chapel to be one of the holiest places in the south of France. Luckily, I am an acquaintance of Abbot Beaufort, the superior of this charterhouse. Monsieur Beaufort is a friend to poor people. You are here as his ward, and I am here to watch over you."

A look of guilt passed over François's face. "My sickness has caused everyone a lot of trouble, especially you," he said.

The monsignor shrugged. "It is my duty to serve God readily and without consciousness of merit. It was He who desired to save you. Your recovery shows that the Lord has reserved some holy purpose for you. In this matter I am just a simple priest, chosen to carry out His divine plan."

"What is His purpose for sparing my life?"

"Monsieur Gervaise, as a child, I once prayed to God for a personal request. I asked Him to save the lives of two people I held dear in my heart: my mother and my brother Joseph. At the time, both of them were fatally ill. My prayer, however, was answered only in part. It was my brother's life that God chose to spare. There is no need to ask why the everyday miracles in our lives happen the way they do. When it is time, the Lord will reveal to you the purpose of His action."

The monsignor sucked his teeth and then continued. "It is now my obligation to offer you a position in my missionary work. You once sought me out to express what I believe to be the most beautiful of Christian virtues: your sublime devotion to God. I have decided to accept your offer of service."

François grabbed his bedcover and pulled it closer to his chest. "Thank you for your praise," he said. "But I am not as noble as you have asserted. I only wished to partake in the most exciting adventure one could hope for. However, sir, in our last conversation, you demanded a confession of my past . . . I must admit, my view on the issue has not been changed."

The monsignor sounded almost scornful. "When a person is gravely ill, he is forced to meet with his own conscience, to listen to his own heart. Monsieur Gervaise, if you insist on protecting your past from confession, then I will respect your wish. I will not ask you to discuss it again. When you choose to do so by your own free will — and believe me, that day will come — I shall be willing to listen. Now, are you well enough to walk?"

"May I ask where we are going?"

"To Avignon. The Tower of Saint John."

CHAPTER FIVE

François drew back the curtains and surveyed the infirmary in which he had lain for three days, delirious with fever. Having washed and dressed himself, he was eager to get his bearings. He saw that his bed was near an entrance. To his right, a large marble basin containing holy water projected from a pillar. Patrons' fingers, through time, had eroded the rim of the stone receptacle, forming a smooth indentation. A white stone staircase rose at the far end of the great hall. These were the clues that had led him to believe that he was in the charterhouse's main chapel. The floor was bare dirt, warmed slightly by the thin rays of sunlight that crept through a series of small windows near the ceiling. The earthy scent failed to mask the stench of illness that surrounded him.

He saw lines of wooden beds, row upon row, covered with grass-filled mattresses. Four or five bodies occupied each bed. Unlike his, most beds had no sheets or blankets, probably to avoid the expense of laundering them, but the crowded conditions helped keep the patients warm. Priests and monks hovered over them, their voices creating a wordless murmur. The faces of the ill were like naked skulls, absorbing the shadows, and he wondered if his face looked any better. Locks of long hair no longer brushed his shoulders, and he realized that his head had been shaved.

The stench of burned fat permeated the hall. It took him a few minutes to realize the odor came from the cremation of the dead. He wondered if these unfortunate souls would be allowed to enter heaven's gates without a proper burial.

He could still feel the shadow of death reaching for him, like a tree root seeking water. All he had been before, all the memories he had carried with him and all the past that had created him, was no longer significant. Although weak, he was aware of his five senses. Thoughts and sensations flooded him until he was left trembling with the sheer joy of being alive.

The monsignor stood leaning against a wall, rubbing his nails with a vinegar-soaked cloth. He observed François with the patience of a hunter.

François gathered his belongings, a routine that had become habit in his life as a drifter. As soon as he untied his bundle, he saw that his clothes were folded more neatly than he'd ever left them.

He felt a pang of panic. How much could someone learn about his past by looking through his meager possessions? He glanced up. The monsignor calmly kneaded his fingers against the cloth. Only his faint smile acknowledged François's questioning gaze.

Searching under the layers of fabric, François felt rough leather against his fingertips. Without looking, he caressed the first of the items he had sought: his private sketchbook. This was not the same collection of illustrations de Béhaine had seen; those depicted people, nature, sleepy villages, and the architecture of cathedrals. Instead, the contents leaped to his mind's eye: the private pictures of Helene, her graceful nude poses, her face, her gestures, the swell of her breasts and her derriere, all of which had once consumed his every thought.

Turning his back to obscure his movements, he untied the strings that bound the cover and took a peek at the pages. Her eyes painted on paper, blue and detached, stared into his. Every sketch seemed to be intact. The images stirred his feelings with an intense mixture of relief and pain, for he was happy to have retained the sketchbook, but also felt that he would never again love anyone or anything as completely as he had loved her.

Trying to keep his mind in focus, he rifled through the rest of his things. Again, he searched for an item of importance.

Someone in the next corner was gasping. Two male nurses mounted a wooden device over the patient's mouth to pry it open while the third poured in a thick, black liquid, forcing him to swallow. He could hear a priest intoning a prayer in Latin over the sputtering sound of struggling lungs. The stone walls of the tower echoed the moans of unseen patients, the rattle of tin jars and basins, the squeak of heavy litters carrying still bodies. Like the others, he had been brought to this place of quarantine to die. Although he did not understand why he had been spared, he knew clearly that his destiny was not to be one of them.

His fingers grazed a leather pouch, and he felt relieved — until he opened it and found it empty. It lay at the bottom of his knapsack, gaping open, as if leering at him. *Who could have stolen that cursed dagger? A thief? A priest or monk? Or could it possibly be the monsignor himself?*

The dagger's absence shook him with a mix of feelings — terror, rage, excitement. The image of the knife hung foremost in his mind, its shape, the keen double edges, and the handsomely engraved family crest on its handle. For as long as he could remember, it was always sharp and shiny, ominous, valuable, and ready to strike. He had never held it for any purpose other than honing the blade or staring raptly at the handle, which resembled an Egyptian ankh. The family crest was outlined in emeralds and a ruby, along with two carved columns, one made from black ebony with the initial *E* on it, and the other of white ivory with the initial *C*.

To hide his preoccupation, he asked, "How did I get here? How did you find me?"

"After you left, I went to search for you," replied the monsignor as he smiled down at him. "For a few coins, a whore led me to you. She was your neighbor in the forest shelter. I'm sorry to say she died yesterday afternoon. You are fortunate to have survived."

François stared into his sack. Without looking, he could list every article inside it. The linen shirts and woolen breeches — the finest of his clothing — took up the most room. Next to them were a few pairs of knitted stockings, some towels, a tin cup to hold water, writing paper, paintbrushes, and some vials of colored powders that he mixed with linseed oil to make paint. There was no sign of his dagger. But to ask about it would invite the very questions that he had been trying to avoid.

"That poor woman," François said. "May God have mercy on her soul."

"Shouldn't we go?" asked de Béhaine.

"Yes, I am ready," said François, swinging the bag over one shoulder to mask his reluctance.

A blast of wind blew out the candle in de Béhaine's hand. The hallway that led to the side exit of the infirmary was gray and chilly. The monsignor took a monstrous key and inserted it into the keyhole. Inch by inch, the two men lifted the oak bar that hooked through paired brackets. When they cracked open the heavy door, the outside air assaulted them. François shrank back. The sun pummeled him with a thousand fists, shocking him as they mounted the steps to ground level.

Two pairs of guards, dressed in the abbot's bright yellow livery, jumped to attention at their appearance. They drew their muskets and held them in shaky hands.

"Halt! By whose permission do you leave the house of the plague?" the tallest guard near the entrance barked at them.

"Do you know who I am?" said the priest, removing his hat.

The guard lowered his musket. "Monsignor de Béhaine, I didn't recognize you. Who is your companion?"

"Never fear, my good sir," said the priest. "I assure you that none of you will catch any contagion from this gentleman. He has been blessed by God and is being released with the permission of Abbot Beaufort. Let us pass!"

His confidence reassured the guards, who fell back.

François took a few steps. He felt as feeble as an infant.

At the end of a gravel path, a hooded carriage drawn by a pair of chestnut horses waited. Its door swung open. The horses tossed their heads and neighed. François blinked away a sunbeam that bounced off the carriage's window.

The same gray-haired monk who had brought François to the monsignor's room stepped out of the coach. His cheeks were pink from the cold. He and the monsignor acknowledged each other with slight bows.

"This is Brother Angus," de Béhaine said. "He will take you back to my cell in Avignon."

"What about you, Father?" François asked. "Are you not coming with us?"

The priest shook his head. "I have a few matters I need to attend to. When I return in a few days, we shall meet again. In the meantime, Brother Angus will look after your needs."

Still light-headed, François accepted Brother Angus's hand. He crawled into the carriage and sat next to the window. The springs swayed, and he had the sensation of floating in time.

The old Benedictine monk crept in next to him.

The rocking motion of the trip lulled his senses.

Resting his head against the window, François watched the trees that slid past him. The wet grass, crushed under the iron-rimmed wooden wheels, gave off a fresh odor. He was silent, conscious only of his breathing. Except for a small tremor where the side of his face bumped against the door frame, his body was barely aware of the journey. A monotonous rhythm caressed his limbs, making him drowsy.

He wondered about de Béhaine. The monsignor's guarded nature prevented him from displaying any hint of friendliness. His black tunic and the broad rim of his hat concealed all his thoughts. François had sought more than once to make eye contact during their conversations, but all he encountered was a vague, undefined smile.

Why had the priest left him so abruptly after putting so much time and care into nursing him back to health? They were both strangers in Avignon; François a drifter and the priest on a mission to recruit new disciples. There seemed to be no reason for de Béhaine to take a new journey at this time unless it pertained to his search for more priests. But if that were the reason, why should he leave the papal palace, where most of the Christian activities were centered? Or could it be that he had rejected François and moved on?

"Is it wrong of me to ask you the whereabouts of Monsignor de Béhaine?" he asked Brother Angus.

"No, why should it be? On the contrary . . . But why do you ask me? Hasn't the monsignor told you his itinerary?"

"I didn't think of asking him," replied François. "He appears so preoccupied with his missionary work that I was reluctant to bother him. Where did he go? Will he soon be coming back to Avignon?"

The monk adjusted the cushion he was sitting on. "I believe . . . ," he said, "the monsignor mentioned that he is taking a two-day trip to Villaume."

François gasped. The missing dagger. His village. The priest's self-satisfied smile. Suddenly everything made sense. Villaume would be the best place for de Béhaine to gather information about his past. *If I were in his position, I would have done the very same.* François's nails dug into the palms of his hands.

"I need to find him!" he cried.

A chill made him shudder. His ears were ringing. The throbbing inside his head threatened to return in full force.

"Monsieur Gervaise, are you well?" came the monk's voice. His hand reached for François's shoulder.

"No!" François sprang out of his seat. "I must stop him from going to Villaume. That is the way!"

The monk stuttered, "W-what do you m-mean?"

"Halt! Halt!" He jutted his head out the window and shouted at the coachman. The driver hauled at the reins, and the wagon came to a halt.

"Get down!" he barked at the stunned man. And to the monk, he ordered, kicking the door open, "You, too, get out!"

At the first touch of the whip, the horses bolted forward, charging in unison on the hard-packed dirt. The main road to Nîmes was simple, and he had traveled it once before. The trip to Villaume would take almost an hour. Far on the horizon, across a large field where the sun was looming in a haze, he could see the village's outline. Nature's cool breath was on him: the odor of fresh air. The path beneath him was a melting gray that reminded him of a river, flowing in the opposite direction.

The road became more rutted, and the wagon swayed on its wheels. The horses galloped at a steady speed. François held tight to the reins. His muscles were taut, as if he were flying instead of riding. He watched every group of passersby and studied their faces as he overtook them. Some of the women glared at him, annoyed at his recklessness. His mind was frozen on one thought: he must prevent Monsignor de Béhaine from entering Saint Magdalene Priory.

He saw a dark shape on the side of the road. Even from a distance he recognized the familiar black-robed figure riding on the mare. The animal was moving at a slow canter. With a shout he charged closer, pulling alongside and then advancing past the rider before he made a sharp turn to block the road a few paces ahead. His carriage skidded as the wheels locked. He fell back in his seat, gasping. Out of the corner of his eye, he saw the monsignor, looking on with his usual knowing expression. It was as though he had been expecting him all along.

"So, Monsieur Gervaise, you decided to find me," said the priest. "Are you ready to deliver a confession? Or should I hear about your past from your guardian, Father Dominique, the superior of Saint Magdalene Priory?"

"Father, you leave me no choice in this matter," replied François bitterly.

"I must know what kind of man you are, and understand your nature, before I can employ you." The monsignor reached inside his robe and retrieved the bejeweled dagger. The sharp blade quivered with the reprimanding tone in his voice. "The crest of this stiletto belongs to a noble family. How can a vagabond like you possess this valuable weapon? Is thievery one of your sins?"

François cringed at the priest's accusation. "I'm sorry," he said, sobbing.

"Did you steal this dagger?"

He gasped, "Worse than that, Father. But before I tell you, please answer me this: would you employ a murderer to carry out God's sacred work?"

His question tugged a furrow across de Béhaine's forehead. "It is not the law of man that I am concerned about," said the priest. "It is the wrath of God and the eternal damnation of our immortal souls that terrify me. Whatever of God's commandments you have broken, whatever grave mortal sins you have committed, even though you may think you are beyond redemption, our Lord is a just and forgiving God. Confess to me, and I shall give you absolution."

François remained silent, his eyes shut. Another sob broke from his lips — a wounded cry of pain and regret. "Please do not enter Villaume," he begged.

"You must give me a reason not to."

Tears fell on François's cheeks. "The mention of my name could be enough to kill Father Dominique. My disgrace is a heavy burden on his frail shoulders. Please do not trouble him."

"Enough of your evasion," the priest shouted. "Stop this dance of deceit and tell me the truth."

The mare skittered.

François was being swept away by the priest's force of will, with no strength to retaliate. "As you wish," he said. "That dagger in your hand belonged to my rival, Vicomte Étienne de Charney, son of the governor of Villaume. You can see the vicomte's initial carved in its handle." He looked away and lowered his voice. "I killed him in a duel. It was an accident, but he died — all because of my selfish indulgence, led blindly by a licentious woman. I keep his weapon as a reminder that I have lied, fornicated, and taken a life. Because of these crimes, as well as the anger of de Charney's family over the loss of their firstborn, I was forced to abandon all that was dear to me in this world: my childhood home, the monastery." He covered his face with his hands. "So you understand my reckless effort to leave France and begin a new life elsewhere."

The monsignor dismounted from his mare and extended his open hands.

François jumped to the ground, grabbed the priest's fingers, and buried his tear-streaked face in the sweaty palms.

"Hush," whispered the monsignor soothingly. "Be still, my son, and let us pray for your sins."

François nodded without looking up.

The priest intoned, "Dear Lord, I am very sorry to have offended Thee."

François repeated the words.

The prayer continued. "For Thou art infinitely good, and sin is revolting to Thee. I firmly pledge, with the help of Thy grace, never to disappoint Thee again and to do penance humbly and sincerely, from the depth of my soul."

He lifted François's chin and stared at him with his honey-colored eyes. "By the rite of confession, I grant you absolution of your immortal soul. Will you wholly submit yourself to God? Will you become His shepherd, a painter for God, secluded and shut apart from society until you are ordained? Will you rescue the souls of others and turn God's house into a temple of beauty?"

François nodded. "I will."

"Then I shall send you to study discipline and virtue for the next two years at the University of Avignon. As soon as you complete your education and are ordained, you will join me. I have no fame or fortune to offer you. What I can give is the single most valuable secular gift our Lord has granted me: freedom. Once you step onto the soil of Annam, you will be free to perform God's work in whatever way you see fit. You can travel to any Annamite city, accept novices, teach the Bible, serve the Annamese king as a counselor, or even join in his army — anything to wrest Annam from impiety. My son, your choices are endless. Through your hands our Lord's magic shall prevail."

François wiped the tears from his eyes and said, "I am glad to have heard you speak so candidly. My mind is clear now. Take me, Monsignor. I want to go."

"You may join my next expedition to Annam," announced de Béhaine. "But first you must be ordained a priest. As a missionary, you must swear allegiance to the pope, as well as undergo questioning as to your fitness for this mighty undertaking. It is, I must warn you, an extreme vow, not for the weak at heart." He raised his voice. "*Iustum necar reges impius* — it is just to exterminate impious kings, heretical governments, and barbaric rulers."

"When will your next voyage be?" François asked.

"My son," said the monsignor, "there is more. You will be taught to act the dissembler: among the Roman Catholics you are to be a Roman Catholic. Among the Reformers, to be a Reformer; among the Calvinists, to be a Calvinist; among the Protestants, generally, to be a Protestant. You must obtain their confidence to gather information for the benefit of our order as a faithful soldier of the pope. For without the shedding of blood no man can be saved."

The severity of his words dampened François's enthusiasm. "But would God desire bloodshed?" he asked, sniffing.

"The pope is the vicar of Christ — the purest form of the divine in human flesh. A true gentleman needs nothing more but to give his word. You have shown your sincerity. Now it is my turn to show mine. I have a good friend who is the captain of a sailing ship called the *Wanderer*. It is now January 1771. You have much to do to prepare yourself to leave France. You must be in Marseille by May of 1773 to embark on this ship. I will arrange for everything, including your passage. I need new missionaries. You have a choice, my son, either to join us in an adventure that few have dared to dream of in an unexplored world, or to return to the streets and paint your insignificant pictures. The next time we meet, I hope it will be in Pondicherry, India. That will be our intermediate stop on our way to our holy mission in Annam."

And so, on the moss-covered path that led to Villaume, François surrendered himself to God.

CHAPTER SIX

Paris, 1772

At the age of thirteen, Henri Jacques Monange had already acquired the habit of looking back at his life. In a few short years, he had accumulated more experience than many could in a lifetime. Often, his memories were saturated with despair, but he had learned that the best way to overcome his disappointments was simply to accept his fate.

The decision to entrust himself to destiny had proven its merit, considering that the events of his life had always seemed beyond his power to change. Like many before him, he had been preordained to a lifetime of destitution. Born in Geneva as the oldest of seven children, he became the only surviving child at the age of ten. None of his siblings lived beyond a few years.

Henri's family descended from the Auvergnats, who originated in the volcanic mountains known as Plomb du Cantal. His father,

Maurice Monange, devoted his life to the occupation he had learned from his forebears, that of a coal merchant. When Henri was still a young boy, he too was taught the skills of the trade.

The sole possessions of his family consisted of a farm cart harnessed to a horse and a barrel in which to store coal. From these meager tools they earned a living, coming to Paris by way of the Allier River and the Briare Canal to sell wood as well as coal. Afterward, they would return home to begin the migration all over again. The difficult journeys wore away at his father's health, like the rust that ate through the yoke of his family's cart.

One night, as they entered the city, the temperature had dropped more steeply than usual. The winter came early that year. The winds, blustery and penetrating, whipped at their tattered figures, searching for what little skin was exposed through the holes in their cloaks. Henri, then twelve, walked between his parents behind the wagon, their bodies shielding him from the squall. His frozen fingers gripped the cart's handles, and he let himself be drawn along by the weary horse. The streets were so rough that wooden planks had been thrown down to provide smoother access. Far away in the mist, their destination, the boulevard du Temple, was dusted with snow, silent and empty except for a few passing beggars.

In a small clearing outside the Hôtel Dieu, the hospice for the poor, a man sat on a bundle of rags near a small torch, a heavy club in his hand. He stood up to search their faces, lingering on Henri's mother's. Henri watched as she sank farther into the shadow of her cape.

"I cannot allow all of you inside," the man said. "The place is overcrowded, and the rule is that only sick people are welcome. The child and his mother can enter as they wish, but there won't be any room for you." He jerked his bearded chin at Henri's father.

The boy felt his father's hand against his back. In the still night, the horse rasped through its flared nostrils.

"Go on in," his father said, baring his teeth in a forced smile. "You've been walking without rest for days. Get some sleep. Besides, I must stand guard over our barrel of coal."

"No," his mother replied, shaking her head. "We stay together."

"Don't be stubborn. Think of the boy and sleep well, for me too." He pushed them toward the warmth of the building.

His mother took off her cape and spread it on the wagon, making up a bed.

"Roll under my cloak when you lie down to sleep," she said to his father; then she turned away, pulling Henri along with her.

The man stepped away from the entrance to give them admission. He whispered in Henri's mother's face, "Welcome to the Hôtel Dieu. But don't forget that you now owe me a favor." Henri could smell the alcohol on his breath.

Without waiting for them to respond, the man threw his scarf over his shoulder. Henri could tell that under that thick layer of wool, he was smiling as they walked past him.

Inside, the dwelling was packed with vagabonds. Some twelve hundred beds were occupied by more than five thousand people. Many sat on their haunches, propped upright in their ragged clothes and stacked against one another to keep warm.

Henri and his mother poked around in the forest of human limbs, hoping to find an unoccupied space to rest. At last they were forced to bed down beside the dying and the dead. A dozen or so corpses had been sewn up in sacking, piled in a heap near the entrance, where they waited for the morning pickup. From there, in the shelter of the carcasses, Henri could look out a window at his father, who was positioned behind the barrel of coal. The guard came in a few minutes later, humming. Recognizing them, he walked over and wedged his boots between Henri and his mother.

"What do you want from us?" his mother asked.

Henri could hear the weariness in her voice as she sat up from her reclining position.

"I come to ask you for the return of my favor," the man said.

He ran his club along her blouse, tracing the outline of her breast. A grin deepened on his face.

She shrank away from his touch. "I don't have anything to give. That is why we came here to find refuge, for the sake of my son."

"Leave us alone," Henri whispered. "Or I'll fetch my father."

"Why don't you just do that?" the man asked. "Or better, why don't I just throw the two of you outside?" Turning to Henri's mother, he said, "For your son's sake I gave you both a place to sleep. You don't have anything to give? What I want won't cost you a sou." He crooked an eyebrow at her.

His mother sighed.

"Do not look at me," she said to Henri. "Turn to your side and go to sleep."

He turned away. His eyes were wide open. The man gave a hollow laugh before he hovered upon her. His cloak spread like the wings of a gigantic bat and swallowed her in its pouch. Their bodies pressed against the mountain of body bags. She did not resist him.

Outside, Henri's father's gaunt face melted into the darkness, but there seemed to be two drops of water where the eyes had been, mirroring the sky. The winds howled. Snow was falling in earnest, rippling across the streets in soft, fluffy clumps like raw wool. Henri watched the shine in his father's eyes grow duller as sleep came, even as he endured the rocking of the sacks that he was leaning against. The guard's panting mixed with the incessant coughing throughout the room. An odor, like pig's urine, stung his nostrils.

The next morning, they discovered the frozen body of his father, wrapped around the barrel of coal in a final attempt to safeguard the goods. He had died sometime during the night, at the age of thirty-two. His wife's cloak was clutched in his still fingers.

Unceremoniously, the dead man was thrown into a sack and buried in the paupers' cemetery at Clamart. Henri's mother sprinkled the grave with quicklime, and then they went to the market and sold the coal.

Without his father's strength, he and his mother were forced to abandon the hard labor of transporting fuel. For a few months they lived off the money from the sale of the coal, renting a room on the second floor of a cheap hotel on the rue de Lappe, commonly known as the "Street of Crime" among the residents. The dingy, derelict alley was home to an assortment of foreigners, common laborers, and thieves. Many of its ground floors served as shops, bistros, and rudimentary cafés, selling coal and wine not only to the locals but also to the bourgeois of neighboring precincts.

Henri was all too aware of their dwindling savings. His mother had been ill ever since the night they had spent in the Hôtel Dieu. She spent most of her time in bed, wheezing and coughing into a handkerchief. No longer was she able to bake bread in the stove or boil soup in her iron cooking pot. They hardly talked to each other. At night, when he caught her stare in the dark, he would look away, wrapped in his father's cloak instead of a blanket and pretending to be asleep. He could not forgive her for accommodating the guard, and he blamed her for his father's death. Silently, he mourned the loss of his father, but he would not share that grief with her.

To further avoid his mother, he was obliged to eat in the cafés, and this was much more expensive than having his meals prepared at home. He indulged himself sparingly, realizing in desperation that his growing body was getting longer and lankier. But he was not the only one who was being tormented by a food shortage in the city. Thousands of laborers were unable to support their families. The winter wore on, bleaching the city white with snow.

By late January, most of the populace of the rue de Lappe was suffering from hunger, the death toll escalating. The animals that were left outdoors endured the same destitution. Often, in the morning, when the city workers raked through the streets, Henri would help them load the carcasses of dogs, cats, and birds onto their hand-drawn carts. One day, he added his beloved mare to the heap of the winter's casualties. The frost had grayed her eyes to the same dullness he remembered seeing in his father's not long ago. As hungry as he was, the thought of eating her flesh was repulsive to him.

In the third month of their stay in Paris, Henri announced to his mother that he would begin a new career as a water carrier. He needed her help to pull the wagon. The same barrel they owned could be cleaned out and used as a vessel to bring fresh water to the rich households, where it would be sold for bathing. Paris was inherently grimy. For his new trade, the demand appeared high.

But there was much that he needed to learn about the water business. Quickly he discovered that the water carriers fell into two categories. The first group, the more successful and wealthy Auvergnats, had their own wagons and horses, which could haul eight to nine hundred liters per trip. They also paid an official to reserve certain fountains so they would not have to wait in long lines. The less fortunate would have to be satisfied with two buckets of a few dozen liters per day, which they attached to a yoke and carried over their shoulders.

At first the sight of the long queue of people outside the public reservoir was shocking to him. The men bundled in their leather and fur coats resembled a trail of animals coming to the river for a drink. With his cart, he stood in line, waiting for his turn at the tap. To pass the time, the laborers gossiped about opportunities to obtain work on the sailing ships that were exploring the New World. According to the older men, the fastest-growing city in France was Marseille. Even though Henri had never heard the city's name before, he listened with keen interest, allowing his imagination to come alive.

The waiting drove him mad, and he could not conceal his anger. Mostly he was furious with himself for not learning about this work sooner. He could have saved some money all those wasted months. The rage inside him mounted, pulling him deeper into loneliness.

Drawing and selling water grew difficult. The city was overrun with wretched souls like him, all competing for the same business. The rich consumers took advantage of the water carriers' plight by demanding higher levels of service. For a few sous, they wanted their baths delivered with heated water, and if one drop were to spill, the carriers would be penalized.

Each morning up and down the boulevard du Temple, men

and women clad in rabbit pelts dangled pails of water over their shoulders. One after another, they bellowed the familiar street cries to attract the customers' attention, *Oia! A l'eau!* Each syllable was sung from deep within their diaphragms, guttural and resonating so that the invitation could travel all the way to the top floors.

Henri, with his hands clasping the handles of his pushcart, followed the stream of people as they sidestepped mounds of ice that sparkled like broken glass. In spite of the cold, beads of sweat dotted his forehead. He had gotten used to the weight of the barrel. His body grew stronger and taller, and he no longer needed his mother's help with the cart. How many months had it been since they migrated to the city? Twelve, maybe fourteen, he could not remember. It did not matter. Every time he pushed his wagon down the boulevard, his loneliness reminded him that he did not belong in Paris and never would. The gloomy buildings threatened to close in around him, and the shadows of merchants lurked like wolves under the scant rivulets of sunlight. He kept a fast pace, his eyes focused on the splashes inside the barrel, and his mind clung to joyful memories of the days when his father was alive.

But Paris was not always an intimidating place. There were days when the crowd did not bother him as much, and delivering water was in fact exciting. He especially enjoyed the mornings when Madame Leyster, his favorite customer, took her bath. The young wife of a busy wigmaker, she was one client he always desired to see, and the thought of her would make him smile behind the brim of his felt hat.

Over the months, he learned her disposition. He did not mind her habit of haggling over the full price of three sous to fill her tub. One Christmas, she hid money in a pair of green wool socks and gave them to him as a present. These he wore with great care underneath an older pair of stockings so that they would not get ruined. They made him think of her — the soft fabric rubbing against his feet, suggesting the velvety texture of her skin. The sensation got so overwhelming at times that he felt he would burst with longing.

At the turn of the street, Henri hoped to see Madame Leyster on the front stoop of her home. He would prefer to approach quietly rather than shout for her attention in his cracked adolescent voice. He shuddered at the thought of how absurd he must sound. She had made fun of him before. As a result, he avoided conversation, only speaking when he needed to. Despite his attempts to modulate his tone, his traitorous voice, without warning, would shriek like the crowing of a rooster. Sometimes the pitch would get so high that it became inaudible.

Her house came into view, one of the few that had been converted from wood to a stone foundation and brick walls to protect against the risk of fire. No one was in the clearing outside the front door. He ventured closer, and around the shutter of a small window, he saw her. She sat behind the glass panes, using a pointy tool to try to replace a clump of hair in a wig. Red flames roared in the fireplace. The sun shone through the glass, but its weak rays faded before the aggressive fire. He watched, marveling at how the heat had ripened her cheeks until they glowed, before he tapped a finger on the window, grinning.

Madame Leyster looked up from her seat. A white snood pinned at the top of her head restrained her hair, but a few golden strands, a shade darker than Henri's, escaped to trickle down her breasts. Her sharp face wore a frown, but her large brown eyes were so innocent that it looked as if she had stolen them from a baby. She didn't seem to recognize him. He pointed at the barrel and grinned again. They were only a few steps away from each other.

"What is it?" she asked. Her voice sounded small behind the thick window.

"Madame, your bath," he said, keeping the words short and simple.

A hint of recognition appeared on her face.

"Has it been one month already?" she asked, examining her nails. "My hands are not yet dirty."

As if to prove her point, she pressed her palms against the window to show him. Between her fingers, he could see the discoloration of grime, but he was not about to argue with her.

"I'm sorry, Madame," he said. "I'll come again next week."

He pushed the cart away from her house.

"Hey, Auvergnat boy, wait!"

She glided through the room to meet him at the entrance. Her red underskirt dragged along the path, hiding her feet.

"How much heated water do you have?" she asked.

Henri stepped away from his wagon, at the same time lifting the heavy covering behind the barrel to reveal a copper pail of simmering water on top of a small stove.

"Thirty liters," he said, and thought, *If you wish, I could make more.*

"Then what are you waiting for?" she said. "Carry the water to the basement and prepare my bath. You remember how I like it, don't you?"

He had memorized every detail of her bathing habit. He knew how to pour just the right amount of water in the tub so it would not spill when she submerged her body. He learned to place the hard soap with soda — the scented kind from the Mediterranean coast that smelled like a field of hyacinths — on the floor within her reach. Now, as he stood near the bathroom door, he could hear her moans of pleasure coming from the other side, the water splashing. Through the gap under the door, steam escaped in fragrant wisps, a good indication that the temperature had met her satisfaction.

He inspected the bathroom door. It had a crack in one of the corners, the dark rim gawking back at him. His common sense told him to leave. When a lady took her bath, he had no right to linger. But the basement was empty. There was no one in sight, except for a small yellow cat taking a nap. Its furry body was stretched out by the foot of the stairs. He knew that as long as the cat slept undisturbed, he was safe.

Excitement and fright shot through his body. He held his breath and crept closer to the door until his cheek brushed against the rough surface of the unfinished wood. It was a tense, feeble grope for the right angle, but eventually his eye found the crack. Inside, the mist was heavy. He looked. And his mouth went dry.

For a moment, he thought he saw Madame Leyster soaring through the air. Her white blouse, the bodice, and the scarlet skirt rose through the fog, floating as though she were dancing. The writhing figure twirled and trembled like a ghost, stopping his heart. Then he saw the clothesline that held the items suspended in space and realized he was seeing just the garments, not her. Even so, the rippling air gave them an eerie aliveness.

He heard her soft voice, humming. In the middle of the room sat the large tub, made of wood and bound with hoops like his barrel. He saw her fair body steeping in the water. Her back was to him. Her lovely blond hair was wrapped inside a cap. He could see the glistening drops trickle down her long neck. Like nectar from a lily, he thought, and clenched his fist.

At the bottom of the stairs, the cat gave a muffled yelp, but Henri was too preoccupied to pay attention to it. Madame Leyster raised one of her elbows high so she could clean the fuzz in her armpit. He was drawn to the swell of her left breast, heavy and thrusting. The ring of her nipple deepened from the heat; its erect knob quivered in response to her vigorous scrubbing. He tried to take a breath, but something lifted the back of his coat, choking him.

What happened next was over in no more time than it took to blink. Henri found himself pulled upward by the nape of his neck. His body dangled a few inches off the ground.

"Emmanuelle," the husband yelled. "This idiotic water boy is watching you bathe. Such filthy animals, these Auvergnats."

He could feel the collar tighten around his neck, and his fingers fumbled to loosen its grip. All he could think was how disappointed Madame Leyster would be when she discovered his lewd act. He could hear her screaming from behind the door. The wigmaker puffed. He was a large man, and everything about him was oversized, including the odor of garlic on his breath.

He could no longer hear water thrashing in the wooden tub.

Instead, he registered the sound of wet bare feet slapping the stone floor; then a small object struck the door with a hollow sound, followed by a loud thud and a scream that modulated into a muffled, painful whine.

Still struggling to breathe, he watched the bathroom door shake with each blow from his kicking feet until it flung open. Her husband spun him around, and the cloak ripped away from him. He fell, sagging on the ground as his hand came into contact with the bar of soap on which Madame Leyster had slipped. She lay on her back, naked except for the parts that were covered with her hands. One of her legs was bent at an odd angle. He saw the pointed tip of a broken bone jutting through her skin, and underneath, a small pool of blood spread from the wound. She was looking at him, her eyes glassy with agony.

The excitement he had felt as he spied on her was now overwhelmed by shame. He was trying not to think of the terrible consequences of his act, of the husband's condemnation: *filthy animals, these Auvergnats.* He wished he could disappear like the steam from her bath. Desperation spurred him to spring up and run toward the stairs. The wigmaker did not stop him, nor did any of the servants. No one reacted to Henri's escape because all attention was riveted on Madame Leyster's broken limb.

He ran through the streets. Mounds of snow loomed like anonymous graves that had been sanitized in quicklime. He did not stop until he reached his home. He ascended the two flights of stairs and wept silently before he entered the little room, wishing the tears would wash away some of his humiliation. But he could not shed the memory of Madame Leyster's haunting expression, and the way her brown eyes had turned icy when she stared at him.

He found his mother by the window, her blanket drooping to the floor. For the past months, she had spent most of her time sitting there. The frost etched new wrinkles on her gaunt face, turned her lips blue, and made her hands tremble. He wondered whether she had seen him running and crying through the streets.

"Forgive me, Mother," he said. The words flew faster than he could think. "I must leave Paris at once, and I cannot take you with me. You have to go back to the Hôtel Dieu and wait for me. I will return in a few months."

"Are you in trouble?" his mother asked.

He replied to her query with silence.

"Why can't I go with you? I don't want to go back to that place."

The responsibility she placed on him felt like an iron yoke around his neck, cutting into his windpipe. "You have no choice, Mother." His voice was uneven. "You're ill, and I can't take care of you anymore."

She winced as if he had struck her. Without a word, she handed him the cloak of thick, felted wool that had belonged to his father. He put the coat on, fastening it tight under his chin and pulling the hood well forward to cover his face. They left the apartment in a grim mood, heading toward the Hôtel Dieu.

Silence gnawed at them, interrupted only by her convulsive coughs and sporadic murmurs. He avoided looking at her. At the Hôtel Dieu, under the scrutiny of the same watchman, he pulled her shawl closer around her shoulders. She tried to kiss him, but he averted his head. If he showed his mother any love now, he knew he would be trapped in this place with her forever.

"Go inside, Mother, where it is warmer," he whispered.

She clutched him to her with surprising strength. "I forgive you, son," she said. "I hope someday you will forgive me."

He wrenched himself away from her and ran.

The gossip at the fountains told him the wigmaker was looking for him for revenge. Paris became a forbidden city — a place of waiting punishment and dishonor.

From the boulevard du Temple he followed the route back toward his old home in the mountains. He was surprised to discover the trail was narrower than he remembered, and several new homes had sprung up next to it. So much had changed that he became unsure if he was still on the right path. He wondered what Plomb du

Cantal would be like. But a volcanic mountain was a mountain like any other, where he would have to fight for a miserable existence. The prospect of a lifetime toiling in the coal trade, only to reenact his father's final tragedy, was unsettling to him.

Halfway through the journey, Henri sat and rested under a leaf-less chestnut tree where his family had paused many times before. Ahead, the road forked. The unfamiliar path, which had always seemed alluring, now beckoned him to explore. There was no one to tell him what to do. He abruptly changed his mind.

Instead of returning to the mountains, he would go south to Marseille. The fantastic stories he had heard from the water carriers were still fresh in his mind. He imagined a city of wealth, adventure, and opportunity. It was also a distant land, far enough for him to be inconspicuous among the other strangers. He would find work there, and — most important of all — an ocean, where he could get a job at the port. He was young and alone. The sea offered the most exciting prospect he could hope for.

CHAPTER SEVEN

Marseille, 1773

*T*hree months later, in mid-spring, Henri reached his destination. It was noon, and Marseille was veiled in a light rain. He was footsore and hungry after a long journey, one he had survived through begging alms from religious houses and, occasionally, petty thievery. Unlike his picturesque fantasies, the city that stood before him was stricken with poverty and pestilence, and filled with refugees like himself. Outlines of sailing ships bobbed on the murky waters. The port and its waterside were clogged with animal and human waste, spilling a vile smell into the surrounding coast. The rats played on the dock under a dripping sky.

The noise of boat passengers shouting in the harbor rose to a hysterical pitch; animals crowed, barked, and neighed; and the rattling chains of ships' anchors being dropped through portholes roared like thunder. The sweeping rain added moisture to the muddy ground, and stagnant water collected in green puddles.

Sailors from every nation strolled the twisted streets looking for whores. Brigands lurked in alleyways, waiting for an opportunity to rob travelers of what little money they might have. Peasants from the nearby countryside poured into the marketplace to exchange their supplies of meat, milk, and eggs for the cargos of grain and flour that arrived on the ships from America.

Henri watched in amazement. His stomach rumbled, a reminder of how hungry he was. He searched his pockets in vain, not sure what to do next. There must be some way he could exchange his labor for food and lodging. Near the pier, a merchant stood on top of a raised platform. A thatched rooftop shielded him from the drizzle. Henri's heart leaped at the sight of laborers lining up before the man, anticipating work. He rushed to join the queue.

"I need twenty men to unload my cargo," announced the merchant. His stout frame, barely five feet tall, was draped in finely tailored clothes and topped with a three-cornered hat. "The *Mighty Gale* has arrived from Boston."

He pointed his index finger at the workers, selected a few faces from the crowd, and shouted, "You! You! You!"

The chosen ones moved away from the mass and walked toward the pier head, where they stood next to a train of mules and waited for the merchant.

He glared at Henri. "Hey, boy! Are you new here?"

"Yes, sir," replied Henri, excited at the possibility of being chosen.

"How long have you been in Marseille?"

"I just arrived, sir."

With a shrug, the merchant dismissed him and moved on to another laborer in the crowd.

Raising his voice above the noise, Henri called out in disappointment, "Why don't you take me? I am strong. I can work hard."

The merchant's face was a mask of indifference.

"You aren't qualified," said a voice near Henri.

The worker was a tall fellow of about twenty-five, with jet-black hair and dark eyes. He could have passed for being handsome if his face weren't so lean. His stooped shoulders, sagging eyelids, and tight mouth gave him a sinister appearance that troubled Henri. A piece of brass filigree hanging from a miniature S-hook dangled from his left ear.

Catching Henri's questioning stare, the man bowed, folding one arm across his chest with exaggeration. "I am Jérôme Bianchi," he announced, and chuckled. Even his laugh sounded unscrupulous.

"Henri Monange," the boy replied.

The man grew serious. "You are inexperienced. To get the job, you have to be a citizen of Marseille."

"A citizen?" Henri asked, mostly in disbelief. "What must I do to be qualified?"

"You must either be a resident for ten years, possess property, or be married to a local girl. You are too young and too fresh to have done any of those things. But that is the law."

"Then how can someone like myself earn a living? I need to eat."

"You can ask for a job on one of the large ships that will be sailing to the colonies. They're always looking for sailors. I was fourteen when I was made a cook's apprentice. With proper training you too can become a seaman. The ship I'm now on will depart in a month and two days, if the wind permits. I can speak to the first mate about you if you like."

"Yes, yes, please," he replied without hesitation, but in the same breath, a pang of fear struck him. "Does it mean I have to leave France?"

Again the tall stranger chuckled. "What do you have to keep you here, your wealth and castle? Or are you worried that Louis XV would miss you?"

They both laughed. Then a thought flashed through Henri's mind. "But what will I do until the ship sails?"

The stranger scanned the harbor with a look of contempt. "Look at those rich merchants," he murmured between his teeth, pointing at a group of well-dressed men. "Do you see their folds of fat? I wish I were a mosquito; I could feed off them and not have to worry about ever being caught. Do you know what I mean?"

Henri nodded, although he wasn't sure he did.

"I am glad that you do," his companion said. "Follow me. I know where we can get something to eat. But tell me, what brought you to Marseille?"

In a dark and muddy alley later that day, Henri sat near the back entrance of a tavern to keep out of the rain, slurping beef stew from a wooden dish. A patch of clouds, cranberry-tinged by the setting sun, made the gloomy sky blush. After the last afternoon rays died away, the town began to light up. Shimmering embers glowed through the windows of thatched hovels. He could hear the noisy chatter from the other side of the wall as customers squabbled over a game of dice.

While they were waiting for the food, he had told Jérôme about Paris life, his experiences as a water carrier, and the death of his father. But he omitted the story of his mother, the Hôtel Dieu, Madame Leyster, and the unfortunate incident that had expelled him from the city.

Now, as Henri ate his supper, Jérôme's shadow loomed near the opening of the alleyway, hovering over a dark-haired woman. The strings at the front of his breeches were unraveled, exposing part of his buttocks as he clasped his hips to hers. She was the one who had brought them their dinner. Leaning against the wall, she bared her breasts to her lover. Her red-stained lips became a gaping hole in the dark. One of her hands rested across his shoulder, sharp fingernails clutching the night. Every time he thrust himself into her, she hissed as though he were punching air out of her lungs. After a while, the rain began to smell rancid to Henri as he listened to her growls of pleasure.

Ignoring an occasional glance from passersby, they coupled savagely, like two stray animals. With a loud grunt from Jérôme, it was all over. Henri watched his friend arch his back, then push away from her while clutching his pants. The woman lingered long enough to give him a kiss on the forehead before she retreated back to the darkness.

The sailor drew closer to Henri, fastening his trousers. A contented smile hollowed his face, and he seemed to be possessed with a new burst of energy. Whistling a tune, he splashed through a puddle.

"That is my wench," he said proudly.

"She seemed very nice, Jérôme."

The sailor spat in the air. "All women are whores. This one is a prostitute, but I always get it for free. Judging from the way you were gawking at her, I suspect you are still a virgin."

Henri looked down at his feet.

Jérôme's eyebrows came together, and he peered down at Henri from under them. "I thought so. We have to find you one like her — a benefactor to break you in and to take care of all your needs."

"I don't want a woman to take care of me," Henri said.

"Then you will die! Or become a thief to stay alive. There is no job for you here. I am an experienced sailor, and I still have to struggle to find work. And while I am waiting, I have to eat. All those fat merchants, they just keep getting fatter. But someday I won't have to persuade peasants like you to see what I am seeing. I am going to be an important person. You'll see! And you'll thank your friend Jérôme." He caught Henri by the elbow for emphasis and pulled him to his feet. "Join me! I need a hand to help me. I'll teach you how to survive."

He pulled his arm away from the sailor's grip.

Jérôme cleared his throat and spat again, this time aiming at

Henri's foot. When he spoke, his voice was filled with equal parts anger and disgust. "You have scruples now because my wench has stuffed your belly with her food. But wait till tomorrow when you are hungry again. Do you think anybody cares what happens to scum like us?"

He started to walk away. The truth of his words struck Henri, and the boy felt utterly alone. At least when he was living in the rue de Lappe, he had his mother.

"Please wait," he called to Jérôme. "Don't go!"

The tall man stopped. His back was to Henri as he said with a slight turn of his head, "Whether you realize this or not, I am the only friend you've got in this town. The reason I let you eat was that I thought you understood me, and that we could be mates. If I leave now, you will soon be rats' food on the dock."

"I understand you," whispered Henri.

Jérôme wheeled around. "That's better," he said. "Why else did we end up in a backstreet of Marseille together? We need each other."

The boy stammered, "W-what are we going to do?"

"Aha, a smart question! I'll teach you everything I know. First, we need to set a trap."

"A trap for whom?"

Jérôme did not reply. He was rummaging through a heap of trash near the back entrance of the tavern. With the door closed and the moon in its last quarter, hardly any light shone on the alley. Henri could not see what his accomplice was searching for. He felt foolish and frightened. He wanted to run, but curiosity held him in place. In the dark, the sailor seemed a large dog digging for a bone.

When Jérôme straightened up, a long, black, twitching object dangled from his hand. It was difficult to distinguish, but Henri was certain that it must be a snake, and he jumped back.

The sailor gave a coarse laugh. "Relax, it won't bite you. It's only a rope."

He whipped it through the air, shaking off the excess dirt. To Henri, he continued, "I am going to catch myself a moneyed pig. Do you suppose you can help me trip him and make him fall?"

"With this rope?"

"Yes, doubtless," replied Jérôme. "My plan is crude, but it will work if you follow my instructions. I've done it before." He handed Henri one end of the rope and explained, "Take this and go to the other side of the street. Conceal yourself in the dark. When I pull on the cord, you hold it as tight as you can so we can trip someone."

Henri nodded as he began to understand. "I know this game. My father and I did something similar to catch wild animals in the forest."

"Very well then," the sailor said. "Remember, tonight we are going for bigger game. Aim for his neck so that you can knock him back with as little force as possible. Do not attack a horse or a carriage. We just want to rob a person walking alone. We don't want to fight unless we have to."

Henri walked to the other side and crouched next to the wall. The rope swung gently in his hand. Sooner or later somebody would wander through the alley. He could only hope that it would turn out to be a drunken merchant instead of a vagabond. It was impossible to make such a distinction now, in the thick of night. He was nervous, and the fear unsteadied his hands.

He could hear the chatter of people talking in the distance, as well as the rumbling of horse-drawn carriages and the barking of a dog. He had other worries in mind. If this plan did not work out, and he got caught, the authorities might learn about the crime that he had committed in Paris. He feared that he would be put away in the most dreaded prison of all, the Château d'If. His mother would weep if she found out. The seething anger he had once felt toward her abated. The thought of her alone in the Hôtel Dieu flooded him with guilt.

The rope in his hands jerked three times. It was Jérôme's signal that someone was approaching. Henri stiffened his back against the wall, held his breath, and listened. Footsteps reverberated in the night. He wanted to drop the cord and run away as fast as he could. But before he could move, a figure appeared at the curve of the narrow street, walking toward them at a brisk pace. He had no time to think. The rope tugged at his hands. He gave a mighty pull. It lifted, and the target let out a muffled cry before crumpling to the ground.

A three-cornered hat flew in the air and landed on the cobblestone street.

Henri caught a glimpse of the victim's half-hidden face. His thick, dark hair was shorn in a straight line over his brows. Beneath his bangs, his eyes seemed to have been bleached white with pain. The outline of a silver cross on the man's chest reflected a weak trace of moonlight. Realization shot through him: he had wounded a holy man — a priest. Jérôme sprang from his hiding place. As though he had a sixth sense of where the money was hidden, he reached and found the purse.

"Curse my luck," he howled, "it's empty."

In frustration, he kicked his fallen prey. Henri's hands dug into Jérôme's shoulders, pulling him back.

"Don't hurt him anymore," he pleaded.

The sailor spat contemptuously, "Don't be afraid! He's just a stinking Jesuit." He bent down to the priest and snarled, "No judge would hang me for killing you."

Then, to the frightened boy, he said, "Leave him!"

Henri stumbled to follow but stopped when he heard the man's moan. Ahead, his partner's shadow dissolved into the black ink of the night.

Henri hesitated, angry that his compassion outweighed his judgment. Behind him, the choking sound kept him still; he was unable to leave an injured person unattended.

"Help me, somebody!" came the cry.

Henri tiptoed back to get a closer look at the victim. The priest stirred. Confusion, then surprise, then acknowledgment registered in his eyes. Already the boy regretted turning back.

"Thank God you are still here," the priest rasped. His voice was hoarse, probably because of the injury to his throat. He reached for Henri's hand.

"No," the boy screamed, jolting away. "Let me go."

"Do not fear," the priest said, swallowing with difficulty. "I will not condemn you for what you did. If God can forgive you, so will I."

The words rang in Henri's head. Forgiveness was something his mother had given him. Bending, he lifted the priest to his feet and offered a shoulder for support. The wounded man was barely able to stand upright.

Henri struggled to find his voice. "Where are we going?"

As they stumbled down the alley, the priest whispered, "Help me walk to my seminary. I am grateful you decided to come back to me. I am Father François Gervaise."

Henri muttered his own name in reply. As they emerged from the alley, the light from the nearby dwellings brightened their path. Henri could feel the priest staring at him.

"Dear God, you are so young," he said. "Why are you doing this? Why rob people? Where is your family?"

Henri said, "I am by myself. I arrived in Marseille this morning. I tried to find work, but no one would hire me." Meeting Father François's sympathetic gaze, he felt encouraged to explain further. "I left my mother in Paris. I met Jérôme a few hours ago."

"The man who took my purse? You would be wise to never see him again."

Henri walked silently beside the priest as they made their way through the narrow streets along the harbor. The weight of the wounded man seemed lighter on his shoulders with each step.

"Do you have lodging for the night?" asked François.

"No, sir."

"There is room at the monastery, if you'd like to stay."

Henri's lips moved, but his "yes, sir" was inaudible.

The monastery where Father François resided was located on a hill looking down on the harbor. The moon had descended. The stars were too weak to illuminate the way. They managed to find a crude path leading to the residence. The front door was unbolted.

When they crossed the threshold, a harsh odor greeted Henri, the smell of rotted wood beams and kerosene lamps. Sitting inside the entrance, the night watchman had nodded off. The sound of their arrival woke him. He rubbed his hands over his face and assumed an alert expression, which turned into concern when he saw the wounded priest. He raised a metal lantern closer to them.

"Oh, Father!" he cried. "Why must you insist on going out so late? Now look what happened to you." Turning to Henri, he said, "Since we were forced to close our university, few people in this town have respect for the Jesuit order. Just this week alone, there have already been four assaults on our priests. I can't understand why they must attack us. We are just missionaries. The only reason we have this seminary here is so that we can wait for ships."

More priests gathered, drawn by the watchman's voice. Shoes scraped the hallway, shadows brushed across the wall, and Henri heard voices whisper, "Dear God!"

The priests took François to an inner chamber to tend his wound. Ignored, Henri stood by the door, his shoulders hunched. There was a hint of rain in the air, but the night was warm. After waiting for what seemed like a long time, he left the monastery. Apparently Father François's offer of a night's lodging was an empty promise.

All was quiet outside. Henri was alone.

He had not gone far when a soft wail escaped his throat. He remembered the tiny room in the rue de Lappe where he had lived with his mother. It was the last home he had known. He missed his mother's warmth, the gentle way her ribs rose and fell when he lay next to her, her quiet enjoyment of his company. What chance did she have in the Hôtel Dieu among the sick, with no means of support? Had he paid attention, he would have recognized the boundless love she had for him. But he had been angry at her betrayal of his father — too angry to care, too selfish to see, and too eager to leave. If she knew that he had harmed a priest, her heart would be broken yet again.

Overcome with repentance, he burst into sobs. He did not begin to calm down until a hand rested on his shoulder. He wiped his face with the tail of his shirt, blew his mucus to the pavement, and turned.

The watchman stood before him, scratching his thick white hair.

It was plain that the old priest had not expected to find Henri in such a state.

"Come, my child. Father François is waiting for you," the priest said.

He led Henri back to the open door of the monastery.

In the corner of the room, Father François lay in a wooden bed, under a sheet. A white bandage was wrapped around his neck. On the nightstand by his bed was a washbasin containing a cloth, along with a burning candle and a crudely carved cross.

"Sit here," said Father François, pointing to a chair. "I want to talk to you."

Henri came forward and sat down. He turned his face away, hoping the priest would not see that he had been crying. But Father François leaned over and wiped a tear from his cheek.

"These tears," he said, "tell me that you are a boy with a good heart. Will you promise me that you will love God and serve Him by following His commandments?"

"Father, I don't know if I can."

The priest seemed to take the measure of Henri's soul. "I came here to embark on a ship," said Father François. "I need someone to help me in my missionary work in the Far East. And here you are. You can be my assistant. Would you like that?"

"Does that mean we would go to sea?"

"For at least seven months, possibly a year."

Henri pressed his hands on his knees to keep from trembling. Going to sea had been his desire. And helping a missionary would make his mother proud.

"When will we be coming back?"

Father François thought for a moment. "I don't know when or even if I will return. But you will be free to leave any time you want."

Henri cleared his throat. "I don't want to be like Jérôme, but Father, I don't want to lie to you. I don't love God the way I should."

He closed his eyes, expecting to be chastised by the priest. But Father François propped himself on his elbows.

"I too have a confession," the priest said. "I don't think I love my God either, the way I am supposed to. In many ways, we are alike. I think we can help each other."

In the company of the priest, Henri was cleaned and fed. He would never have imagined that by helping Father François, he would change the course of his destiny. A few weeks later, he became a novice in the Jesuit Society of Foreign Missions, a branch of Catholicism that explored distant worlds.

The choice came to him quickly. Unlike most adolescents, who believed that their lives would go on forever, Henri was aware that his life on Earth had its allotted span of days, months, and years. And in the end, inevitably, it would cease. In his mind, the only certainty was Death, whose presence stretched through an infinity devoid of light. To him, Death had always been the ultimate God because it was unyielding, irreversible, and eternal.

Meeting Father François introduced him to a new way of thinking that was the opposite of everything he had learned. Watching the priest sit and read his daily devotions, he wanted to acquire the same patience and tranquillity. He wondered why this order of men had such an optimistic belief in a divine being. Clearly, by being one of them he could learn to both achieve this contentment and avoid facing the uncertain future alone. In Father François's care, he was safe. The priest had assumed the role of a provider as well as a teacher.

To prepare for his voyage, Henri took with him his single possession: Madame Leyster's woolen green socks, which he wore around his neck under his ankle-length cassock. He did not want to use them, for fear that they would be worn through. And in doing so he had made certain that the gift served its purpose well: to be near his heart.

Normally, a candidate entering the Jesuit society was required to pass a series of examinations conducted by four or more experienced priests. But because their ship was to disembark in a month, and because of Henri's lack of education, Father François accepted the responsibility of teaching Henri. The training of a novice should last at least two years. On its completion, Henri would be well versed in philosophy, theology, mathematics, and languages, and would take a vow of religious obedience and chastity.

On May 12 of the year 1773, one month after their encounter, Henri joined the young priest for the journey. France had offered him nothing but hunger and destitution. Annam seemed a fantastic world, and he was eager for adventure.

Influenced by his teacher's tales, Henri had his own picture of the exotic land. He dreamed of a place where dense masses of gigantic trees and monstrous flowers wound together to form wild forests, and where the sun burned so brightly and so close to the Earth that dark brown was the common skin tone. And the natives — he envisioned little clay statues that moved like pawns in a game of chess. These thoughts only intensified the excitement Henri had felt since he first learned about the voyage.

The waiting was over. The wind blew due east, and in the early morning, the harbor of Marseille bustled with travelers hauling heavy burdens. A ghostly sun stretched its limbs of light above the rippling water. Three large ships were anchored and bound together in a series of mooring places, apart from the steady stream of craft down the port.

The boy ran to the edge of the water and splashed his feet in the breaking waves. He was delighted to feel the cool ocean. His clothes, wrapped in a bundle, hung over his right shoulder. The green stockings around his neck flew in the air, catching the wind.

"Look over there, Henri," the priest said, pointing across the bay to the dock. "The white one nearest to us is our ship, the *Wanderer*. Next to her are the *Saint Ignatius Loyola* and *Saint Raphael*. Ignatius is the founder of the Society of Jesus; Raphael is patron of the travelers and one of the seven archangels who stand before the throne of the Lord. The name Raphael also means 'God heals.' You may notice that the last vessel is slightly larger in size and armed with cannons. That is the *Hercules,* which is a warship. Her job will be to protect the other three."

Henri halted, apprehension in his eyes. "Why do we need protection?"

Before the priest could answer, a loud, continuous whistle cut through the heavy air. Its noise prompted the men-at-arms to begin boarding, most of them heading toward the *Hercules.* Over the taffrails of their caravels, the four captains appeared, their hats off in salute to the passengers. Seven monks were praying together on the quay, along with three nuns. Like Henri's and François's, their belongings were contained in a few modest packages. Their garments were made of crude black wool. Small identical metal pins, each adorned with a cross, fastened their coats at the neck. The priest identified them as Portuguese members of the Dominican order.

Henri lingered. His anticipation grew, and now and again he turned to look at the city behind them, still sunken in fog. The sounds and smells that came from the dirty streets reminded him of Paris. The thought of not seeing France for a long time was frightening. To his embarrassment, he felt like crying.

Henri and François stood in line behind a few merchants, who were directing their cargos into the watertight compartments below deck. Toward the stern of the vessel, the sailors stowed large sacks containing dried beef, rosewood crucifixes and rosaries, gunpowder, and rifles.

With a rush, the wind came upon them, making the rigging clank against the masts. Henri and François walked up a long ramp to the ship. The Portuguese monks and nuns followed them. Once on the deck, Henri took a deep breath, smelling the air. A putrid odor greeted him. The water below was dark and slimy with fish carcasses and discarded refuse.

"It smells foul!" he said, holding his nose. "The water, the wind, the air — everything stinks of rotting flesh."

The captain lumbered forward — a thickset man of medium height. His face, made leathery by the sun and wind and dripping with perspiration, beamed a generous smile. His sun-bleached hair, his reddish beard, and his muscular upper body gave him the appearance of a Nordic king. A pewter pipe with a reed stem dangled at a corner of his mouth.

"Yes, yes, and so do I stink!" he replied. "But that doesn't matter because we will set sail soon." Turning to the priest, he said, "You must be Father François Gervaise. Monsignor de Béhaine has informed me about you. He was very accurate in his description."

The priest nodded, appearing pleased.

The captain continued. "I am Captain Petijean. Welcome aboard the *Wanderer*. Would you be kind enough to bless my ship before we depart?"

"Indeed," the priest said, and intoned a heartfelt prayer.

Henri's education began a few days after they left Marseille. Being young and impressionable, and having an appetite for knowledge, the novice readily absorbed information from his teacher. He retained most of what he learned, and sometimes he even surprised François with difficult questions. On days when the ocean was calm and the vessel was gliding along with every sail full of wind under a blue sky, they sat on deck exploring the boundaries of knowledge and faith until their minds were exhausted. Never did they run out of subjects to talk about. When he looked at the beauty of the sunrise or sunset, he was amazed to think of the ignorance that had blinded him in the past. Now he was able to read passages of the Bible, listen to the sailors' singing with a keen ear, and appreciate the beauty in his teacher's paintings.

One day, as they sat on deck watching fluffy clouds drift across a bright sky, the priest described to him the splendid painting by Leonardo da Vinci of a woman with a mysterious smile.

"That is the greatest achievement on canvas ever done by a human being," said François. His voice trailed dreamily as he described the image.

Henri closed his eyes and tried to visualize the colors and brush-strokes. He could only see the face of Madame Leyster, and he was satisfied.

The priest continued. "Do you know the difference between man and God?"

Henri shook his head, not knowing how to reply. The possible answers to that question were endless.

François smiled. "The painter takes his brush and dips it into all of the different colors of oil. And with each stroke, he applies his talent to give birth to an image of life and makes the viewers see what he sees. But the image in itself is still, and that is all the artist can do. When God smiles, He breathes life into the painting."

It was an excellent analogy. Yet Henri felt that something was lacking. As much as he tried, he could not share the priest's faith. François seemed to be secure in his belief that God created the universe and controlled humans' lives. How could a world so magnificent exist, he argued, without the hands of a masterful creator?

But the more Henri pondered the question, the stronger his fatalistic convictions became. He could not imagine some being up in the clouds ruling all life. Deep inside, he felt that his existence in the universe occurred merely by chance.

Four and a half months into their trip, Henri was on the way to becoming an educated man. He had mastered reading and writing, and acquired some knowledge in conversational Latin and simple mathematical problems. The *Wanderer* and its accompanying ships sailed northeast toward the mysterious Indies for an exchange of passengers in Pondicherry, India. There they rested for a week and gathered new supplies before continuing their journey to Cochin China.

Among the newcomers was the famous Monsignor de Béhaine — the man whose vision had inspired many French priests, including François, to journey to the Far East. Henri was by now familiar with the monsignor's background, from his unwavering belief to his devotion to the missionary work. According to his teacher, the monsignor's power of healing had saved François from the clutches of cholera. This and other tales of miracles had helped raise this man above all other clerics.

One evening before supper in the galley, the monsignor expressed his desire to bless Henri. To earn this generous act, the boy had to recite the first five verses of the Bible in Latin. Henri had already learned that no one disputed the monsignor's commands and desires, or opposed his opinions.

They were standing face to face. Henri was a few phrases into the recitation when the older priest reached for the crown of his head. The boy started at the unexpected contact and fell silent. As the pressure continued, Henri raised his head, allowing the fingers to brush through his hair. His eyes fixed on a jagged scar that ran across the monsignor's neck.

Then he felt the strength of the monsignor pushing down on him, as if making a dog sit. He fell to his knees.

De Béhaine's hand slipped down Henri's collar and grasped the green wool stockings. He gave a tug. Henri saw the precious gift being pulled from his body. He uttered a cry and reached for them. Disbelief mixed with panic at the thought that he might lose his beloved possession. The monsignor slapped Henri's hand away.

"No priest should be allowed to own such colorful articles of clothing, let alone to wear them inappropriately like any common sailor," de Béhaine said, looking sternly at the novice.

Henri wanted to leap up, to snatch back his stockings. Instead he opened his trembling hands. With shame and panic, he begged, "May I please have my things returned to me? I promise I will put them out of your sight."

"No, you may not," the monsignor replied. With a flick of his wrist, he tossed the stockings overboard. "You are a novice," he said.

"First you must learn the lesson of detachment. Material things should have no value or meaning to a priest."

The boy watched the last thread of his past disappear. In his eyes, the monsignor had acted more like a common man than a saint.

CHAPTER EIGHT

South China Sea, 1773–1774

The sea had many voices. In his private berth, Pierre could listen to all of them. Unlike other passengers, he had not grown accustomed to the roar.

To ease into sleep under such conditions was difficult. It had been two weeks since he had embarked on the *Wanderer*. He was leagues from shore. All night the waves slapped against the rough outer boards of his cabin. Sometimes they were great watery columns; sometimes they were splashes, murmurs, and retorts that sounded almost human. He learned to anticipate the lull that followed the last wave of each interval. The rhythm was never monotonous to him.

In the bulkhead outside his room, an oil lamp was burning. He kept his door open in order to admit its light, which shifted from one grimy wooden wall to the other. The confined space was cold and drenched in sea dew. His bony frame shivered, his mind drifting. The relentless insomnia trapped him in his past.

Lord, hear our prayers and be merciful to your daughter Mathilde, whom you have called from this life. Welcome her into the company of your saints, in the kingdom of light and peace.

He saw himself at the age of ten, standing by his mother's bed. A white shawl was draped over her head to cover her eyes. Her ashen skin sagged downward to freeze her face in a ghastly grin. His father, in red breeches and dirt-colored shirt, stooped and examined a stump — her right leg had been severed. A moistened animal bladder sealed the wound to stop the bleeding.

Leaning over Pierre's mother and praying loudly, Father Jean-Paul drew a red cross in the form of the Greek letter tau on her forehead to indicate that she was a victim of Saint Anthony's fire. A smell of rust permeated the air. In Pierre's arms, his two-year-old sister, Mercedes, gasped as though she were suffocating. He looked down and loosened his clutch on her.

Without turning around, his father shouted, "Mademoiselle Tournelle, where are you? Help me with the children. Get them out!"

The governess nudged Pierre toward the door. He took one last look at his mother. Everything about her was immobile, except for her shadow, which quivered in the lantern light.

Along with his seven brothers and two sisters, he had attended her funeral. Everyone wore black, including him. The women hid their faces under long, dark veils. Origny was cool in the morning. The sky dripped down sheets of mud-colored rain onto the cemetery where they had gathered. Father Jean-Paul intoned a liturgy. Pierre was teetering on the edge of the grave and could see his reflection on the slick black wood of the casket. His mother seemed so distant. He could not endure the thought of her lying in the open field for an eternity, her round face melting, her body becoming a puddle of carrion.

Voices were whispering. Among them, he heard Mademoiselle Tournelle wailing, *What is going to happen to the children, having no mother? The oldest one is barely ten years old.*

His father tapped the crown of his head with his large hand. *Pierre will assist me with my work at the hospital, won't you, my boy?*

Mommy, please don't leave us, whimpered his sister Theresa, clinging to the tail of their father's coat.

The ship staggered and plunged in the weltering sea. Above him the masts groaned to the whistling gale. He sat up, looking into the indistinct hallway. His lungs gasped for air, but the bitter salt condensed in his throat. He felt trapped. The walls around him flowed into a wooden coffin, and the fear of being buried alive drew him into the past that was seizing him.

He rushed toward the door.

On the main deck, the world was peaceful. Despite what Pierre had felt from his berth, there was no storm in progress. The sea was rolling and slick, like crude oil. The sky was dull, with only a sliver of a crescent moon, creating a darkness that seemed to have no end. Walking fore and aft on the deck were two sailors on their watch. Behind them, and fencing them in, was a black rim of gunwale with a metal railing. Beyond that, he could see, by the fluttering sails, that the wind was growing stronger. The clear air calmed him, but the steady moan from above was still unnerving.

One of the seamen emerged from the darkness, his movement startling Pierre.

The man was bare-chested despite the coolness. A cotton bandanna was wrapped around his large head, and a small corner of it hung over one eye. When Pierre stared at his face, the sailor nodded.

"No one is allowed to walk on deck after midnight except us crew," he said. "You should turn in for the night, sir."

"Let me be," Pierre said, annoyed at the disruption of his solitude.

"But, sir . . . up here it could be dangerous."

"Go back to your post," snapped Pierre. "Even your captain would not use such tone to me."

His haughtiness found its aim. He could see the sailor's muscular arms rippling in the dark and the flash of his teeth. *Good! Get angry,* he thought, and felt his own rage abate. Straightening his robe, Pierre walked away. The path to the stern felt wet and slippery under his bare feet.

"I blame you, Petijean, for your men's insubordination," he

muttered, his voice lost in the creaking of the spars. In a more grating tone he added, "That sailor should be flogged."

There wasn't a cloud or a star to be seen in the sky, but the ocean was twinkling. When he looked over the rail, he thought he saw the reflection of his own shadow. The wind returned, as abrupt and powerful as he had anticipated, threatening to scrape him off the gunwale and into the watery pit. Pierre gripped the handrail, dizzy with fear, until he regained his balance. To be thrown overboard in front of the sailor he had just insulted would be more irony than he could bear. In one instant he would lose not only his life but also his work and his ambition. A thin laugh escaped his throat.

All caution, he moved away, reaching the center of the deck by holding on to the rigging. The watchman had moved to the other side of the ship, invisible in the thick night. The wind cried again. This time, he heard a voice. The sniffing and words of entreaty were unmistakable.

Pierre strained to listen. His hand clutched the crucifix around his neck. The cry seemed to be coming from the sails over his head. He looked up and saw a dark figure perched among the yards, booms, and ropes that connected to the main mast.

He lifted his hand to his mouth. Nothing could have surprised him more. It was Henri, the novice François Gervaise had recruited in Marseille. How and when did he climb a post ten feet above the ground without being caught? The lad seemed too distraught to be aware that he had been discovered. The weeping that broke from him was piteous. *Mother . . . Mother . . .* was all Pierre could hear.

The monsignor stood leaning against the mast. The first time he had encountered Henri, he was not impressed, mostly because of the novice's age. He remembered feeling furious at François's decision to bring one so young to a place as dangerous as Annam. Weakness and inexperience could pose a major threat to the mission's survival. This evening's discovery confirmed his apprehension. Still, the thought of Henri dangling while François slept, unaware of his novice's plight, left him boiling with rage. *How irresponsible of that priest.*

He decided not to intervene. The first rule he had learned as an explorer was that upon encountering trouble between the natives, it was best to leave matters in the hands of God. The boy was François's problem.

Pierre turned and went back down to his cabin.

After seven months at sea, François noticed a growing restlessness among the passengers and crew. Even in January, the temperature was unbearable. Each day, the tropical heat burned the deck and stripped the wood of its dark varnish. The sea was shimmering; all he could see was blue or orange, and as brilliant as the sun. And the billowing waves were relentless. They constantly tossed loads of seawater over the *Wanderer*'s deck, discouraging his explorations. With each knot the brigantines sailed, France and all of her familiar comforts receded farther into memory.

In the heavy swells, the ships drifted. Their motion was directed by the wind and the ocean's currents. Many of the missionaries had been struck with seasickness, including François. The acid from his stomach reached up his throat, spoiling every morsel of food he tried to swallow. Even the sea vapor, which he had once found so invigorating, made him ill. Every day, he covered himself in wet cloth and salted water. Every night, he sweated in a damp berth that he shared with his novice, Henri, and three of the seven Portuguese monks.

The monsignor seemed to have no difficulty adjusting to the harsh conditions. With the skills he had learned during his past expeditions to Annam, he used folk medicine to treat such ailments as headache, stomach troubles, and kidney complaints. Seeing that François and the others were seasick, he introduced a remedy to strengthen their bowels.

"The treatment is simple," he explained one morning after catechism. "One must cut and search into the bellies of large fish for the smaller fish they have consumed but not yet digested. Remove one of these fish, clean it well, then cook it in a broth of fish sauce and pepper. Eat it with rice at supper. This will impart vigor to the stomach so that you will feel no nausea while crossing the ocean."

He nodded at François. Henri, wrapping his arms around a wooden column twenty paces away, looked on with a frown.

Miraculously, the medicine worked. After his first meal of the fish-within-a-fish, François suffered no more seasickness. During the day, he strode the length of the ship with his novice. He scanned the horizon, looking for land. But all he could see was an empty sapphire sea stretching out to infinity.

Behind their vessel were the *Saint Raphael* and the *Saint Ignatius Loyola,* each floating a half league from the other — close enough for François to see the figures on the other boats, but too far away for him to hear their conversations. Ahead was the *Hercules,* leading the way.

At night, the air turned chilly. Tucked under a blanket on a hammock slung between coils of rope, Henri tossed and sniffled in his sleep. Sometimes the priest would find tears on the youth's cheeks, which he wiped gently with his thumb. François found himself caring for the boy as precisely as he tended to his paintbrushes.

Like the Portuguese Dominican monks, he was bearded now. His wavy brown hair was shoulder length. The two younger nuns, Sister Natalia and Sister Lucía, had abandoned their black wimples and habits. Instead, they wore short, sleeveless dresses that they had made from a bale of cloth — a gift from Monsignor de Béhaine from the market in Pondicherry. With the leftover fabric, they cut triangular scarves and wrapped them around their shaved heads to ward off the blazing sun. Despite the heat, the oldest nun, Sister Regina, hid herself in the heavy folds of her order's prescribed garb.

The constant exposure to salt air and heat, the cramped space onboard, and the excessive humidity drained the energy from the passengers. The oldest monk, Brother Jorge, battled scurvy and exhaustion. During his last hours, he shrank in a corner of the deck as though trying to hide in a crack in the gunwale. François watched the monk's rotting teeth, blackened like segments of a leech, drop from his mouth. Monsignor de Béhaine tried to heal the dying man with spiritual communion and folk medicine. In the end, the captain and two of his seamen shrouded the monk's still body in a canvas sheet and tossed it overboard, while de Béhaine chanted a prayer. The others surrounded him, heads bowed.

The following morning, the captain announced that they had not far to go. The world around François was a hazy mist, vague and formless. Just when he thought he could no longer endure the incessant rocking of the ocean, he was roused by the lookout's excited cry of "Land, ahead!" Straining into the glare from his hammock, François made out a series of gray lumps in the distance.

The captain heaved a sigh. He had utilized every inch of caulk available onboard to repair the ship. The white sails were tattered and mended in layers of large, discolored patches. The names of the ships had been washed by the seawater until only an outline was visible. As they drew nearer, the phantom flicker of approaching bamboo trees, the green of the rice fields, the dark figures of water buffalo chewing on grass, and human silhouettes bending over the earth were coming into focus. Everyone onboard watched the sights: they knew that within these shapes hung their new fate.

François fixed his gaze on the unknown land. A new world was waiting. Above him the wind abated. He noticed a hard-shelled husk of a coconut palm bobbing in the water, flanked by a large rotting palm leaf.

He heard Captain Petijean give the order for his helmsmen to drop the anchor.

"It's over!" the captain shouted happily. "The journey is done."

François drew out his crucifix and held it tight in his palm. For him, the journey was far from over. This day would mark the beginning — his beginning of a new life as a man of God among the heathens.

The sealed book of Indochina was about to be opened to him.

PART TWO

The Mission

At noon, François was leaning against the rail when he heard the sound of moving oars. Strange chanting was behind him and before him — eerie, anxious inflections rising above the rhythm of drumbeats. The Annamites were rowing out to meet the ships in their canoes.

The ocean had turned crimson. He wheeled about. The captain and his men were grinning. Small red torches whirled below as dark figures seized the ropes dangling from the *Wanderer*'s gunwales and shimmied upward. The natives' shiny, blackened teeth clenched torches whose flames reflected in their ebony eyes. Sister Lucía made a fearful groan and drew behind the men, clinging to the arm of the oldest nun, Sister Regina.

"What are they doing?" François asked de Béhaine. Without waiting for an answer, he turned to Captain Petijean. "Where are we?"

The first boarder reached the main deck. His copper-tinted skin glistened with sweat. A piece of cotton, passed between his legs and around the waist, was his sole garment. Most of his head was hidden beneath an oversized conical straw hat, like a thatched rooftop. The blaze in the man's hand sizzled. Something told François that he was about to be captured! He wondered if these heathens were cannibalistic.

"We are offshore at Quinion," said the captain.

"Do not overreact!" added the monsignor. "These people are usually harmless, but you never know what cultural differences may cause them to be violent."

"But why are they carrying torches in the daytime?" asked Brother João. He was a handsome-looking friar, a few years older than François. A lock of his dark hair fell over one eye, but he was too excited to notice.

"Remove your boots immediately!" commanded the monsignor.

François noticed that the crew members had already removed their footwear. Without questioning, he untied his laces. The captain had informed him of this custom before.

The monsignor explained, "The Annamites believe in many gods. If they cannot see your feet, they will assume we are white demons that floated in from the sea. Demons and ghosts in their culture are depicted as gliding through the air without feet."

The first Annamite came forward, and so did Monsignor de Béhaine. He raised his palm in a greeting and said to the frightened clerics, "They use fire to purify any bad omens that come from the sea. Just allow them to carry out their rituals and breathe in the smoke of the sandalwood bark that they burn as incense. You will find it refreshing."

The fire was in front of François, burning with the smell of sage and gingerroots. In its light he saw the face of the native for the first time. He looked with total wonderment at the man's high cheekbones, his flat flaring nose, and his mouth full of gleaming black teeth. His appearance was indeed strange, but his expression seemed open and kind. François inhaled deeply.

With the help of the natives, the missionaries came to the beach one by one. Feeling curiously out of balance, François walked close to

Captain Petijean and the monsignor. Still offshore, Henri seemed to have developed a strong attachment to the savages and their canoes. He made them all laugh as he pushed and pulled, rowing an oar with both hands to propel his vessel toward land.

François walked briskly on his heels. The sand scorched the soles of his bare feet. Its texture was a combination of finely ground shells and coarse granite that sparkled in the sun. Here and there he saw a rainbow reflection of mother-of-pearl, fragments of ruddy coral, transparent quartz, dark-blue mussel shells, and dull, purplish porphyry stones, all clean and soaked in the brine. Coconuts littered the ground, and beyond the white strip of sand lay the thick jungle. *Mercy! Mercy!* cried the bottoms of his feet.

Everywhere he looked, François saw short dark figures dressed in rags. They all looked alike to him. Their exposed thighs and backs were decorated with blue tattoos of unrecognizable shapes. The women wore black or brown skirts that reached a little below the knees. A triangular piece of cloth was worn over the bosom. Their jet-black hair was smooth, slick, and glossy. They ornamented their necks and arms with copper or silver bands. Men and children ran about in a state of near nakedness. No one wore shoes. Their feet appeared flat and broad, the color of terra-cotta.

Some of the natives withdrew into the shade of the trees. Fear mixed with curiosity on their faces. The monsignor spread out his arms, which were draped with strings of large, colorful glass beads. He moved, and their shine caught the women's attention. They chirped to one another like magpies. Some of the children squirmed free from their mothers' clutches.

"See our feet," shouted Monsignor de Béhaine, first in Latin, then in their native language. He lifted the hem of his robe to reveal his right foot. "We are not white sea devils."

His fluency in the Annamese tongue sent a jolt of surprise through the crowd. They erupted into laughter.

"Take my gift of beads as a token of my friendship."

He threw a handful of necklaces into the air. The children ran to catch them. Two boys wrestled for the same strand of beads. They seized each other, punching and growling. A handful of villagers approached with curiosity, and as François watched, the crowd grew larger, until all he could see was a wall of thick black hair. Some of the Annamites tugged at his cassock, and then, growing more daring, they reached their fingers upward, pulling at his hair and stroking his cheeks.

"I have a precious pearl," announced the monsignor.

The natives screeched with delight.

"This pearl is far more valuable than any of the glass beads that I have given you. It is more prized than any jewel in a king's crown. And it is so cheap that even the poorest among you could obtain it. Who among you is ready to accept this magnificent gift?"

Hands lifted in the air, waving at de Béhaine. "*Thầy, thầy,*" they called. It was a word François understood, for it meant "teacher." He exhaled with relief. Of one thing he was certain: he had been welcomed.

"Very well, my children," the monsignor continued. "Let me tell you more about that precious pearl. It cannot be seen by human eyes, but it can be felt by your spirits. It was formed in God's hand, bright and pure. But when it was placed into your body, it became corrupted and soiled because of your original sin. This pearl is your soul. And only I can teach you how to make it shiny and pure again . . . through the holy water of baptism. With this gift you shall be led to an eternally safe —"

He stopped. Forcing its way through the peasants was a team of eight soldiers dressed in blue silk uniforms and armed with drawn swords. The natives dispersed. A woman screamed. Silence fell upon the beach. Among the clerics, no one moved. Together, the nuns recited a prayer.

The leader of the guards approached de Béhaine. He tilted his straw hat back using the pointy tip of his sword.

"Would you like some necklaces?" asked the monsignor. His right arm reached forward. The beads made a soft clanking sound.

François held his breath.

"You . . . come with me," replied the guard, lowering his sword.

He had a shrill voice that made his pronunciation impossible to understand. Most of what he said François understood only from studying his hand gestures and expressions. Certain words seeped into his mind slowly. "No stranger . . . enter . . . Quinion . . . first . . . Mandarin Chi Tuyền . . . meet."

The monsignor adjusted his robe. "The mandarin wants to meet us? Then you must take us to him."

A dozen canoes took the voyagers down the brown tide of a sluggish river toward Quinion City. For a long time, François did not see his novice. It seemed that wherever de Béhaine was present, there would be no Henri. The boy had avoided the monsignor ever since de Béhaine had confiscated his green stockings. He chose to ride with the Portuguese monks instead of sitting next to François.

Slowly they moved forward. Each boat was manned by four to six natives. Ahead, the river narrowed into smaller streams that vanished into the mountains. Thickets of forests turned into rice paddies and small villages, and then back to forests again. François could no longer feel the sun beating down on him. Green curtains of leaves blocked the sky, cooling and dampening the air.

The canoes came to the mouth of a brook, which tumbled down a ladder of rocks amid foam and spray to churn the river. François gripped the wooden bar that separated him from the passenger in front of him. The vessels tossed, the first few dashing against one another. Cries rose in every direction. But the danger was quickly over, and the stream resumed its calm meandering.

The forest grew thicker and darker, a luxuriant wall alive with bright flowers. Near the front of François's canoe, Monsignor de Béhaine studied the mountains with his brass spyglass. François had the feeling that he and his company were not alone. He felt small, insignificant, yet uniquely visible, and he knew that somewhere in the mighty trees along the banks of the river, creatures were watching them. The rustling of leaves, the sound of squirrels frisking among the branches, and the chirping, squeaking, crying, and trumpeting of various species of birds, monkeys, and elephants all created a symphony of dread around the explorers.

With ramrod posture, François perched on his seat. He could not tell how close the creatures were to him; certain sounds seemed as near as a breath against the nape of his neck. In his heightened state of alertness, he became aware of a pair of eyes scrutinizing him. He felt the quick, flashing, golden gaze of a jungle cat. He turned and saw the monsignor looking at him through the metal eyepiece of his telescope.

The monsignor pointed to the line of canoes behind them, stretching down the stream as far as the eye could see. Each boat carried a dozen soldiers who had disembarked from the ships. There must have been more than a hundred men-at-arms, pulling along five iron cannons on bamboo rafts.

"Always remember, Father," the monsignor said to him. "You have the power of France by your side."

At length, the waterborne caravan reached a cluster of thatched huts at the edge of the forest. To François's surprise, he saw that most of the irrigated plains surrounding the houses were left unattended. Their brown earth turned the sky gray. The sun was setting — a pink orb hanging over the desolate landscape. Black buffalo, their bloated abdomens inches away from the wet ground, chewed mouthfuls of grass. The children that rode on their backs played sweet melodies on bamboo flutes. One of them waved to François.

The priest no longer felt strange being in the heart of this tropical scenery. All it took was the friendly smile of a child to eradicate his fear.

He heard the voice of the Annamite leader. "The sun dark. We sleep here. Tomorrow, we go see Master."

In just a few moments, he would dismount the canoe and walk on this feral land, where he would settle into a new life, with new opportunities. Never would he think of his past again. It was indeed God's will.

"Monsignor, have you ever been to Quinion?" he whispered to

de Béhaine. "All that we have been seeing are straw huts, rivers, and trees. Where does a governor of a province reside?"

The monsignor gestured to the leader of the guards and spoke to him. When he turned to François, his face was almost jovial.

"The city is at least fifty kilometers away, about another half day on the water. We'll be leaving at sunrise."

In the background, François could hear Henri's laughter. The novice was running through the rice paddies as if he had known the place forever. Each new thing he discovered broadened his smile in the wan dusk. The Annamite children, with their brown skin and round bellies, chased after him. They seemed to have no fear of the strangers. Two precocious youngsters clung to Henri's long legs. Meanwhile, a group of village women surrounded Sister Natalia and Sister Regina, marveling at their height and touching their pale skin with blatant curiosity.

François listened to the voices around him, high-pitched and loud in the sultry air, and he tried to recognize some words. He had spent the past eight months on the *Wanderer* learning the Annamese language and culture from Captain Petijean. But even though he had easily mastered Latin during his novitiate, understanding these brown people was impossible. Clearly he would need more practice, more time. He must learn the virtue of patience.

A woman in her midtwenties twitched the side of his tunic. Silently she offered him a coconut, cracked open at the top to reveal a murky liquid inside. She pressed it against his lips as if to gesture for him to drink, and so he did. The juice tasted sour and tepid. François grimaced, and the woman shrieked with delight. He joined her merriment, threw back his head and gulped down the liquid, and returned the empty shell to her. The woman's child, a little girl, clung to his fingers. He bent and lifted her in his arms. She nestled her head on his shoulder, her tiny hand toying with the crucifix he wore around his neck.

In the clearing at the edge of the village, a large fire was being built. To provide food for the travelers, Monsignor de Béhaine purchased a buffalo and two full-grown pigs from the village chief and paid him in silver pieces. François could see the farm animals being led to an open area near the fire by the owner and two youths. A large stake was driven deep in the ground, knives were sharpened, and wooden vats of rice wine appeared.

"Welcome to Kim Lai," said the Annamite leader, bowing with solemn hospitality.

A circle of spectators, mostly children, formed around the frightened beasts, and above the locals' dark heads, François saw the buffalo. A rope was wrapped around its thick neck and tied to the stake. Before François could prepare himself, one of the youths raised an enormous mallet and signaled for the others to get out of the way. He aimed at the beast's forehead. A dull and heavy *thwack* rang out. Sister Lucía let out a hoarse cry, hiding her face against Brother João's shoulder. Sister Regina scratched furiously at her back; her old hands shook. François saw Henri, standing tall among the natives, watching with fascination.

Night fell. They camped in the rice paddies. Swarms of mosquitoes tormented the uninvited guests. The insects' bites were intensely irritating, but their faint buzzing was drowned by the calls of crickets and toads. No one could sleep.

The bonfire crackled. Sparkles of embers added glitter to the starry sky. The crescent moon was as slender as a misplaced silver eyelash. François lay on his side, wrapped in his cassock. Facing him, Henri was awake but deep in thought.

The wind rose, filled with menacing voices. The world around François seemed hostile. More than ever, he longed for morning.

A hand touched his shoulder, and with it came a musty scent that brought him back to his childhood: the smell of an old Bible Father Dominique had often carried in a pouch beneath his tunic. François wondered if he had just dozed off and was dreaming of Villaume. He rubbed his eyes, and then he saw Henri's grim expression.

It dawned on François that the presence he sensed was that of Mon-signor de Béhaine. He sat up to face the older priest.

"Well, Father François," said the monsignor, "I am not disturbing your rest, am I?"

"No, sir," grumbled François. "However, the mosquitoes are."

The monsignor laughed.

"And what about you, sir? Can you sleep?"

"I don't sleep," replied the monsignor. "I am going to take a short walk. Come with me? A stroll may help you rest better."

De Béhaine offered his hand to help pull François to his feet.

François hesitated.

"Come now, Father," the monsignor pressed. "You know that I will always protect you. It is time for us to continue our lessons. I must show you the proper way to establish your own congregation once you settle in this country. What I know, I learned from years of experience and hardship. Peace comes to men of great patience and to those who are willing to be trained."

He walked to the campfire and pulled out a burning branch. Its red blazes glowed in the dark, serving as a torch. François got to his feet. The monsignor led the way, the flames showing a short distance ahead. Soon, the earth turned muddy at their feet; they left the camp and the other travelers behind.

For a hundred feet or more they did not speak. The monsignor held his head high and showed no sign of weariness. It was disturbing to see him always so resilient, so in command of himself and events. Even with the rising heat from the earth, François felt the chill ema-nating from the monsignor, like an impenetrable shield that set him apart from the rest of them.

François broke the silence. "The way you approached the savages on the beach this morning was a revelation to me. You not only speak their language but also seem to have a clear insight into their nature. I see that I have a lot to learn."

The monsignor stopped walking. "It is acceptable to think of them as savages when you are at home in France," he said. "But it is dangerous to have that perception here in their land. You will never understand their nature by thinking that way. To reach out to the peasants, you must recognize their customs and their pagan beliefs, which have existed for thousands of years. Our job will be to eliminate that nonsense and introduce them to the true religion."

François released a discreet sigh.

"Are you feeling overwhelmed?" asked the monsignor.

"I realize how little I know of this place," replied François.

The monsignor grasped his shoulder and turned so that he could look into François's eyes. "I give you these simple truths. Understand them and you will find a way to triumph. The Annamites, like the Chinese, worship three sets of superstitions. The first is Buddhism, the creed of the king and the royal family, which reveres the material heavens and the stars. The second is idol worship, which holds past kings as deities. One of their false gods is Confucius, who created a set of laws and writings. The third belief is Taoism, founded by a man named Lao-tzu. It is by far the most pernicious because it is widespread among the many sorcerers and witches. They devote their service to the devil. Only when you know their belief systems can you meet their challenges and attack them at their roots."

He raised his forefinger. François looked and gasped in surprise. On the monsignor's finger he saw a large, ancient ring. The light in its glittering stone matched the silvery flame in his eyes. François knew what the ring signified. He bowed and placed his lips on its smooth surface.

"Why didn't you tell us that you were made bishop?" he muttered. "All these months we have been together, and you said nothing of this."

"I chose to travel with you as a priest, not a bishop," said de Béhaine. "But now that we have reached our destination, I must exercise my power."

CHAPTER TEN

*T*he next morning, the procession of missionaries, led by Captain Petijean and his soldiers, approached the east entrance of Quinion. Their purpose was to seek the governor's approval of their presence in his territory. Pierre had abandoned his black attire, exchanging it for a brown Annamite robe from the elder of Kim Lai Village. His new clothes were traditional, with large sleeves and a stiff collar, and the front buttoned down under the right arm. His three-cornered chapeau was replaced by a simpler handwoven straw hat.

Only François Gervaise and his novice followed his example and adopted the local wardrobe. The Dominican monks felt they had to honor the Council of Trent for ecclesiastics and kept their brown silk cassocks and brown silk overcoats. Mimicking the natives, François let his hair fall in long braids to his shoulders. Next to him, the nuns had replaced their habits with simple black dresses. Their shaved heads appeared pale and delicate. They walked close to one another, clutching their rosary beads.

Sister Lucía chewed at her fingers. She was thin and piteous, with a small face filled with bewilderment and fear. Her look reminded Pierre of his own as a child. He imagined her agony at having to face the world outside the safety of her convent, and he prayed she would adjust to the new life she had chosen. Both her companions, Sister Regina and Sister Natalia, seemed to have a bit more confidence. These were the lives he was now in charge of.

Pierre knew about Lucía's nail-biting habit, just as he knew about the mysterious rash on Regina's back and Natalia's compulsion to crack her knuckles. He had learned so much about these missionaries that it was difficult to make fair decisions about their future and well-being. He wondered if God would be more merciful if He knew less about the human race.

Before them, Quinion was built like a fortress, with a tall wall surrounding it. Beyond these barriers, the ancient city, with its myriad twisting streets and pastel buildings arranged in a circular pattern, drowsed under a hot sun. Deep within its core sat the mandarin's mansion, the heart of the metropolis. The guard who escorted Pierre and the other foreigners referred to this home as *Điện Mã Não,* "the Amber Manor," because of its yellow marble construction.

For reasons of security, only the missionaries and the captain were allowed to enter the city. The other foreigners had to remain beyond the city limits. The priests walked within a protective ring of Annamite soldiers, who hauled boxes of offerings and five cannons on wheels. From far off came the cries of a child. The streets were crowded with the ragged citizens of Quinion, mostly women and children. Other than the soldiers, there seemed to be a general absence of men.

They weaved their way through the town until they were led to the mandarin's property. Settled on a hilltop, the dwelling was built in the round and gave off a golden-orange glow in the sunlight. Lanterns hung from the curving tips of its red-tiled roofs. At the main entrance, a large burnished-copper cauldron served as an incense burner, puffing balmy smoke and giving the place the air of a Buddhist temple. Pierre covered his nose with his sleeve.

They didn't wait long to be received. The news of their arrival must have preceded them, because he could hear the shuffling sound of footsteps behind the thick wooden gates. An old man pulled open the gate. Behind him stretched a large courtyard, with red and orange orchids everywhere. Servants and maids in blue uniforms scurried about, paused to stare at the foreigners, and quickly fell into rank on both sides of a pathway. The light reflected off the marble walls; the glossy flowers seemed transparent. All was bright and lavish. Brother João instinctively made the sign of the cross.

The Annamite guard stepped forward. Pierre stood behind him. He did not want to announce his own arrival, so he waited with impatience, staring at the guard.

"The white men from the sea request an audience with Mandarin Tuyền, governor of Quinion City," the guard announced.

The old man repeated the call to a servant, who then called out the same message to another standing close to him. It was echoed several times, until it disappeared into the main house.

The scarlet sun gleamed through a curtain of mango trees. They waited in silence.

Captain Petijean's face grew slick with sweat. He took two steps forward and abruptly marched back. Then he scratched his mane of white hair, pulling at his collar as if struggling with an invisible foe — a force that was suffocating him.

The echo returned from within the grand house, passing from one servant to another until it reached the missionaries.

The old man said to Pierre, "Master has agreed to grant you an audience. You may enter."

At the far end of the main hall, Mandarin Tuyền sat in an official chair, acting out his role as the governor of Quinion Province. Surrounding him were twenty bodyguards. Each was equipped with a weapon, from spears to sabers. In front of the mandarin, incense smoke curled around a large, veined desk cut from a single piece of ironwood.

The old servant removed his shoes, seated himself on the floor, and bowed before his master. Pierre entered. The yellow-faced, black-whiskered man on the armchair looked familiar to him. His jaundiced appearance and sluggish movements seemed to be an older representation of someone he had once known. He searched his mind in vain.

With a snarl, the governor blinked and jolted forward. Recognition filled his face.

"*Cha Cả!*" he exclaimed.

The acid in Pierre's stomach churned to his throat. It was his Annamite name many years ago, used largely among his followers. It meant "First Father." A flash of memory entered his mind — the burning of his seminary in Hatien City in 1769. After this catastrophe, he was forced to escape to Pondicherry. The voice brought him back to the memory of a face. He shuddered, remembering this man — a government official who had converted to Christianity. The thought sent a flow of warmth throughout his body.

"Do you remember me, First Father?" the governor asked in Annamese. "I am the one who pardoned you from prison."

"Yes, I will never forget," replied Pierre, nodding. "You and the sea captain saved my life. I also remember when I baptized both of you." He looked up, pleased that he was still able to speak this language with such fluency, his eyes searching the great hall. "Never did I imagine you would abandon our God and surrender yourself to false cults and idols."

Tuyền laughed. "I no longer believe in the religion of the white man. I returned to my Buddhist roots. I can't imagine you alive and preaching the Gospel again. When did the king of Cochin China grant you permission?"

Pierre quoted an Annamite proverb: "'A king's orders are not as vital as the laws of a village.' I am here to ask you as the governor of Quinion to allow us to spread the words of our God to your people. You could see this as a business proposal, if you like. We'll bring you Western firearms and goods and anything else you request."

He stepped aside to present to the governor the five cannons and boxes of gifts. "These are but a few examples of what Captain Petijean can give your army. You need to protect your city and the large population of women and children I just saw on the streets."

He could hear the whispered exchanges between the guards — murmurs of awe and incredulity. Above them came the cracked voice of the novice Henri. "I can't follow their conversation. My Annamese is useless. Can you understand anything, Father François?"

Pierre glared at them. "Be silent!" he hissed.

Governor Tuyền fingered a corner of his embroidered robe. "I have no use for your glass beads."

Confidence gained on Pierre with rapid steps. "Of course you don't," he coaxed. "Your position deserves much more. These boxes contain gunpowder, clocks, and rare books."

His words seemed to satisfy the governor, but still, there was uncertainty in those small, dark eyes. Pierre waited, holding his breath.

"If I agree to admit your priests, when will the next shipment arrive?" the governor asked.

Pierre gave a discreet nod in the direction of Captain Petijean, who moved forward. Beads of sweat glistened on his forehead. "It would take at least one year, sire." Slowly the captain added, "Provided that it would be a smooth journey."

Tuyèn smiled. "Very well. I shall expect to collect what is due to me in a year." He stared at Sister Lucía as he added, "I hope for your priests' sake it is a smooth sailing." To the rest of the missionaries, he said, "Welcome to Quinion. Make this land your home."

With a wave, he dismissed them.

"Your novice is unruly," Pierre complained to François when they returned to Kim Lai Village.

The two men were walking across an empty field. The ground, under the severe temperature, cracked like the scaly skin of a crocodile. In the distance, Pierre could see the village, hidden behind a tall bamboo fence, where the sea captain and the others had settled in. He lagged in order to have a private talk with Father François.

The priest had a confused look, which irritated Pierre all the more. "He should know better than to speak while I am negotiating for our survival," he grumbled.

"Your Excellency, he is young. In due time, he'll learn."

A hundred paces away, Pierre could see Henri perching on a tree branch and waiting for them. He knew that the novice avoided him, yet was unwilling to stay too far from his teacher.

"Look at him," he said. "He is probably wishing me ill at this moment."

The priest replied, "You threw away his only possession, Bishop de Béhaine. He is hurt, and probably furious every time he sees you. But sir, I assure you my student harbors no malice in his heart toward you. I will vouch for him before God if necessary. His purity is genuine."

"How can you vouch for what is in another person's mind?" asked Pierre with sarcasm. "Besides, as I explained to him, a cleric should not grow too attached to material possessions. You, of all people, should understand that concept. Henri needs discipline."

The priest stared at Pierre. "Are you accusing me of poor judgment in choosing my novice?"

"To put it bluntly," replied Pierre, "yes, I am. I have been watching you. I know you, Father, in more ways than you think. You are young and inexperienced, and adamant in your opinions. By questioning me, you doubt my authority as your leader. I sometimes wonder if you believe that you know more than I do about missionary work."

His mind conjured the image of the fire that had consumed his mission in Hatien. He had been overconfident. As a result, all was destroyed, and he himself had been given a death sentence. His students and other catechists he had trained, all young men, had been flogged, their heads shorn, and one finger removed. Could this agony have been avoided? If only he had tried harder to understand the heathens' thinking.

François looked away. "I would not dare to entertain such thoughts, sir. I am just eager to begin my work here in this village after you all depart."

Pierre made a sweeping gesture with his hands. "Father, I think you are making a lot of assumptions about your role in this mission. I do not condemn you for thinking favorably about your strength and ability. After all, it is your ambition that brought you here, is it not? But I am unsure whether I should allow you to establish your own congregation or continue to keep you under my supervision. I don't think you are ready to be on your own."

"You cannot go back on your word!" François cried. "It was our agreement in Avignon that I would be free to carry out God's work in any way I saw fit." He drew a breath and added, "Why don't you let me prove what I can do?"

"Ah, Pride! I know thy name well," said Pierre. A faint smile passed over his face. The priest's reaction was exactly what he had expected. "You are confident that you will not regret this decision, Father François?"

"I cannot answer that. But I shall try my best not to disappoint you. I pray that I will make you proud someday."

"Very well, Father. Kim Lai Village is yours. I shall leave with my troops early tomorrow morning. We will accompany the Dominican monks to another community. They will begin their work some twenty kilometers deeper into the forest. I will assign ten men bearing arms to stay behind for your protection. And besides young Henri, I also want you to watch over the three nuns."

"I favor peace," François replied, struggling to keep a look of triumph from his face. "God will be my savior and my defense, the only army I ever need. For my missionary purpose, the soldiers' muskets are ugly, intimidating, and useless. Please take all your men with you, Bishop. The nuns can stay, as long as they respect my authority."

Pierre nodded. "Remember, I have warned you about the dangers and difficulties of this land. Many French missionaries have been cruelly massacred at the hands of the peasants that they themselves had converted. These men died alone and in frustration, because their work was left undone. It's now up to you to understand the natives and their culture in order to survive. The rules for success are constantly changing, but our primary goal remains the same. Be wary always!"

It was all that he could say. Like himself, François must make his own mistakes in order to find redemption. Pierre swallowed and said no more.

CHAPTER ELEVEN

Kim Lai Village, 1774–1775

François built his first church out of bamboo stalks, palm branches, sugarcane leaves, and planks of wild pine. It was located at the far end of the village, surrounded by rice paddies on three sides and the Bạch Lu'o'n River on the other. First he and Henri cut down trees, planing them, twisting vines to hold the beams in place. Slowly, a crowd of curious villagers formed to watch them. François kept his plans a secret, answering their questions only with a smile. His reticence increased their interest, just as he planned, and each day more people came.

One morning, the chief's youngest son approached them, carrying a large basket full of animal excrement. His name was Lộc, and he was a buffalo tender. Gesturing broadly, he showed them how to soak their timber in it, to preserve the wood's texture and to ward off termites. Soon other villagers joined in, plastering every wall of the structure with a mixture of mud and cow dung. François and Henri communicated with them mainly through gestures and pantomime.

The village chieftain, Mr. Sú', helped the priest create a traditional roofing pattern, which would maintain a balance between function and aesthetic expression. They first built an outdoor kiln to bake black terra-cotta tiles. The roof was then formed using an ancient yin-yang pattern — a convex tile interlocking with a concave tile. With difficulty, the old man explained to François the purpose for its design, to denote the three happinesses: good fortune, wealth, and longevity. As with all their dialogues, this one was slow and cumbersome. But when the concept was at last conveyed, both men shared a hearty laugh.

Next, a deeply curved eave was created, pointing up at the four corners. It was believed that if the devil were on the roof, he would slip and fall and be speared by this motif. François was delighted to learn that the primitive locals also feared a hell. That belief would help him to introduce the concepts of God and a Christian heaven.

With his limited vocabulary, François needed another means to teach his message of faith, so he turned to his skill as an artist. In the village and its rural area, Western-style art supplies were nonexistent. After he used up the items he had brought from France, he had to invent new ones. Through trial and error he learned to use a China ink block; to grind and purify rocks, earth, wood, and animal bones for pigments; to gather hog's hair for brushes; and, on a glorious afternoon, to combine fabric with rice flour to create a kind of paper superbly suited for painting. Like a research chemist, he experimented with every available substance to achieve his goals.

After numerous frustrating failures, François discovered a way to mass-reproduce his images. First he engraved religious figures on blocks of wood: Christ on the cross, with his head drooping on his naked chest and blood trickling from his wounds; the Garden of Eden, with Adam and Eve; Noah and his ark; angels standing by heaven's gate.

He chose Palm Sunday, four months after his arrival in Kim Lai, for the first Mass in his church. The reason for it was simple. Palm Sunday closely followed a day when the natives honored their dead by hanging palm branches outside the doors of their huts. The greenery served as a spiritual key to allow their ancestors to reenter their home.

Early that morning, François dressed in a silk ceremonial robe that he borrowed from Mr. Sú. He even donned a new pair of wooden clogs, which thumped merrily on the terra-cotta brick path they had built in front of the church. Henri and the nuns gathered a pile of palm leaves as a growing crowd looked on, anticipating that something new was about to happen.

"Just like your deceased ancestors, all those who receive these palm leaves may enter my temple," he said, while Henri distributed the fronds.

With a flourish, he parted the thatched door of the church and entered, beckoning them to follow. The children were the first to come in, then Mr. Sú̓ with his family. Henri held the hand of a village elder, guiding her. Before long, most of the peasants had ventured in.

Inside, the church's simplicity was almost monastic. At its front, a wooden table draped with a crimson cloth served as the altar. Above it hung a tapestry depicting Christ's crucifixion. Mass was celebrated with a chalice brought from France, but the communion wafers were made of rice. Instead of sitting in pews, the congregants rested cross-legged on the dirt floor.

As a house of worship, it was crude and malodorous. But its unpleasant smell and humble appearance seemed to reassure the citizens of Kim Lai, making them feel at home. To François, the chapel was beautiful beyond his wildest imagination.

He began his ceremony by distributing sheets of paper on which he had printed religious scenes using his woodcuts. Without a word, he stepped back and watched as dismay spread through the audience. Everyone recognized the image of hell. Still silent, he handed out a new set of woodcut prints, this time showing Christ's martyrdom.

"This is Jesus Christ, the Son of God, and He has died for your sins," he enunciated carefully.

Before the shock could leave the audience, he placed his hands on a few foreheads for emphasis. Those who were touched gasped.

In the following weeks, François saw familiar faces among the Annamese who came to listen to him and to watch him depict the Bible in ingenious sketches. He chose the five men who seemed most interested to become his disciples, for he perceived a need to recruit and train native priests to help him with the daily routine. The first among his acolytes was the young buffalo keeper, Lộc. The slender, wide-eyed youth could sing the Ave Maria and the Paternoster with reasonable skill, yet without understanding what they meant. However, the simple melody conveyed a genuine feeling that moved those who listened.

Within the year, the mission compound expanded to include a

dwelling for François and Henri, another for the three nuns, and a kitchen area consisting of an outdoor stove, a table, and chairs. In the long evenings, as François sat sketching, he felt at home. More important, he reveled in the certainty that God had led him to this strange place to carry out a divine plan. He no longer missed France.

Everywhere François looked, he saw green fields and thatched huts that stretched in endless repetition toward a shimmering horizon. Under every roof, well within his reach, were ignorant souls that had yet to awaken to the power of prayer. They were waiting to be rescued, and he was God's messenger. He preached with increased confidence, knowing that Bishop de Béhaine would return someday to inspect his mission. When that happened, he hoped to reveal to his mentor neither his talents nor his accomplishments, but the miracles of God's endless wisdom expressed through him.

The Portuguese nuns, too, grew accustomed to the harsh climate, the strange culture, and the savage nature. Diseases attacked them, heat weakened them, yet they remained devout. Prayers were their strength. Still, François sometimes noticed a sense of emptiness among the women. Sister Lucía, the youngest, let her hair grow long. Before dawn each day, she sat on the levee overlooking the watery fields. The dawning sun danced on her blond curls and brightened them to a richer shade of gold. Sadness glistened in her eyes, and she would burst out in tears if anyone mentioned Brother João or Brother Tiago. There was no correspondence among the missionaries.

Unlike the mournful Sister Lucía, Sister Natalia was a robust yet quiet nun just a few years older. Her physical being was as unremarkable as her personality. Working outdoors gave her plain face a healthy glow. The two young nuns recited their prayers together, often in a whisper. They were gentle and secretive, like doves.

The eldest of the nuns was the lanky Sister Regina. In the morning, when the first round of roosters crowed, she roused herself from her hammock and left for the fields, wearing a straw hat that she had woven with the help of the village women. Her face, long and bony, was nearly as pasty as the stack of rice cakes she brought along for breakfast and lunch. No amount of hours under the sun could make her skin darken. Even the strongest noontime rays only added more freckles and wrinkles. The children put together a few French words they had learned from Henri and teased her with a new nickname: *ma Sœur Pâle* — "my Pale Nun." She ignored them the same way she ignored François's orders, clutching a simple cherrywood crucifix around her neck and mumbling under her breath.

Ma Sœur Pâle dedicated her time to cultivating rice in a field that the village chief had designated for the use of the *cha sứ,* as the locals called the missionaries. Sisters Lucía and Natalia spent most of their day teaching the women and children basic lessons in language, history, and hygiene, as well as nursing the sick. When they washed their laundry along the riverbank, they were often joined by giggling women and children, who chattered to them in Annamese and sang songs that sounded like an out-of-tune violin.

As an artist, François found it difficult to appreciate the native music and culture. Their paintings were limited to crude, repetitive, and unimaginative themes such as birds, trees, and flowers. They had no concept of sculpture or works of art in three dimensions, except for a few rudimentary forms of pots and vases. Their literature was mostly borrowed from the Chinese.

Sometimes, as he rocked in his coarse hammock, François was troubled by the void in his heart where he knew a Jesuit missionary should feel compassion for his flock. This, he deduced, would come with time.

He entered his second monsoon season, a period from May through October in which the weather could bring pounding rains or brilliant sunshine seemingly without warning. The field grasses grew so tall that elephants and rhinoceroses could hide in them. As the monsoons faded and the peasants began the heavy work of harvesting their crops, he realized it had been more than two years since he had left France. His life back in Villaume had taken on the hazy contours of a distant dream. It seemed to him that he had been in this exotic land forever.

He grew thinner. His gaunt cheekbones protruded noticeably. His new diet included mostly rice and vegetables, and when meat was served, it had little to none of the fat he had been used to; but he never made his complaints known. Other obstacles demanded his attention. One morning, Sister Lucía discovered, much to her repugnance, that tiny black insects had infested François's hair and beard. She had to shave his head. From then on, with his brown peasant outfit, dark eyes, and bare, shiny skull, the villagers could easily mistake him for a Buddhist monk.

Word spread of the tall, round-eyed foreigner who practiced strange rituals, and peasants from nearby villages came to him out of sheer curiosity. Some said he was a holy man; others claimed that he was a white wizard sent by a Western god. These rumors were reinforced after they saw him and witnessed the beauty of his art. To them, he was a man of mysteries, distinguished from the other foreigners by a wall of superiority.

François prayed with the villagers outdoors, performed the daily Mass, and baptized newcomers into the fold. His faith and commitment to his church, spurred by his success, soared like a kite. But unlike other missionaries, who had eagerly become a part of the new environment and adopted the parishioners as newfound friends, he kept most of his private time to himself.

In solitude he rocked in his woven hammock, observing the world beyond the rectangular frame of his window. There, he would either add new entries to his French-Annamite dictionary or record his daily journal in a series of sketches.

He knew it would be the achievement of a lifetime to establish Christianity here among these needy souls, and although his progress was slow, he believed his goal was attainable. But his efforts crumpled one gray, gusty day in October.

Fast and cruel and furious were the stallions that galloped across the bamboo hedges. From where he stood, knee-deep in the river and halfway through a baptism, François could see about two dozen riders — bearded men with silk headdresses and fine embroidered attire. They were armed with swords, scimitars, and lances — the typical weapons of the East. Nearing the river, they slowed their advance. Harsh-voiced equestrians herded a crowd of villagers together like cattle.

François was confused. The howls of men in pain, mixing with the terrified cries of children and women and the blasts of a horn, terrified him. Panic spread through the congregation that had gathered at the riverbank. Fighting his urge to run, François stepped out of the water and looked for Henri.

To his relief, he spotted his novice, his five Annamese disciples, and the nuns standing in front of the mission. All appeared to be in shock. The Westerners had been convinced that the Annamites were a peaceful race who were only capable of singing love songs, making babies, fishing in the river, and planting rice shoots in the paddies. The sight of the armed riders and their warhorses, plunging and rearing behind the frightened crowd, was hard to comprehend.

Grabbing one another's hands, the nuns ran behind a large willow tree and watched the marauders pull to a halt a hundred feet from the mission. The peasants fell to the muddy ground in front of them. The soldiers' banners, high on bamboo poles, snapped in the wind, and their brass horns blasted terrifying sounds.

Following them came a horse-drawn wagon piled high with sugarcane, bamboo shoots, dried tobacco leaves, and two large cylindrical earthen jars. From behind the cart, Mandarin Chi Tuyèn, on a spirited gray stallion, pressed forward and regarded his captured peasants. The cord and tassel of his cummerbund flicked around his slim frame like a silver python. As he faced the villagers, his men stretched out on each side to form a half-circle wall and box them in. There was no escape, except for the river, its golden haze behind them.

Some villagers had already plunged into the water and swum

away. Others turned around and rolled up their sleeves, prepared to fight; but their will and courage were quickly dimmed by the fierceness of the army. A sunbeam pierced the day's dull glare, and for a moment, François could see nothing but the brilliant flashes that reflected from the soldiers' weapons. The aroma of fish sauce and fresh mud permeated the air — the distinct odor of the peasants. Henri held out his arms and enfolded Sister Lucía's delicate white shoulders. She pulled the other nuns along with her.

It was noon. François pushed his way through the peasants until the missionaries were finally clustered together.

"You know who I am," the mandarin shouted. "Why are you trying to hide? For two years your village has neglected to pay land taxes and perform its annual statutory duty to the king. Today you must settle these debts or face dreadful consequences. Where is your elder? Where is that Sú? Let him come forth!"

The horse neighed as if to emphasize its master's words. No one dared to speak. The naked children hid behind their mothers' ragged skirts.

François watched the mandarin's yellow face, beaded with sweat. His features were distorted into a grimace of hate and exhaustion. It had been more than a year since François had seen the governor. Time had worn his withered body. It seemed to the priest that this was not a healthy man. He wondered if he should speak up on the villager's behalf, but decided it was not his place to interfere.

"Where is that elder of yours?" the governor shouted, devouring the captives with his eyes. "Who among you will show me the hut in which that rat is hiding? Make haste and speak up! I don't like to be kept waiting."

A murmur spread among the huddled villagers. The governor veiled a triumphant smile beneath his fringe of whiskers. Before anyone could speak, Sú, the village elder, pushed forward, leaning on a black staff. His footsteps dragged on the damp earth. He wore the brown ceremonial robe, the same one that François regularly borrowed to celebrate Mass. From his waist, the long skirt of the tunic separated into two panels, tattered and caked with dirt. The governor gave a thin chuckle.

"Oh, Master Tuyền," said Sứ, "there is no need to set a price on me. I am of no value. Must you come here in person, armed with guards so strong and so full of rage? You frighten the women and children."

"I've come to collect the king's taxes," snapped the governor.

"We are poor peasants, Mandarin Tuyền," said Sứ, pointing at the few acres of rice paddies around them. "As you can see for yourself, we have very few young men to plow the soil. Many have run off into the mountains. Without a large crop, we have no means of paying our tribute. We barely have enough food to feed ourselves."

Anger flashed in the governor's eyes. His hands gripped the horse's reins and pulled back. The animal gave a cry and reared its front legs upward. One flailing hoof kicked the wooden staff from Sứ's grasp. He lost his balance and fell to the ground.

"Then what do you do all day, old man?"

The elder opened his mouth to reply. But before he had a chance, Mandarin Tuyền interrupted him. "It would take more than a few hectares of uncultivated lands for you to convince me that you are destitute. Any dog, cattle, or creature that lives in this land must pay its taxes to the king, and so must the people of Kim Lai. How can you be so disloyal? Not only have you stopped paying your public dues and encouraged your men to run away, but you are also harboring these white ghosts who preach the words of a foreign god. If their god is so powerful, why didn't he bless you with gold and silver and many healthy sons?"

Sứ fumbled on the wet ground in search of his staff. François, unable to remain still, strode forward, picked up the rod, and handed it to him. The old man leaned on François's arm. The warhorse's breath was above them, hot and impatient. Despite his fear, the priest kept his expression calm. God's strength was within him. His disciples were watching. He retreated back into the crowd out of respect for Mr. Sứ. This was a secular matter. The old man must handle it his way.

"But the people have nothing to offer you," said Sứ, returning his attention to Mandarin Tuyền. "It is you that force them to run away, sire. Your very presence makes everyone want to flee."

"Don't flatter me, old man," said the governor. "Your people have one thing that I could put to use: the children."

The village chief cried out in disbelief. His tunic's skirts whipped in the wind. The crowd behind him shuddered. Mandarin Tuyền's men drew closer. Rattan ropes with grappling hooks flew from one soldier to the next as they prepared to attack. The women sank down on their haunches and clutched their children to their bosoms. Their husbands and fathers formed a circle around them.

"You would not be so cruel, dear sir," croaked the elder. "Beware of your retribution in heaven's eye. The children are all we have left in this village. Take the cattle and the oxen. We will pull the plows ourselves. Or take us. But please, spare our young."

Tuyền stayed motionless. François thought he saw the mandarin furrow his brow. He prayed to see some compassion come alive on the governor's face. Surely if François entrusted his fate to God, he would be rewarded with a miracle. He must!

But the mandarin remained adamant. François heard a clamor behind him. He turned and saw that a few guards had spurred their horses to charge through the crowd. Some of the villagers were caught between the animals, fighting the soldiers with their bare hands. The air filled with anguished cries. Among the voices, François heard Sister Lucía's scream.

A soldier rode his stallion at a gallop into the group of nuns, shouting to frighten everyone else out of his way. With a clenched fist, he threw a punch at one of François's disciples. It was Lộc, Mr. Sứ's son, who had been François's first convert. The boy fell to the ground, his face bloody. In the same motion, the horseman leaned forward, wrapped his arm around the waist of the blond nun, lifted her off her feet, and flung her facedown on his saddle. She let out another cry that echoed through the barren fields. Her white legs, like the wings of a trapped moth, kicked in desperation. The soldiers cheered. Her captor's hair and beard streamed as he made a circle around the prisoners.

"Stop, you fools!" cried the mandarin. His voice was shrill and high.

At once the guards returned to their original posts, waiting for their master's next command. François felt he had received an answer to his prayer — the mandarin had revealed his empathetic side. Without thinking, he ran toward the soldier who was holding Sister Lucía. Her frightened, flushed face was being forced downward by the soldier's burly hand. Soft locks of her long blond hair dangled below the horse's belly.

"Release her!" His voice quivered, weak as a child's.

The eyes of the mandarin were upon him. He prayed for God to be on his side. Whatever happened now was beyond his control. Suddenly he became aware of the silence he had just created.

"Man from the evil land of the West," said the mandarin, "I have warned your kind not to make empty promises to me. It has been over a year; where is my tribute? Where are my cannons, gunpowder, and all the supplies I was guaranteed? How dare you preach your religion or build your home in my province without paying your dues? Now you are turning the peasants against me with your falsehoods. No one works anymore. You have brought nothing but misfortune to my land. Compared to the mountain rebels, you are even more dangerous."

François gathered courage. "You must have patience, sire. Captain Petijean is a man of his word. If he promised to bring you those things, he will, as soon as his ships arrive."

Tuyền cracked his riding crop. It stung as it slashed against François's face. He could hear the governor's voice roar in unrestrained fury. "White devil, I have waited long enough. I blame you and your false cult for everything that became ill fated. Today I shall teach you a lesson for disrespecting our culture, our laws, and our ancestral deities." Turning to his guards, he commanded, "Arrest all the foreigners and those that follow them."

The crowd slid away at the sight of the soldiers' advancing horses. Henri and the two nuns stood frozen on the riverbank, as if paralyzed by the mandarin's venomous hatred. Nearby, Lộc rose to his feet. Blood and sand trickled from a large cut on his upper lip. He spat a tooth on the ground, turned to the mandarin, and cursed. His voice was lost in the tumult.

The horseman that held Sister Lucía laughed and asked, "Master, will you reward us with this female devil?"

His request received a cackle from Mandarin Tuyền.

"Let me go!" Sister Lucía screamed. Her accent ignited a burst of laughter from the soldiers.

Ma Sœur Pâle sprang forward, brushing past François. She grabbed the blond nun's feet and tried to whirl her off the saddle, but was too weak to succeed. In a rage, she pounded her fists on the mounted soldier's leg. The man stopped laughing. He had not expected this reaction from the nun. He clutched his reins as his horse spun away from her. François thought she would be trampled under the charging steed. But she clung on, sinking her teeth and nails into the soldier's flesh. He roared in pain.

Another soldier came to his rescue, thrusting a pitchfork straight into her back. So great was the force of his blow that the implement's spikes slipped right through her. Ma Sœur Pâle fell against the horse. Inside her muddy black robe, her long, bony limbs jutted outward in a convulsion. The guard lifted her off the ground, allowing her body to stiffen before he thrust it back down. It was a long, agonizing moment watching her die.

Sister Regina lay still on the ground.

The horse that carried the other soldier and his blond captive continued turning until François came face to face with Sister Lucía. She was screaming uncontrollably. But her cries ceased when she saw the corpse of the older nun.

She looked at François, eyes wide with horror. Then a surprising calmness overcame her. "If you live to see Brother João," she said to François, "please tell him that I have always loved him."

One of the royal soldiers came from behind François and struck the side of his head with a club. He fell on his face. The pain was almost bearable, but the ringing in his ear was deafening. From the muddy ground, he looked up, searching for Sister Lucía. The soldier had taken her away. He saw a few thin strands of smoke coming from the roof of his mission. From inside, red tongues of fire reached upward, consuming the entire year of his labor.

CHAPTER TWELVE

Quinion, 1775

Mandarin Tuyền, governor of Quinion Province, was furious as he neared his home three days later. Sitting astride his gray stallion on a small hill overlooking his properties, he frowned at the untended rice paddies and burned remains of cornfields. The deserted, tumbledown thatched huts of his villages were as dispiriting as they had been when he left. His failure to collect taxes from his farmers added to his frustration. Behind this devastation were the rebellious peasants who called themselves the West Mountaineers. In this dilemma, Tuyền stood alone.

The opulent city of Quinion was about three hundred kilometers south of Hue City, the capital of the South Kingdom. To travel this great distance would take several days, and to get aid from King Due Tong's military troops would take at least another six months. His Majesty was only nineteen, and the actual ruler of the country was his chief adviser, Vice-king Truong Loan, who would never authorize an army unless he received a substantial bribe. The rebels understood Mandarin Tuyền's weakened position and took advantage of it. They raided his granaries, torched his fields, and stole his cattle. Even if the peasants' forces overcame his stronghold, it would take weeks before the young king could learn the news and take action. By then Hue City, too, would be in danger.

The leaders of the Mountaineers were three brothers: Nhạc,

Thom, and Lu. To Tuyền, they were not strangers, for the eldest brother, Nhạc, had been employed in his service as a tax collector. Two years earlier, after collecting large sums of money for the government, Nhạc had yielded to the temptations of gambling, and in an evening of recklessness, he lost the entire fortune to a group of Chinese businessmen from Wuchow.

The punishment for his crime was a death sentence for three generations: Nhạc and his brothers, his father, and his children. Having no other choice, the family had retreated deep into the mountains. Nhạc and his brothers lived as outlaws, stealing from the wealthy landowners. They began recruiting peasants, woodsmen, and forest people to join them. Soon the three brothers were able to assemble a ragged army from those who were angered by the corruption and wealth of the noblemen.

As the number of rebels grew, Mandarin Tuyền would wake up every morning to news of their actions. In the cloak of night, the bandits crept into his city, robbing from the rich houses like rats chewing at a sack of rice. They would distribute their spoils among the downtrodden, and this strategy steadily increased their popularity, strength, and numbers. Soon the roads to other towns were blocked, and his province stopped functioning. The well-to-do relocated to Quinion Citadel to be near the soldiers' protection.

Through two meager harvests, Mandarin Tuyền watched his estate decay around him while he lived in fear. His rage, finding no release, manifested itself in ailments. He frequently felt ill, with an acid burning in his throat, and his stomach bloated until it was taut with pain. One morning, he woke up to find chunks of his hair on the pillow. All the rare herbs and therapeutic needles prescribed by his physicians failed to ease his pain. To his chagrin, he could no longer find an interest in his concubines. Even the tiger's testicles — the most potent of all remedies — could not reignite his passion.

To make matters worse, his household was burdened by an expensive and demanding houseguest. It was the practice of Vice-king Truong Loan to send members of his family for extended visits with the warlords of outlying regions. It was a clever strategy that served

two purposes — planting spies within the local authorities and placing the cost of their upkeep on the shoulders of local rulers. Prince
Hoàng, King Due Tong's twenty-seven-year-old cousin, had been
soaking up Quinion's resources during the past eight years as Tuyền's
guest, and there was no end in sight.

Mandarin Tuyền made an impatient gesture to his retinue and
turned his horse's head back toward Quinion. A man in his forties, he
was tired, bloated, and itchy. The snug cummerbund he wore
squeezed his belly, making the ride on horseback unbearable. A
group of twenty-some bodyguards with swords at their belts followed him, pulling behind them cages of trapped prisoners from
Kim Lai Village. Recognizing their master's dark mood, the men
plodded along in silence.

Tuyền thought of a golden past when the earth offered abun-
dance and small trips to collect rents, such as this one, had brought
sheer satisfaction. Now his life was just a string of disappointments.
Even with a fair harvest this season on the cultivated fields, most of
his tenants refused to render what was due to him. He could no
longer force them to sell their cattle or their tools to pay their rent,
for he knew if he did they would simply abandon their homes and flee
to the forest. Brewing his rage in silence, he had no choice but to
treat them well.

On his journey, Kim Lai was the last village that he had visited.
There he faced more of the same problems he had encountered
throughout the countryside. He was convinced he was losing his grip
on the farmers. Unable to discipline them, yet knowing he had to
punish someone in order to reassert his authority, Tuyền was at his
wits' end when he encountered the Western missionaries. To save
himself, his family, and his fortune, the mandarin released his wrath
on the foreigners. They were dispensable, and they would serve as a
good lesson to the others.

A trial was unnecessary to condemn the missionaries. All would
be put to death, including the two Frenchmen and five of their Annamite disciples. As for the two nuns who survived, he gave them to
his soldiers as their prize. None of these decisions caused him any

remorse. On the contrary, his renewed sense of accomplishment helped restore his peace of mind.

Before long, he and the guards approached the east entrance of Quinion. To his surprise, two strangers were waiting for him at the gate, seemingly a father and son. They looked alike, both with deep-set brown eyes and strong jaws. Their clothes were made of fine black silk. The style of their attire and the queues hanging at the back of their heads told him they were Chinese.

As his horse neared, the older one, his face taut with politeness, stopped the animal by grasping its bridle. The younger one remained standing at the edge of the stone wall, clutching a straw hat with both hands and acknowledging Mandarin Tuyền with a bow. As Tuyền studied the two of them, he found no trace of dirt under the long fingernails. A scroll was half hidden in the opening of the older man's sleeve. Both men glanced at the prisoners with curiosity.

"You are Mandarin Tuyền?" the Chinese man asked.

The mandarin stared at the narrow face and pulled at his horse's reins, breaking the man's hold. "Yes, I am," he replied.

"I am here to warn you that your enemy is coming."

It took Mandarin Tuyền a moment to realize what the stranger meant. "The West Mountaineers," he croaked.

"Indeed. Their leader, young Nhạc, is heading this way."

Surprise, incredulity, then panic overwhelmed Tuyền, and he gave a little laugh to mask his fear. "Who are you? And why do you come to me with this information?"

"I am called Wang Zicheng from Wuchow, and this is my son Qui. We are your neighbors. For five years we have owned a gambling house in Song Cau."

"I have heard your name before," Tuyền said with shock. "According to rumor, that dog Nhạc lost all of the government's money to you. Do you know it is a crime to keep that wealth, even if you won it from a gambler?"

Wang reached for the note in his sleeve and handed it to Tuyền. "This is a letter I received from him, requesting a night of gambling at my club. I know he plans to rob me before he attacks Quinion. Sire, we both know that you haven't got the military power to hold him back. I propose to capture the rebel and turn him over to you in exchange for a modest ransom. His head is far more valuable to you and the young king than it is to me."

The mandarin unrolled the scroll and glanced at it. With his left hand, he twirled a long strand of his whiskers and pulled it upward, giving the impression of a smile at the corner of his mouth. Staring down at the Chinese, he said, "Wang Zicheng of Wuchow, name your price — although I doubt that you can capture that wily fox."

The man gave a grunt. "You don't know the shrewdness of a casino owner. I may have possession of a gambling house, but I never gamble. I can deliver the goods in exchange for two hundred silver coins and two of the best stallions in your stable."

Tuyền opened his mouth. But before he could utter a sound, Wang raised a finger. "Mandarin, you have no ivory chips to bargain with me. That is my final offer. When we meet again, have your money ready, for my son and I will bring your fox in a cage."

Mandarin Tuyền's first action was to order a handful of soldiers to take the condemned prisoners to Hue City, the capital of Cochin China. Under imperial law, the executions would take place there, for Vice-king Loan reserved the ultimate power — that of capital punishment — for his own precincts. Sending the missionaries to the vice-king would show the ruler that Tuyền was carrying out his duties as governor of Quinion despite the difficulties caused by the peasant unrest. It would also give him a chance to plead his case. Along with the captives, Tuyền sent his most trusted aide, his oldest son, to beg the king for reinforcements. Still, he knew that any help from the seat of government was likely to be too little, too late.

Resigned, he spent the next few days preparing for war. Inside his home, his concubines disappeared into their apartments, bundled their valuables, and made ready to flee. He had no time or means to plan a thorough counterattack against the rebels. In fact, the near impossibility of the task frightened him. What would happen to his lovely Quinion if Wang Zicheng were correct about the raid? What would happen to him and his family? He had no place to run.

It had not occurred to him to ask the casino owner about the bandits' strength, how many men were in their army, what sort of weapons they had ready for battle, or what direction they would take to enter Quinion. Tuyền had been so startled by the news that by the time he could gather his thoughts, the two strangers had already departed. Now his only option was to wait.

Mandarin Tuyền ordered his men to place a series of ladders along the walls of his fortress to reach the parapet from the inside. The soldiers and townspeople worked together to transfer heaps of rocks from the ground to the battlements so they could be thrown down on the attackers. In groups of three or four, under the shade of banyan trees, the women whittled arrows from bamboo stalks. Some of the barbs were wrapped in rags and dipped in kerosene; others were coated in red arsenic and cobra venom.

Mandarin Tuyền walked up and down the great wall to look for signs of the enemy. Any time he spotted a cloud of dust in the distance, terror would seize him. But each time, the mirage proved to be only a caravan of passing merchants. Whenever a black crow screeched for its mate or a spider fell from a branch, he saw an omen warning him of misfortune, and the familiar, bitter taste of bile rose in his throat.

The Chinese man's arrogance made Tuyền feel that the casino owner would not go back on his word. Surely Wang Zicheng and his son had concocted a plan to capture the leader of the bandits. He suspected that as part of the scheme, the government would be indebted to Wang for turning in the rebel Nhạc and therefore would not pursue the purloined tax money. In addition, Wang and his family would benefit from assisting Tuyền, as such an act of loyalty would guarantee the continuance of their gambling establishment.

Tuyền desperately held on to these convictions, since this scenario meant that a war could be avoided. On the other hand, history had taught him that in the game of war, the Chinese were not to be trusted. No one could outwit them. Like it or not, he had to prepare for battle.

Walking back to his mansion, Tuyền mentally examined each aspect of his preparations one more time. In the front yard he lit large stalks of incense, burned paper money for the dead, and made offerings of rice and salt to the gods, entreating the sovereign lords of the terrestrial world to bless his land.

As he was immersed in his prayer, the barking of a dog startled him. A lad of fifteen was running barefoot through the street, waving his hands and holding what seemed like a clump of fur. He shouted, "Master, Master, the Chinese are here."

Townspeople, concubines, and servants ran in every direction. Mandarin Tuyền leaped to his feet, dropping the incense to the ground. He grabbed the boy by the back of his neck. "What are you saying? Who is coming?"

"The Chinese," the boy repeated, panting. "They are waiting outside the north entrance. They need your permission to enter the gate. And they said to give you this." He uncoiled his fingers, and the mandarin saw that in his hand the young messenger was holding a bloody foxtail.

It was midday. The sun spilled through the side windows of the community hall and spread across the bleached wooden floor. Every time Tuyền held a meeting in this spacious hall, under its vaulted ceiling, he felt a sense of importance. His men stood nearby, weapons in hand. From the balconies, with their carved banisters and ornate spindles, the local citizens watched the spectacle below as though it were an opera. Their loud chattering, mixed with the noise of children crying, reverberated through the cavernous space.

Mandarin Tuyền ran a finger inside his collar in a vain attempt to release the heat trapped inside his official uniform — a long, blue silk tunic with detailed embroidery. With his other hand he produced a current of air around himself with a delicate folding fan, holding it at the pivoted base of the sandalwood frame but making sure that the sight of the phoenix embroidered on his tunic was in full display. This was the first time in many years he did not feel racked with illness, because his enemy was locked in a bamboo cage twenty paces from his upturned shoes. Safeguarding the crate were Wang Zicheng and ten of his men. Their weapons had been left at the gate.

At the first series of drumbeats, silence fell on everyone, including the smallest children. Tuyền used the fan like an extension of his fingers, pointing in the direction of the prisoner, whose head was bowed low and locked in a wooden ladder–like yoke. The barred enclosure was so small that he had to crouch on his palms and knees like a savage dog ready to attack. A heavy chain around his ankle anchored him to a large metal ball.

"Lift his head," the mandarin said to Wang. "I want to see the face of my enemy."

The prisoner looked up, and the onlookers in the balcony, like a chorus of singers, uttered a fitful moan. The rebel's blood-streaked face was mostly covered by his long, black, wavy hair. Yet through the thick tresses his eyes were burning with defiance. His full lips, parched by thirst and the beating sun, parted to bare a mischievous grin.

Wang broke the tension. "Do you recognize this man, Your Highness?"

Tuyền pushed himself up from the carved wooden chair, strutted around the desk, and advanced until he was inches away from the cage. Poking his fan through the closely spaced bamboo bars, Tuyền replied with mild amusement, "It has been two years, but he has changed little. I never forget the brazen face of a scoundrel."

Peals of laughter broke out above him, echoing among the timber columns. Tuyền nodded in satisfaction: here within the glittering city, its rich citizens were still on his side. But before he could draw another breath to savor his victory, the gleeful noise above him was cut short.

The convict grabbed the horizontal rods above his head. With a hoarse cry he sprang up from his crouched position, breaking his jail apart with a loud crash. Mandarin Tuyền gasped, blinking. His enemy tossed the cage's ceiling toward Wang, the casino owner, who leaped and kicked his legs wide. Catching the structure with one hand, Wang ripped it apart with the other. Concealed within each of the hollow bamboo bars was a long, thin blade. Wang hurled the weapons to his warriors while the prisoner tore apart the yoke around his neck.

What followed happened so fast and with such precision that every detail must have been choreographed by a grand kung-fu master. Mandarin Tuyền could hear the clashing of swords all around him as his guards engaged the intruders, while the spectators wailed above. In their desperate attempt to escape through the narrow staircases, people pushed one another with such force that a portion of the banister broke away. Shattered pieces of wood and bodies came hurtling to the main floor. A few clung to the remaining rails until their strength gave way and they, too, smashed to the ground.

On the floor below, the former prisoner reached for Tuyền's throat, but the mandarin staggered a few steps back. The rebel's hand seized the front of his uniform, tearing away the phoenix symbol of his rank. With a whimper, Tuyền fell to the ground.

One of the guards thrust his spear toward the escaped convict. Nhạc twisted his body away and, at the same time, grabbed the shackle that bound his ankle. He lunged forward, flung the heavy ball over his head, and smashed it against the thronelike armchair. The sturdy piece of furniture broke into pieces, and the massive orb made a dent in the wooden floor.

Metal javelins shimmered through the air as Tuyền crawled on hands and knees away from the mayhem. He saw the bandit swing his weapon once again, this time aiming it at the guard with the spear. A hollow crack and the soldier sank to his knees like a wedge being driven into a board. Blood from his fractured skull sprayed the mandarin. Too frightened to move, Tuyền huddled in a fetal position. His lips were moving, but he could not hear his own voice.

All around the two men, the fight continued, until one by one the guards of Quinion City were overpowered. The pastel walls were streaked with crimson, blood dripping slowly in the hot sunlight. Body parts and the wounded were scattered about the hall. The coppery smell of blood attracted flies, and before long the buzzing of their wings replaced the screams of the rioting men.

The convict towered over the crawling mandarin, dangling his ball and chain inches over Tuyền's frightened face to stop him from moving any farther. Tuyền could not look at the bits of flesh that adhered to the gruesome sphere. Instead he looked up at his opponent's wicked grin, which seemed to mock his piteous supplication. The bandit grabbed Tuyền by the collar of his inner shirt and lifted him to his feet. "Now, as promised, I've come for my ransom," he said.

The stately doors of the community hall were flung open, and more of Mandarin Tuyền's guards appeared beyond the threshold, bristling with weaponry. Nhạc stepped forward, pulling his prisoner by the collar.

"Put down your swords," he said. His voice boomed like the striking of a gong. "Do it now, or I shall take his life."

He raised the metal ball. Mandarin Tuyền closed his eyes when he heard the first sound of weapons dropping on the pavement. The battle was over.

On the highest parapet of the fortification, the rebels' solid red flag billowed in the wind. Underneath it, the earth undulated with hordes of people flowing in all directions. All were pushing and shoving; none had the slightest idea of what to do or which way to run, but the main tidal wave of people kept pouring toward the city's exits.

With his head locked in the bandit's brawny arm, Mandarin Tuyền was dragged along the concrete road that led to the north gate. His soldiers stood helplessly at either side, their palms opened, defenseless. Fragments of brass shoulder pieces and breastplates lay scattered on the ground. Tuyền tripped over an iron spearhead, and its sharp blade stabbed the side of his foot.

Warm blood seeped from his handmade shoe and smeared the pavement. The mandarin found, to his surprise, that his mind remained quite lucid in spite of the throbbing wound. He did not try to escape the viselike grip because he knew any attempt on his part would be like trying to break a rock with an egg. His face was inches from the rippling muscles of his captor's arm, so close that he could smell the man's perspiration. Fearful of the iron ball, he resisted the urge to scratch and bite.

They stopped a hundred feet from the ancient gate that marked the boundaries of the city. On its surface, the wooden carvings of the mystical animals, once so regal, were now weathered with time. Even in the bright sun, the mandarin could not distinguish one figure from the next. He remembered a time when he had wanted to restore this entrance to its former beauty. Now the chance was gone forever.

Upon a signal, the men hauled back a sturdy log that bolted the entry. The untamed beating of the bronze drums, the fierce shrieks of the brass horns, and the rhythmic thumps of approaching horsemen rose to a crescendo as the two heavy panels creaked open. What waited behind the great wall was beyond Mandarin Tuyền's wildest imaginings.

Standing before them were thousands of peasant soldiers, each carrying a crude weapon. In the center of the crowd, soaring over everyone, was a man perched high on an elephant. The wind rippled through his hair. His broad eyebrows slanted up toward his temples like two dark blades. He rode the animal bareback, commanding it with only his voice. On the ground, his followers chanted, "King Nhạc, King Nhạc, King Nhạc . . ."

Around Mandarin Tuyền, Wang and his men fell to their knees at the sight of their leader. The bewildered mandarin could not understand what he was seeing. He had been led to believe that the man in the cage was Nhạc. Blinking, he looked from his captor to the man on the elephant.

As if reading his thoughts, the rebel by his side laughed. "What did you expect, Tuyền?" he said. "Surely you did not think that our king of the poor would risk his life and be trapped in a cage, did you? My name is Thom. I am his younger brother." And to his soldiers, he pounded his fist in the air and shouted, "Quinion is ours. Hue Citadel is next!"

CHAPTER THIRTEEN

Hue City, December 1775

O n the day of his execution, François woke early.
    In a dark prison cell behind the soldiers' quarters inside King Due Tong's palace, he sat against the cement wall. The peasant shirt he wore was ripped at the back, and his bare skin was pressed against the chilly blocks of stone. A shaft of light, broken up like tendrils of fog, wafted into the room through a small rectangular porthole set high on the wall, near the ceiling. The early sun painted the metal spikes and barbed wires of the window in a faint red glow.

The journey from Kim Lai Village to Quinion, then on to Hue City, had taken more than a week. He was bruised, scraped, and blistered from being transported, along with Henri and their five Annamese disciples, inside a splintery cage drawn over pitted roads in a horse-drawn cart. Their meals were infrequent, and they were denied even the most primitive means to relieve themselves. François felt light-headed and repulsed by his own odor, which stirred in him the memory of Villeneuve and his bout with cholera. But this time his main concerns were not for himself but for his companions.

He hoisted himself up to meet the sunlight. His feet were fettered inside the round openings of two wooden planks fastened together. Each time he tried to move, the sharp inner metal rings around his ankles would dig into his flesh. François gritted his teeth against the pain. For his last morning on Earth, he longed for the warm touch of the sun on his face. Silently and methodically he prayed, reciting the familiar chants in his head, reassuring himself that he was not alone. The destruction of his mission in Kim Lai, the murder of Sister Regina, the uncertain fate of Sisters Natalia and Lucía, and his own impending end — surely these horrifying experiences must be part of God's unseen plan.

Around him lay the dark outlines of eleven other prisoners, clutching one another, motionless. Most of them were men. But here and there he saw the feminine curve of a breast rising under the loose garments. Like the men, the women were bound and shackled. Dawn was now robust enough for him to discern the cuts and bruises on the prisoners' limbs; some of the injuries had begun to fester. On his face, he could feel the tingling sensation where the sun touched his skin, like a torch. Next to him and sharing the same shackle was his sixteen-year-old novice, Henri. The boy was still asleep. His mouth was open, emitting a soft wheezing noise that sounded like a teakettle whistling.

With his bound hands, François scratched his shaven head, feeling a twinge of envy. He had never seen Henri exhibit any signs of fear, even when their death sentences had been pronounced. He believed that the novice was too young to fathom the terror of what was to come. Or did he simply accept his fate? François closed his eyes and tried to pray.

As much as he had tried to envision his death, he couldn't. He saw himself painting the most spectacular work he could ever imagine as an artist in a cathedral, and he saw himself growing old. He felt that when his final hour arrived, it would be the most fulfilled and completed experience, and not delivered at the hands of an executioner. Because of this presentiment, reinforced by his unwavering faith, fear had not yet consumed him.

He had always associated heaven with blissful harps played by angels, whom he had only seen in paintings and heard in dreams. In his mind he saw paradise as the ultimate freedom of his spirit, an eternal existence devoid of suffering, but only to be achieved after he had completed his mission on Earth. He had one regret: that he had never visited the Holy See in Rome to ask Pope Clement XIV to bless him. There should be another chance for him. It couldn't end this way.

He heard his name called, and the warmth of the sunlight disappeared from his closed eyes. When he opened them, Henri was waving his large hand in front of him. Outside, a horse neighed. François gazed at the novice and summoned a smile. With his stocky frame and already six feet in height, the youth seemed like a giant compared to the others. His cheeks blushed from the cold. At a slight angle, François could see the blond fuzz outlining Henri's jaw, reflecting highlights as if a thin layer of gold dust were sprinkled on his face.

The novice adjusted his tattered garments with his trussed hands. The Annamite prisoners were also waking up. Only five of them had been arrested with Henri and François. The rest had been detained for other crimes. Among his disciples, François was especially concerned for the youngest, Lộc. The boy was as sound as a bull, but a bull with no horns, for he was still growing. Two front teeth were missing from his mouth. The wounds in his gum had become infected, causing his upper lip to swell to twice its normal size. In a cracked adolescent voice he cursed at the guards and pounded his fists against the rock wall, shaking dust loose from the ceiling. Droplets of saliva flew from the gap in his mouth and sprayed with his slurred speech.

The rest of the prisoners scrambled to their feet, wailing and trying to keep the dust out of their eyes. A ripple of tension ran through the dungeon as a loud gong rang out, followed by a series of drumbeats. These strident sounds intensified until the walls that detained the prisoners shuddered and the ground vibrated. The significance of the noise was clear: it signaled their execution.

With help from Henri, François stood. Locked in the same wooden shackle, the two men had to move in unison. The time had come for him to confront his destiny. The thought made him weak at the knees. He bit his lower lip and drew a deep breath, then felt Henri's hands pressing against his fingers.

"Pray to God, dear son," he whispered.

The iron door of the cell creaked on its hinges. From a corner, a woman cried out in fright. The guards' footsteps were getting louder. He could hear the reverberation of the men's flat-soled sandals in the cement floor. He resisted the impulse to turn away: he did not want his followers, especially Henri, to see his fear. It was imperative that he, an ordained priest, set a good example. Besides, he still had hope in the mercy of God.

The sunny morning flooded the room as the door swung open. He stared at the entrance, concentrating on the faces that looked back at him. Most of the soldiers were young, their taut bodies clad in the imperial red uniforms and conical hats. They wielded gleaming metal swords in their hands.

"Get up," they roared, even though the prisoners were already on their feet.

Following the soldiers, two male servants pushed in a farm cart, raising a cloud of dust from the dirt road behind them. The wagon held two barrels, each hollowed from the trunk of an oak tree. Once the heavy lids were removed, the smell of stale rice soured the chilly air. As the men drew near, François also detected the aroma of salted fish, and his mouth salivated. The primal urge to satisfy his hunger surpassed the horror of death. Perhaps it was thoughtless to crave food in his last few hours; but he was, after all, still a human being, and he had not eaten for days.

One of the kitchen help, a thin man with skin so dark he seemed to be made from soot, announced, "Dead men's last meal. Come forth for your rations!"

He grinned at the foreign men, waving the wooden ladle toward them. His partner counted the inmates over the steamy mist that rose from the cauldrons. Inside the pot of soup, which was still bubbling, fish heads bobbed in a murky broth.

He looked at the pushcart, at the guards, and then at the servants. There were no plates or spoons in sight. No one offered the prisoners any tools to hold the food. But that did not seem to bother anyone except him. Bound together, the inmates shuffled forward in pairs. Lộc leaned against the wagon of food, hitched up his shirt, and sniffed the air. The bony kitchener shoved his ladle in the rice container to scoop up a healthy serving and dumped it in the shirttail of the hungry youth. Next, the other cook pierced a piece of salted fish using the sharp ends of his chopsticks, piled it on the rice, and then topped it with a spoonful of thick soup. Soon it was François's turn to face the wheelbarrow. He watched the thin man cackle, a toothless grin over the barrel of rice.

The priest flushed red. There was no need for this cruel treatment, he felt. He turned and looked at Lộc. All the boy could do was grab his shirt with his bound hands and bend his head, shoving his wounded mouth into the food like a beast. The broth seeped through his clothing and dribbled down his thin rib cage. François's stomach gave a painful twist.

"Move along, foreigner," the kitchen servant said, flicking a few specks of rice at François with his thumb and forefinger. His smile revealed his blackened teeth. "You want to eat or not?"

"I cannot," François said, looking down at his filthy shirt.

"No place to hold the rice?" the kitchener asked. "Hold out your hands."

He complied, opening his palms to form a bowl. How could God do this to him? Even Jesus had had his final repast in the refectory with his disciples around a table. This cross was getting too heavy to bear. For the first time, he felt angry toward God.

The scrawny cook was relentless. With a quick thrust he emptied a spoonful of hot rice into François's hands. The heat scorched his palms. He nearly gasped, but he would not succumb to the pain. His shoulders drooped, blood drained from his face, his eyes closed, and he moved to the next cauldron. There he received a thick, syrupy layer of soup. The agony went past the threshold of pain and sent him into a new state that bordered on bliss. He opened his eyes and looked at the others. Lộc was still lapping at his shirt and ignoring everyone else. Henri was looking on with horror.

"It's all right," François muttered, mostly to himself. The pain was so intense that it reaffirmed the inevitable. "Soon I won't have much use for my hands anymore."

He bent his head and began eating his last supper.

The path from the prison to the execution site connected King Due Tong's palace to that of Vice-king Truong Loan and stretched for about a mile. At the intersection in front of the king's fortress, a traveler could turn east to exit the city toward the Perfume River, or west to the market, the mandarins' quarters, and the vice-king's castle. Following the imperial guards, the prisoners were forced to turn west. They had heard a rumor among the soldiers that they were going to die in the shadow of Vice-king Loan's palace.

The sky shone with a fresh brilliance, so vast that everything on Earth appeared minuscule in comparison. There was not a cloud, and the sun hung at its midday peak, a cruel patch of orange in the serene ocean of blue.

The road was narrow, and all the lower-ranking soldiers were on foot, arranged according to their station. First in line were two common criers, carrying funnel-shaped instruments made from buffalo horns. When the men blew into them, they made deep groaning sounds, vaguely resembling the trumpeting of elephants. Another pair of menservants swaggered a few steps behind, a bronze gong slung from a bamboo pole between their shoulders. Occasionally, as if to mark the time, they struck it with a wooden mallet. The people of Hue watched the solemn parade while hurling insults at the captives.

The soldiers of higher rank were mounted on horses, surrounding the son of Mandarin Tuyền, who had transported the Kim Lai prisoners here. He was dragging François and the other convicts at the end of a rope tied to his saddle. The priest's hands were trussed together in front of him. The yoke that had cuffed his bare feet had been removed so that he was able to walk. Each time he fell behind, the rope around his neck gave a painful tug.

Around noon, they came to a stream. The rushing hum of its current could be heard from many feet away. When they descended toward it, the ground became muddy and slippery, making it difficult for François to keep up with the strutting horses.

A group of peasants sat on a brown bed of grass on the bank. They were drinking from the brook as they ate. The smell of braised catfish and scallions was pungent in the muggy atmosphere. As the prisoners walked by, the female farmers remained sitting with their heads bowed, holding their portions of food. A man rose to his feet and stared at the passing procession, specks of rice clinging to his wispy beard.

Above the branches of a banyan tree, a flock of crows flew by; their black bodies pierced the azure sky like arrowheads. The rope cut into François's neck, pulling him along.

When they had splashed through the brook, the party was joined by people going in the same direction, toward the market. To prevent the crowd from getting too close to the prisoners, the guards banged their metal gong and blew their buffalo horns. The martial sounds warned the spectators away.

In the confusion, François was pushed to and fro by the desperate convicts. He grasped Henri's tunic so they could stay together. While the sun pounded on him from above, he staggered through an entrance and into a boxlike square surrounded by dwellings, homes of the low third- and fourth-class-ranking mandarins. There, above the yelling of voices around him, a bell tolled. Looking at the ground, François saw his shadow, trembling.

Located on a plot of land behind the mandarins' quarters, the execution ground was teeming with townspeople. Above the heads of the multitude, the back of Vice-king Loan's palace was visible on a twenty-foot stone foundation.

François glanced toward the building, mesmerized by its many towers and pagodalike roofs. Dragons, carved from blocks of granite and functioning as railings, ran the length of the two stairways, which were separated by a circular terrace. At the side windows, white triangular fanions with black rims were hung from the awnings to herald the deaths of the prisoners. With the wind gusting from the east, the flags billowed in waves like the swells of the river.

He was thrust into the middle of the square, surrounded by jeering spectators. *They all came to watch me die,* he thought, and was struck with utter humiliation. With nowhere to hide, he wiggled his fingers inside the tight knot, trying to get comfortable. The pain from the morning's scalding food had dulled to an ache, and it no longer bothered him. As the rest of the captives reached the center of the square, he saw a row of three-foot wooden poles, which had been anchored in the soil a short distant from each other. The crowd grew denser. He knew from the wild faces of the onlookers that they were excited at the spectacle, and he was the main event.

The noise from hundreds of people suddenly fell to a hush. Lộc inched closer, hiding behind François's shoulders. Ignoring the boy, he looked around. In the silence, the sea of bodies parted, starting from the outer rim of the square and splitting inward until a path was formed.

Through this passage he could see a road, which ran alongside a marketplace. Rows of bamboo trees on either side formed a canopy of vivid green. In the distance, a structure resembling a marquee atop a platform glided forward. Its parallel columns supported an open roof of wooden rafters draped with white transparent silk panels. The onlookers fell on their knees and elbows.

As the float came into full view, he saw two lines of porters dragging the miniature palace on wooden wheels. The columns at its corners had been painted white and gold, and they glistened in the sun. Silver bells hanging from the eaves chimed softly to the swaying of the structure. To François, in his weakened state, the vision seemed to shimmer like a mirage.

He heard whispers: "The queen, the queen."

Inside the float was a woman in her early thirties, dressed in royal costume. It was the wife of King Due Tong. Like a porcelain chess piece, she sat under a saucer-shaped rooftop, and around her, the sheer hanging fabric sighed under the touch of the wind. Her skin was concealed beneath a thick layer of white powder. A large silver headdress framed her forehead, hiding her hair. Strands of pearls decorated the crown, making her face seem small and flat.

Peeking through the blank whiteness of her face were two dark eyes, glinting like black agate. A vertical furrow between her brows intensified her expression. Even when her eyes were closed, the wrinkle stayed, hollowed out like a deep scar. François stared at her broad nose and thick upturned lips, reddened by the constant use of betel leaves and areca nuts. The features were far from the European ideal of beauty, but impressive nonetheless.

On the left side of her throne sat a boy of about twelve, dressed in gold, the color of Asian royalty. His appearance was austere, and he acted much older than his years. He straightened his back against a silk cushion, his legs crossed, a hand on each knee. François knew the boy was too young to be the present king. But judging from his outfit, the features he seemed to have in common with the queen, and the air of authority in his gestures, François realized the child must be some important member of the royal family, perhaps the king's cousin or younger sibling. Behind the palanquin walked a row of mandarins and their wives.

At the entrance of the square, the floating palace came to a stop. The porters dispersed in two directions, giving the royals full view of the execution ground. A figure stepped from among the mandarins and approached the queen. He wore an Annamite robe, but his eyes were light in color compared to the others. To François's amazement, he recognized the face of Bishop de Béhaine, barely exposed under an official cap.

The chimes stirred as the Jesuit said something to the queen. A breath of wind from the river tossed the curtains aside, and the bishop looked straight at François.

I am safe, he thought with joy. It was the miracle that he needed to see from God, and the bishop was His messenger. God had not deserted him. He was going to be saved. Next to him, Henri uttered a loud sob. The novice had also recognized the severe gentleman beside the queen.

Tall among the Annamites, de Béhaine gazed at the condemned priest. François beamed, unable to stop a flood of joyous tears. He waited for a sign of recognition from his sponsor. But the bishop looked through him. The bright sun made his sunken eyes appear as gray as bones. Then de Béhaine turned his attention back to the queen.

François felt abandoned. His next thoughts came with a more objective scrutiny as he tried to understand the bishop's behavior. By acknowledging the convicts, de Béhaine might have put himself in danger. But why would he be here, among the very rulers of a society that denounced Christianity? Was the bishop here to save him with some hidden plan or simply to witness his execution? François was more confused than ever.

Then he noticed Henri on the ground. One of the guards had his foot on the boy's head, pushing his face into the dirt.

"What happened?" François asked when the soldier turned away.

The novice spit mud from his mouth and said, "I tried to call for the monsignor's attention, but these men hit me."

"Be patient, my son," François whispered. "God has a plan." And then he muttered to himself, "It has to be. I just can't die like this."

De Béhaine retreated until he was no longer in view. The queen whispered in the prince's ear and raised a finger to the crowd, which roared in response. Like ink spilled into a basin of water, the excitement spread through the masses. François saw the terror that shook the other captives' bodies, as though they all knew something that he was unaware of.

"Prepare for the execution," shouted the official who had transported the prisoners.

It was all he could do to keep from falling. His hands gripped the restraining ropes. Bishop de Béhaine did not seem likely to interfere with his destiny today.

Drumbeats rumbled against the sky, and the birds scattered from the bamboo shrubs, screeching. Their scarlet bodies fluttered above him like little balls of flame.

From the left side of the queen's pergola, three men, clad in black linen, marched toward the prisoners. Bristly beards and mustaches concealed their mouths. Each of them carried a sword across his shoulder, the long blades wrapped in black cloth so that they became a part of his uniform. He knew beyond any doubt that these men were going to be his executioners.

He closed his eyes. Someone seized the cord around his neck, and he felt it dangle for an instant before it jerked him forward. He lost his balance and fell to the ground.

Helpless cries were all around him. He was dragged through the dirt until his head collided with a wooden stake. An odor of dried blood forced him to reopen his eyes. There were dark stains on the posts, and he could almost hear the screams of the past prisoners who had died there.

"Please, our Father in heaven," he shouted, unthinkingly reverting to French. "Deliver these people from evil. And save my soul, for my life is now and will forever be in your hands."

Someone took hold of his collar, lifted him to his knees, and settled him with his heels pressed against his tailbone. His back arched until he leaned against the post. His head tilted backward to rest on it. A few feet away, Henri struggled vainly to untie himself, his face white.

Turning to François, he said in a calm voice, "Father, you are a good teacher and an excellent friend. Do you remember the first time we met, in a dark street, a month before we left Marseille together?"

François did not answer. Instead he prayed louder and continued to search the sky above. His face was wet with tears. "Dear Lord, how long will You let your children suffer? Take my soul now and purify it with your eternal love. Help me bear the pain of what is to come. Do not leave me, for I am frightened."

Henri spoke again. "I never regretted following you to this land. Never, Father. Every time I think of that day, I am happy. Thank you for saving me."

François realized that except for his own faltering enunciation and Henri's whisper, no one else spoke. All was hushed in the square, and he could hear the wind rustling through the leaves. The young prince stepped down from his cushion and walked toward the prisoners. His long golden tunic, edged with embroidery and silk fringe, dragged across the mud. The three executioners knelt and bowed their heads. In the mounting tension, people seemed to have stopped breathing — they had never seen a royal so close. The prince walked straight up to François.

On his knees and wilting, the priest was face to face with the boy-prince. Although the boy's skin was smooth and the rest of his features seemed childlike, an ancient spirit peered through his round, birdlike eyes. The prince tilted his head back slightly and, from that position, was able to look down at the priest.

"Who are you praying to, foreign monk?" he asked.

"My God, Lord Jesus Christ, Your Highness," François answered.

"If your Jesus is a god, can he save you from death?"

François licked his lips. "I have accepted my fate. It is whatever God wills."

The pagan boy-prince asked, "Will you renounce your God in exchange for your life?"

François swallowed hard to suppress the loud resounding *yes* that struggled to burst from his mouth. He was quickly overcome by shame at his surprising and unbidden thought.

"Dear Lord, help me," he moaned.

"Well?" The boy-prince pressed. "What is your answer?"

"No," he whispered.

"Will you then renounce your God in exchange for your life and the lives of your fellow missionaries?"

François looked at Henri and his disciples. He saw his own fright reflected on their faces. They pleaded with him silently. He shut his eyes and nodded.

The prince turned to the mandarin-in-charge and gave an order. "Release this man and his followers. Kill the others." To François, he said, "Remember this day, priest. Your god, Lord Jesus, did not save you. I, Prince Ánh, spared your life. Now make sure that you never preach the words of your false cult in my country again. If we meet once more in a similar circumstance, I will not be so compassionate."

He made a swift turn and walked away.

François slumped against the post, defeated. He had been saved from the claws of Death, but his soul was shattered. He could no longer feel the presence of God or, worse, believe in Him.

CHAPTER FOURTEEN

Henri could not grasp that he had been set free by a boy who could not have been older than twelve. For the past year living in Annam he had been happy. Unlike the older missionaries, he had had no trouble easing into the new culture. It was as though he had been born in this land. But in prison, all his comfort had been shattered. He had prepared himself to die. Now that he'd been given a second chance, his most fervent desire was simply to live.

He knew that at any moment the queen of Cochin China might override the prince's ruling with a simple hand gesture. His heart lurched. He could see the impatience on the faces of the executioners and of the queen's guards, eighty to a hundred men. The metallic glint of their drawn swords mimicked the sun. They were all eager for the sight of blood.

The instant his ropes were undone, he dragged himself away from the post. The prisoners who were not pardoned remained kneeling. No one made a sound, but the site was tense with anticipation.

He realized that he must get away before the crowd demanded a greater spectacle. He did not want to witness the executions of the others. He ran to François, who was lying on the ground in the fetal position with his hands clasped over his head.

"On your knees," a guard shouted.

Henri ignored him. "Come! Help Father François," he yelled to Lộc.

At the center of the square, the executioners were advancing on the prisoners. His voice was drowned by the pounding drums that seemed to rise up from within the crowd. Lộc walked away as though he did not hear him.

He had to get himself and Father François out of this city.

"Kneel down," repeated the guard, standing behind Henri. His drooping mustache curved across his face like an exaggerated black frown.

He did not have time to comply. He felt a violent pain at the back of his head. From the corner of his eye, he saw Lộc fending off a pack of sentries. The sky seemed to become brighter, and the sun hovered above him with the menace of a fireball. It wasn't long before the sun smashed into him, and the earth caught fire.

He collapsed next to François and hugged the ground with his outstretched arms.

The smell of blood brought Henri back to consciousness. He could hear the buzz of horseflies. He had been turned over on his back and was looking upward. The evening was approaching. In the soft, red dusk, the sky was closing in like a coffin's lid.

He sprang up, gasping for air. Then he felt the iron manacle wrapped around his neck. It was a crude collar, rough in design, making it hard for him to breathe. A blacksmith must have forged it on him during the time he had passed out from the guard's blow.

He was still in the courtyard, but the floating pagoda, the crowd, the sentries, the executioners, and the royal family had all vanished. Before him, six decapitated corpses hunched over, tied to the poles. Flies were feasting on their severed necks, where pools of blood had coagulated. The view and its stench were so gruesome that he wondered if he had entered hell. But his headache reminded him that he was still earthbound.

His stomach gave a painful squeeze at the overwhelming aroma of death. Coughing, he staggered across the square.

With each gust of wind the sunlight faded. He heard a moan, and a voice called his name. A dark figure huddled close to the wall. It was his teacher.

François staggered from his refuge. He, too, wore an iron collar, welded around his neck. Written on it was a series of characters in red paint that Henri could not read. François appeared drained. Still, the sight of him flooded Henri with relief. He threw his arms around his teacher. The priest's body felt as though it would collapse.

"Where is Lộc and everybody else?"

When there was no answer, he grabbed François's head and examined it for wounds. There were none.

"Gone," sighed the priest.

"Are they dead?"

François shook his head. The look in his eyes was vacant.

"Thank God we are still alive," Henri said. "Come with me. It is getting dark. We must leave before the gate is locked."

To his surprise, the priest stood motionless. Henri took his teacher's arm and guided him forward.

They chose the main road, heading east. If they hurried, Henri thought they could reach the Perfume River in less than two hours.

He was eager to leave the citadel. Finding refuge among the peasants would be their only hope. In some remote village he and François might have a chance. Once they were safe, the priest would be able to decide what to do next.

When they came to the east entrance of the fortress, the gates had already been shut. Fifteen or twenty imperial guards stopped the two travelers from advancing farther. François retreated behind the boy. The guards talked among themselves, pointed to the iron collars, and burst into laughter. The priest covered his ears with his hands.

"May we pass?" Henri said, half pleading.

One of the sentries replied, "Criminals are not allowed to walk the same path as the king's citizens. If you want to leave the citadel, crawl like an animal."

He pointed his sword at a small opening beneath the wall; it had probably been dug by a dog. From above, a yellow moon sprayed its thin glow on the slope that led to the hole.

Henri swallowed, reminding himself to control his temper. If he wanted to leave this place alive, he had no choice but to do what they ordered.

He turned to François. "Father, we must do as they say. Please go first. I will be behind you."

The priest obeyed, his eyes fixed on the dark opening. Another burly guard aimed a kick at him and pushed him forward. With a cry, François fell face-first into the pit. Henri was trembling with rage. Still he said nothing.

A voice boomed like thunder over the soldiers. "Stop your harassment at once!"

They all turned, and Henri saw the high forehead of de Béhaine above the light of an oil lantern. He was escorted by a group of soldiers in red uniforms. The two sides stared at each other, and the novice called out in excitement, "Monsignor!"

Standing beside him, the guard who had kicked François repeated like an anxious parrot, "Monsignor!"

De Béhaine halted. His face was devoid of all expression as he removed one of his black silk gloves, taking his time. Then he looked at the guard, gesturing with his bare hand. "You! Come closer."

The frightened man approached.

"What did you just call me?" de Béhaine asked him, ignoring Henri and his teacher.

The guard, sensing hostility, shifted his eyes back to Henri as if searching for an answer. When he received nothing, he whispered, "I called you *Monsignor, sir.*"

The priest's eyes flared in indignation. His glove swung in the dark, and he slapped the man's cheek.

"I am not a monsignor," he said in a soft, conversational voice. "I have been Bishop of Madras for almost two years now. How long have I been the private tutor of His Majesty? Haven't you learned anything, fool? You must address me as Your Excellency. Do not forget this title. Ever!"

He glared at Henri, and the boy flinched, wondering if he should have known about de Béhaine's promotion. The bishop turned to the guards.

"What are you waiting for?" he barked. "Get out of my sight."

The Annamite soldiers faded into the darkness. The bishop's men also retreated, taking the lantern with them.

The bishop's face blended into the night, masking his expression. To hide his nervousness, Henri moved to his teacher's side, helping François to rise. The priest trembled, unsteady on his feet. The bishop studied the two of them.

"What is wrong with Father François?" he asked.

As if you didn't know, you pompous priest, Henri thought. But he swallowed his resentment and replied, "I think the near escape from the execution has affected his mind." He threw a furious glance at de Béhaine, and added, "Your Excellency."

The bishop came closer. A frown creased his forehead.

"You think what happened to you and Father François is my fault," he said. "You think that I should have interceded with the queen to spare your lives. What makes you think that I didn't try to?"

Henri continued his reproving frown until his rage incited the bishop.

"How dare you?" de Béhaine roared. "A novice is accusing me of his misfortune with such a look? The rice of your last meal is still wedged between your teeth. Who do you think arranged it for you?" Drops of spittle flew from his mouth. "What do you know about God's will, or about the politics and diplomacy between nations? Do you think my mission in this land was only to rescue failed missionaries? Or do you believe that your lives are worth more than the importance of the Church, which I have worked so diligently to establish over all these years?"

Henri blanched. His anger turned to fear.

The bishop's voice became rueful. "Or are you convinced I am heartless and so cowardly that my fear of death overpowers any desire I might have to save you?"

Those had been Henri's thoughts. He needed to stop the bishop from talking so he could have time to think. "Why are you here?" he asked. "In our last meeting you told us that you were going to return with Captain Petijean in a year with supplies."

The bishop unhooked his stiff collar and caressed his neck. When he spoke, his eyes were closed, and the pale moonlight bathed his austere face in its glow. "You might have met death this afternoon, but I live with it every day. Life is cheap in this land. I came to the Far East ten years ago, when I was only twenty-four. Like you, I was pursued by misfortune. I have repeatedly been subjected to imprisonment, torture, and death threats. But I never accepted defeat. I have sworn an oath to God.

"The main test of my faith came five years ago, when the governor of Hatien Province ordered his men to burn down my mission. My entire life up to that point, all of my hard work and effort, was destroyed. The native students I recruited either are dead or have renounced their faith. I alone survived that catastrophe. I had to flee Annam and seek refuge in India, where I was appointed Bishop of Madras. My heart and soul still belong to Cochin China. I am now the private tutor for the royal family in Hue Palace. I do not preach

Christianity to them. I only give them some knowledge of the Western world. As they learn more about me, I learn more about them. Prince Ánh is one of my students. You must know who he is. He spared your life this afternoon."

He opened his eyes and looked at François, who returned a blank stare. The bishop stepped closer and said in his ear, "Father, I know who you were before you came to Avignon. And I know more about your past than you think. None of that matters now. In Kim Lai I warned you about the difficulties you would encounter, from the destruction of your mission to the test of your faith. You didn't listen. Neither God nor I has abandoned you. It is you who abandoned God. I was there when you renounced our Lord to save your life. When forced to choose between survival and faith, many of my missionaries have preferred to be martyrs, but not you. You decided to save your skin, not your soul. You are not fit to be a missionary."

He turned to Henri and moved his hand to expose his neck. The scar was visible under the moonlight. "So you see, novice, I too am familiar with humiliation and fear. And I know what it is to wear the collar of denouncement."

Henri touched his own iron brace.

The bishop continued. "Yes, that iron ring will tell the citizens that you are a religious outcast. The writing says that you don't believe in their traditions and values, or their gods; therefore, they are making you renounce your own God as punishment. You cannot remove it. Any attempt to do so will be punished by death. It will scratch and gnaw at your neck for as long as you wear it. It will remind you and others that your faith is not as strong as your urge to live. As for me, I knew I had to wear the collar in order to continue the Lord's work. But look at your teacher — he is dazed and unable to speak. His ordeal has broken his spirit, and he is wearing that collar for a different reason than I did. Therefore, take him to Quinion and find Captain Petijean. He will take you both back to France. I hereby release you from your vows."

François gasped.

Henri reddened. "But —"

The bishop overrode him. "I am the Bishop of Madras. This title was granted to me by His Holiness, Pope Clement XIV. You must do as I say."

"Will our sins be forgiven?" Henri asked, mainly for François's sake.

The bishop's serenity was more severe than any anger Henri might have had.

"There is only one who can answer that question," he said. "Ask God."

CHAPTER FIFTEEN

Henri and François walked for hours through a field that stretched behind the citadel. The path forced them to climb to the top of a rocky promontory, where they sat for a few minutes looking back down on the walled city where they had narrowly escaped death. As they continued walking east, the land became more desolate, and the air was heavy with moisture.

Late in the evening, they heard the babbling of the Perfume River. Henri was too tired to go on. There was no village in sight, but in the air he detected a faint smell of cooking spices. The breeze brought the smoke to them from far away. He had a few silver coins, given to him by the bishop, which he had hidden in a band around his waist. The money provided the only touch of promise in their otherwise bleak future.

Above them, gloomy clouds framed the silvery moon. Large, spherical drops of rain fell, shiny as mercury, on Henri's head. They soaked his clothes and plastered them sheer against his skin.

Henri and François were alone. The novice peered ahead, but he could not penetrate the darkness. François murmured incoherently, his face a mask. Henri hoped that his teacher's confusion would be temporary. The priest wandered aimlessly on the road.

"Please, Father François," he said, "we have to get out of the rain. I need you to be stronger."

François did not seem to hear him. His fingers curled into fists and drew up under his armpits. He marched to the middle of the road, turning his back to Henri. His clothes sagged under the weight of the rain, outlining his body. From behind, with his shoulder blades sticking out, he looked like a bat, ready to fly into the night.

The bitter smell of wet soil was getting stronger as the breeze changed direction. Henri wiped the water from his eyes. The thought of leaving his teacher seeped into his mind. But the land ahead was dark and desolate. More than ever, he needed companionship.

A clap of thunder boomed, and by the lightning that followed, the novice saw a cluster of huts on stilts, clinging to the soil. Dead trees stabbed the sky with clawlike branches. In the distance, the Perfume River glimmered behind a row of rocks. The rain splattered on the rippling water, turning its surface into reptilian scales. Then all became dark again.

They walked through a sunken path toward the village. By the time they could hear raindrops hitting on the thatched roofs, a swamp opened before them. The mud rose to their ankles, slimy against their skin. Henri waded past a row of tree trunks toward the nearest hut. A foul stench, stirred up by his movements, carried rotten vapors in its waft.

He climbed the wooden ladder, dribbling a trail of muck behind him. He knocked, but instead of hitting a door, his knuckles scraped against a curtain that was hanging from the door frame. A small strip of light shone under the fabric. Inside, cautious footsteps stirred, and moments later, voices whispered, nearly muffled by the rain. The creaking of his weight on the old rungs must have awakened the occupants.

A voice shouted, "Who is there?"

"We are two travelers in need of shelter," replied Henri.

As soon as the words came out of his mouth, he realized his mistake. His foreign accent had given away more information than he would have liked. Behind the burlap, the murmuring stopped. He leaned against the frame and waited, shivering.

"Please help us," he begged. "We are wet and cold."

The only sound he heard was the pounding rain.

"We have money."

At Henri's feet, the faint glow brightened into a flood of light. He looked up to see the burlap part. Blocking the entrance was a man in his midthirties, without clothes except for a bit of cloth that covered his loins. He was holding up an oil lantern. Its flame illuminated his bronze face and added glints of copper to his beard. As he caught sight of the iron collar on the novice's neck, he took a step back.

"I cannot let you in," he said.

Henri turned around and searched for François. The priest stood on the ground beside the ladder. His face was lost in shadow. Behind him, the swamp glowed.

Henri had no more strength to look for another shelter. The room behind the Annamite man was warm, and the smell of fried fish and steamed vegetables made his mouth water.

He cleared his throat. "If we leave, my teacher surely will die from the cold and exhaustion. He is not well. Please let us in. We will depart in the morning as soon as the rain stops." Sensing the man's hesitation, he added, "I'll pay you, sir."

"I know who you are," replied the peasant. "Foreigners teaching the forbidden religion. You are criminals. I can't harbor you even if you pay me. I have a family to protect."

He stepped aside, and Henri saw identical twin girls, hiding behind their father. Wrapped in a mat woven from rush, the children could not have been more than twelve. They looked at him with a quiet expression as their father hugged them closer to his side. The light from the lantern hovered above their heads. Although the girls seemed frail, their cheeks were rose-colored, and their long black hair glistened in the amber light.

Henri was stunned by the beauty of the two girls. They looked like fawns in the forest. The bonds of happiness among the three people before him pierced his lonely heart. With nothing else to say, he bowed his head and bade them good-bye.

"What kind of Buddhists are we if we shut our door to these suffering souls, husband?" said a voice from a corner of the room. "How will you teach our children kindness when all they witness from you is indifference and fear?"

The man turned around. His lantern swept the room until it came to rest on the slight figure of a woman. She lay on a bamboo bed, facing them. Dried skin was peeling from her lips. She had long, thick hair — a trait that the twins had inherited — that flowed over the pillow to touch the floor. It seemed to be her only healthy feature. She acknowledged Henri by nodding in his direction.

"B-but —" the man stammered.

"Their only wish is to be our guests for one night," she said. "Of all the sheds in this village, they chose ours. It was destiny." Her eyes were large and feverish, conveying more of her thoughts than her words. Her husband heaved a defeated sigh.

"Please bring your companion inside," he said. "My wife and I and the children welcome you to our humble home."

In front of a terra-cotta stove that crackled with burning wood, they were each served a bowl of rice topped with fried bass. To Henri the fish came as no surprise, since it was the main diet in this region. But the pork fat and heavy seasoning that flavored it turned it into a delicious treat. He ate rapidly, grabbing the fish in his fingers and biting into its crispy skin until the comblike bone was clean.

Nearby, François squatted on his thighs and leaned toward the stove. He chewed the food slowly. It was impossible for Henri to guess what his teacher was thinking. He seemed far away, absent-minded, lost. The twins huddled under the blanket with their mother, watching him. All of them were curious about François's state of mind. But Henri knew it was not their custom to ask questions.

When the guests finished eating and their clothes had begun to dry from the heat, black tea was served. Its bitterness curled the novice's tongue, and his forehead broke into a sweat. He savored the warmth of the tea, feeling his limbs relax for the first time in days. Outside the window, a bird cried over the din of the rain.

"Y Lan and Xuan," said their father, "it is considered bad manners to stare at the guests. The black cuckoos are calling. That means it will be dawn soon. Go to sleep with your mother."

The little girls crawled under their mother's arms and giggled.

The father mumbled to the priests, "Forgive them; they have never seen a Western man before. They don't understand why you don't have black hair and narrow eyes."

"That is enough," said the woman. "Do not cause any more discomfort to these gentlemen than they have already experienced."

The husband fell silent. Henri decided to change the subject. "What happened to the trees?" he asked. "So many are dead."

"They drowned," she replied.

Henri looked at her husband, unable to imagine what she meant.

"Too much water, too much water," said the man. He stood up, spreading his arms to make a sweeping gesture as he explained. "The flood came and stayed for many days. Some trees were uprooted and washed down the river. Others rotted away. We are fortunate because our home still stands. My father and I built this hut together when I was your age. Without it, we would have nothing. If the water continues to rise, we will lose everything."

"Husband, please sit. You must not preach with your arms open. The loincloth and that light make you look like the Jesus man."

Her eyes squinted, and she winked at her husband. He stifled an embarrassed laugh.

Henri hid his thin smile behind his cup of tea. Even François, in his perplexed state, seemed amused by the hostess's unexpected humor. But the laughter was short-lived. From under the blanket, one of the girls shrieked. And soon after, her sister joined in with her own scream. They sprang out of the bed. Their mother tried to soothe them, but suddenly she too was struck with horror. Her husband ran to her side.

Henri was taken by surprise — he had not anticipated any danger inside the hut. He followed the man and caught a glimpse of a snake as it slithered through a small crack on the bed and blended into the darkness of the wooden floor. It had moved so fast that the novice did not have time to see it clearly. For a terrible moment, he imagined how its slick body would feel gliding along the inside of his tunic. He bit his lip to keep from cursing.

With the snake out of sight, the Annamite man shifted his attention to his wife. She sat up and leaned over the edge of her bed. He helped her to her feet. She drew a labored breath, dragging herself along beside her husband. Her hair, thick and glistening like a silk shroud, swallowed him. He placed her against the wall, and gently he picked the hair up from the ground with both of his hands, rolled it around one palm, and twisted it into a large chignon at the back of her head. Henri noticed her swollen abdomen, pushing beneath her blouse in spite of her emaciated frame. She was at least six months' pregnant.

"This is very bad," her husband murmured.

"What is happening?" Henri asked, wondering if the snake was considered a bad omen.

"Hold her, please," the man said.

She leaned against the young novice, who supported her among the confusion. In the cooking area, François remained sitting. Only now, he had his arms wrapped around the twins, who were silent. Their father ran toward the entrance. He grabbed the curtain with both hands and ripped it away from its frame.

At first, Henri could not understand what the man was searching for. All he saw was a view of dead tree branches crisscrossing a dark sky. Then silhouettes of dangling vines that cascaded down from the roof came alive and recoiled in a rhythmic motion. A few of them slipped to the floor.

The children began to cry again. Henri felt a chill when his eyes at last acknowledged the familiar forms of the snakes — hundreds of them seemed to be falling from the sky, along with the rain. They slithered across the floor with incredible speed, avoiding the humans.

"W-what is happening?" Henri asked, his voice quivering.

"The flood is rising," the man replied. "The snakes are trying to reach higher ground. We have to get out of here."

A cold wetness licked at the soles of Henri's feet. The hut gave a violent shake, and a gurgle rose from below. Water seeped in between the cracks of the floorboards, rising in a continuous flow.

Henri stood frozen, watching in disbelief as his feet disappeared into the growing tide. The air bore a heavy, penetrating smell, like overturned mud mixed with an undefined floral fragrance. A sharp blow stung the side of his face.

"Are you listening to me, foreign man?" said his host. "Or do I have to slap you again?"

Henri recoiled, and the man struck him again.

"Whatever you are planning to do, tell me." His voice sounded weak in his ears.

"Help my wife and daughters. We must get to the roof now."

His teacher stood on a windowsill and lifted one of the girls to the top of the hut. The other twin waited by François's side, clutching his shirt. Snakes were crawling everywhere, wrapping themselves around the girl's limbs. She cried each time one fell on her, but despite her fear, she grabbed the reptiles by their tails and swung them over the ledge into the water.

"Don't worry, darling," her father reassured her. "They are grass snakes, the harmless kind."

Henri lifted the woman in his arms and carried her to the window. Outside, the first rays of sun turned the sky a faint gray. The water surged.

He was the last person to reach the top of the hut. But their misery was far from over. While they huddled there, the flood continued to rise, coming after them with white, fuming waves like the crowns of a thousand swift horses, shrieking madly in the wind. Lightning flashed across the sky, leaping from one cloud to another in red and blue streaks. As the water mounted higher, the Annamese man sliced away the vines that connected the roof to the hut's walls. Once detached, it was swept away by the current, twirling with the refugees on its back. The downpour unraveled the woman's chignon, and her hair flew free. She tried to gather it back in her hands but was too weak.

"Oh, no," cried one of the twins. "The house is drifting away."

The man reached for his children. "Don't be frightened," he said over the screeching bellows of nature. "Lie flat on your stomach and hold tight to the palm leaves so the wind won't knock you over."

"Be still," added the mother. "*Má* is here. Soon it will be over. We will be safe."

The parents looked at each other, and in a pulse of lightning Henri caught a secret exchange of despair between them. He kept his body low as the flood spread farther into the delta, taking them through a newly formed maze of lagoons and channels. Ahead, Hue City slowly disappeared as the water redefined the borders of the Earth.

Nothing seemed to withstand the flood's wrath. All that was left, as far as they could see, was a handful of rooftops that had been turned into floating islands with people on them, clinging like colonies of ants. Teetering above the waves were the heads of a few palm trees and the leafy branches of wild oaks, filtering the water that coursed through them.

The raft gave an unexpected jolt as it collided with a tree. The water's momentum kept it spinning while the undertow pulled it forward as though it were caught in a whirlpool. The woman screamed. She reached for her husband, but her hands could only grab the empty space in front of him. She floundered for an agonizing moment before she was pulled into the water by her hair, which was tangled in the tree. Her cry was stifled when she sank beneath the waves.

"*Má!*" screamed the twins simultaneously.

Without hesitation, their father plunged into the murky water after his wife. Henri stared at the place where the pair had been. Their sudden disappearance was more frightening than his wait for the executioners, for now he was left in command. He knew he had to find a way to stop the makeshift barge from abandoning the couple.

He thrust his hands blindly into the tree's branches. They kept sliding and slipping until he found a limb that he could grasp. He wedged his feet between two roof boards to serve as an anchor. But nature's force was unyielding, and the water was stronger than he was.

"Help!" he screamed to François.

The priest wrapped his arms around Henri's legs to anchor him as he searched for the Annamite pair. The woman's long hair clung to the tree as her husband struggled to untangle her. The river beneath them continued to swell.

Henri gritted his teeth. His strength was dwindling, and he could no longer hold on to the branch when it retreated in the water. Something indomitable was sucking it downward. With a quick jerk, it slipped through his fingers, and the tree vanished into the deep. Like a fish caught in the tentacles of a sea monster, the woman was submerged with it, her husband clinging to her. All that was left in Henri's hands was a cluster of leaves as the raft was swept away.

The river churned. A surge from its belly propelled the tree upward again, with its captives entwined in its branches, rising some twenty feet in the air. The woman looked at him with the sad acceptance of a saintly martyr. The twins shrieked, reaching for their mother. François held them back. With a crashing sound, their parents disappeared for the last time.

Henri fell back, exhausted. The river raged on, and the rain pummeled him with its ice-cold beads until at last the sky was drained.

CHAPTER SIXTEEN

*T*hroughout the morning, the flood continued to rise, washing away all life in its path. Only with ceaseless effort could Henri and his team maintain their grip on the tossing rooftop that had become their sanctuary. Sometimes lying on their stomachs, then crouching on hands and knees, the castaways laced their fingers and toes through the roof's rough timbers until they bled, while under them the waves hammered the bottom of the raft like a thousand angry fists.

Seizing a branch from the rolling waters, Henri used it as a crude paddle, doing his best to guide the craft. Toward midday, as they floated toward drier ground, the river slowed its pace. Above, the clouds shrank to mere balls of unthreatening cotton. The refugees lay sprawled on the battered rooftop, while a few rays of sun beat down on them.

Gliding through blankets of thick reeds and tall grass, Henri at last was able to catch his breath. Trailing his fingers in the water, he examined his surroundings. A floating graveyard of debris surrounded his vessel, with furniture, mats, clothing, and rags entwined in its planks. His hand brushed across a fleshy mass beneath the water's surface. The face of an infant, frozen into a grimace, floated a few inches away. He stared until the baby disappeared among the dark oak logs that bobbed next to him.

Part of his mind told him he should feel repugnance at touching the corpse, but he was numb. Dimly, he regretted how callous he must seem to the twins crouching a few feet away. Even their suffering no longer stirred him.

The wind and current drove the raft forward. More corpses passed by, some with long tendrils of hair that drifted in the water. One of the twins leaned over the edge to turn over the cadavers in search of her parents. Her shirt was as muddy as the water. Large patches over her shoulders and elbows showed her mother's attempts to mend the torn fabric. The sunlight glinted in her eyes, exposing her sadness.

Inside François's embrace, the other twin swayed to the water's rhythm. Unlike her sister's, her blouse was pink. It hugged her torso in a way that gave her a more mature appearance. To Henri, the little girl's bright top only underscored the dismal situation they were all in. But it helped him to make a distinction between the two girls — the one in gray carrying out her grim task while her sister, in pink, watched.

They were entering a sunken plain surrounded by jutting mountains. The current flowed between steep banks, forking into smaller streams. To their right they could see the roofs and parapets of the citadel of Hue City. The fortress's high walls had so far acted as a dam, shielding the inner city from the flood. But even from this distance, Henri could see the waves crash against the structure, and he wondered how long it could withstand the mounting pressure. Squinting, he could make out the forms of sentries, armed with bows and arrows and naked swords, poised atop the fortress's walls as if they were ready to battle the flood. Their voices echoed along the water's surface as they called and relayed orders.

Henri looked for a place to dock their raft. After floating for some eight hours, they were back where he and his teacher had rested briefly the night before. The flood had erased their entire journey, as if it were nothing but a bad dream. Now he and the others were weak from hunger, thirst, and exhaustion.

Grasping his oar, Henri paddled with all the strength that was left in him, steering the raft out of the main current. After forty brisk strokes, his lungs were burning, but the river's edge was too steep to permit a landing. The raft made slow progress along the inhospitable shoreline, following a sparrow that skimmed a short distance ahead. Its dark wings fluttered against the sky like a lost punctuation mark and blended into the haze of the afternoon.

A short distance downstream, the landmass closed in around them, and a thick fog blurred the inlets between the crags. As they rounded a rocky outcropping, the little girl in gray crawled toward Henri. She raised her head and stared up at the dark shape of the approaching mountain.

"What's your name?" he asked.

"I am Xuan," she muttered. "My sister is Y Lan."

"Do you know where we are?" he asked.

"My father called it Ngự Bình Mountain," she said. "We came here often to gather mushrooms."

The mention of happier days seized her, and she let out a sob, using her sleeves to cover her face. The force of her tears made her dwindle back to the little girl he had encountered the night before.

Henri turned away, unable to think of an appropriate way to act. The memory of his mother came to his mind, and his eyes welled up. He waited for that grievous moment to pass with the same will that he had drawn on to weather the storm. Although he sympathized with the girl's misery, he was reluctant to reach over and comfort her. The twins were now parentless; but unlike him, they still had each other.

He leaned forward, grabbed the nearest rock, and pulled the raft to shore. *Ngự Bình,* he understood, meant, "the king's screens." The name was now infected with a touch of irony, as its sole purpose was believed to be to shield the citadel from catastrophes. The mountain pushed its indifferent, slanted chest forward, oblivious to those who suffered. He helped the others disembark from their tipsy craft, climbed a few paces up the slope, and looked back to make sure they were following him.

The mountain was a mass of granite and shale, with a coating of soil that nurtured only a few thin pine trees and scattered underbrush. Beyond a succession of rock formations, Henri came to a narrow trail.

The sun hid behind the folds of the mountain. The sparrows returned, circling the sky in search of their nests. Once again, stillness mesmerized the land, and everything seemed to sink into a stupor as the light of the sunset faded on the rocky walls.

Henri looked back at his companions. A few feet behind him at the side of the trail, Xuan stood on a steep bank, leaning against a large stone. Her shadow lay motionless on the ground.

"I can hear a horse," she whispered.

Henri listened. At first he heard nothing, then something that sounded like heavy rain reverberated across the cliffs. Images of the guards on the citadel's ramparts flashed in his mind.

He stared ahead on the trail but saw only scattered rocks and stunted grass before the road made a sharp turn to the right, preventing him from seeing beyond. He knelt and offered his hand to Xuan. She ignored it and, instead, threw her arms around him. He lifted her until her head was even with his own, and when he saw the fear in her eyes, he felt as though he were gazing at his reflection in a mirror.

"Hurry, Father François."

Y Lan and François caught up with them. The priest walked hand in hand with his young companion, their faces sharing the same absent gaze. Their calm infuriated Henri.

"Father François," he said, "have you taken a vow of silence? Or have you gone completely mad? Answer me if you've heard anything I've said. I am sick of having to take charge because you decided to forgo your responsibilities. I ask you, sir, where is your courage? Where is your faith?"

The priest lowered his eyebrows. He flinched but did not reply. The little girl in pink shook his hand to get his attention. He turned to face her.

"I know your fears," Henri went on. "So, your God has abandoned you. And now your faith is in doubt. But look around you, look at the devastation! This is life and we are still living it. These things happen because they happen, and not for any other reason —"

He could not finish his sentence. An explosion shook the very ground they stood on. From above them, a deep rumbling filled the sky. The air smelled of gunpowder, the mountain groaned, and thousands of boulders and rocks came tumbling down toward the water's edge. As Henri and his companions stared in dismay, the avalanche thundered down the hillside in front of them.

The children screamed. A wall of dirt and debris knocked him to the ground and darkness engulfed him, stealing his breath.

When the bombardment ceased, he found himself flat on his back on the narrow trail, with his hand caught under a large stone. A numbness spread from the tips of his fingers to his elbow. The boulder that had kept him from being swept into the river was crushing his hand.

Xuan and François lay facedown beside him on the cold, damp ground, surrounded by the rocks that had been dislodged from above. Y Lan, the twin in the pink blouse, was nowhere in sight.

Henri threw his shoulder against the rock that pinned his hand. When he was able to pull his hand free, he saw that it was covered in blood, and the last two fingers were twisted backward. Pain shot to his shoulder like a dart. Struggling to his feet, he found that he could not raise his arm. He was weary, chilled, and unable to stop shaking.

"Y Lan, where are you?" he cried, searching the dim landscape for her colorful garment.

A moan came from below the trail. He bent over the bank. At first he saw nothing. The moaning came again, scarcely audible over the stirring of the waves. At the water's edge he saw a thin, bare arm, frozen in motionless calm, reaching up from a ravine. The pink sleeve was hidden from view. While he watched, her fingers stirred as if to beckon him.

"Y Lan! Y Lan!"

He scrambled to the rocky ground below, holding his injured arm. The footsteps behind him were a reassuring indication of his teacher's presence. He heard the little girl's muffled cries.

More explosions resounded. The flooded land glittered in streaks of orange as if it were being struck by lightning. This time, Henri was able to look beyond the shadow of the hilltops, and dread seized him when he recognized what he was seeing. On the other side of the

citadel, warships emerged from the fog. He counted more than fifteen vessels, gliding on top of the water like dragons, their sharp
keels splitting the air. The emerging moon lit them from behind with
wisps of silver light.

High amid the ramparts of the tall fortress, the people of Hue's
inner city shouted at the incredible sight with a sense of doom. Henri
realized that he was witnessing the capital of Cochin China under
attack. But who were the attackers?

The first boat advanced toward the northeast entrance of the
citadel. Out of the openings in its wooded gunwales bristled a line of
heavy artillery guns, each attended by a unit of soldiers clad in bamboo armor. From within these dark, cavernous mouths the weapons
spat their cannonballs, bombarding the city's fortifications.

The air filled with fire and ash. The harmony of the fortress's
walls was marred by black columns of smoke that rose above the con-
flagrations within. As the cannons continued to fire, some of their
balls overshot the target and landed in the river. Others traveled farther, to jar the mountainside where Henri was standing. He realized
that an earlier cannonball must have caused the avalanche that had
swept them off their feet, and that another could occur at any moment.

He ran down the slope toward Y Lan, stepping carefully across
the wet ground. Her head was trapped under a rock. Her chest heaved,
specked with dark blood. He shut his eyes and used his uninjured
hand to roll the stone off her. A gurgling sound escaped from her
throat.

In the flickering dimness of the ravine, Henri saw a hole where
her nose and mouth once had been. It was as if a red carnation were
blooming on her face. The sharp edges of broken facial bones protruded from the wound. Upon seeing him, the girl closed her eyes.
The muscles of her cheeks moved slightly in an attempt to readjust
her face.

Around Y Lan, the dusk of evening glowed lighter as the moon
climbed into a clear sky. Henri saw her face more clearly, and a new
agony gnawed at him. Her lower lip moved. From within the bloody

wound, a piteous, faltering voice whimpered. Behind him, he heard François weeping.

"Help me, Father!" he called to his teacher.

His voice was lost in the clamor of a new cannon blast. The mountain trembled, and stones rained down on them. Henri set his shoulder against the wall of the ravine and hovered over Y Lan to shield her.

With surprising alacrity, François jumped between Henri and the wounded girl and scooped her up in his arms. A burst of light glinted off the priest's shaven head and gave his metal collar an eerie glow. Henri turned. In the water's surface he caught the reflection of the citadel burning. A portion of the wall had collapsed, and through this newly made fissure the flood was pouring in. The tide swept through a horde of people, hurling them this way and that, and pinning them against the walls. Across the dark sky, flaming arrows arced toward the ships like shooting stars. One struck a boat's mizzen sail on the right side and set it on fire.

With a cry, François sprang forward. The girl slumped in his arms, her head back, her hair cascading away from her forehead and dripping blood. On the trail above, Xuan saw her sister for the first time since the avalanche had swept her off the slope. She stared at the unrecognizable face, and then screamed. But her cry was drowned by a greater sound of clomping and chanting that seemed to come from inside the mountain. The ground quivered with the echoes of hoarse laughter.

Henri looked up. Under the fire from the citadel, he saw the dark forms of men spread down the mountainside like termites flushed from their nests. Their deep, unintelligible voices churned the night, a solemn counterpoint to the clash of steel weapons.

As they grew nearer, he saw that these men wore no bamboo armor, and the clothes on their backs were tattered. Still, the sense of menace was overwhelming as the black figures swarmed, weapons lifted above their heads.

He took Father François's arm and urged him across the rugged riverbank. The descending men were getting closer with each second. Leading the troops was a herd of elephants, ten or fifteen of the enormous beasts lumbering in the perfect formation of an arrowhead. A flag that swept over a length of four yards billowed above their heads, red as blood in the firelight.

In the northeast, the warships were now riding over the damaged ramparts to enter the citadel. Behind him, the chanting grew louder as shadows bearing torches raced closer. Within minutes, Henri was swallowed in a sea of men.

King Nhạc! King Nhạc! King Nhạc!

Their voices rolled into the night, accompanied by wild drumbeats and horns that maintained their cacophony even when the troops reached the edge of the water.

He felt a blazing light on his face and saw the flames lick the darkness away. Among the strange countenances that surrounded him and his teacher, one pushed forward, grinning. He recognized at once the swollen upper lip and missing front teeth of the young Kim Lai convert — Lộc.

"Teacher Henri, Father François," the boy said. "We meet again."

Henri knelt on the ground and wept, whether from relief or despair he did not know. Around him, the chanting penetrated the night.

King Nhạc! King Nhạc! King Nhạc!

But the novice had stopped listening. Before darkness claimed him, he caught a glimpse of Xuan, hurrying to the side of Father François and the limp figure of her twin.

CHAPTER SEVENTEEN

*I*t was past midnight. The peasant army that had teemed along the steep mountainside was settling down to rest. Clusters of men sought comfort around low-flamed campfires on the damp, uneven ground. Near a tropical almond tree, five soldiers stood guard over François and Henri. A rope, wrapped around the tree trunk, bound their ankles together; their wrists were tied in front of them. Two other peasants placed the orphaned twins in a rope hammock and carried them out of sight.

Among the guards was the familiar, bruised face of the buffalo keeper. "Come, Teacher Henri," said Lộc. He raised his sword toward the citadel and licked his puffy lips. "Join our army. Bring your god along to help us crush those who have wronged you and your religion."

A group of peasants huddling nearby mumbled and nodded in agreement. Henri trembled. The moon had moved beyond its pinnacle and was sailing westward, casting its shadow on the ravaged landscape. He could see the flood ripple over clumps of rocks a few feet below the campsite; fog hovered above the water's surface.

In the distance, the sounds of battle were dwindling, and the fires inside the fortress were waning. Black smoke rose like tall pillars and mingled with the clouds. Even with a fire nearby, Henri could not stop shivering. He was feverish and weak.

Visions of his mother, triggered by the horror of witnessing the two young girls lose their parents, refused to leave his mind. Even when Lộc was talking to him in his high-pitched, excited voice, her face flickered. He saw the deep creases of her suffering. He remembered the redolence of her unwashed clothes, like decomposing leaves after a rain. And her eyes, drenched in agony the last time he had looked into them. He wished he could again walk through the door of his apartment on rue de Lappe and see his mother sitting on the windowsill, wrapped in her thick cloak. The campfire before him spat.

Drops of moisture fell on his cheeks, but they were too cold to be tears. Henri touched his skin and felt the dew. He examined the two broken digits, bent atop the back of his hand, but he lacked the courage to reset his bones. Blood from the wound had coagulated, and the swelling intensified. He could no longer feel his fingers. The lack of sensation shocked him; he would have preferred pain.

Around him, the mist grew thicker, and the buffalo keeper blurred from view. Henri lay down and tried to sleep. The rope around his ankles limited his mobility, and the supine position made it difficult for him to breathe. Father François was twisting in his sleep. His soft snoring vibrated in the night.

Henri gazed at the sky. His mind drifted above his battered body with a sense of loss. The sky above the campfire was a wall of blue indifference. And the moon — a severed head — floated in a puddle of its own blood. Scattered thoughts rushed through his brain.

He fell asleep with his mouth open, as if preparing for a scream.

Morning came with a burst of sunshine. The brightness penetrated his eyelids and forced him to blink. His thoughts echoed, slow and remote, as if from a well. His first whim was to return to sleep, but approaching footfalls quickened his pulse.

Around the mountain, the moving forms of the peasant soldiers circled in groups of four or five to practice their combat skills. The mud smeared their feet; their clanking swords and scimitars mirrored the sun. Beyond them, the dark outlines of trees and shrubs climbed the mountain peaks against a blue sky.

Henri stretched. His right hand passed over his brow against the glare, and he realized he was no longer bound to the tree. The flood had receded during the night. The ground was exposed in small patches, forming a broken path toward Hue Citadel. Still, the current was churning too strongly for the rebel army to cross. Through a black mist of ash he saw a crumbling battlement. Here and there in the marshland jutted the upturned hulls of sampans that had been wrecked the night before while attempting to flee the city. The attacking fleet appeared to have entered the citadel. The acrid smells of gunpowder and sulfur tainted the air, making his eyes water. He thought he could hear cries from behind the fortress's walls.

A hand clasped his shoulder, too rough to belong to François. He turned, and the buffalo keeper looked down at him. In the daylight, his body seemed scrawny and stunted. A formless black garment cloaked him to his knees. He narrowed his eyes in a grin.

"They are hunting for King Due Tong," the boy said, pointing at the citadel. "A spy reported that he saw him escape last night with what remained of his army. I hope I can catch the soldier who knocked out my teeth. When I do" — he folded his hand and threw a punch in midair — "I'll break every tooth in his mouth so he'll spend the last of his days tied in a barn and slurping soup from a manger."

Henri squinted in puzzlement. He had witnessed a great battle, but he understood little of what he had seen. He could not tell who was fighting, or who was winning. Lộc's anger made him uneasy, even though it was hardly a surprise. He wondered if he should preach to the native boy the philosophy of turning the other cheek. But he was no longer a missionary. The iron collar around his neck reminded him to hold his silence. Using his healthy hand, he rubbed Lộc's shoulder.

With a weak smile, he said, "I forgot how strong you are. The poor sentry, it would be his most unfortunate day on Earth if you ever got your hands on him."

Lộc snorted his appreciation of Henri's sentiment.

Henri realized that his teacher was missing. "Do you know where Father François is?" he asked the boy.

"I released him early this morning, while you were asleep. He went to visit the wounded girl and her sister."

"What do you mean by 'released him'?" asked Henri. "Are we not your prisoners?"

"It would indeed be an offense against your god if I detained any of you holy men," said Lộc. "I've stated your innocence to my superiors and told them what we have endured together. They agreed to free you. You can leave whenever you wish, Teacher Henri. But if you depart from Ngụ Bình Mountain, you will not be under our protection. I urge you instead to join us."

"I cannot, and neither can Father François," replied Henri. "We must continue with our journey. My teacher is not well. He should return to France. And I intend to go with him wherever he goes. As you know, I am his only companion."

Seeing the disappointment on Lộc's face, he pressed on. "Please take me to Father François. Besides, it would be ill mannered for me to leave the poor orphans without saying farewell."

Henri followed Lộc up the mountain along a path of footprints. As they ascended, the two young men passed through some thirty or more crude campsites. The main body of the peasant army clustered on the side nearer the river, while the leaders bivouacked two hundred yards higher, where they could observe the entire Hue region laid out like a map.

The trail twisted over slippery cliffs and past steep ravines until at last they came to a cave. In a clearing near its entrance, an empty hammock hung between the trunks of two banyan trees. No one was in sight. Henri peered into the darkness where the mountain was hollowed out. Beyond the opening lurked an unfamiliar dampness. The native boy went in, followed by Henri. He crouched to keep his head from hitting the low entrance.

Inside, coolness engulfed him. Toward the back of the cavern, a smoldering torch flickered. Black soot was smeared on the dome-shaped ceiling. The smells of wild herbs and rice alcohol were in the air.

Y Lan, the injured girl, lay on one side with her knees drawn up under the pink blouse. Her face was wrapped in a cloth that seemed to be bathed in some kind of plant sap. Nearby sat her sister on a rock, her chin resting on one knee. There was someone else, a woman, whose profile was lost in the surrounding blackness. A scarf was wrapped around her head. At her feet, a stone mortar held a thick reddish liquid. She soaked a round banyan leaf in the potion and handed it to Xuan. The girl then held the leaf over Y Lan's face and pressed it lightly against the bandage covering her sister's wound.

"Bỏ Y Lan, ba hồn chín vía, Y Lan, về đây," she chanted. The magic invocation entreated the wounded twin's spirit, beckoning for her return.

A small fleck of red light illuminated Xuan's exhausted, fearful face. François was nowhere in sight.

Xuan ceased her ritual to gaze at Henri. With a happy shout, she leaped over her sister and flew into his embrace. Henri was surprised, first by her reaction, and then by his own. A sudden warmth flooded his heart, and he pulled her closer to him, peering through the loose strands of her hair.

Under the torch, the woman rose to her feet, turned around, and removed her scarf. Her hair was golden, its sheen reflecting the flames. And while Henri looked on, she walked past him to exit the cave. It was Sister Lucía. Whether or not she recognized him, the nun showed no expression.

The other twin watched them from her bed. But before he could react to the shock of Sister Lucía's presence, he saw pain course through Y Lan's bandaged face. Henri broke away from Xuan. Her fingers, wet from the medicine, left purple marks across his tunic.

"You found us," Xuan whispered. "We couldn't bear to be trapped here alone. But now you've come."

A cry escaped Y Lan's throat. Her face became red as she struggled to sit up. The dressing gripped her skin. Xuan ran back to assist her, reaching for the banyan leaf to soothe her face. She resumed her chanting to the rhythm of her hands. Bỏ Y Lan, ba hồn chín vía, Y Lan, về đây.

Henri came closer. In his confusion, he wondered where Sister Lucía had gone. His shadow draped over the twins.

"I believe she is trying to speak," he said. "What shall we do to understand her?"

"I know what she wants to say," replied Xuan. Her voice sounded thin and weary. "She cannot endure the pain."

She placed the leaf on Y Lan's face. The wound soaked up more liquid, and her masklike bandage reflected the fire.

"Hush," she muttered. "Don't try to talk. It only makes your wound bleed more."

The injured girl lowered herself back on the nest of leaves. Her neck tightened, and a few sounds escaped her throat. This time, Henri could understand her anguished cry.

"I want my *má!*" she called out. "Where is *má?*"

Xuan choked back tears. Lộc sat on the ground next to Y Lan. He lifted her head and laid it in the cradle of his arm. To Henri's surprise, Lộc took the leaf from Xuan's hand and continued the strange practice, calming the sick girl with his tenderness.

"*Bỏ Y Lan, ba hồn chín vía, Y Lan, về đây,*" he sang. "Y Lan, I retain thy three souls and nine spirits in thy body. Do not dare to depart! Instead, I command thee to heal thyself."

Without thinking, Henri said, "Why are you chanting that superstitious hymn?"

Lộc raised an eyebrow to look up at him. "I am no longer your disciple, Teacher Henri. If you decide to stay with us, you can teach what healing power your god possesses, and then we will listen."

The soft light inside the chamber grew dark, and an outraged voice exploded from behind Henri. "Nonsense!"

The word echoed against the walls. Henri turned and faced a group of peasants. Some of them were clad wholly in black; others wore protective armor made from bamboo.

Standing in front of the rebels was a young man in his early twenties — undoubtedly the mightiest Annamite man Henri had ever seen. His wavy jet-black hair fell to his broad shoulders. Except for the horsehair string of an ivory bow wrapped across his muscular torso, he was bare-chested, and over his shoulder a quiver of arrows was visible. His tanned, smooth upper body towered over the other peasants. With his handsome features and firm posture, he reminded Henri of an oak tree.

On his right stood a woman warrior, clasping a naked sword. Its handle, half-hidden in her grip, was adorned with jewels that sparkled with a rainbow of color. Unlike the weapon, she seemed crude and earthy, with a weathered face and a long, flat body. Her thin lips were pressed together, and her eyes, much too far apart to be considered attractive, looked at Henri with a scrutiny that made him divert his stare.

Next to her was François, cleaner than the night before. In place of his dirty rags was the same black garb worn by the peasant soldiers. Henri realized that his teacher no longer wore the metal collar.

"Prince Thom!" exclaimed Lộc. He bowed his head.

Xuan fell to her knees.

Thom opened his arms and smiled, showing a row of straight, white teeth. "You must not pressure anyone to join the West Mountaineers," he said to Lộc. "We are an army of volunteers, and our warriors are fighting for freedom. If the foreign teachers do not wish to stay, they can leave of their own free will."

Henri looked at the rebel prince. Thom spoke Annamite in a pure form, much like the language Henri had absorbed from Father François while on shipboard, and the novice could understand him far better than he could the other peasants. Still, he was so full of questions, he did not know where to begin.

He asked, "Who are the West Mountaineers? And why are you attacking the citadel?"

Thom put one foot on a rock and assumed a relaxed pose. His voice was gentle when he replied to Henri. "Foreigner, you speak our language well, but I see that you understand little of our political affairs. Let me inform you about our history. Seven years ago, when the boy king Due Tong was crowned, he was twelve years old. Since he was unable to rule the kingdom on his own, he appointed Truong Loan as his vice-king. Loan became a fiend and in a short time had gathered enough power and wealth to govern the country.

"The vice-king decided to raise and collect unlimited taxes. They were so high that the peasants were unable to pay them. Those who could not pay were forced to give up their lands, or to sell their cattle, or, worse, to send their children into slavery. Loan himself sired many offspring, and he arranged for them and the king's relatives to be raised in wealthy houses throughout the land, where the families were forced to support them in royal style. In order to accommodate this heavy load, the local rich in turn robbed their poor. As for the king's army, any warrior who did not wish to go to war could buy his way out with ivory, gold and silver pieces, or other treasure. The country was racked by corruption, hunger, and injustice."

He drew a deep breath. "My brothers and I are the only hope that the peasants have. We are fighting for our survival and freedom, and for a fair government. You asked who the West Mountaineers are. They are each and every one of us — the peasants of Cochin China. We have not yet attacked the citadel because we are not strong enough. The northern kingdom of Tonkin is trying to crush the South. It was their war boats and cannons that you saw last night. We are here biding our time."

Henri asked, "Why are you coming to the battle if you are not going to fight?"

Thom said, "In many ways, the northern army is far better prepared than we are. Like the southern king, they know about us and also consider us rebels. Our goal at this time is to capture the royal family of the southern kingdom as they flee the citadel, and then turn them over to the North. In that way, we can establish an alliance with the northern king and ensure our survival and safety. They need our help because we are the farmers. We are the men who work the land. Without us, their wealth will dwindle to nothing."

"But, Prince Thom, clearly you are an educated man. How can you be both a prince and a farmer?"

He gave a boisterous laugh. "A prince of the poor is a peasant nonetheless. I wear their clothes and carry their banner. My education came from a few years of schooling. You can address me as Thom."

"Why are you telling me all this?" Henri asked.

His boldness seemed to exasperate the woman warrior. She glared at him.

The prince replied, "You saved our children even when you were in danger, as any true holy man would. Every year, more and more of the white ghosts enter our country. We have no choice but to learn their ways. In return for the freedom I am about to grant you, I want you to tell them about our plight so that they can understand who we are and what we are fighting for."

He turned to the female warrior. "This is Lady Bui, one of my chief commanders. She is so skillful with her sword that she can remove an enemy's eyes during battle without taking his life. She will now release the yoke of denouncement from your neck."

The woman strode forward and her sword flashed. The blade's tip snicked into the lock that held the collar together. Then she twisted her wrist, pulling Henri forward. His neck was inches from the blade. After a few such thrusts, the lock broke in half. When the woman withdrew her weapon, the collar slipped to the stony ground with a thud. He clutched his neck, expecting to feel a gush of blood, but instead, his fingers glided across smooth skin, itching from the brisk air. At last, he was able to breathe again.

"Teacher, you are a free man," Thom said. "Now, you can go."

In the clearing outside the cave, the missionaries divided their scanty possessions into two bamboo baskets. Most precious among them were the gifts of food and clothing given to them by Thom, the peasant prince. Fresh fruits, cooked rice, and chunks of sun-dried venison wrapped in banana leaves formed tidy packages for their journey. In addition to the clean garments they had on, each man received an extra article of clothing, made from the same heavy plain-woven fabric and dyed in vegetable ink to a muddy, nondescript color.

At Thom's command, one of the soldiers produced a donkey to carry the goods. Henri attached the baskets to both sides of the saddle, making sure to distribute the weight evenly. He was able to feel his fingers again, thanks to a shaman who had reset and splinted them. Their dull ache reassured him that they were still part of him.

As he prepared the donkey, the peasant prince perched a few feet above him on the branch of a banyan tree. Thom was looking down at the city with steady concentration. His bow and arrows were slung from a branch near his fingertips, within easy reach. His attention was riveted on things that Henri's untrained eyes would never see.

Through a deep green curtain of leaves, the sun dappled yellow dots of light on the hard soil, and above him the trees tossed their limbs in the wind. When the pack was secured on the donkey's back, Henri looked up at François, who was staring at the ground with an absent expression.

"We are ready to leave, sir," he said to Prince Thom. "With your permission."

Behind him he heard a sniffle. He turned and saw Xuan standing in the shadow of the cave's entrance, with her arms wrapped around Sister Lucía.

"Where is Sister Natalia?" he asked the nun.

"Dead," she replied.

"How did she die?"

Lucía rubbed her temples with the palms of her hands.

Prince Thom answered, "We rescued your friend from the house of Tuyền when we invaded Quinion. She was the only one who survived. We are grateful to have her helping us with the sick and wounded."

Lady Bui added, "The shaman has been teaching her his healing skills."

The news of Natalia's death left Henri speechless. The fact that Lucía had survived the brutality of the soldiers amazed him.

"Where are you planning to go?" the prince asked. Pointing to François, he added, "He's obviously not well."

Henri frowned, thinking. The speckles of sunlight grew rounder on the ground. It was almost noon. Soon he would be somewhere on the graveled trail, taking François away from Hue City, and these dis-

mal events would become little dots of memory, stored in the darkest places of their minds. He could feel his veins pounding with the
desire for motion.

"I want to take my teacher to Quinion Port," he replied. "There
we will find a ship that will take us back to France. Since Father
François is unable to make his own decision, I think it is best for him
to return home. I have a mother waiting for me in Paris, so I am
going with him. It seems a terribly long time since I left." He gave a
low gasp, suddenly aware of the import of his words. "I can't stay
here any longer. I must go home."

Turning to the nun, he said, "Sister Lucía, come home with us."

She shook her head. "I prefer to stay here with the rebels. You
can see I am no longer a nun; therefore, you have no responsibility
toward me."

"Do you all understand that you are welcome to stay?" said
Thom.

"Thank you, but I must take my leave," replied Henri.

He felt something touch the hollow of his palm. A hand encircled
his forefinger. Henri turned reluctantly. Standing beside him was
Xuan. Her tears had left little tracks down her dusty cheeks.

"Ông Tây," she said. A tone of pleading muffled her voice. "Can I
go with you?"

Henri looked away, understanding her pain but unwilling to add
it to his own. "I can't take you with me," he said. "You are safe here
among these men. Your sister needs your help, and you must take
care of her."

"But I don't want to stay," she said, clutching him with both
hands. "I feel safer when I am with you."

"No!" said Henri. "I can't."

He pulled away. François fumbled to untie the donkey. Henri
took the rein from his teacher. With a heart full of guilt, the novice
led François down the winding road, trying his best not to look
back at Xuan. On the slope, he could not help breaking into a run.
François struggled to keep up. The rope in Henri's hand forced the
animal into a gallop.

"We can't stay, we can't stay!" Henri chanted, almost in a trance. "We'll be someplace else this time tomorrow."

His mind was fixed on the image of the *Wanderer*'s large white sails billowing in the wind.

CHAPTER EIGHTEEN

They walked under the hot sun until Henri was no longer sure if he was traveling in the right direction. From Prince Thom he had learned that the Port of Quinion was two hundred miles southeast of Hue Citadel, but the flood had erased the paths. Any landmarks that might have been there a few weeks earlier no longer existed.

He looked around for a familiar rock formation or pagoda, but nothing triggered his memory. All he saw were the ruins of abandoned villages, littered with the corpses of their former occupants. A stillness that was void of life — a flat silence from which even the echoes had vanished — permeated the air. Death wafted over the desolate terrain, stirring the vultures.

Over the barren ground, the scavengers waddled, ripping and tearing the corpses with their talons and hooked beaks. Henri had never seen the large, frightening birds so close before, and he watched in horror as they carried out their ancient role. After they feasted, they flew away, leaving only stains on the dried earth, which eventually grew thick with red ants.

As the earth seemed about to melt under the heat of the sun, Henri and François came upon a clump of tamarind trees surrounded by tall reeds. The novice collapsed in the shade while his teacher stood motionless, holding the rope that tethered the donkey. The animal nudged his hand with its nose, searching for a treat.

Tired and hungry, with no idea which way to go, Henri decided that this would be a good place to rest. The weather became gray and overcast, and a cool wind gusted from the east, but as the afternoon grew into nightfall, the sky became clear. The full moon, encompassed by a white halo, illuminated the landscape. Dogs howled. Black birds of prey circled above their heads. Henri moved about, collecting pieces of wood to start a fire.

François bedded the donkey down. From time to time he stared into the darkness. The ruined towns seemed to harbor deep secrets and lurking dangers. Even nestled next to a fire among the wild reeds, tall hyacinth grass, and bamboo shoots, the two men felt vulnerable. Eyes seemed to peer through the thick night to spy on them. Now and then, the priest stiffened and cocked his head. But when Henri sat up and joined him, he could see nothing.

To ward off the eeriness, Henri opened one of the bamboo baskets and took out a bundle of food. The donkey bumped his elbow, as if hoping for some grain.

"Eat your grass, little friend," Henri said, petting it behind the ear.

As if it understood, the animal lowered its head to the ground. Henri unwrapped the banana leaves, layer after layer, until a spicy odor of roasted meat burst into the air — the distinct, seductive aroma of wild game. His mouth watered. His teacher wetted his lips and leaned toward the food.

The reeds rustled, and there came a hissing of breath too sharp to have been created by the wind.

Henri stood up, grabbed a burning branch from the fire, and faced the darkness where the sound had come from. There was another hiss and a thump as something hit the ground. He whirled the makeshift torch toward the intruder. His teacher came to his side, holding a long knife that Prince Thom had given to them. The donkey straightened its ears.

"Who is out there?" Henri shouted.

The land replied with a sigh.

Again he thrust his fiery wand forward. "I know you are out there. Reveal yourself."

A small black figure darted forward and hurled itself at Henri. Its long mane of hair whipped in the wind. Recognizing Xuan, he heaved a sigh of relief before surprise overcame him. He dropped the torch back into the fire, sending an explosion of embers up toward the sky.

The little girl buried her face in his belly. Her voice erupted into rapid speech. "Please don't send me back. I promise I won't be any trouble. I won't get in the way."

He was too shocked to speak. His teacher reached to pat the child's hair. A small smile crossed his face. Xuan gathered both men with her arms.

"I couldn't stay there another minute," she said. "I want to be with both of you."

Henri stammered, "B-but y-your sister —"

"My sister is going to die," she interrupted. "I've lost my mother and father. Please don't make me watch Y Lan die too."

The image of himself running away from his mother flared in Henri's mind, choking him.

"Xuan, your very presence might have helped her," he argued weakly.

She sank to her knees. "The medicine man says the hole in her face may be too large to retain her spirit. I covered it with the penny-wort leaves and cloths, but nothing worked. The forest lepers came and took her away. They claimed she is now one of them. There is nothing more I can do."

Henri was about to speak, but François pressed a forefinger against his own lips. "Feed the child." The words escaped him in a whisper.

They walked for three more days before signs of life reemerged along their path. The brown muddy soil blossomed slowly into an emerald green. Away from the rotting corpses, the air became fresh. Sweet-voiced songbirds replaced the screeching vultures.

The destruction of the flood was behind them, but its aftermath was still evident. He could see the famine had taken its toll on the survivors. Except for their donkey, they encountered no living animals of any kind. All had been hunted down and eaten; even the rats could not escape the province's hunger.

The beggars they passed eyed their donkey. Perhaps it was the missionaries' foreign appearance, or their tall stature — something held these people back from attacking them and stealing their animal. Instead, they merged together, drifting and swaying after Henri's caravan as if hypnotized.

The gathering behind them did not disturb Henri. His mind was consumed by other predicaments. He was uneasy with the responsibility of caring for his teacher, and he could see that Xuan would become a burden once they returned to Quinion. He would not be able to smuggle a young Annamite girl onto a French ship, nor did he want to. At the same time, he could not bring himself to abandon her. He knew what grim fate would befall a defenseless child. As they passed through the stark villages, he kept hoping some family would have enough compassion to adopt her. But with each step he took, he saw corpses and hungry faces staring back at him.

The landscape grew hilly. Ahead of them the road narrowed, running like a furrow between rugged rock formations. Boulders and cliffs frowned down on them like the stone dragons that guarded ancient temples. They continued southward for another mile, and Xuan began to slow down and stumble. She clutched the panel of his shirt and would not let go.

He noticed how pale her face had become. The dark hollows under her eyes spread. He had nothing to feed her — they had finished the food in the baskets the night before — and he did not want to stop for rest. He lifted her onto the donkey's back. Wearily, they pressed on, and the parade of beggars followed like an expanding shadow.

The path twisted until it opened to a clearing. Ahead was the beginning of a dense forest. Already the sun was in the west, and the sky shifted from bright blue to canary yellow. Patches of grass and clumps of wildflowers dotted the road.

Coming toward them out of the forest was a small group of men, pulling a cage on a wheeled platform. At first it appeared to Henri that they had captured a bear. But then he recognized the barred enclosure, and it brought back his own experience as a prisoner.

The structure was about four feet in height and built out of bamboo poles that were latched together by rattan palms. It served to jail a convict. His head protruded through a hole on the top, keeping him in place. Even though the cage appeared primitive, it was efficient and impossible to break.

The men approached. With great effort they wheeled the cart up the uneven road, gaining only a few feet at a time. When they came closer, Henri could see that they were peasants with swords like the Mountaineers he had met, not the trained soldiers of a royal army. Fourteen men made up their group. All wore the same harsh, drained look of starvation.

Henri lowered his head, avoiding their stares, and in his mind he tried to will himself invisible. Their sullen hostility repelled all within their path. A few more steps, he assured himself, and they would be out of sight. From the corner of his eye, he saw a mandarin's figure in the cage as it went past him, so close he could touch it. Unable to help himself, he looked up and saw the face of Bishop de Béhaine. His eyes, glowing with expectation, burned into Henri.

Inside the enclosure, the bishop sat with his legs crossed like a Buddhist monk in meditation. His silken embroidered robe, once so striking, was shredded and dusty. The wooden panels at the top of the cage held his neck in place. As the structure bounced along, his head bobbed in unison, giving the illusion that it had been severed from his body. The wood's edges had broken the skin on his neck, drawing blood. Seated on his lap was the boy-prince Ánh — the child who had pardoned Henri and François.

François let out a whimper. He too had recognized the prisoners in the moving cell. Like the bishop, François turned to Henri with a look of expectation. "Save them," he said.

A plan flashed through Henri's head. He did not have time to sort out the details. He had to act.

Ten paces on his right was a sloping rock formation that rose up to a broad crag overlooking the road. He grabbed Xuan and lifted her off the donkey, handing her to François. Then he took the rein and led the animal up the rocky path. It became frightened and refused to move. Henri had to pull with all his might to get the creature to the top of the cliff. Panting, he looked down at the crowd. The peasant captors stopped. Their leader took several steps forward in anticipation. Henri waited until all eyes were on him.

He spread his arms toward the heavens. "Listen, Annamites!" he shouted. "Our Lord Jesus Christ has delivered this gift of food to you."

He reached into the basket and pulled out a knife. Holding it firm with one hand, he plunged it into the donkey. The knife sank all the way to the handle, piercing the base of the animal's neck.

The creature howled in surprise and agony. Its forelegs folded. The blade had cut through an artery, and jets of blood sprayed Henri. He could taste it, warm and salty. A terror clutched his heart; he shook, unable to control himself. Never in his sixteen desperate years had he taken a life. But it was too late to turn back. All of the peasants, beggars and troops alike, were advancing toward him. The leader of the captors was the first one to crawl up the narrow passage.

He stabbed the animal several more times, until its body spasmed in the throes of death. It seemed to question him. Blood dripped from its mouth, and the last flicker of life was extinguished.

He retreated, the stained knife trembling in his hand. Fierce voices shouted from beneath him: the starving crowd was climbing to the sacrificial altar. Waves of peasants pushed one another up the tapered path. They parted to give Henri enough room to descend. Without delay, he bolted downward.

The sight and smell of the carcass turned each man into a savage. One of them seized the donkey's hind leg and tried to drag it off the cliff. Others stopped him by gripping the other limbs. In the struggle, the animal was torn apart, its torso ripped open.

Once the meat was separated and the intestines were spilled, more hungry men were able to join the bloody banquet. A man picked up a rock and struck another in the face, knocking his opponent off the cliff so he could claim his booty. Others panicked and bit wildly into the flesh, taking in as much raw meat as they could swallow. The tumult of shouting and cursing echoed through the gorges.

Henri ran toward the abandoned cage. François followed him, pulling Xuan along. Prying with the knife, Henri broke the panels apart. Prince Ánh sprang from inside the bishop's embrace. His royal tunic was torn at the shoulder, exposing his dark skin.

"Help me out," the prince ordered François. His voice was as arrogant as ever.

François frowned, and for the first time, the vacant expression left his face.

He asked, "Do you remember me, Your Highness?" His voice was hoarse from disuse, and he had to clear his throat to regain its tone.

"Dear God," moaned the bishop, white with fear and panic. "This is no time for confrontation, Father François. Hurry, free us before the rebels return."

François raised an eyebrow. "So you too wish to escape death? Have patience, Bishop! If God intends to have you continue His work, then you shall be saved." He turned to the boy. "Recognize me?"

"Yes," came the whisper.

With his right hand, his teacher made the sign of the cross over the boy's forehead.

"My Christian God, Lord Jesus Christ, has now freed you, Prince Ánh," he said. "A short week ago, it was He who saved my life in the execution ground so that I can save yours today. At first I did not understand the depth of His wisdom until I saw you again." To the bishop, he said, "You are wrong, Your Excellency, I do have a purpose in this land. Never forget this miracle!"

He offered his hands to help both prisoners down from the cart. Together they ran down the narrow and pitted road.

Nobody on the cliff saw them running. Nobody cared. The natives' attention was riveted on the feast. Henri and his group raced away and didn't slow until they could no longer hear the peasants.

They eventually came to a stop, blinded by the oncoming night. Their exhausted bodies could not move another step. Henri tried to catch his breath, while his legs throbbed with pain. He had tramped on so many unseen stones that his feet were bleeding. In a whisper he gathered them together, calling each by name and waiting for the reply to make certain that everyone was accounted for. They were!

Almost weeping at the priest's recovery, he asked, "Where should we go now, Teacher?"

"We are not returning to France," said François, resuming his responsibility. "You'll join the bishop. I shall go where I am most needed."

The words stung Henri. "But I came here with you —"

His teacher replied, "There is so much that you have not yet learned in this journey. Your view of God is very limited, and so is mine. I feel that I have failed to educate you. Henri, you have so many questions, which I don't have answers to. I know the bishop's experience and knowledge of the divine could be beneficial to you, if he is willing to accept you as a novice."

He turned to de Béhaine. The bishop had been watching him.

"What happened to your collar of denouncement?" he asked.

Even though the question wasn't directed at him, Henri felt compelled to speak. "The lady general of the Mountaineers removed it with her sword."

He felt his teacher's finger pressing against his lips, urging him to silence.

The information enraged the bishop. He snorted. "Don't you know those rebels are King Due Tong's enemies?"

François replied, "Your Excellency, you once taught me the Jesuit Oath of Induction, 'Among the reformers, be a reformer.' I only do what is required of my duty as a missionary."

As fast as it appeared, the bishop's exasperation abated. "Father,

God chose to speak through you. Your will should be His will. As for the boy, I shall take charge of him from this moment."

"Thank you, Your Excellency," said François. "I now leave him in your care."

Henri objected, cross with frustration. "But Father François, you are my teacher. How could you leave me after what we have been through together?" His voice broke. "You are my only family."

The light touch of François's hand brushed his forehead. Henri felt the priest's warmth even though his body was cloaked in darkness.

"When God tested me, I failed. To redeem myself I must go alone and face my next trial. This time my faith will not falter. You too must find your own way."

"Please don't forget me," said Xuan nervously. "What will happen to me?"

The boy-prince answered, "I need a servant. She comes with us."

The bishop chuckled at the prince's demand. "What say you, Father François? Should Xuan come with us?"

There was no answer. All that remained in front of Henri was the murmur of the night.

"Father," he called out. "Father . . . Father . . . Father . . ."

CHAPTER NINETEEN

François heard Henri calling his name. He broke into a run, covering his ears. A few dozen yards north, he halted. The night was dense with mist. Henri and his companions were no longer in sight. Without them, the darkness expanded. He seemed to be the last one on Earth.

By saving Prince Ánh, he had set himself free. Even the sorrow of saying good-bye to his only friend, Henri, could not dampen the joy of finding himself. When he had been forced to renounce God, his spirit had withered. But now, he had found a way to reaffirm his faith. He felt restored.

The trees moaned under a restless wind. A swarm of fireflies surged around him. All the living souls that were sprinkled across the valley were asleep, waiting. He could see that he had been the one who was chosen to safeguard this strange flock, teach them the mercy of God, and lead them to salvation.

He smiled. It was a new beginning. His next destination was clear in his mind: the King's Screens Mountains. Prince Thom of the West Mountaineers had offered him a place in his army. If anyone could help him reestablish his church among the peasants, it would be Thom.

François reached the mountain at dawn on the fourth day. As the morning fog receded, he saw clusters of the West Mountaineers camping along the riverbank. He went up the familiar path to search for Thom.

To his right, a pair of Annamites clashed their weapons in a mock battle. As he walked past them, neither man seemed to notice his presence. Here among the poor, his ragged clothing brought him acceptance.

He scaled the hill, panting and calling for Lộc. His faltering enunciation drew a few suspicious glances. He waved to the onlookers, and they slipped back to their activities. He headed toward the cave, expecting to find Lộc or Sister Lucía, because it was the last place he had seen them.

A shout from behind the fence to his right drew his attention, only to be drowned by the prolonged lowing of an animal. He gazed into a dense herd of elephants and horses. Among their massive bodies he saw Lộc's impish face. Behind the boy stood Lady Bui, the female warrior. The long sleeves of her shirt were rolled past her elbows. Blood smeared her hands.

Lộc sprang up, beaming his sunken smile. Raising his arm, he whipped a stalk of sugarcane in the air to greet the priest. Then, with a shout, he raced across the stony field and leaped over the animal pen's bamboo railing. Like Lady Bui, he was splattered with thick, red fluid.

"Father François, you are back."

"Yes, I am," replied François with equal enthusiasm. As the boy ran closer, he said, "I am glad to find you here, still camping on this mountain." Concern eroded his joy. "But what's this? Is that blood on you? Are you hurt?"

The agonizing trumpet of an elephant shook the ground.

"Lộc, come here," Lady Bui shouted. "I need your help."

The boy gave François an apologetic look. "I am fine, but I must go. One of the elephants, Mia, is giving birth."

He vaulted the fence and ran back to the female general.

François followed. He could see the leathery face of an elephant hovering above him, one big, dark eye glaring with distrust. Its skin, stretched painfully at the midsection, hung on a wall of ribs. A wave of contractions rippled along its belly. He heard it whining as it shifted its lower body about the field, and he found himself touching it, massaging the rough surface that was caked with dried mud, trying to soothe the creature's pain.

"This ground is forbidden to strangers," Lady Bui said without looking at him.

"I want to help," he said.

Her arms were raised toward the elephant as she turned to François, squinting. Then he saw the crimson stream streak down the animal's hind legs. A stubby tail arched in midair.

The priest stood transfixed.

Lady Bui said to him, "Do you see that bucket over there? Fill it with water so you can wash Mia and keep her cool. Behind the hut there is a stream. Lộc, show him!"

The boy led him across a dusty pasture and toward the woods. The moans of the elephant came louder.

"Why hasn't the army moved on?" he asked Lộc once they were out of the female general's sight.

"Prince Thom is waiting to meet with the leader of the North Army," Lộc said. "So far we have no permission to enter the citadel. We're still looking to capture the king of the south. Father, you came back —"

He gave François's arm a rough squeeze and then broke away in embarrassment. Turning anxious, he asked, "Where is Teacher Henri? Have you seen Xuan? I could not find her anywhere. Sister Lucía said that Xuan has run away to look for you."

They reached the stream. The priest placed his hand on Lộc's shoulder.

"Do not worry!" he said. "Xuan is safe. Henri is looking after her."

"But who is looking after Henri?"

"God is, dear child. It is time for the boy to find a mission of his own. I feel certain we shall see them again someday."

Lộc turned in the direction of Lady Bui and said, "I am worried about Mia. I hope she won't bleed to death."

François nodded. When they returned to the birth scene, the elephant did not move. Humbly, she was leaning against a tree, making a low-pitched moan. Somehow, during their short absence, the beast had given birth. Her baby lay in a puddle of blood and afterbirth, still connected to her by the umbilical cord.

Lady Bui took the bucket from François's hands and splashed the water on the new mother. She whispered in the animal's ear. The elephant responded by massaging the lady's back with her trunk. François noticed the jagged edge of a broken tusk a few inches above Lady Bui's face.

"It's a boy," she said proudly to François.

The priest chuckled.

"Since you wanted to help, priest," she said, "you can name him."

Her compressed lips hinted at a smile. For the first time, he looked at her closely, and he noticed a certain motherly appeal in her face. He scratched his head, at first unable to think of a name. Then a thought entered his mind.

He said with conviction, "Tín." It was the Annamese word for faith.

Comprehension washed over her face. With a generous thrash of her hand, she smacked her knee and beamed her approval.

"Good name. From now on, he is Tín."

The next morning, François went to the great banyan trees to look for Sister Lucía. The cave was empty. The smell of an infected wound lingered in the air. With every step, he could hear the echo playing off the walls, increasing his sense of desolation.

From the far end of the cave, a flickering light beckoned him. He blinked, looked again, and saw nothing. But as he sat on a boulder, the light flashed again from behind rows of stalagmites.

As his eyes adjusted to the dimness, he could see, farther in a corner, a pile of debris that included broken arrows, damaged swords, and rusty utensils. Beyond that, the end of the cavern disappeared into the darkness, and it came to him that there must be a passage through to the other side of the mountain. He went forward, feeling his way with his hands.

The stone walls were pocked with cuts and crevices, but none was large enough for a man to fit through. He kept moving forward until a cool wind breathed on his face, and his hand reached into emptiness — a doorway. Faintly, he could hear running water. He inhaled and stepped forward. The light was just strong enough for him to glimpse his surroundings.

After several turns, the channel grew narrower. At one point, François had to squeeze his body sideways in order to pass through. He strained for the sound of the brook, hoping his ears would compensate for his lack of vision. At last, a blinding light fell on him from high up above a cliff. As the view opened up, the priest rubbed his eyes, overcome by the beauty before him.

He was facing a clear lake, which was surrounded by rising peaks of jagged cliffs. Nature had made these walls so steep that it was impossible for anyone to climb up or down. He felt as if he were at the bottom of a dormant volcano, reaching for a patch of blue sky above. A few paces away, near a green bank, a bell-shaped gong dangled from an arched frame. Next to it, from a wooden armature, hung a log, waiting to strike.

A shaft of light fell into the lake, glittering on the white feathers of a flock of painted storks. Along the perimeter, flowers of rainbow colors hosted hummingbirds and butterflies. To his right, a trio of glossy-maned colts nosed through the grass in a lazy search for food. He could see their mirror images in the water. Their presence suggested that there must be at least one other way to enter the valley.

Feasting his eyes on the beautiful scenery, François noticed little cave dwellings in the rocks. Each had a white door, along with window frames and shutters that were also painted white. A few figures crept alongside the shaded paths, but he was unable to distinguish who or what they were. One of them stepped forward into the light, and François recognized Sister Lucía. Like a vision, she was bathed in a golden aura.

With a shove, she sent the log flying into the gong. Its resonant sound stirred the painted storks into the air as it boomed against the mountain walls. As if answering its summons, more of the inhabitants emerged from behind the white doors. Their faces and parts of their bodies were wrapped in white linen. He saw a stick-thin old man who was missing an arm, a younger one thrusting his legless trunk across the rocky ground. To the priest's right staggered what looked like a rotting, living corpse of a woman. Her child dangled in the folds of her tattered clothing, sucking on her discolored breast. Among the faces, he saw Y Lan. Beneath the girl's bandage, her agonizing look had been replaced by a dull tranquillity.

Hearing François's gasp, Sister Lucía turned and saw him.

"Oh, Father, you've come to join us," she said.

François retreated several steps.

"Who are these people?" he asked. "And why are you here with them?"

"Welcome to Lepers' Cavern," she said. "These are God's unwanted children."

His voice shook as he said, "B-but they are h-highly contagious. You c-could turn into one of them."

Her expression was serene. "I am one of them. I may not have sores on my flesh, but my insides are decaying."

He heard Lộc calling him from a distance, a thoughtless adolescent voice: "Father, where are you?"

He took Sister Lucía's hand. "You are beautiful. In God's eyes and in mine."

Lộc called again, "Father, Prince Thom is waiting. You must come at once."

Lucía drew her hand away. "You should go," she said.

He muttered a good-bye. "I'll see you again."

He turned and forced himself to hurry back through the cave.

The rebels' seat of government was high up on the mountain, on a ledge where the leaders could oversee their entire army. To get there, François and Lộc had to climb a tortuous path, which grew increasingly narrow and difficult. On either side, the forest, with its twisting ancient trees and deep ravines, was home to a thousand dangers. Above him, the sharp pinnacles were indistinguishable behind thick white clouds.

They walked toward the faint, reedy sound of a flute that rose through the rocky gullies. Even though he made no comment to Lộc about Lepers' Cavern, François was still disturbed by what he had seen there. As much as he tried to regain his composure, he knew the shock must be evident in his stiff body.

Ahead, on a patch of green grass, stood a row of bamboo huts. Nearby, a brook foamed over the rocks. But the sight of war and its devastation could be seen in the distance, where the City of Hue still smoldered.

"As you know, Father," Lộc said, "it is important for the royal family to live high above its people. This way, the king will be closer to the heavens than to Earth. And even our peasant king must have his rightful place under the sun."

At the entrance, two soldiers sprang to their feet and barred the way with lances. The bamboo plates of their mail banged together and made a clanking noise like wooden chimes.

"This is Father François, the Western priest," announced Lộc to the grim-faced guards. "Prince Thom expressed his desire to meet with the holy man when and if he returned to the mountain. I am bringing him to His Majesty as I have promised. Go and report that we have arrived."

One of the guards nodded to his comrade. "What the boy told us is true," he said. "I remember seeing this man a week ago. It was the master's will to keep him here among us, just like the white-skinned nun." To François he said, "Only you can follow me. Any weapons you are carrying, take them off now and leave them at the entrance. The boy will keep them as he waits for you."

"I have no weapons," said François.

Under the morning sun, François reencountered the peasant prince. Also present were his brothers — Nhạc, the gambler, self-appointed king, and leader of the rebels, and Prince Lu — along with Lady Bui and a dozen or so other warriors with their weapons drawn and ready in their hands. In the clearing, the three brothers sat side by side. The wicker chairs that had been mounted on the backs of the elephants served as their thrones.

Lady Bui stood a few steps behind Prince Thom, cloaked in her armored uniform. Her lips barely touched the base of a flute. Her eyes were shut. The sweet sound of her music took form like wisps of smoke, like droplets of rain, tenuously at first, then with fuller melody, each note reaching its own inflection, its own mood. Lost in a song, she again shed the fierce facade of a warrior to become a woman, full of grace.

The prince nodded to François but raised one finger to prevent him from speaking. The guard fell to his knees and assumed the prostrate position. François stood, not knowing what to do.

As the last notes of the song fell to a murmur, Prince Thom spoke, his voice full of surprise. "You've returned, holy man. And I see that you are feeling better. What changed within you?"

François didn't know if he was allowed to speak. Under the scrutiny of the Annamite rebels, he bowed. He could feel one pair of eyes, sharper than all the rest, devouring him with unconcealed hostility. He did not dare look up to find out which of the warriors it was. Instead, he directed his attention toward Prince Thom.

"Do not fear," said Thom. "Treat us the same way that you wish to be treated. There is no need for formality in our court. We are only servants of our people."

A snicker came from the king. With no trace of kindness, he shook his head and talked with a mouth full of red saliva — the result of chewing betel nut and lime powder. The concoction made his cheeks flushed.

"My young brother is simple by nature. I have told him that a king must have order in his own court — that is my belief. But we have our different ways of governing. You may have noticed that as brothers, we all look alike. But we do not always think alike."

François looked up. The warrior whose eyes had consumed him with hatred was now whispering in Thom's ear. There was a vague familiarity about the man that made François uneasy. He searched his memory, trying to recall an incident that would explain the man's animosity. Then, with a chill, he remembered. In that moment, he foresaw his doom.

The warrior had led the peasants who were transporting Pigneau de Béhaine and Prince Ánh when Henri had sacrificed the donkey to save them. Two splashes of donkey's blood, flicked across his straw hat, refreshed François's remembrance. Surely the man was report-ing the bloody subterfuge to the prince. François sighed and awaited his fate.

Thom rose from his seat, adjusting his golden robe. He was much taller than the rest of his men. In his opulent garment, the prince seemed a different man from the one François had met outside the cave days earlier.

"Tell us, why did you return?" he asked François.

"I've come to ask for your protection," said François. "It is my Lord's wish that I remain in this country as a missionary. But my task is impossible without your help."

"Can your god protect you, priest?"

"He must, as he led me to you."

The king spat a glob of red fluid. It landed a few feet from François. Nhạc interrupted. "This is idle talk. There is no doubt that you need our protection. But why should we help you? How do we know you are not a spy that was hired by either the north or the south king?"

François chose his words cautiously. "I am a foreign priest who was condemned by the government of the south king. I almost lost my life and was forced to wear an iron collar to denounce my God. This humiliation precludes me from ever working with the forces of the south. Until a few days ago, I had never heard of the Tonquinese or the North Army. So, Your Majesty, as you can see, your enemies are my enemies. Besides, I do not answer to any mortal. My master is the Lord in heaven. If you protect me, He will protect you."

The doubt remained in the king's eyes. "Will you fight our foes alongside us, or does your religion forbid you to kill?"

François felt cornered, yet at the same time confident in the face of the king's challenge. They had not yet condemned him for helping the boy-prince escape. There was still hope. He recalled the Oath of Induction: "Among the reformers, be a reformer."

"If that is what it takes to establish a kingdom of God in this land," he answered, "then let me be your soldier. But I will fight with God by my side. I won't be alone. With the Lord's blessing, we shall never fear losing any battle. Our Father will always protect us, watch over us, and satisfy our every need. I will never question His plan or His everlasting wisdom."

"For now, I have decided to trust you," said Thom, pressing his hand on the priest's shoulder. "Come, from this time on, you are one of us."

CHAPTER TWENTY

*T*he sun bloomed like a red dahlia, petals ablaze.

For the last twelve hours, the bishop and his three young charges had been walking south along the shore of the South China Sea. They were eighty kilometers away from Quinion, a small fraction of the nine hundred kilometers they would have to travel to Saygun. There, the royal family had agreed to reunite after their flight from Hue City. Pierre had shed his mandarin's uniform in favor of peasant garb. The wide-rimmed hats he acquired for himself, Henri, and the Annamite children were a necessity to deflect the scorching heat. They also provided an element of disguise.

His clothes were damp from sweat; salt accumulated in the rough fibers. Unlike the boy-prince, he, Henri, and Xuan went barefoot. Their feet, inured to abuse in this tropical climate, had become leathery and flat, with toes that spread apart. Their callused soles made it easier for them to walk on the hot sand. From time to time, when the surf washed over the beach, they would step into it. The waves massaged their tired flesh and made their journey bearable.

The sea and land surrounded them under a copper dome of brilliant sunshine. No one else was in sight. Perhaps all the inhabitants were dead or had fled from the recent war and flood. In the white emptiness, they were like strands of grass, clinging to one another on the shoreline.

The children were exhausted. None of them had ever walked for this long before. But the reminders of war were everywhere — the black smoke of burning forests, pieces of wrecked boats and ships, and the occasional neighing of a distant horse. Their pace dragged. The waves — foamy and good-natured — erased the imprints of their passage.

For a long time, Henri carried the prince on his back. A thin boy of sixteen, too tall, with long arms and legs, he sprinted along the water's edge like a spider. But his strength was fleeting; in the end, he stood teetering on the tips of his toes, gasped for air and coughed, then collapsed. His face was gaunt, a bleak caricature of the hearty novice Pierre once knew. But his eyes were still as green as the ocean, and his sun-bleached hair was curly and bright like a patch of fabric sewn under his hat's brim. The Annamite prince, half-asleep, reluctantly rejoined the caravan and walked on his own.

In front of them, a cluster of coconut trees dangled limp branches toward the water. Nearby stood a hut, twisted off its foundation and barely retaining its shape. Its wooden skeleton moaned with each gust of wind. Pierre thought of entering the cabin to hunt for food. It was dangerous — the structure might collapse, or it could harbor bandits. But what choice did he have? The prince needed nourishment. His little Annamite treasure. He had a vision of placing this child on the throne of Annam.

He said to Henri, "Go in the shade and collect some coconuts. Look for some sharp stone to open them. Do not come out until you hear me call you. If anything should happen to me —"

He fell silent, unable to finish his thought. He couldn't possibly entrust the prince's safety to this youngster. If anything happened to him, he could not imagine anyone, at least not in his flock, capable of carrying on his missionary work. It would take a rare combination of fervor, determination, and political expertise to bring the true religion to this heathen land.

François Gervaise, although ambitious and intelligent, was a coward. Ignorance and lack of faith, the priest's greatest enemies, had nearly destroyed him. Now among the Mountaineers, would he be true to his mission? The priest might easily be frightened again; what little he had accomplished would be lost.

As for Henri, the novice had been brought to Annam merely through an accident. Pierre couldn't see that Henri possessed an ounce of the piety that would make it worthwhile for him to educate the boy.

He walked closer to the hut. The opening that served as a window allowed him to look inside. Nothing moved. Still, Pierre could not banish the sense that he was trespassing, a feeling that was reinforced by the foul and familiar odor of rotting flesh. The flood had been here and left the footprint of its fury. The structure seemed ready to collapse.

He thrust his shoulders back and climbed through the opening, reminding himself that his presence had often prompted miracles. Nothing in the shed could harm him, for he was a servant of God!

Inside, the stench slithered down his throat. A decomposing corpse sagged between an upturned cot and a retaining wall. The naked body was silvery gray with soft blotches of blue, like a marble statue. He averted his eyes and saw a small earthen jar, sealed with a wooden cap. It lay on its side, on a bed of soot.

Pierre covered his nose and mouth with the inside of his shirt. When he uncapped the jar, its contents spilled — a mixture of seawater and uncooked rice, soggy from soaking too long. Still, it was edible.

All he needed now was a pot and some dry sticks to build a fire.

In the shade of a coconut tree, they ate the steamed rice balls that Pierre prepared and drank coconut juice to wash the salty taste away.

There was not enough food for everyone, so the bishop gave his ration to Ánh. The boy gulped down the crude meal without chewing, without looking up, and without taking time to taste it. Then he eyed Xuan, expecting her to give up her portion as well. The girl was terrified, but she did not stop eating. Ánh screamed and stamped his feet. Henri placed himself between the prince and Xuan.

The bishop grabbed the girl's wrist.

"Give him half of your share," he ordered. The word *half* caught in his throat.

She hid her face under her hair.

"Just half," Pierre said. "You are the prince's property. Your duty is to serve him." His cheeks burned with shame. But he had to safeguard the prince.

Henri took a small bite of his food and thrust the rest to the prince. "Here! Take mine. I am not hungry."

Ánh took the morsel from the novice's palm. Henri licked the few grains that clung to his skin. He gave a forced smile to Xuan.

She divided her food, offering a portion to Henri. He took it and they swallowed simultaneously.

Pierre averted his eyes.

The afternoon breeze from the sea lulled the children to sleep. The tide was rising toward the palms. Pierre sat against a tree with his back to the ocean. He wanted to have a clear view of land in all directions in case they were being followed.

A few colorful sea snails burrowed in the wet sand near his feet. He watched the little bits of formless flesh, each hauling a tower of shell on its back. He wondered what vital force drove these tiny creatures to fight for their existence. Was God's strength even within them?

He was afraid to rest. He dreaded the awful plunge of surrendering himself to sleep — the loss of control. He tried to sleep with his ears cocked toward any sound, but it wasn't enough. Worry hung over his head, holding him awake.

The weight of the prince pressed on his lap. Ánh lay quietly, sipping the air with his mouth. At his waistband a silken pouch bulged with a square object. Looking inside, Pierre saw a heavy block of jade, topped by a carved dragon holding the Earth. Pierre uttered a soft sound of surprise. It was the jade seal — the national treasure that proclaimed the king's power, the only possession that the Mountaineers had somehow not found. *How clever of the royals,* he thought. Giving the seal to the youngest member of the dynasty was the surest way to protect it. Pierre straightened the boy's clothing, causing him to stir.

Prince Ánh waved his thin arms, fumbling for his toy. Pierre placed it in his fingers, and he turned quiet again.

Sifting his fingers through the sand, Pierre gathered a few stones that had been washed white in the saltwater. He stored them in an empty coconut. With the sap collected from the roots of a cactus, he would seal the opening and turn the shell into a noisemaker. The prince could shake it to let Xuan and Henri know when he needed them. When night fell, the sound would help others to locate the boy.

Pierre had to save this boy's life. Ánh was young enough to be molded and conditioned into the type of ruler the bishop could control; and besides, the boy had a trace of ruthlessness that Pierre found promising. It would make him strong against his enemies.

True, there had been at least fifty princes in the palace, each with his own right to claim the throne. But during the attack by the Tonquinese, Pierre had witnessed several of King Due Tong's brothers and nephews being slaughtered, along with their families. Truong Loan, the powerful vice-king, had been executed in front of a crowd, his possessions divided among the Tonquinese leaders. How many more had died since they abandoned Hue Citadel, he had no way of knowing. In order for the West Mountaineers to gain sovereignty over the kingdom, they would have to obliterate the entire Nguyen royal family. From what he had seen, the rebels seemed capable of doing just that.

And in the event the present king survived, Pierre was sure to find favor. Rescuing the ruler's favorite nephew would certainly help build a bond of trust between the Annamite monarch and the Jesuits. Whichever way the events unfolded, the bishop stood to gain.

That is, if the South won the war.

So far, the king's army had proved to be impotent. Soon Due Tong would realize how much he needed the help of France. As a bishop, Pierre would be the perfect mediator to plead for French military aid to Annam.

Then and only then would he be able to convert this kingdom to a Catholic, French colony.

They traveled by night to avoid the oppressive heat and risk of being discovered. The evening's coolness soothed their wounds, but the dripping moisture soaked their clothing. The relentless sound of thrashing waves kept their nerves on edge. Far in the sky, the half-moon floated on soapy clouds. Its light penetrated the thick darkness, creating strange images that danced across the glassy ocean. The children bathed in its glow, their thin limbs swaying like tree branches.

Pierre had traveled this way before. The coastline would take them back to Quinion Province, where they could seek refuge in the Portuguese monastery with Brother João and Brother Tiago before continuing the long journey to Saygun City.

The moon seemed to hum with energy. They came to a small shrine at the fork of a crossroad, an indication that a village was near. He looked into the dark, hollow interior of the ghostly house. Incense wisps lingered inside.

He prayed that the monastery would still be standing. *What if it is no longer there?*

Pierre wondered if he had enough strength to continue his journey unaided and with two children and an adolescent he still mistrusted.

For the first time, he received no guidance from the voice of God inside him.

CHAPTER TWENTY-ONE

March 1776

François squatted on the branch of a banyan tree, gripping a lance. It was a crude weapon, a stout iron bar laced to a pointed spearhead, but practice had made it rest naturally in his hand. His body, bare except for a brown cloth wrapped around his midsection, was coated in mud. The dirt's earthy odor served to mask his human scent from his prey. A dagger was looped through his waistband.

He sat unmoving, quiet and alert, with his back leaning against the tree trunk, as he surveyed the greenery that encircled him. His face, freckled by the filtered gold of the sun, studied the forest with the patience of a leopard. There was no sound, no movement, except for his breathing and the blink of his eyes.

In a tree nearby, a shadow stirred, breaking the silence. One of the other hunters had grown restless. François tensed. The squirming ceased, and the jungle fell back to a tense stupor.

For the past three months, since returning to the King's Screens Mountains, François had made himself a part of the rebel force. For the first time since his arrival in Annam, he felt that he comprehended the role of a missionary. No longer could he rely on the Bible or his expressive drawings of Christ on the cross to get the peasants' attention. He studied their ways of thinking, asked them about their hopes, their dreams, and their fears as well as their beliefs. Only when he was truly accepted as one of the natives could he contemplate building another church.

Under Prince Thom's direction, he had been assigned to join a legion of fifty men whose task was to hunt and gather food for the community. From the start, his Western stature, strength, and stam-

ina gave him an advantage over most of the Annamites, and his eager-
ness to learn intensified his skills. As days passed in basic survival
exercises, his palms developed calluses. He allowed his hair to grow
wild like the majority of the men. Like them, he shaved his beard
daily to keep his face clean.

Every day he devoted himself to his insatiable new interest in the
Annamites' culture. Now François could identify a person's origin by
the inflections of his dialect. He questioned everyone around him to
learn the history of East Asia, memorizing the war strategies, ruses,
and deceits of kings and emperors of past eras. In doing so, he discovered the depths of loyalty the Annamites had for one another and for
their sovereigns.

His hard work was noticed, and he was advanced to the leader-
ship of a band of ten hunters. In the eyes of the peasants, he was no
longer a foreigner — a white ghost — who had invaded their land.
They had accepted him, even Annamizing his name. He was now
known as Father Phan.

From his roost, he heard the beaters crashing cymbals from a distance. Anticipation rushed through his arm. With his weapon, he
could kill any animal, large or small. He flexed his bicep, raising and
lowering his weapon in his hand, expecting the arrival of the prey.

He felt, before he could see, the thunderous stampede. Then a
herd of wild buffalo charged toward him, running from the noise-
makers. There were hundreds of them, slick black and rippling with
muscular humps, climbing the slope in unison, trampling everything
in their path. Their red eyes seethed like molten lava. As they poured
past him, he tightened his fingers around his spear. His hunting
instinct, formed in Villaume and heightened by time in Kim Lai,
prompted him to search for that one single beast that would present a
perfect target.

He spotted his choice. A bull! It sprinted away from the rest of
the herd with its head down. Its elongated, pronglike horns thrust
forward, stabbing at some invisible foe. A loner! In its round eyes,
bright under a shaggy mane, he detected no fear, only rage.

The cymbal sound was coming closer. Instead of fleeing, the bull stopped and turned toward its pursuers, lowering its head and kicking the dirt. From where François hid, the buffalo's heavy forequarters were almost directly below him. He could see every swell of muscle beneath its massive bulk.

He lunged from the tree branch and landed on top of his prey. With his left hand grasping the bull's horn, he jammed his lance through the thick hide below its right ear. The beast jolted as blood sprayed from the wound. It flinched, snorted, and swiveled, struggling to topple its enemy.

François held on. A season with the West Mountaineers had renewed his strength and confidence. His fingers slipped from the horn but caught the buffalo's mane, and he let the animal carry him through the woods. Around him the forest remained as before, green and brown and dotted with gold, only now the colors blended together like a smudge on a canvas. Where were his companions? Their plan had been for François to select an animal and make the first attack; the others were to help him finish the task. For now, at least, he was alone with the wounded, enraged beast.

When the bull slowed, he gripped the spear, pulling hard. It yielded to his strength, tearing the flesh on its way out with a loud ripping noise. His right hand was red and slippery. He saw the wound, just for a moment, before the hot crimson stream stung his face. The buffalo gave a powerful shake, tossing its head. It hurled him through the leaves, and he landed in a bed of damp black earth. The buffalo shuddered, snorted blood, and broke away into the deep forest.

He sat, catching his breath. There was no one else in the clearing but him. He heard his teammates' voices, calling to one another, following the same trail of blood he had pursued. The sound of cymbals was growing nearer.

"You cannot escape," he said aloud.

He staggered to his feet and picked up the lance. The forest around him was strewn with crushed leaves and broken twigs. He sniffed the air, detecting the odor of blood. He was sure he had inflicted a fatal wound on the animal. It could not have gone far before it weakened from blood loss. He walked through the woods, following all signs of the bull's desperate flight.

The closer he got to his prize, the bloodier the path. He found it standing behind a flowery shrub, trembling and rolling its eyes at him. He advanced. Both his hands lifted the spear, ready. The bull glared back; a hoof scratched the dirt.

With a bellow it charged him, a soaring wall of black fury. The air churned. He stood still. When it came close enough, he plunged his spear into its shoulder, feeling the trident head reaching for the heart. The buffalo's massive force crashed into him, and he was hurled through space, while it collapsed on its forelegs. He landed on his back. The animal let out a last bellow of desperation; its lips trembled. From the kneeling position, his prey tumbled to its side and rested its head in its own blood.

When he approached, it was too weak to move. The spear protruded from its neck. Standing over its body, he waited for it to die. At last, its belly swelled in one final forceful heave, and it expired, just as Lộc and three other West Mountaineers caught up with him.

"Father Phan!" Lộc cried. "You've done it! You're the master of the hunt."

Outside the City of Hue, the rebels camped patiently, waiting to gain entrance. So far the conquerors — the northern army of Tonquinese — were silent within the protection of the citadel. They had attacked the South in order to seize the kingdom's wealth, and they had succeeded. Having forced the southern king and his family to flee toward Saygun, they now held the famous capital of Cochin China at their mercy.

Inside the wall, the citizens suffered. Each day brought new reports about the cruelty of the invaders. Only the captors knew the fate of the southern kingdom. Who would be its new ruler remained an unanswered question. The three brothers hoped that the Tonquinese had come only to plunder the citadel, not to conquer new territories. The rebel forces could not wage a long war.

It was mere luck that the Tonquinese war boats had been able to take over Hue City without a struggle because of the recent flood. There were few skirmishes between the armies of the North and South. The campaign was mostly an ongoing massacre of innocents. As the Mountaineers waited, the civilian death toll continued to rise.

The three peasant brothers would seek to form an alliance with the northern army so that they themselves could assume power after the invaders departed. So far, all their requests to meet with the Tonquinese officials had been rejected. Though the intruders' arrogance was intended to humiliate the West Mountaineers, it failed to discourage them into withdrawal. In fact, defiance anchored them, and the longer the rebels were forced to wait, the stronger their will became. With every day they remained on the King's Screens Mountains, they grew in numbers, as peasants from the valleys, hills, and jungles joined their force. All the while, across the Perfume River, their enemy, like locusts, swarmed over their once stately capital city.

King Nhạc, like most monarchs, was invisible to the public view. He resided high on a hill, isolated from his subjects. The youngest brother, Prince Lu, remained by the king's side as his guard. Among the warriors, no one seemed to have captured the rebels' respect and affection more than Prince Thom. François often saw him walking through the campsites, accompanied by the female general, Lady Bui, and the Chinese casino owner, General Wang Zicheng. They made the rounds to help the peasants with their makeshift shelters of bamboo branches and thatch coverings, or to train them in the martial arts, always exuding an air of self-assurance and authority.

At times, François caught a glimpse of the prince alone, standing under a tree, practicing his kung-fu steps. His bronzed body, as if sculpted from the Earth's purest clay, reflected the burning rays of the tropical sun. His hair cascaded in a rippling tide. As he moved his arms and legs in a deliberate, meditative fashion, the mountains loomed above him. Often the prince would acknowledge François with a nod, never holding his stare long enough to create any bond. When he departed, Thom seemed to leave a part of himself behind, whether it was a musky odor, or the imprint of his feet in the sand, or the lingering energy of his being.

December 31 of the lunar calendar — mid-March on the Western calendar — was the first day of the three-day celebration of the Annamite New Year. That morning, the West Mountaineers received a messenger from the citadel. He presented an official document sealed inside a hollow bamboo tube to the three peasant leaders. The news spread quickly across the mountainside: the Tonquinese were now ready to receive the rebels' representatives.

The next morning, when the sun climbed above the walled city, the New Year began. A storm of booming firecrackers exploded over the mountainside. The sky pulsated, jolting François from his hammock. Birds were screeching and leaping from their nests. For an instant it seemed the rebels were being attacked from every side at once. But over the clamor, he heard laughter.

In the smoke, the dragon dancers swayed to the beating of the drums. The face of Lộc, the buffalo keeper, flashed through the papier-mâché mouth of the dragon's head every time it turned in his direction. Through the air the creature rose and spun, a colorful and festive sight that was believed to ward off evil spirits. Five other dancers hid under its long yellow tail, their feet stomping in time to the hypnotic drums.

"Father Phan, join us!" Thom's voice came from behind him.

François turned, disoriented.

From the clearing of the forest appeared five riders, sitting bareback on their horses. He was able to distinguish their faces beneath their full combat armor. Leading the group were the brothers Thom and Lu, accompanied by the three warriors: General Wang Zicheng, Lady Bui, and her husband, General Sam Le. In one hand Thom held his favorite weapon, a bow carved from ironwood with ivory inlay, while his other hand guided the reins of his horse. Trotting alongside him was another stallion without a rider. The prince leaned over to pat its back, motioning to François.

"Come along, Father Phan," he said. "It's time for us to meet the Tonquinese."

François was surprised. "Me?" he asked. "You want me to accompany you?"

Thom handed him the animal's reins. Even though François was not looking forward to reentering the citadel, he mounted the horse.

Thom reached into a pouch at his cummerbund and pulled out a piece of green jade carved in the shape of a fish.

"This carp," he said in a soft voice, "I have carried with me for eighteen long years; once it belonged to my mother. It was her talisman that she used to drive away evil. In her last moments on Earth, she gave it to me. I believe that as long as I have this charm, no bullets or arrows can harm me." He returned the fish to the silk compartment. "You have escaped death many times. So to me you are a jade carp."

François was pleased.

"If you are my friend," continued the prince as they rode off together, "I want you to be close to me. However, you've committed a grave error against us."

The smile disappeared from François's face. The prince was so close to him that their two horses were rubbing against each other.

There was no mercy in Thom's voice as he went on. "You helped an important prisoner escape. And for that my brothers want your death. But I defended you."

François looked into Thom's dark, unblinking eyes. "Why?"

"Because you've made the game more interesting, but harder to play. If you were my enemy, I would keep you just as close. Now, ride forward!"

Thom broke away, heading toward the open field.

When François entered Hue City, along with the five members of the council, his hands were clammy. Too confused to think, he concentrated on following Prince Thom's horse ahead of him.

The warriors brought with them several wagons filled with bounty, including honey, sandalwood, bamboo shoots, gold, and the finest betel leaves — exceptional gifts from the mountain. The last wagon was built like a cage. It contained ten female slaves and a mysterious prisoner, whose head was covered in a red silk sack to conceal his identity.

After a brief stop at the south entrance, where the rebels had to leave all their weapons with the gate wardens, the caravan continued on its way. A Tonquinese official and a small troop of soldiers escorted them deep into the fortress that had once belonged to King Due Tong of Cochin China. It was now being occupied by General Viet, one of the important commanders who served the northern vice-king, Trinh Sam.

François searched the scenery around him for traces of familiarity. All he could see was destruction. Floodwaters had reshaped the land, but clearly the main devastation in the city was not caused by nature.

Down a long, narrow road they made their way behind the soldiers. Several times they had to snake around because the main passage was blocked by fallen trees and collapsed houses. There was no echo; the city sank in muted silence. Ashes floated in the wind, and he could feel them choking him. Heaps of corpses rotted under the hot sun. Their stench permeated the air. No one tended the dead. Their only companions were the black crows who picked diligently through the refuse.

The living dared not appear on the streets unless they were members of the Tonquinese military. Frightened survivors lurked behind the half-burned walls of the brick houses like animal scavengers. It was difficult for the priest to remember how teeming and opulent this city had seemed when he was brought here for his execution.

"Don't be afraid!" said Thom.

It was too late. He was already afraid.

Lady Bui and her husband whispered to each other. Prince Lu and the Chinese fighter, Wang Zicheng, kept a short distance behind, watching and listening.

They entered the inner fortress through a structure of four pillars that made up one main entrance and two side doorways. The air grew cooler, and the foul smell faded away. They dismounted and walked across a long courtyard, hauling the wagons with them. High-beamed ceilings above shielded them from the sunlight. Through a succession of circular doorways forming a long corridor that led them from one gallery to the next, François caught glimpses of mysterious stairs and arches, strange passages and dark tunnels. He let himself be led over the thresholds of many gates, bewildered by the complexity and repetition of the vast structure.

Through court after court they passed, until they reached the central chamber, which was heavily guarded. The doors were ajar. From the inside they heard voices. The official who had brought them to their destination stepped forward and announced their arrival. His proclamation resonated through the halls. As the sound faded, François heard the faint scuffling of bare feet approaching.

The doors grumbled on their hinges and opened wider. A current of incense engulfed them. From the fog peered two androgynous faces, both whitish, frail, and hairless. They spoke simultaneously with a shrill voice.

"Enter!" said the strange creatures, pointing inside with long, slender fingers.

Thom whispered to François, "The vice-king's eunuchs."

"Oh?"

It took him a few seconds to realize what those words meant, and he flinched before the look in the creatures' eyes. They seemed ageless and untouched by the sunlight.

The Mountaineers entered. On the tile floor, remnants of things that once belonged to the royal family were scattered: jewel boxes, embroidered silk clothing, broken furniture, and smashed vases. The once-striking walls, decorated with gold leaf, painted scrolls, and hanging calligraphies in an ancient language, were now cracked with jagged fissures and gaping holes. The trickling sound of water came from an unseen fountain, peaceful in spite of the dreariness.

At the end of the great hall, the gilded throne sat on a dais, still impressive in size even though it was missing its inlaid precious stones and pearls. They had been gouged out, and all that was left was the empty shell of the chair. Sunbeams poured through the openings in the ceiling to illuminate a seated man who looked to be in his early forties. A black silk headdress circled his brow, and at its center sparkled a diamond. His thin, straight beard ran down his chest. Like his guests, he was garbed in the traditional bamboo armor.

Behind his chair and partially hidden by a gauzy screen stood what appeared to be a woman clad in white. At the man's feet sat a group of warriors with crossed feet and arms, all sharing the same expression of menace.

The man on the throne spoke first. "Thom, the Man of Many Arrows," he said in a rumbling voice, "we meet again."

The mountain prince nodded. His voice was sharp. "General Viet, this is the first time we have met outside of a battlefield. We brought you many gifts to celebrate your victory over Hue Citadel in the dawn of the New Year."

The general chuckled. "Hue City was the first to fall, and many more cities will follow. As part of the campaign of Vice-king Sam, I am making Saygun our next target. I am a man of few words. You have been invited here today to discuss the fate of your kingdom, Cochin China. Your messenger claimed that you have a present for us, something more important than spices and slave girls."

Thom approached the throne. The Tonquinese guards sprang forward to form a barrier between him and the general. Their hands flew to their weapons. Thom halted. His brother and the other warriors took a warning step forward.

"Let him be," said the northern general.

Again, Thom bowed with respect.

"Show us what you have brought," said the general.

Ignoring Viet's request, Thom said, "Surely you are not planning to invade Saygun with the army you possess. Your soldiers are exhausted and grow wearier by the day. The climate and conditions of the South are far more difficult than what you are accustomed to in the North. Also, on your northern border, China watches like a cobra, ready to strike your kingdom the moment your military is occupied with other matters. Furthermore, you cannot preside over our government. The citizens of Cochin China will never accept the Tonquinese king or any foreign king as our ruler. For these reasons, the war will continue long after our bones are rotting in the ground."

"Rumors said that you and your brothers have anointed yourselves to sovereignty," said the general, laughing. "Are you presenting yourself or one of your brothers as the new king of Cochin China?"

"You are a very wise man," Thom replied. "But no matter how much we imagine ourselves as kings, we are not of royal blood. In the eyes of our people, we are just like any peasants who work the rice field. What I brought to you today is royalty."

He turned and signaled to Lady Bui and her husband, who pushed forward the cage that contained the mysterious prisoner. The prince unhooked the gate and dragged the captive to his knees.

Standing before the general, Thom announced, "You have executed the vice-king, Truong Loan. Due Tong has fled. This shall be the new king of the South."

He removed the red sack that bound the prisoner's head, revealing his face. Behind the strings of dark hair, a blue birthmark the size of a coin dominated the left side of the man's face. He shivered and swayed, oblivious to all around him. General Viet's shocked expression was replaced by a gleeful look of recognition.

"Prince Hoàng!" whispered the general. "We have been searching for this man to replace Due Tong. We were told that Hoàng was dead. But look at the birthmark —"

Thom placed a hand under the prisoner's arm, propping him up. "When we overthrew Quinion Citadel, we discovered the prince's hiding place. His cousin, King Due Tong, had placed him in the care of the governor of Quinion, Mandarin Tuyền, whom we have since executed. As you can see, he does not talk. He does not care about politics. He doesn't even know where he is. All he asks is to be fed his daily dose of opium. He is the perfect ruler."

The general threw his head back and barked a loud laugh. The prisoner opened his eyes with a look of fright.

"There is one major flaw in your great scheme, Thom the Warrior," said Viet. "Without the royal seal, he cannot be made king."

"I commit my full service to the security of my nation," said Thom. "Just tell me who possesses the seal and I shall retrieve it."

"We searched the entire palace," said the general. "It is not here. I believe it is in the possession of King Due Tong or a member of his family."

"When they fled Hue," Thom said, "the only place they could go was farther south. You have let them slip away. It is not a secret they are now residing in Saygun and will be rebuilding their army to retaliate."

"Then you must chase after the dragon and sever its head. Do it before it can breathe fire."

"This is our kingdom and it is our problem," said Thom. "Let us finish what you could not. But it will take time. Saygun is deep in the south. Before we can get there, we must strengthen our army and restock our supplies. With a new king, what Cochin China needs now is peace, even if it is temporary. Our people cannot endure any more hardship. We urge you to remove your troops from the citadel and return to Tonkin."

"Do not forget the most important part," said the general. "What would our reward be if we withdraw?"

Thom's eyes were keen with defiance. "You in the North always regard us as a poorer extension of your kingdom. You believe that it has been written in heaven's law that your emperor is the rightful ruler of all the land. Our king should be here only to serve yours. A thousand years ago, Tonkin and Cochin China were born one country. We have since been divided but still share the same language and culture. We have been at war for hundreds of years. It is time for peace. Once we rebuild our cities and lands, we will be able to pay tribute to you. For now, your reward will be that we kill King Due Tong and his family."

He grabbed the prisoner by the collar. "In the name of all things we the Mountaineers hold sacred, I vow this puppet shall be the new ruler of Cochin China and will carry the royal jade seal."

General Viet nodded. "So be it," he said.

PART THREE

Slaying the Dragons

CHAPTER TWENTY-TWO

Saygun, 1778

Henri hurried through a dense forest that formed the south-west border of Saygun's citadel. A smell of ripe mushrooms rose from the bed of leaves on the ground. A soprano voice wove its way through the woods.

> *We stay detached, with folded arms in the realms of glory and notoriety.*
> *How many times have I escaped the unexpected calamity?*
> *In the moonlight gleamed the silver plum blossom;*
> *And rustling in the wind were the silhouettes of the bamboos.*

It was high noon in midsummer. The light around him was delicate, like streamers.

> *It is not that I overlook my patriotism and devotion to the prince,*
> *But in a day, I cower away from all the choices — torn between right*
> *   and wrong.*

I have trekked over several mountains and rivers:
How many perilous places have I been in the world!

Henri reflected on the folk song's theme. How many perilous places had he been in the world? From the day he was born until he set foot on this shore, his life had been a long journey.

Through the foliage, the watchtower of the king's fortress followed his movements. The babble of a waterfall rose above the melody. He knew where the singer was, but he enjoyed sensing her from a distance.

From high on the mountain, water cascaded down rocky stairs and emptied into a small lagoon. On its banks grew wild peach trees, their branches covered with tiny pink blossoms. Through the dense leaves, hummingbirds flitted in search of hidden nectars. And on the ground, the roots twisted and tangled, embracing one another like lovers. With every breath of the wind, more petals slipped into the water, turning it a deeper shade of rosé.

Xuan stood knee-deep in the pond, under the waterfall, with her face toward him. Her body blended with the mist.

His eyes could have registered many splendors in the scenery, but all he saw was her. She was a butterfly in a background of bright liquid droplets — silver and gold, black, white, blue, and green. Her face was tan and lovely. The triangular crepe-de-Chine blouse clung to her chest like wet rice paper, and her skin shone in the sun.

But she was not being deluged with water alone. Along with the splashing torrent pouring on her came wave after wave of slick, red carp. They came from the springs above to lay their eggs, and the falls brought them to the lagoon. Xuan held out her hands to scoop the fish as they flew in midair. A sweet and pungent smell rose from the stream. Each time she caught a fish, she would toss it in a bamboo basket that floated nearby. Her hands were pink from the peach blossoms.

He walked into the ray of mist. The washed gravel crunched under his feet.

Xuan's face lit up when she saw him. The mournful sound of her singing stopped.

"Ông Tây," she called out.

They had known each other for almost three years, but she still addressed him with the name the Annamite children used for a foreign man, meaning "Mr. French." Somehow, though, her intonation made it clear that the title no longer bore its original message of respect. Unlike other Annamites, she never made him feel like a foreigner.

"I was afraid you couldn't come," she said. "Look at how many fish I caught. Help me carry them home."

She glided the basket in his direction. Fish flopped inside the wicker container. It took all his strength to avoid staring at her. Beneath the tattered hems of his breeches, he was conscious of his bare feet, which seemed grossly enormous beside hers. To hide his awkwardness, he leaned over the basket and dipped his fingers inside, touching the fish. They felt slippery and cool.

"The song you sang," he said. "Was it a poem by Scholar Khiêm?"

Xuan lifted both her hands to wring the excess water out of her hair.

"I don't know," she said. "Was that what Cha Cả taught you?"

First Father. Henri recalled the classroom where he had sat among the princes, a rare privilege granted him because of his status as a novice. The bishop's lessons were about the histories of Europe and Annam, their poets, writers, and scientists.

"You were snooping," he teased her. "You probably were hiding outside the window, taking everything in."

"I was not." Her eyes narrowed. "Let's get the fish back to the kitchen so I can make the prince's dinner."

When Henri bent to lift the container, he felt a slight tug at the loose waistband of his trousers. Something cold, wet, large, and slimy slithered inside, squirming frantically. He let out a yelp, jumping up and down and shaking his clothes. It seemed like a long time before a small carp slipped down his pant leg.

Xuan covered her mouth and laughed. She peered over her fingers, and his expression made her laugh even harder. His panic resolved quickly into embarrassment and then a desire for revenge. Picking up the fish, he jumped over the basket and chased her around the lagoon.

"Stop! Stop!" She ran, trying to keep out of his reach.

He reduced his speed, but stamped his feet to magnify his effort. She ran from the forest toward the citadel with exultant cries.

Henri waved the fish like a sword. "You have done a foolish thing, Xuan. First I'll catch you, and then I'll punish you."

"No, no, I am sorry, Ông Tây," she shouted back, giggling.

A few feet ahead, he could see the rainbow-hued arch of a bamboo bridge that connected the forest to the southwestern part of the citadel. They dashed across its brightly painted floorboards, and she made a sharp turn to the right. A fence of bamboo and bougainvillea vines blocked the path. From beyond the greenery rumbled the voice of the bishop. "The concept of the steam engine — do you understand it now?"

At first Henri wondered if he was supposed to answer the question. Then he realized they had come too close to the edge of Prince Ánh's quarters, which were off limits to all but a few.

"Well, Your Highness?" the bishop prodded.

"I don't understand. Tell me again." It was Prince Ánh.

Henri saw Xuan approach the fence. He was astonished to see her do something so daring. He could hear the murmurs of the prince's wives. It had been nearly three years since he and Xuan had seen the royals in Quinion City, when they had escaped together from the Tonquinese army. Time had changed the rules. Now, besides the mandarins, only eunuchs and ladies-in-waiting were allowed to see them in their private quarters.

Whenever you believe you must act on your impulse, for heaven's sake remind yourself twice that you are a man of the cloth. Henri heard the reprimanding voice of the bishop in his head. He caught Xuan's wrist and pulled her back.

"Don't," he warned her.

She slid into the shadow of the fence.

He looked about uncomfortably. His habitual aversion to the bishop made him want to flee, but the thought of sharing a dangerous moment with Xuan was too exciting to pass up. Besides, he wondered what de Béhaine meant by a steam engine. The anticipated answer lay ten feet away. *It is just a lecture,* his mind said, even though his instinct insisted otherwise.

Henri placed his arm protectively over Xuan's shoulders and peeked through the leaves. She withdrew from his touch. The scene on the other side opened before them, stirring with activity. On a stone veranda that ran the length of the palace, the bishop and his student stood regarding a strange apparatus — a glass cylinder connected to a boiler, which was placed above a kiln. Inside the cylinder, a sliding brass valve was attached to one end of a seesaw-type armature. A carriage harnessed to two horses was fastened at its other end.

Henri could see the sun's reflection on the glass — it was too bright to stare at for long. Fifty paces away, the queen of Cochin China, who had been present at the execution site at Hue Citadel, lounged on a settee under a gold-fringed parasol, while her lady-in-waiting waved a fan of peacock feathers. Her companions, the three wives of Prince Ánh, sat at a nearby table, surrounded by a cluster of female servants. They were no longer the same terrified refugees Henri remembered. Something the queen said unleashed a burst of embarrassed laughter from the women. Xuan, like Henri, was too far away to hear the comment. Still, the girl giggled along with them.

With a swift glance at her, he drew a finger to his lips.

"Look at the strands of pearls on their necks," Xuan whispered. "They were gifts from the prince of Siam. Have you ever seen anything so beautiful?"

One of the princesses got up and went over to her husband and the bishop. A tuft of her hair, glistening with coconut oil, hung at the end of her headdress. With each step she took, her hair bounced like a rooster's tail. Her body had not yet lost the shapelessness of childhood — she was barely fourteen — but her midsection already swelled with pregnancy. Henri surmised that she was Lady Jade Bình, the infamous third daughter of the Tonquinese king. For months, the news of Ánh's expected first child had been the topic of gossip all over the citadel.

Prince Ánh smiled at the princess. He reached for her belly and held it in both hands. "What are you all laughing about?" he asked. "Do you find me a poor student?"

Even though he was cheerful, his questions startled his mistresses. The oldest one, twenty years old, holding an embroidery of peonies on a silk cloth, looked up with concern. Her younger companion, his third wife, displayed a grin full of dyed-black teeth.

Princess Jade Bình nodded at the queen. "We would never laugh at Your Highness. Her Majesty told a funny tale about a Chinese man's experiment with fireworks."

The bishop, who had been waiting to regain the prince's attention, seemed to find the topic of fireworks interesting. He turned his stare from the sky to the princess.

"What tale, madam?" he asked.

"A tale of transportation."

"Oh, what do you mean?" He looked at her.

"There was a rich mandarin from China named Van Tu, who dreamed of flying," she said, watching the queen's face for approval. "With the help of his many servants, he assembled a chair under a large kite. Fastened to the back of the chair were fifty firecrackers —"

"Rockets," the queen corrected, sipping her cup of tea.

Lady Jade Bình swayed toward the bishop and repeated, "Rockets. On the day of the experiment, Van Tu sat in his chair and gave the command to his fifty servants. At the precise moment, they all ignited the rockets with their torches."

The women, including the ladies-in-waiting, giggled with anticipation.

"Madam, please," said the bishop, "continue with your story."

"The flames created a thunderous roar and a billow of thick smoke. When the air cleared, Van Tu and his chair had vanished. All that was left on the ground were his skullcap and a bent finial. He was never heard from again. Most villagers believed that the force from the rockets was so strong it flew him to a mystical land. Except —" The princess embraced her stomach to restrain her laughter.

De Béhaine took a breath, swallowing his impatience. "Except for what?"

"Except that the queen thinks he blew himself to pieces with the fireworks, along with his wicker chair and the kite."

Forgetting herself, Xuan joined the ladies' chorus of laughter. Henri sealed her mouth, but it was too late.

The bishop turned in their direction and shouted, "Who's there? Where are the guards?"

Henri saw him peer through the gaps in the bamboo and into his eyes. He jumped back in fright.

"Hurry! Hurry!" cried Xuan.

He felt her pulling at his shirt. Together they ran back across the arched bridge into the thicket. The women's screams tore through the palace's solitude. But to his relief, no guards pursued them.

They returned to the stream where they had left the basket of carp. As she walked alongside him, Xuan crossed her arms over her breasts in an effort to conceal herself. Her thin shoulders drew in as if she were cold, and she didn't look up from the trail.

To avoid the Rainbow Bridge, they took a path that wound in and out of the forest — a much longer route back to the citadel. Inside the basket strapped to Henri's back, the fish barely moved. Xuan walked behind him, heavy-footed. She had rolled her thick hair into a knot and put on an extra blouse, which she buttoned all the way to the top. A terrible silence separated them.

Henri turned and waited for her. She walked to the other side of the road. A strand of hair was caught between her lips, and she chewed on it.

"Are you all right?" he asked, scratching his head.

She lifted her eyes no farther than his knees. "No."

He had to strain to hear her.

They continued to march under the sun. Out of the corner of his eye, he saw her wipe perspiration off her forehead, using a sleeve.

"Don't get upset because of what just happened," he said. "Thank God that we didn't get caught."

"I am not upset," she said. "I am ashamed of my behavior. It isn't ladylike, this curiosity of mine. I just wanted to see their pearl neck-laces."

Henri licked his lips and began to sing, swaying his hips to mimic the mincing steps of a soprano. His voice, out of tune, at first was too soft to hear, but then it rose offensively.

> It is not that I cower away from the prince's slimy touch;
> But in a day, I was torn between obsession and delusion.

The song, whose lyrics he had deliberately distorted, brought back the laughter that he longed to hear. She poked him playfully.

"Stop! You are destroying my ears."

He continued to sing off-pitch and to make up words as they walked. His antics kept her in giggles for the rest of the trip.

CHAPTER TWENTY-THREE

Pierre tugged on the rope that connected the apparatus to the horse carriage, checking its tautness. He was fuming with frustration. It was already past noon. Still, he was unable to demonstrate the principle of the Newcomen steam engine to his student.

Prince Ánh always insisted on having an audience of all of his wives, who never went anywhere without an entourage of servants, ladies-in-waiting, and eunuchs. Their chatter disrupted the prince's concentration. Instead of listening, Ánh constantly looked over his shoulder, eager to display his affection to each of the princesses and take part in their silly gossip. This morning, Queen Thụy, the first wife of King Due Tong, had decided to attend Pierre's classroom, having heard that he was planning to perform an act of magic. Her presence was a source of stress for him. The sound of her laugh, forceful and condescending, grated on his nerves.

He worried about offending her. Even though he had lived among the Annamite royals for many years and had acquired an important position in their court, sometimes the cultural differences still created danger for him. The language continued to challenge him. Each word was a monosyllable with a number of meanings that depended on the six different tones given them as they were enunciated. One wrong inflection and not only would he be misunderstood, but the effect his words had on his audience's mood could also be altered.

At court, he often witnessed the queen's outburst at the slightest misusage or colloquialism. The royals' nature, unlike the peasants', was complicated, and the dialect of court was even more intricate than everyday usage. Once, at a celebration of the New Year, an opera singer and the chorus sang an aria about a thief named Due. Upon hearing the refrain, the queen commanded her guards to seize the entire theatrical troupe and flog them on-site, each with thirty blows of the cane. Blasphemy was their crime. The queen expected them to avoid any reference to King Due Tong's name in association with a villain. Since that incident, Pierre was extra careful when speaking at a formal affair.

More than anything, he wanted to impart his knowledge to Ánh, for he knew it would help the prince become a great leader in the future. Pierre had planned a curriculum, pages long in his mind, of science, mathematics, geography, politics, and war, but time was of the essence.

As King Due Tong assumed authority over Saygun Citadel from its previous ruler, who was one of his kinsmen, the royals settled into

their usual life of comfort. But it was a time of uncertainty and waiting. Around the citadel, and in the rest of the communities in the
South Kingdom, the attack of the Tonquinese and the royal family's
defeat had affected all lives, great and small. The threat of the three
mountain brothers hovered over every household, and the mention
of their names ignited dread among the citizens. The rebels, growing
stronger with each day, could attack Saygun at any moment. Due
Tong's forces had been decimated at Hue and now consisted primar-
ily of a handful of high-ranking officers. Pierre knew they were no
match for the enemy, even when combined with troops already sta-
tioned in Saygun.

A eunuch, who had been using the front panel of his tunic to fan
the kiln all morning, jumped back with a cry of excitement. The fire
was at last ablaze. At the same instant, there was a stir from within
the bamboo bushes a few steps away, but Pierre's attention was di-
verted by a shriek of laughter from the women. He inhaled deeply
and gazed at the vast motionless sky above. Prince Ánh stole another
glance at his wives and grinned sheepishly. Pierre, racked by frustration, reminded himself of his purpose for being there. With the fire
at its peak, he was eager to woo his audience with magic.

Much to his dismay, one of the wives, Princess Jade Bình, drew
nearer. Fully seven months' pregnant, she carried her stomach in one
arm and supported her back with the other. Pierre rolled his eyes.
His major failure was his inability to prevent His Highness from com-
mitting one of the gravest of all sins — polygamy. But he had to keep
his objection private. His opposition to this practice had been one of
the factors that had led to his expulsion from Cochin China on his
previous expedition.

The princess stood next to her husband, studying the device.
Inside the boiler, steam began to rise, pushing the piston upward. The
armature went up, and on the opposite end, it descended. The rope
attached to the horses went slack. It needed an adjustment to make it
taut again.

He heard the prince questioning his wives. "What are you all
laughing about? Do you find me a poor student?"

"We would never laugh at Your Highness," said Lady Jade Bình. "Her Majesty told a funny tale about a Chinese man's experiment with fireworks."

With reluctance, Pierre shifted his attention to the pregnant girl. His curiosity was aroused by the word *fireworks*. Could he in some way use their gossip as a lesson on the principles of gunpowder?

"What tale, madam?" he asked her.

"A tale of transportation." Her happy little laugh told him that she welcomed his intrusion.

"Oh, what do you mean?"

She repeated the queen's story to him. The others hung on each word. From the clearing beyond the bamboo and bougainvillea vines came the rustling sound again. While he listened to the princess, he supplied the rest of the remarkable story from his own speculation. Her annoying giggle kept interrupting the tale. He thought of the Chinese who had attempted to fly. The man's courage and aspiration, to him, were an example of the kind of human ingenuity that had formed the basis for modern science. But the laughter from the royal listeners revealed their indifference to the scientist's unfortunate end.

From behind the fence, the squirming noise returned, unmistakably accompanied by whispers and a soft laugh. Someone was watching them. He made a swift turn toward the bushes and caught a sliver of an eye among the green leaves. He made his voice sound stern.

"Who's there? Where are the guards?"

The shrubbery shook, and the women screamed with fright. His Highness raised his hand to summon the guards, who streamed from within the palace, confused and excited. Some clustered around the queen, who clutched her chest with breathless alarm. Pierre strode toward the fence. What he saw ignited in him an ashen, simmering rage.

Running across the meadow toward the Rainbow Bridge and holding each other's hands were his problematic pupil and the prince's servant girl. She seemed half naked, and he was barefoot. What sins might they have committed beyond spying? Pierre looked at the prince and signaled with his hand. "Stop the guards!"

"What?"

"Your Highness, stop the guards!" he said. "I saw a pair of harmless children. They have already run away. I think they've been frightened enough."

The prince shrugged. The women's cries ceased, and the sunshine forced them to retreat under their parasols. One of the horses shook its head and whinnied. He soothed the animal with a pat on its snout and readjusted the rope. The steam within the boiler was still rising, but the piston had reached its pinnacle. It was time for the magic to begin.

"Your Highness, do you really need that servant girl?" he asked.

"Which one?" replied Ánh.

Pierre said, "The orphan girl. The slave." He searched for her name. "Xuan."

The prince touched the cylinder with his fingers wrapped in his sleeve. "I enjoy her cooking." He cocked his head. "But tell me, Bishop de Béhaine, why are we discussing this insignificant servant?"

Pierre gave the rope a final tug. "I think it is time for a matchmaker to find her a suitable husband before she gets into trouble. A girl that age should not be without supervision."

Leaving his student baffled, he turned a valve that released water into the boiler in order to stop the steaming process. Slowly but powerfully, the piston was sucked downward, pulling the armature with it. On the opposite end, the horses struggled in vain against the force that pulled them into the air, where they hovered, kicking their hooves and neighing.

The audience gasped. Prince Ánh was astonished. He turned to Pierre, speechless.

Rising from the settee, the queen clasped her hands and shouted with enthusiasm, forgetting her station.

"What good would this do?" asked the prince.

"Your Highness," Pierre replied, bowing. "What you just witnessed is power!"

Night fell over the citadel. In the thick, humid air, the chanting of Buddhist monks joined the rhythm of the crickets' chirping. Fireflies drifted through the dark branches.

In the southern section of Prince Ánh's palace was the monastery — the living quarters for foreign guests and monks of all religions. For centuries, before Pierre and the Portuguese missionaries arrived, it had been a Buddhist pagoda, surrounded by many smaller towers like a man-made mountain of sandstone. For the past three years, the temple had served as their home.

Much to his dismay, he had to live with the Oriental idolatry that dominated the interior of his new refuge. Tall, meditating Buddha statues seemed tranquil in the fitful candlelight, but their size dwarfed everything in sight. Under the protection of the royal family, the carved stone figures challenged his authority.

Even though Pierre was not officially allowed to preach to the royals, they didn't object when he held services for the Portuguese monks and the natives who had been converted in the past. His Christian sanctuaries were two small chambers on either side of the grand hall. One was used for baptismal ceremonies for the occasional new convert, and the other for administering the Eucharist and penance. Despite the government's effort to eradicate Catholicism, its seed continued to grow. It gave Pierre the greatest pleasure to reconnect with those he had baptized years earlier, those who still practiced the true religion.

Ignatius Khanh, Patrick Châu, and Vincent Họp were among Pierre's students, living in their own quasireligious community in Saygun after the deportation of the missionaries in 1770. They had been bound to the Church by their three vows. The first was to be chaste and not to marry until receiving permission from the bishop. The second was to share all their possessions. And last, they must, without question, obey their elder, whom Pierre had chosen to be their superior in his absence.

He walked to the door of the great hall and stood, legs apart, hands clasped behind him. A bright star smudged the sky. Far beyond the inked outlines of the temples, across an unrecognizable empty space, lived the prince and his wives. He thought of Henri, his wayward novice, imagined him alone with the seductive servant girl. Their lust for each other polluted the night, like the odor of musk.

Like it or not, it was time for him to take charge of the young man before he lost his grip on him forever.

He surveyed the largest statue under the light of a handheld lantern and caught his reflection in a Pa Kua mirror that a heathen worshipper had hung from its neck to ward off evil spirits. He stared into his own eyes, deep-set and weary, squinting from under bushy brows, and a corner of his upper lip lifted with distaste. He removed his hat and opened the collar of his tunic. A tuft of chest hair, dusted with gray, was visible under his chin.

In the dim chapel, two Portuguese monks, Brother João and Brother Tiago, leaned on a desk, both with their heads bent over their daily Breviary. Brother Tiago sat with his back straight, applying the devotion he had honed with his advanced years. Nearby, the younger monk, Brother João, slouched on his tailbone, his blue eyes moving as he read. Across the courtyard, light shone through the green slats of a closed window in a pagoda that housed a group of Buddhist monks. Their monotonous chant resumed. *Life is a journey, death a return.*

"What can I do to silence those simpleminded fools?" he asked the idols in irritation. "If we come from nothingness, and death is the return to nothingness, then explain to me, how can a soul continue to transmigrate through time?"

It wasn't the first time he had expressed his disdain for the Buddhist doctrine. He wondered how the Orientals, Chinese, and Indians alike, who were so advanced in culture and knowledge, could accept such a nonsensical religion. His frustration was directed toward the silent stones. He had petitioned the royal family numerous times to have the statues removed. Each time the queen denied his request, his resentment increased. As long as the idols reigned in his house of worship, they reminded him of his inability to influence the young prince and, therefore, of his failure as a missionary.

He stood and pointed his forefinger at the stone carving. "One day I will demolish all of you and wipe out this false religion once and for all."

The chanting stopped. Then, as if to challenge his authority, it returned with renewed intensity, reaching a high-pitched crescendo. Pierre spat, facing their monastery's window. The lantern flickered, and a yellow blade of light swept across his face.

Outside, the rain came, rolling down the tiled roof, collecting in the bamboo gutter. From there, it rushed into another bamboo shaft, which poured into a vat. He could still hear the Buddhist monks, but the words were now washed in the drone.

"Where are you, Henri?" he yelled into the darkness.

The two Portuguese monks looked up from their prayer books.

Rain splashed in his face; the taste was almost as salty as seawater. The sultry weather in Saygun reminded Pierre of Marseille. It was, after all, an open city for commerce. Foreigners from many countries sailed in and out of port with their goods, trying to set up businesses. When King Due Tong and his surviving family arrived at the citadel, they had brought with them nothing except for the royal seal, which helped them gain dominance over the people. To recover the fortune they left behind, and to rebuild their militia, the king took control of the trading and enhanced it to an art form.

The holy temple became a refuge for eminent foreign guests. Among them was the captain of the *Wanderer*. Like the other traders, Petijean was attracted to the richness of Saygun. Ivory tusks, rhinoceros horns, sugar, rare woods, ginseng, rice, and other exotic resources were available for export. In exchange, the captain would deliver to the palace his cargoes of muskets, gunpowder, iron armor, and cannonballs. Besides providing the king with artillery, he offered his expertise in Western combat strategies and, on occasion, would sell the king a battleship that would be added to Cochin China's naval fleet. All around Saygun, brothels, gambling casinos, and taverns were flourishing, thanks to the influx of sailors.

Pierre rarely ventured outside the citadel. Three years had made little difference in the lives inside the palace. He confined the missionaries to a lifestyle of religious rigidity — praying, preaching, and administering the sacraments. From Captain Petijean, he learned precious but limited news about the outside world. But the information was generally linked to the captain's own detailed and sometimes humorous stories of his adventures.

Sloshing footfalls approached on the muddy path. The bishop peered into the dark and saw the novice, walking in the rain. His anger, which had been brewing since the morning, pushed him toward the entrance steps. Surprised, the novice gave a yelp. He was soaking wet.

"Where have you been?" the bishop demanded.

Henri looked at him as if he didn't understand.

"What possessed you and that servant girl to spy on us?" Pierre barked. "Have you any idea what would happen if the prince caught you spying on his royal women? In a time of war this is an act of treason. When you see me giving the prince a private lesson, what does that tell you about the secrecy of the subject?"

The youth's silence and his expression of shock infuriated the bishop. He continued. "It meant for you to keep away."

"I am sorry, Your Excellency," replied Henri, straightening his posture. "I just wanted to see how a steam engine works." He came into the great hall, shaking off the excess water as he walked past Pierre.

"You should have asked my permission. Since we've been together, you have accomplished nothing except for wasting time and causing trouble. What did you study with Father François for almost two years? For the length of time that the Church has invested in you, you should be ready to take your vows."

A shadow moved across the room toward Henri, and Brother Tiago whispered, "Take this cloth and wipe thyself."

"What do you mean by taking my vows, sir?" asked Henri, ignoring the Portuguese monk.

Pierre slanted his eyes at the novice. "You know very well what I mean. You are not that dim-witted. What do you think we are training you for?"

Henri ran his hand through his wet hair. His voice came out in a tense whisper. "You want me to become a priest? Now?"

Pierre answered with a loud grunt. "You will be more than a priest. You have been trained to be a soldier of God, a missionary. Since I am your superior and we are in Annam, this will be the sacred place for you to be ordained. Tonight we shall rehearse your ordination, which I have decided to hold on the eve of the Good Friday service."

"During Tenebrae?" Henri exclaimed. "But that is only a month away."

"Your ordination is an important event, which will be included in the Holy Week ceremonies. I advise you, Henri, to set a better example of humility and repentance in your behavior, especially during the Mass of the Presanctified, during which you will pledge your devotion to God and to me."

The novice looked at Pierre, speechless. There was a faint odor on his body, a mixture of flowers and fish — a fragrance that Pierre associated with the female sex.

Pierre continued, "Your ordination will make you a priest, with the power to consecrate the Eucharist and to forgive sins in the Sacrament of Penance."

To Pierre's surprise, the novice pushed his chest forward and said stiffly, "I do not wish to be like you. I have done missionary work without becoming a priest. I want to continue my duty this way."

Pierre started — had he given this youth any indication that he would tolerate a negotiation? He shouted, "If you didn't want this life, why did you come here?"

He thrust his open palm straight into Henri's chest, sending the boy backward. Henri staggered, clinging to a stone column for balance. There was anger in the way he held his fists.

"Are you going to strike me?" asked Pierre.

When Henri didn't answer, Pierre raised the paper lantern closer to the novice's face and watched him squirm.

"How dare you to have such a thought!" he roared. "Ignorant fool! You have damned your eternal soul because of that savage."

Henri shook his head and swallowed. "I know you well, Bishop. You want everyone to live in your miserable world, void of any happiness. Others must share your loneliness or you will find a way to cast them out. You separated Sister Lucía from Brother João because of their affection for each other. And now you are trying to do the same to me and Xuan."

A cry escaped Brother João's lips. The glow of the lantern revealed his ashen expression.

"Ask him for the truth, if you have the courage," said Henri to the Dominican monk.

Brother João turned to the bishop.

"Don't!" said Pierre with exasperation. "No one judges me. Chastity is required in both monks and nuns. What I did was for the benefit of your eternal souls, both of you." To Henri, he said, "Leave. You are no longer welcome in the house of God. May you burn in the fires of hell forever."

Henri hesitated.

Before Henri slipped into the rain, he turned to look at Pierre. His voice was calm. "You may condemn me to hell all you like, but, sir, you are truly in your own hell."

He ran out the door and down the steps. Pierre watched the novice turn and gaze at him one last time, and he was struck with the urge to call his name and forgive him. But he gave up the thought as soon as it took form. The rain closed its curtains behind Henri.

Pierre blew out the lantern.

CHAPTER TWENTY-FOUR

Henri stepped into the unknown.

Behind him stood the bishop, brittle and diminutive among the statues. De Béhaine lifted the lantern. Their eyes met as he extinguished the flame.

Henri had never imagined he could find the courage to defy the bishop. But now that he had done it, he felt more liberated than frightened.

He plunged into the night, oblivious of what his bare feet might encounter. The darkness was impenetrable. A hand reached from nowhere to seize his shoulder. With a shout of surprise, he leaped forward.

"Hush," whispered a soothing voice. "It's me, Brother João."

"Brother João, what are you doing out here?"

"I want to ask you about Lucía," said João. "How do you know about us? When did you see her? Did she ask about me? How is she? And where is she?"

"Why does she matter to you now?" asked Henri bitterly. "You have chosen Christ above all things."

"Tell me if she is all right. I just need to know."

Henri shook his head and walked away.

"Please!" the monk cried after him. "I beg you."

He replied without looking back. "The last time I saw her, she had been rescued by the rebels in Ngự Bình Mountain. She was living with them."

"Praise be to God," said João. "I thank you for your kindness. If you apologize to His Excellency, he will forgive you and allow you to reenter the fold."

Henri turned. "I will not apologize."

"Don't be foolish. Without the bishop's protection, how could any of us ever survive in this land?" He reached out his hand. "The best thing for you is to come back with me. What else can you do? Where will you go?"

Henri was unconvinced.

"Have you thought how much it will hurt Father François when he learns of your decision to forfeit your vocation?"

The mention of his teacher pained Henri. "Don't try to make me go back there."

"Why not?"

"Because if I do, I will become like you."

A sob escaped João's throat.

"I understand," he said in a dejected tone. "Go! Find yourself. I must confess I envy you." He touched Henri's chin, quoting Saint Augustine, "'Love and do what you will.'"

When Henri entered Prince Ánh's grounds, it was midnight. The imperial guards were changing shifts. Silhouettes of palms and weeping willows stretched against the black sky. The light from the sentries' torches made the peripheral area seem darker. He was confident that no one could see him among the shrubbery.

The palace was a series of single-story buildings, linked together by a gold-tinted roof. On the front terrace, a row of four blue-and-white ceramic vases housed a rare species of pine tree. The branches were coiled in demotic characters, whose meanings were unknown to Henri. Two guards marched outside the prince's bedchamber.

The summer rain pierced the night like needles. He took a short-cut through the orchid garden to get to the women's quarter, located at the end of the compound.

As he navigated the soggy path, overgrown flowers thrust themselves into his face. He forged through the vines, ripping their tentacles apart until his hands were sticky with sap.

Before the night was over, he must find Xuan. In a few hours the sun would be up, and so would everyone else in the fortress. He would have to leave this place. The moment he had shouted his defiance to the bishop, he had lost his right to stay.

A lantern lit the window of her room in the servants' quarter. Xuan sat on the dirt floor with her back toward him. He crept closer.

With one hand, she removed a jade pin from her chignon. Her hair fell down her back. She combed the long, thick, black strands. Henri envied the instrument in her hand, imagining its tortoiseshell teeth as his fingers. The lantern flickered, trickling over her river of hair to give it an identity, a life of its own. He had seen her using a brew of coconut oil mixed with crushed wild peach flowers to maintain the rich luster. But it was Henri's gentle stroke that many a time had untangled the knots caused by the unruly winds.

From within the mosquito net that draped her bed, someone stirred. Henri saw the face of an aged person. Alarmed, he retreated into the rain.

To see Xuan, he had to wait until morning.

After a fitful nap under a clump of sugarcane, he awoke feverish and impatient. The breeze that wove through the orchid garden only heightened his anxiety. As the gray in the sky spread, the air was heavy with moisture, forecasting more rain. He rose from the piles of leaves that had been his bed. His muscles ached under his damp clothing. From his hiding place, he watched until he saw Xuan emerge from her bedroom. Her blouse was not yet buttoned at the front. A brown undershirt, the color of her skin, preserved her modesty. She was more beautiful now that her hair was tied neatly in a knot, exposing her face.

She stepped into her clogs and walked outside to the well where she kept the fish basket. Following her was an old matron. This was the shadowy figure who had occupied her bed. Leaving the apartment, the woman limped toward the palace. Xuan fished into the wicker container for two carp. They writhed in her hands, gills pulsating. The fish must be alive as she prepared them for the prince. To serve him a fish that had expired would be disrespectful — a punishable crime.

During his travels with Xuan and the prince, Henri had developed a taste for her cooking. He knew she always made more food than necessary, so there would be some for him. Most of her dishes were simple. The ingredients she used were of the peasant style, prepared with imagination to yield an assortment of delicious flavors. Henri delighted in her everyday inventions.

In the courtyard, servants and eunuchs went about their daily chores. To Henri's relief the sentries were no longer at the corridor.

He approached the well. Preoccupied with her work, she did not notice him.

With one hand she gripped a carp by its gills, allowing its protruding stomach to face upward. She slid the thumb and forefinger of her free hand across its thick body. Jets of reddish-orange eggs shot into a waiting bowl, translucent and bright as pomegranate seeds.

After harvesting the eggs, she scaled and gutted the fish, removing the vein along its backbone. When she was done, the two carp lay twitching on the cement floor, their abdomens gaping open, their eyes glazed. Both her hands and the knife were red with blood.

She stuffed the fish's bellies with mushrooms, swallow's nest, fresh spices and herbs, and then tied them closed with palm fronds. In two clay pots, she placed the carp, one under a blanket of large-grained sea salt, and the other in a mixture of mud and honey. Henri watched, forgetting himself.

From inside the kitchen came the scent of wood smoke. She raised her head and saw him. Fish scales stuck to her cheeks and forehead, and her eyes were the color of black currants. Startled, she shrank back in the shadow of the well.

Recognizing him, she calmed, then looked concerned. "Are you well, Ông Tây?" she asked.

He sneezed.

She wiped her hands on the front of her blouse. "You are ill," she said in a determined voice. "Come in the kitchen so I can make you a cup of lemongrass tea."

He blurted out, "I can't, Xuan. I have to leave the citadel."

As she was lifting the two clay pots, his words stopped her. "Now? How long will you be gone?" she asked.

"Once I leave, I will not come back."

She gasped.

He explained hurriedly. "It's the bishop. He tried to force me to take the vow of the priesthood. I refused. And so now I must go."

"But where? This is your home. He cannot ask you to leave, can he?"

He reached out to caress her cheek. The skin felt soft on his fingertips. Unable to conceal his emotions, he looked away.

"Don't leave me!" she said. "You are all I have."

"Then come with me."

She withdrew from his touch and shook her head. He swayed, feeling his blood race downward. He had to hold on to the stone rim of the well for balance.

"Please come with me," he said. "You and I, we can find refuge in the Saygun Harbor, among the French and the Chinese. I can work on the docks, and I am sure I can find a safe place for you."

"I can't."

"You can't or you won't?"

Xuan looked past him. She seemed to be on the verge of tears. "You are kind, Ông Tây. But I can't! This is where I belong. Besides, last night the prince sent a matchmaker to my bed. For the next two weeks, she will monitor my sleeping habits. Unless I have a trait that she finds disagreeable, I will be his concubine."

Flashes of lightning tore across the heavens, followed by a drumroll of thunder. "Don't marry him," Henri shouted over the clamor. "You know what he is like. He is sixteen and already has three wives and seven concubines. You will never be happy."

The rain returned, pounding the earth. He stood silent and watched her shiver. Her hair came loose. The full, heavy strands fell to her shoulders, down her back, and past her thighs like a waterfall.

"I will have fine clothes, servants, and respect from everyone," she said. With a sniffle she sang softly, "*I have trekked over several mountains and rivers: How many perilous places have I been in the world!* Forgive me, Monsieur French, but I don't want to run away anymore. If I leave with you, I will always be running."

In the gray light, he could see that her eyes were red. Her lips were parted, and moisture dripped down her face.

"The old woman will be back soon," she said, summoning a rueful smile. "Grant me one last favor. Say nothing more."

He closed his eyes and did as she asked him.

"Farewell, Ông Tây," he heard her say.

When he opened his eyes, Xuan was gone.

CHAPTER TWENTY-FIVE

The April weather in Saygun was erratic. Even with the rain pouring down, the heat was sweltering.

For two weeks, Xuan had not noticed the weather. She lived in anticipation. Soon she too would sit in the rose garden, sipping imported white tea from a gold cup and wearing a pearl necklace. No longer would she be dressed in the blue uniform of a servant. With her beauty, the matchmaker had assured her, Xuan would lead a life of luxury.

The old matron filled her head with wonderful stories of court life as well as gossip about other concubines. Xuan envisioned herself wrapped in fine embroidered clothes, with her own private apartment and a succession of ladies-in-waiting and eunuchs. In exchange for this opulence, she would have to meet the prince's every need.

"What must I do?" she asked the old lady. Even if she taxed her imagination, she could not fathom what a master and his mistress did behind the red curtain of matrimony. She wondered what she could do to please him. Over the past two weeks, she had learned so much, yet understood so little.

"Never deny His Highness. Your body and your soul must belong to him the moment you enter his bed." The matchmaker batted her rheumy eyes and cackled. The years had drawn her smile downward. "Remember, child, never look directly at the prince. It is one thing to be his trusted chef and another to merit his love."

"What do I do behind the red curtain? Is there a song or a dance he would want me to learn?"

Again the woman laughed. "My wisdom is costly. For a girl of your station, I have but one bit of advice. Patience, child! As with all things in life, you must allow nature to be your guide."

Her mind invented fantasies that her body ached to experience.

Each day, a terrible excitement consumed her. Each night, under the matchmaker's scrutiny, she feared sleep, afraid to reveal an unpleasant habit that she herself was unaware of. Her head whirled with thoughts of the prince, Henri, the poverty of her past, and the possible wealth of her future.

Inside the western wing of the fortress, the living quarters of Prince Ánh, it had just begun to grow dark. The weeping willows that flanked the palace's moat quivered in the wind.

Clutching a basket of food in her arm, Xuan walked on the familiar path. Slanted shafts of rain pricked her cheeks. She did not bother to wipe her face. It was more important that she deliver the prince's supper on time.

Outside Ánh's chamber stood two sentries at attention. Their faces gave a hint of recognition. Each day at the same time, she met them there, guarding the entrance, so formal that she never could gather enough courage to speak. One of the guards would take her food to another servant, who would test for poison before he served it to the prince. While His Highness dined, Xuan had to wait outside the heavy doors, never allowed to look at him.

This evening, something felt different. The food-taster was nowhere in sight.

The sentries bowed. One of them said to her, "You may enter, madam. His Royal Highness is waiting."

The shock of the guard's message weakened her legs, and the sentry offered her his arm. Adjusting her blouse, she glided through the doors before he could change his mind.

The living room of Prince Ánh's apartment was ablaze with lanterns of various sizes and shapes; many of them were suspended from the great carved and painted beams that supported the ceiling. The rain knocked on the tile roof with a relentless clatter. Humidity hung on the wooden columns like fish scales.

Beyond an oval arch was the bedchamber, perfumed by scented

candles. On an ornate bed with a wooden canopy draped with many layers of silk, Prince Ánh reclined on a red quilt. His face was turned from the light. She had never thought she would see him again alone. Up close, he was larger than she remembered; his shoulders wider, his face more angular.

She placed her basket of food on a table, loosening the top tray from its handles. Every object in the room was made of gold or porcelain or ivory, rare and exquisite, reflecting the lanterns' light. Unlike her, each item occupied its rightful place. She saw her image, multiplied in an array of light and shadow, and the sight choked her with disappointment. Her clothes were plain and disheveled. The rain had drained the color from her face and made her pale.

Her hands shook, spilling some sweet-and-sour quail-egg soup onto the inlaid table. To her horror, it dripped onto the sandstone floor.

"I've been waiting. What has taken you so long?"

His voice made her jump. She stood clutching the rattan handle of the basket, her back to him. His movement made the bed creak. Looking down, she caught a glimpse of his foot, dark and slender, as he crossed the floor. His fingers encircled her arm, spinning her so that they stood facing each other.

"Ah, you have become such a beautiful girl," he said, a statement of surprise more than a compliment. "I can see why the bishop has expressed his concerns about your future."

Never look directly at him. What an incredible struggle it was to keep her eyes downcast! She focused on a hanging scroll on the wall, then shifted her attention to his embroidered robe, his thin neck, a flash of his pinkish tongue, his flaring nostrils. A nagging stubbornness took hold of her. Unable to resist, she lifted her gaze and encountered a pair of dark, blinking eyes.

His brows furrowed. He squeezed her chin and turned her face away.

"If I catch you looking at me again, it will be the last thing you're ever going to see."

Though his voice was deeper now, she still heard the petulant tone that had been his everyday mode of expression when they were children.

His fingers tightened around her jaws, making it impossible for her to speak. Slowly he loosened his grip, but she did not dare to move. Too frightened to look at anything, she shut her eyes. He pulled her toward the bed. She stumbled against a piece of furniture. In her new sightless world the only thing she could discern was the lantern light, thick and red. The prince gave a push, and she fell on top of the red quilt. At the same time, she felt his hands at her waist, and then they were pulling her pants past her ankles.

Xuan fought the urge to scream.

His hand caressed her abdomen.

"Open your legs!" came his voice somewhere above her face. She could smell tobacco on his breath.

She felt his hand, clammy and rough, pry into her. Crying soundlessly, she groped for the quilt. In her mind she screamed out for her mother, and then for Henri. But her breath was forced from her lungs as he stabbed her again and again. Sticky fluid dribbled on her face — the stench of tobacco was stronger now.

With a sigh, he collapsed on top of her.

"I am finished," he said. His words were no longer angry. "You may open your eyes."

She rose, brushing her hair from her face.

The cement floor felt cold under her feet as she stepped into her pants and tried to repair the broken string that held them together.

Prince Ánh lay on his back. He was holding a piece of white cloth, which he had placed underneath her. It bore a smear of blood — the evidence of her maidenhood.

She was astonished by what had happened. The mystery curtain had finally lifted. He was the curse of her new opulence. Within her flesh there was a place of pleasure where he could feast, without warning. His clutching hands gave her no time to prepare herself to surrender. She only knew the act was over when he had salivated on her face during his climax. Now that she had nothing left for him to take, she could feel he wanted her to disappear.

They listened to the downpour together, yet remote from each other. She was feeling her own emptiness, and he, his contentment.

The sight of herself in a mirror intensified her humiliation. She gathered the trays together and rearranged them inside the hand basket.

"I am hungry, but the food is cold," said the prince matter-of-factly. "How long would it take for you to prepare another meal?"

She reached for the basket of food.

"Do you hear me? I told you I am hungry," he repeated.

She drew a breath and turned to face him. "Do I still have to cook for you?"

"Why wouldn't you?" he asked, doing nothing to hide his slick nakedness.

She lowered her eyes to the table and retrieved the scattered chopsticks. Through a gap between the door panels, she could see the moving shadows of the guards. She wondered how much of her disgrace they knew.

The prince was close to her. She could feel his hand on her hair. His breath was hot on her neck. She dodged, but he pinned her in his embrace.

"You will continue to cook for me," he whispered in her ear.

His fingers crawled on her skin, reaching under her breastband. His voice came soft and low. "My kingdom is under attack, and my family is in exile. It is your duty to share my sorrow. But once we reclaim Hue City, your loyalty will be rewarded. Now, feed your prince."

With his scent clinging to her like a ghost, she left his bed-chamber.

In the courtyard the two guards fell to their knees when they saw her slip through the doors. Bamboo hats concealed their faces. Xuan stood, bent forward, her hand holding her clothing together. More than anything, she wanted to be alone.

One of the sentries, who was wrapped in a raincoat made of palm leaves, asked, "Where are you going, madam?"

"To the kitchen," she replied, and hurried past him.

"Please wait!" the guard called, reaching for a parasol. "I will escort you there." To his partner he said, "Stand your post. I will return shortly."

Xuan protested. "You don't need to protect me. I can go by myself."

"No, madam. It is my duty. From now on, someone must be with you at all times."

"Why so formal?" she argued, pulling herself away from him. "I am just going to the kitchen. This is something I always do. You've seen me many times coming and going. Just let me be."

She ran down the wide steps. Rain slapped her in the face, awakening in her the shock she had tried to suppress. But before she could react, the parasol floated over her head and shielded her. The guard followed in silence.

"You like being someone's shadow?" she asked.

"I only obey the prince's order."

His answer reminded her that her life was now changed forever. She wanted to disappear, to remove the whole incident from her memory. Henri had been right. She would now live only to regret.

For the first time, the thought of Mr. French brought her sadness. She longed for his warmth and sympathy. If she could see him one more time, she would tell him how much she regretted her mistake.

She let her hands fall to her sides and stared at the wet soil.

They turned a bend in the path. The wind carried petals of peach blossoms to circle at her feet. The garden, veiled in darkness, whispered a secret. She stopped, one hand pressed against her chest. Her instinct sensed his presence.

She took another step and paused, looking into the forest. The guard watched her studying the night. Xuan inched forward, and then to the sentry's relief, she turned and walked to the kitchen.

CHAPTER TWENTY-SIX

A man and his wife give each other their bones and flesh."
Pierre, his back to the altar, lifted his arms wide, looking out at the multitude that stood before him. Tonight, in his black vestments, he led the Mass of the Presanctified, a service to end the commemoration of Good Friday. It felt good to preach again before a large public gathering. He had waited years for this opportunity, which had been granted by Prince Ánh. Brother João struck the gong. By quoting an Annamite proverb, Pierre knew he had captured everyone's attention.

The grand hall around him was gloomy in the broad shadows of the stone pillars. After the weeks of unrelenting rain, the full moon had returned to dominate the sky. Its light, thick as milk, spilled through the windows of the temple. All the Buddha statues had been draped in lavender — a sight that pleased Pierre. At least on this day he didn't have to look at the faces of the false gods. Besides the natural moonlight, the altar was lit only by a bronze candelabrum with fifteen burning branches. Above it hung a crucifix, also shrouded in purple silk.

The crowd, twice the number he had expected, was made up of three main groups. In the center were the Annamite converts, who had been taught the prayers in their own language because of their ignorance of Latin. A larger contingent of pagans, drawn by curiosity and the anticipation of a performance, filled the rest of the temple and its two annexes. Outside, the children clung to the bars of the windows, seeking a view of the spectacle. On Pierre's left sat a few mandarins and members of the royalty, occupying three rows of chairs. The bishop saw his student, Prince Ánh, sitting proudly among his wives and concubines. His newest concubine, Xuan, clad in black silk, was by his side.

Pierre was troubled by the girl's presence. How could the prince possibly have mistaken Pierre's suggestion to marry her off for a hint that he should make yet another marriage? Ánh knew how his teacher felt about the practice of polygamy. Yet because of him, the Mass was now tainted.

"A man and his wife form but one flesh," he said, raising his voice. "Even Lord Jesus Christ, Son of God, true God and innocent man, has taught this with His own divine mouth."

The prince folded his arms. Pierre hesitated. He could feel Ánh's dark mood escalating. Should he change the subject of the sermon? He was a priest, after all. For so long he had compromised to retain the royal support. It was time for him to stand up for his belief, even if it meant upsetting Ánh.

He looked into the crowded room, searching for courage. Eager, innocent faces looked into his.

"At the beginning, God gave Adam only one woman, Eve, and he stayed with her until his death, for nine hundred and thirty years. The same God saw us crucify His only Son on this very eve, on a cross. But His Son was resurrected three days later. Why this miracle? It is because God is merciful and all-forgiving.

"Your own proverb carries the wisdom of Christ. Your law has affirmed that the mutual commitment between the husband and the wife is sacred. As long as one partner is alive, no other partner shall be taken. Polygamy, like divorce, is forbidden under the divine law. Christ has died for our sins. For our part, we must uphold His teaching."

The converts followed his sermon with the recitation of one Our Father, seven Hail Marys, and one Glory Be. The prince, red-faced and indignant, perched on his seat.

It was time for the theatrical liturgy, which Pierre and the Portuguese monks had carefully rehearsed.

Pierre declaimed, "In his last moment, the Lord Jesus cried out: 'Father, into your hands I commend my spirit.' Then, bowing his head, he breathed his last. The earth was shaken."

The converts stomped their feet. A wood floor had been built on top of the sandstone to amplify the sound. The rumbling noise reverberated through the old temple, making the candlelight tremble.

"And there was thunder and flashes of lightning that lit the darkness."

They stomped their feet louder and clapped their hands, accompanied by Brother João's gong and Brother Tiago's drum. Soon the entire crowd joined in the clamor. Pierre smiled. He had successfully re-created the atmosphere of an Annamite operatic theater, with lines of dialogue exchanged between him and his congregation. He gripped the Bible until it hurt his fingers. He shut his eyes as he basked in the success of his strategy.

The heavy doors flung open. All heads turned and looked toward the entrance. Pierre jerked from his trance.

A tall man staggered into the temple, dragging a large wooden cross on his back. The children screamed. An old woman opened her toothless mouth and wept. In the front, two men fell on their knees and pounded their chests in supplication.

"It's God's messenger," someone wailed.

Whispers and calls of protest drowned out Pierre's demands for silence.

The bishop was dumbfounded. This extraordinary occurrence was not a part of his planned ritual. But even though he could not discern the man's features, he knew who he was. That blond hair, those long, spiderlike limbs could only belong to his former novice, Henri. *What is he up to?* One month had passed since he had stormed from the temple. Pierre was buffeted by waves of shock, anger, and annoyance. He swallowed his impatience.

Henri took a few steps forward. His cross grated along the floor. No one spoke. The crowd parted, forming a center aisle. He stumbled and fell with the wood beams on top of him. His clothes were tattered and bloodstained. An unshaven face added to his martyred appearance.

"Father," he pleaded, "forgive me, for I have sinned."

He dragged himself a few more steps and fell a second time. Brother João dropped his musical mallet. Xuan gasped, pale with grief.

"Can you feel my pain? I ask for your forgiveness."

His voice cracked, invoking more sympathy from the onlookers. Many offered to help him rise, but he struggled alone. He fell again, this time at Pierre's feet. The bishop retreated.

The spectators resumed their stomping. Henri looked up at Pierre. His face was wet with tears.

"Please —" he whispered.

The bishop opened his arms, palms up toward the youth. "I forgive you," he said to Henri, making the sign of the cross, "in the one name of the Father, the Son, and the Holy Spirit, amen." To the crowd, he shouted, "I have washed away this man's sins. Who will join him next in the light of Christ?"

Hands were raised. Several rushed forward and formed a line behind Henri.

Xuan rose from her seat.

"What do you think you are doing?" demanded the prince.

"I want to be a Christian, Your Highness," she said, infected by the room's excitement. Her body shook.

"Don't make a fool of yourself," said Ánh. "You will do no such thing."

She turned to the bishop. "Please baptize me, Cha Cả."

"Come, my child," Pierre said to her. "Make your vow to Lord Jesus Christ that you will become a Christian this Easter Sunday."

The prince grabbed her arm and held it tight.

Pierre bowed. "Your Highness, everybody is equal in the house of the Lord and has the right to be christened. With all due respect, you are not a stranger to God's miracles. My Lord saved your life and brought you unharmed to this city. With my prayers, He will continue to protect you for years to come. Please don't try to interfere with a soul in search of salvation."

Xuan tore herself from the prince's clutches. Ánh brushed some invisible dust from his tunic and walked out, followed by his three wives and the rest of his retinue.

After the candles had been extinguished and even the most fervent converts had departed, the priests barred the doors. The temple resumed its dark and isolated mood. A solitary lantern cast its dim light through the cavernous hall.

Henri sat on the floor with his back against a wall. Brother Tiago tended his bruises. They talked to each other in whispers.

Pierre paced the room with angry steps. Conflicting emotions clouded his ability to think. Surely for him the event had been triumphant. At his urging, many had agreed to convert. But that scoundrel! How dare Henri use "the creeping of the cross" to interrupt his homily? No one had the right to perform a religious act without the bishop's permission. Pierre hated nothing more than to be surprised. Clearly, his decision to accept Henri back into the fold had been forced. In front of the natives, he had had no choice.

"Your Excellency," said Henri, pushing Brother Tiago's hand away from his face, "when you said you forgave me, did those words come from your heart?"

"Hush, don't speak now," the old monk advised.

Pierre replied in a gruff voice, "I said it, didn't I?"

Brother Tiago commented with exhilaration, "It's a sign, Your Excellency. He is, after all, the Prodigal Son."

Pierre flushed with shame. Very well, he would accept Henri with open arms, and even rejoice, for the novice who had been lost was now found. But under no circumstances would he trust the youth's sincerity. With Henri's rebellious nature, there was no guessing what he might do next.

Brother João, who had been standing near the barred doors, approached Henri. "The last time I saw you, you were adamant in your decision to leave the Church. Why did you come back? What happened during the month that no one saw you?"

Henri remained quiet.

"It's obvious why he came back," snapped Pierre.

Henri looked up.

The bishop raised his voice. "It was foolish of you to think a native girl would deny her heritage for you, a foreigner. And when she broke your heart, what did you do? You could have left this kingdom, returned to France, or become a sailor, and never come back again. Instead, you decided to plot revenge. Your wish to become a priest serves no purpose but to punish yourself and inflict pain on her. Side by side but unable to contact each other, you will exist in misery together. I cannot allow you to enter the priesthood for such a venal motive."

Henri leaped to his feet. Fists clenched, he thrust his face inches from Pierre's. "I never want to hurt her. I just want to watch over her."

Pierre shrugged. "That has nothing to do with serving God. I am happy that you've decided to return to the church. But you are doing it for the wrong reason." He pointed toward the entrance. "It is not too late for you to walk out. Your whole life is waiting. I promise you, you will love again. A year from now, you probably won't even remember that girl. But if I have misjudged you, if you decide to stay because this is your true calling, you must renounce Satan and all his works. A priest is the minister of divine worship, and the highest form of our worship is sacrifice. You've shown none of that. You may not be a priest, but I might accept you back as a novice. You will surrender all your will to God and recognize my authority as your bishop. Make your choice now."

Without hesitation, Henri fell to his knees, his hands clasped in prayer. "Lord, please help me find the strength to serve you."

Brother Tiago breathed a sigh of relief.

Pierre lay on his cot, watching the night through the window of his cell. From the streaks of silver light traveling across his body, he could tell that it was past midnight. As usual, his mind refused to rest. He could hear the sound of footsteps splashing through the mud, hoarse voices drifting with the night breeze. Someone shouted his name. A guard mumbled. There seemed to be six or seven men speaking — their voices were undistinguishable.

He rose from his bed. The sound was coming from outside the main entrance. It must be important, as it wasn't common for late visitors to disturb a monastery. He rushed to the door. Behind him, Henri and the Portuguese monks shuffled from their rooms. Pierre puffed out his chest and resisted the urge to reach for the door handle.

"Who is out there?" he asked, making his voice deep and commanding.

"It is I," came the angry voice of Prince Ánh as he pounded his fist against the wood. "Open the door!"

The bishop pushed the doors open. The prince rushed past him, followed by the aroma of burning torches. The temperature was dropping. Pierre shivered in his robe. Under the awning of the temple, a palanquin waited, surrounded by six royal sentries.

He shut the doors and bowed. "Your Highness, what troubles you?"

"You and your terrible cult are the source of all my troubles," shouted the prince. "I should never have granted you permission to preach. How could I be so foolish? For years you have been begging me until I gave in. You are supposed to educate me about Western civilization, not influence my people with your nonsense."

"I am sorry, Your Highness. If you had sent for me, I would have come to your quarter. Whatever it was —"

The prince interrupted. "I am too angry to wait. Besides, the last thing I want is for you to be around my concubines. You have caused enough problems in my household already."

Pierre cleared his throat. "Are you upset about Lady Xuan and her decision to become a Christian?"

The prince let his shoulders slump. The anger on his face was replaced by a frown of frustration. "She refused to enter my bed-chamber because you condemned multiple marriages. She claims that she's afraid of being cast into the underworld if she disobeys your law."

Pierre turned to hide a smile in the dark. *Clever girl.* He could not help admiring her resourcefulness. He managed to keep his voice sympathetic. "She is not worth all this rage, Your Highness. Remember, you have others."

Again, Ánh flared. "She is my property," he shouted. "She has no right to refuse me. Cha Cả, if you had any respect for my power, you wouldn't have put me in this predicament. If any woman rejected me, I wouldn't hesitate to put her to death. Except in this case, I do not want to offend your God. You are the wise one — tell me what to do."

Pierre looked at Henri, who stood motionless between the two monks. "You must let her go," he said to the prince.

Ánh seemed startled. Clearly that wasn't the answer the prince had expected.

The bishop stood firm.

"Never!" was Ánh's reply.

CHAPTER TWENTY-SEVEN

*T*oday was Brother João's turn to prepare supper. Henri was sent to the market for bamboo shoots and wild mushrooms. The bishop had been gone all morning, summoned by King Due Tong. Passing through the dusty roads, Henri saw cavalry, foot soldiers, and convoys of military wagons. The news of the rebels' advance had reached the citadel. The city was preparing for war.

The market, at the outskirts of the fortress, was nearly vacant, littered with abandoned platforms and empty baskets. On a wide field of grass, a few peddlers displayed the last of their pigs and chickens.

It had been four weeks since Henri had returned to the Christian sanctuary.

Suffering now acquired a deeper meaning. He felt alone even among his fellow missionaries, whose main concern was to calm the hysterical people of Saygun. The monks' acceptance of their fate had given them a serenity that he lacked. Whether it was his youth or his inability to forgo his love, the gulf between them pushed him further into isolation.

The only thing that kept him sane was the memory of Xuan. She was the string that tied him to life. Their shared hardships had taught them to depend on each other. She was all he desired.

Nothing could soothe the pain of her rejection. An occasional glimpse at her from a distance only deepened his wound.

Although never religious, Henri hoped to find solace in the Church and its rituals. But how could he, when his mind was full of her image, her smile, her voice?

The door to her was shut, Henri reminded himself, and Prince Ánh possessed the key.

He wandered in the hot sun, searching for the ingredients that Brother João had requested. Two little girls held each other inside a clay hut. Their long black hair whipped in the wind. He wondered what would happen to Xuan if the enemy were to attack. Would the prince be able to protect her, among the many others who depended on him?

As if in reply to his thoughts, deafening blasts of cannons tore through the air.

The ground shuddered. He could hear the gongs sounding an alarm. People scattered from their cottages into the streets, screaming and running in all directions. Frantic questions leaped from mouth to mouth. No one could grasp what was happening. Across the road, the two girls hid behind a partition. The roof of their hut was ablaze.

He must find the fastest way to Xuan's apartment. But first, he had to rescue the two little girls he had seen.

He ran to the hut, but when he threw open its door, they had disappeared. The burning hovel stood for a few moments longer before it collapsed. Flaming arrows whizzed past him.

A tidal wave of men, women, and children rushed toward him. The whites of their eyes told unspoken accounts of horrors.

Henri struggled against the current of refugees. Human limbs and tree branches whipped across his face, but he barely noticed. Looking over the crowd, he could see the fortress, shrouded in smoke. Lake Thien Thu emptied into several streams that circled the palaces, forming a moat.

He scanned the landscape for the western wing, where Xuan lived. But Prince Ánh's palace was no longer there! At least, not in the way he remembered it.

In the smoke-filled stream, he saw the inverted reflection of spurting flames. A portion of the stately hall had collapsed, and a hole was coughing up black smoke. He came to the shelf of land bordering the water and paused, taking a long, bewildered look at the scene across the moat. Several apartments in the eastern wing of King Due Tong's palace were also on fire, including His Majesty's throne room.

The drums rolled, and the great bronze gongs inside the fortress brayed. The imperial soldiers formed ranks in a manicured garden behind the ruins, using what was left of the building's bulk to protect themselves against further cannon attacks. Each troop of swordsmen, spearmen, and bowmen held up a banner to identify its unit. From the back of the fortress, soldiers mounted on warhorses surged over wooden drawbridges.

"Dear God!" Henri exclaimed in disbelief.

The women of the court were nowhere in sight.

A man sprang over a block of stone and lunged into him. His mandarin uniform was tattered; his headdress had slipped over his head to embrace his neck; his eyes darted with fear.

"Let me go," he babbled, falling on his knees.

Grabbing the front of the man's tunic, Henri shouted, "What is happening?"

The mandarin pulled against Henri's grip, but there was no strength in his struggle. A large patch of his scalp had been grated away. The skull was bright red and glistened with moisture. Over the man's left ear, the loose skin dangled like a tousled hairpiece.

"Big news!" he slurred. "The puppet king of Cochin China escaped the West Mountaineers' prison and sought refuge here."

"What do you mean?" Henri asked. "King Due Tong is already here."

"No, ignorant foreigner, I am not talking about the true king," the mandarin said with exasperation. "I am talking about Prince Hoàng, the puppet king appointed by our enemy. He has escaped from Hue Citadel, and the rebels are coming after him. They have surrounded us. Because of Hoàng, they will kill us all."

He broke free from Henri's grasp and ran off.

Henri thought quickly. There would be only one way to escape, by the river.

He must find Xuan.

When Pierre had been summoned by King Due Tong that morning, dawn washed the city in thin shafts of light. To his surprise, his palanquin joined the traffic of other conveyances belonging to members of the Nguyen family and their courtiers as they headed to the eastern wing entrance of the palace. The throne room was the only hall inside the Forbidden City that was open to mandarins of the first three tiers. The rest of the city — a series of apartments — formed a fortress, home of the king and his immediate family. For the king to hold this unexpected audience, Pierre realized something of importance must have happened.

Pierre's palanquin, borne on the shoulders of four imperial guards, moved through a sea of black iron mail and muskets. He could not count the troops, but their number had to be in the thousands. In spite of the confusion, the soldiers lined up at attention. Their broad, flat faces shone under sputtering torches.

We are going to war, thought Pierre. It had been nearly three years since the bombardment of Hue City. The imperial troops had recuperated; they had trained and rearmed themselves with imported weapons. But were they ready?

The palanquin jolted as the porters came to a stop. Pierre swung open the curtain, studied the ranks of soldiers, and dismounted. Ignoring the extended hand of an officer, he marched into the grand hall and found a place among the crowd. Prince Ánh and his brothers sat near their uncle, King Due Tong.

Although he was in his early twenties, the king was already graying and looking haggard. He sat on his jeweled throne with his legs astride, one knee quivering.

Partially hidden behind the throne was the queen of Cochin China. She whispered in her husband's ear, while he listened intently.

Despite his close ties to the royal family, the bishop had always disapproved of King Due Tong. In 1765, Vice-king Truong Loan had carried out a coup d'état against King The Tong, Ánh's father, and took control of his government. Loan himself then selected twelve-year-old Due Tong to be the next ruling monarch. Ánh's father and mother were imprisoned and murdered. Through this stratagem, Loan gained power over the people and the throne, thus bypassing Ánh and his seven brothers.

The idea that his ward was cheated out of the throne ate away at Pierre. He picked Ánh in the hope that with his guidance this youth would become a liaison between France and Annam. He believed the prince was the rightful ruler. Like a chess master, Pierre contemplated ways to take advantage of the chaos that the marauding rebels would create within the dynasty.

Losing patience, Ánh rose, shouting into the vast hall. "Your Majesty, we don't need any more debate. We must attack the Mountaineers now, pull them up by the roots. Let's meet them in battle, face to face. Everything or nothing."

Pierre saw an identical flash of anxiety on every face in the hall. On the dais, the prince's seven brothers stood in a cluster, all long-legged and thin-necked and brown-skinned. Years of constant flight had broken their spirits, taming them into a herd. In a few more years, what would become of the Nguyen monarchy? Except in his student, there was no courage left in the line. Unfortunately, Prince Ánh had not yet gained the experience to lead an army.

Pierre emerged from the shadow, the hem of his black robe dragging along the floor.

Before the king could reply, he interrupted, "We cannot go to war against the peasants, Your Highness. We don't have an efficient troop to defend our city. I urge you to consider a retreat."

Overcome with frustration, Ánh kicked his chair. "Bishop, you have no right to speak your opinion here. This is Cochin China's matter, and it should be resolved by our people." He surveyed the noblemen and mandarins, searching for their approval.

"Is this Your Highness's irrevocable decision?" Pierre asked his ward, keeping his gaze steady.

"Without doubt," Ánh grumbled, and looked away.

The bishop approached the throne. "I must hear directly from the king that Cochin China does not need the help of the Christian priests or a European army."

"Be silent!" shouted King Due Tong.

He pushed himself up with the help of his wife. Like an old person, he leaned forward, shoulders bent, and his hands held the arms of the throne for balance.

"Everyone, please keep your peace," he said. "In this time of adversity, I need all of you to be united, not to squabble with one another. There is someone I must introduce to you." He signaled to a soldier who was guarding a door below a staircase. "Bring forth my guest of honor."

Behind the door was a large study, which was concealed by a screen. A man shuffled forward. His body swam inside a large blue tunic. Even though the hall was dimly lit, he held his hands to his forehead as if to shield his eyes from glare. Dark circles emphasized his eyes. A round birthmark was embossed on his left cheek. The assembly of nobles gasped in recognition.

"Gentlemen," said the king, "I present to you my cousin, Prince Hoàng, the king of Cochin China, appointed by the rebels. For three years he has been held prisoner in the Tower of Grace, on the outskirts of Hue Citadel. He never stopped thinking about his people, and for that reason, he escaped the clutches of the enemy to come to us."

Prince Hoàng climbed on the dais with difficulty. The king took his hand, helping him up.

The guest mumbled, "Dangerous rebels . . . I saw them, covered many hills with skilled soldiers. They are chasing me . . ."

Unable to continue, he wiped his eyes with the hem of his sleeve. The king, weeping, held him in his arms.

Ánh stomped his feet. "Fear and self-pity will not solve our predicament. They will just weaken the spirits of our soldiers. Let us take action before it is too late!"

No one paid any heed to Ánh. The king's tears were contagious. Many of the mandarins and court officials sniffed in sympathy, until Due Tong collected himself enough to speak. His voice was hoarse with emotion.

"For too many years I have played the role of leader. During my reign, I have achieved nothing for the happiness of my people. Instead, I have managed to lose most of my ancestral lands. We have lived through floods, famine, plague, and war. Everything has been against me."

The harsh words seemed to calm him. When he spoke again, he looked into the eyes of his noble followers. "I am not to blame. I never desired the throne, nor was I groomed for its responsibilities. Vice-king Truong Loan cast a dark shadow across the land with his misdeeds, and because of him, the rebels were born. When Hue Citadel collapsed, Loan was arrested and murdered by the Tonquinese, but his death was not enough to restore peace and harmony. Our citizens are still suffering hunger and misfortune.

"Except for all of you, I have no allies. I have no plans to improve the future. And, most of all, I have no skills to manage a government. We need to beg for heaven's forgiveness. I believe that the gods will once again favor the Nguyen family's fortune and destiny. But we must promise to reinstate the rightful heir to the throne. That is why I called you here."

Murmurs of surprise and disagreement stirred the crowd.

Pierre called out, "But who is the rightful heir?" His voice was lost among those who asked the same question.

"He is!" Due Tong grabbed Prince Hoàng's arm and raised it high. His skeletal hand dangled like a dead cobra.

A gasp swept the room.

The king continued, "To us and the people of Saygun, this is a prince. To the mountain rebels and the rest of the kingdom, he is king. From the landowners to the peasants, the nation recognizes his ancestry and his stature. I say he has already conquered the minds and the hearts of his men. What he needs is the throne. If I had the jade seal, I would bestow it on him. But since it is missing, our approval is enough."

Pierre and Ánh exchanged a glance.

Prince Hoàng gave a loud moan. To everyone's horror, the prince's eyes rolled up as he fell to the floor in a swoon. Pierre was too shocked to utter a sound. Was the heir apparent an opium addict? Or was he merely weakened from his years of imprisonment and perilous escape? Either way, the bishop could not suppress a bitter laugh. His mocking sound ignited a reaction among the guests. Disputes broke out, voices bellowed, and someone screamed profanities. Such chaos had never been known in the imperial court.

Pierre turned to Ánh. "I am leaving. It is dangerous to stay. If you know what is best for you, you will come with me. Now!"

The prince looked at him with distrust. "Flee, again?" he asked. "No! I have seen the rebels' forces. They are disorderly and poorly supplied. We have thousands of well-trained soldiers, armed and ready to lay down their lives for their kingdom. I am their prince. How can I leave?"

Pierre took in the room with a sweeping gesture. "Look around you. Your king is a weakling. His replacement is an invalid. Your brothers are all cowards. And your men are not prepared. Your Highness, you need more than an army to fight this battle. You need a miracle. You need me."

"You're a fool to think I need you," shouted Ánh with indignation. "I stopped needing you long ago."

An explosion near the entrance made the hall quake. Mandarins pressed forward, clinging to one another amid a cloud of dirt and smoke. The beams creaked from above, and several roof tiles fell down, revealing the sky. Gongs were striking, heavily shod feet were clomping, and a platoon of soldiers ran into the chamber.

Pierre could not see much through the smoke. The acrid smell of gunpowder rekindled the memories of past skirmishes. He reached for the prince's hand and felt it jerk away.

The battle for Saygun Citadel had begun.

CHAPTER TWENTY-EIGHT

From the top floor of a pagoda in the king's palace, Pierre studied the spectacle below. Across the cavernous halls of the Eastern Palace, through the throne room's shattered walls, he could see two towering pillars — the citadel's main entrance. The columns were carved from sandstone to resemble twisted oak trees, forming an arch. From them hung the heavy doors of gray granite, which were open.

As King Due Tong charged through the gate, three thousand mounted imperial soldiers galloped behind him. The king was clad in golden armor and rode atop an elephant. In his hand burned a torch; its red flames were a beacon for his armed forces. Their roars rose with the persistent drumbeats.

Beyond the citadel, the landscape of Saygun consisted of rolling hills and rice terraces dotted by large haystacks. Cannon explosions opened over the plain like parasols of fire, competing with the soldiers' rumbling chant.

Using a brass spyglass, Pierre looked for the enemy troops. In the room with him were Ánh and his wives and concubines. Several imperial guards stood by the door. Outside the pagoda, a second military troop was forming, under the direction of the prince's seven brothers.

Through the magnifying lens, Pierre could see the fields in detail, down to the rice tassels that floated in the wind. Something seemed to crawl like a swarm of black cattle beneath the quivering sheaths. He had heard that the peasants were skillful at making themselves invisible, covering their bodies in dirt and clay to blend with nature.

Pierre saw King Due Tong rise on his elephant. Behind him were the highest-ranking mandarins — the most skilled warriors of the court. Next were the men with muskets loaded with gunpowder, followed by a militia of fighters carrying spears, swords, and bows.

The army faltered as it encountered resistance. The ground shrieked, churned, and erupted into thousands of brown bodies, like corpses that had risen from their graves. Three of the knolls of haystacks morphed into elephants, charging toward the king's brigade.

In the tower, Prince Ánh gave a cry of dismay. Pierre lowered the spyglass. One of the enemy generals who rode the charging elephants was a female. She wore armor made of bamboo slats, and her hair streamed as she stood atop the beast, brandishing a sword. Her foot struck the crown of the elephant's head, urging it into the attack. A horn wailed to signal a charge from the peasants. They advanced, shouting.

The imperial army quailed, vastly outnumbered by the attackers. Frightened horses whinnied and bucked, crashing into one another. Some of the royal guards' muskets slipped through their fingers before they had a chance to fire. The soldiers closest to the rear attempted to retreat into the citadel, but it was too late. The gate was shut. Mountaineers were closing in, forcing them to huddle in the center of the field around their king.

"Fire! Fire!" screamed King Due Tong to his troops.

A rain of arrows from the rebels drenched his army. Muskets barked. Bodies fell. Many bullets struck the peasants, but all too many found targets within their own ranks. Before long, the Mountaineers swept over the royal forces. Weapons clashed in hand-to-hand combat between the two armies.

The female warrior stood on the edge of the battlefield, watching. Her every gesture exuded confidence. As one rebel met his death, two sprang up and took his place. Soon the king's troops were grossly outnumbered. They herded closer together, fighting with all their might. The king turned his head in the direction of the pagoda, to where Pierre and the prince were watching. He staggered and waved his hands in desperation.

"Save the king!" cried Ánh.

A guard ran down the spiral stairs. But below, the army of the prince's seven brothers had already acted. The granite gates screeched on their hinges, revealing a wall of peasants on the other side. The horses covered the green pasture with long strides, keeping no order as they sped from the citadel. The princes' weapons flashed high. One after another, the soldiers descended the vast field, into an arch of sunlight.

Pierre watched the eldest prince hack his way through a throng of rebels. Limbs flew in all directions. Soon his body was soaked in red. However, the destruction that he created was short-lived. From a tree twenty paces away, a black arrow flew through the leaves to pierce his neck. He tilted to one side and slid beneath his stallion. His body was swallowed by a mass of advancing hooves.

A path was clear where a great number of peasants had fallen. The remaining princes and their warriors could now view King Due Tong and his surrounded troops. They were gaining on the rebels, and their only objective was to save their king. Within their ranks, the bowmen took positions, shooting arrows from their horses. Several peasants fell; many more retreated.

The female general yelled and stamped her feet on top of her elephant. Her body twisted in a primitive dance to the rhythm of her shrieking voice. The animal trumpeted in response. Its sound ripped high above the clamor, and the other elephants joined the chorus.

What seemed like another earthquake shook the ground. The rumbling spread as far as the distant forests, where the trees shivered. More peasants surged forward, hatched from within the Earth's bosom. All around the mound on which the imperial soldiers had gathered, a terrible cry reverberated. One by one, the king's soldiers tossed their weapons in defeat.

The fire in the king's torch had gone out. This time, he did not look back at the citadel.

Silence fell. The lead elephant lifted one foot, forming a step for the female general to dismount.

With every eye focused on her, she strode over to the frightened king. Ignoring him, she gestured to his elephant in an unspoken language, then took a few steps back. The beast understood her command. It knelt on its front legs. A group of peasants reached into the king's compartment and pulled him out. She clapped her hands, and all the elephants rose tall.

Together the animals lifted their trunks and released a penetrating roar.

Pierre put his hand on Ánh's shoulder, forcing the prince to look at the battlefield.

"What does Your Highness plan to do?"

The prince sat still, wearing a vacant look.

"You cannot try to rescue your uncle and brothers. As you can see for yourself, nothing can save them. Soon the citadel will be invaded. You'll be imprisoned and tried along with the other royals. None of you will live."

The women sobbed, holding on to one another.

Ánh shrugged away from Pierre's grasp and shouted, "Silent, all of you!" He clutched his temples. "And you too, white devil! I cannot think with you filling my head with such damnation." He lurched to his feet and almost fell.

Pierre was unrelenting. "I am your only friend. Ever since you became my ward, my mission has been to protect you. Your Highness, I'm afraid this time it might be too late."

Outside, the Mountaineers had disappeared from view, taking the defeated soldiers as their prisoners.

Ánh panted. "If it is hopeless, then I shall attempt an escape, or die trying with the last of my men."

Pierre couldn't help smiling. "That is what the rebels want you to do," he said. "It would be easier for them to draw you out there than to break through the walls of the citadel and hunt for you in here. There are traps we can set to counterattack them. Remember, they know that besides Prince Hoàng, you are the only one left that has not been captured. For now, they are amusing themselves at your expense. Your sanity is what they want. That is why they retreated."

His words seemed to reach the prince.

"What can I do, Cha Cả?"

"It doesn't seem likely the rebels will strike anytime soon," said Pierre, pushing his shoulders back and resuming his erect posture. "They are anticipating your surrender. We still have a few hours to prepare a plan."

"What if I don't surrender?"

Pierre replied, "Then they will tear this city apart, brick by brick, to search for you. This day will enter history as one of the rebels' finest achievements — the day they conquered the South. You must —"

A cry cut off Pierre's words. It came from Lady Jade Bình. He threw an annoyed look at her, but that did not stop her from moaning. She was clutching her abdomen. Her face was covered in sweat and distorted with pain. The prince turned to her, bewildered.

"What is wrong?" Ánh asked.

The girl's lips tightened. Pierre watched her press her thighs together in that frantic gesture that children often use to fight the urge to urinate.

A voice came from behind the wives. "Your Third Mistress is about to be blessed with a child, Your Highness."

For the first time since they had entered the pagoda, Pierre noticed Xuan. She wore a simple tunic of honey-colored silk.

The prince's eyes widened. "No! It can't be! Now? But it is too soon, isn't it? How could it be?" he babbled. "Quick, somebody help her. Take her away and get a midwife to help with the birthing. I cannot see this act. It will curse me with ill luck. I cannot survive any more misfortunes."

"Where do you want her to go?" Xuan asked.

Another woman, the oldest of the wives, struck her across the face. Xuan's head swiveled to the side, and her cheek reddened.

"Why did you hit her?" Ánh asked in surprise.

The princess replied, "Twice she spoke without your permission, Your Highness. I cannot just stand idly by."

He pointed at her. "You must never hit her again." To Xuan he said, "Take her to the next room and get a midwife. If there is no one, then get a servant to help you. Let me know the sex of the child when it comes."

He sank back into an armchair, exhausted. Pierre pressed down on his shoulder.

"Pray to God, my child," he whispered. "Surrender yourself to His glory. It is His hallowed sign: in the darkest hours of death and destruction, there is new life."

He moved toward the door.

Ánh tossed his head back and cried out, "Cha Cả, where are you going?"

"To say a prayer for the health of your wife and child."

Without leaving his chair, Ánh reached for Pierre's elbow. "Do not leave me, please," he begged. "I must not be alone."

Pierre smiled.

Pierre could hear running in the hallway, the whispers of servants, and an occasional scream from Lady Jade Bình. The sounds blended into a hum as the day aged into late afternoon. Ánh drew his armchair to a corner of the room, away from the view of the open plain.

Looking out the window, Pierre said to him, "Your Highness, you must see this."

The prince moved slowly. What Pierre wanted him to see required no spyglass.

The peasants' female general had reappeared, her armor-clad body swaying atop her elephant. Behind her, a wall three times the size of the citadel's entrance was rolling on logs. On it was a series of proclamations. DEATH TO THE ROYAL FAMILY AND THEIR SINFUL PAST! ERADICATE THE RULING MONARCH! FREEDOM AND HAPPINESS FOR THE PEASANTS!

As the sun reached the land behind the moving wall, the bishop saw a multitude of marching rebels: men and boys running forward with pitchforks, clubs, buckets, ropes, and torches; old farmers carrying rocks; howling girls and women with babies packed on their backs. Angrily, they charged toward the citadel. Their shouting voices created a blast that pushed the prince back several steps.

An infant's cry rang out.

The prince whispered in disbelief, "No! It can't be."

Xuan entered the room. "A thousand good fortunes, Your Highness," she said. "You have a son, a prince —"

She stopped, her mouth open as she looked past him. The peasants' voices were drawing nearer. Pierre whirled to see what she had seen.

On the open field, the bamboo wall squeaked as it was turned around on a central pivot, revealing its opposite side to the spectators in the citadel. From the top hung the head of His Imperial Majesty King Due Tong, placed on a bamboo tray. His eyes were still half-open, blood seeped from his nostrils, and his long hair spiked through the wicker. Below it, in a row, were the heads of the seven princes, followed in two more rows by those of the high-ranking mandarins. Pierre imagined his ward's head mounted on the wall of shame, completing the final portrait of the Nguyen bloodline.

He said to Ánh in a low-pitched voice, "If I rescue you and make you king, do I have your word you will open your country to Christianity?"

"What?" the prince whispered, unable to comprehend.

"You don't have much time — answer me. Do you swear to have your country baptized into Christianity and guarantee safety for all missionaries during your reign and thereafter?"

"If you could save me," cried Ánh, "my kingdom would be at your disposal."

"Then I have your word?"

"Yes, yes! I promise."

"Very well," replied Pierre. "Go to the throne room now. Brother João is waiting. He knows what to do."

"What will happen to me?"

"You and your son are the last hope of the Nguyen family. More than ever, your survival is crucial. You must go into exile and remain invisible until I am able to bring help. As soon as possible, I will take your son to Europe and plead with the king of France for military and financial support. We each face a long and difficult journey ahead. You must learn patience and wait for me." He held the prince's hand. "From this moment on, I will no longer be at your side to protect you. So, Your Highness, you cannot act on impulse anymore. Use your wisdom."

He reached into an inner pocket and withdrew a velvet pouch.

Ánh took it. The shape and heaviness of the pouch told him of its content. He released the drawstring. In his hand was the royal seal of the Nguyen dynasty.

Pierre bowed and said, "Your Majesty, you chose me to safeguard this seal all these years for today. You are now king of Cochin China. The seal is yours. It is your duty to keep it. God be with you." He made the sign of the cross over his stunned ward.

Reaching into his robe, Ánh pulled out a gold bar and a dagger. With one quick thrust, he cut the bar into two pieces and handed one to the bishop.

"Give this to my Lady Bình as a symbol of my esteem for her. Someday I will return, and these two pieces will help unite us again."

He bolted out the door.

As he passed Xuan, he grabbed her hand and said, "You are coming with me."

She stiffened; he put his arms around her.

"You are my concubine," he said, touching the red mark on her cheek with tenderness.

She pushed against him.

"Please, come with me," he pleaded. "I need you to take care of me."

She stopped resisting.

The new king turned to Pierre. "Look after my son. Keep him from any harm. I fear if I see him now, I would not leave."

"I will protect him just as I protected you," replied Pierre. "I will baptize him in the name of our Father in heaven. Then he will always be watched over by his Christian God."

CHAPTER TWENTY-NINE

Ánh ran down the spiral staircase and through the forbidden garden. Three hundred horsemen still guarded the collapsed throne room. He saw the glow of torches beyond the main gates, heard the voices of the Mountaineers calling out his name. Trembling, he searched the soldiers for Brother João. The monk was nowhere in sight.

He wove through the horses, determination forcing him forward.

There wasn't a face he could identify, except for that of the kitchen girl beside him. Her calm expression revealed nothing of her thoughts. Close to the other side of the crowd, a figure rushed toward him. Ánh let out a soft cry as he recognized the Dominican monk.

Brother João was dressed in the imperial robe and protective metal breastplate, adorned with the dragon symbol of the Nguyen family. It was Ánh's ceremonial costume. He realized that Brother João was in disguise. Behind the monk stood an elephant, equipped with a two-seated throne. On one side sat the hunched form of Prince Hoàng. The other side was empty. Suddenly the prince understood the bishop's plan.

"You must give me your helmet," said João.

Ánh complied. His hair dropped to his shoulders.

"Why are you giving your life to save mine?" he asked.

The monk replied, almost without emotion, "I am doing penance for my grave sin and for the redemption of my soul. What is one life compared to the success of God's mission? I will die a martyr."

His head disappeared beneath the helmet, until only his eyes could be seen. The monk turned and mounted the great beast with the assistance of a hanging rope.

The citadel's gate burst open with a tremendous crash. The barbarians had broken into the sacred city.

Across the back drawbridge, which led to the jungle behind the citadel, Ánh's horse galloped at full speed. Pressed against Ánh with her arms around his waist, Xuan breathed against his nape. Brother Tiago and a dozen soldiers escorted them. Soon a flood of refugees, heading in the same direction, slowed them down.

Ánh and his convoy rode up a hill. Beyond the thick bed of grass was the Rainbow Bridge, made up of concentric bands of painted bamboo. It arched over a ravine, where a swift-moving river flowed toward the sea. The bridge was the only route from the citadel to the forest. He could hear the falling water and smell the cool mist.

If he could get across the bridge, he would be safe. Ánh thrust his heels against the horse's belly, forcing the animal through the crowd of dazed escapees.

An arrow whistled alongside his ear and thumped into Brother Tiago ahead of him. He heard the monk's muted cough and the thud of his body hitting the ground. Another arrow struck a guard on his right. And then the one on his left toppled. Ánh did not dare to look back. His companions were being eliminated in a calculated order, leaving him the last target. Whoever the bowmen were, they were exceptionally skilled. Not an arrow was wasted. He spurred his horse to its fastest gallop.

Ahead of him were two flights of steps: one leading down to the river and the other up to the bridge. He chose the second, guiding his horse to ascend the bamboo stairs. The three surviving men trailed close behind him.

The last rays of the sun reached over the crest of the trees, blinding him. When Ánh was able to adjust his vision, he saw he was at the center of the bridge, and the trees and shrubs at the edge of the forest had altered their shapes. It came to him that he was looking at a wall of peasants. Ánh halted, using both hands to steady the horse. He made a headlong turn around.

He was trapped between both ends of the bridge. Looking at him was a tall bowman, likely the one who had killed most of his men. The hunter was a muscular, dark-skinned man, with full, black, wavy hair. Ánh realized, from the legends he had heard and the skill that he had witnessed, that he was facing the notorious archenemy of the Nguyen family: the self-proclaimed Prince Thom of the rebels.

In a daze he watched them advance. No longer afraid, he felt a white-hot rage seize him.

"Get down from the horse, Xuan," he said. "Save yourself!"

Her arms did not loosen from his waist.

"Did you hear me?" he said. "Dismount! And save yourself."

"It's too late. That won't save me," she replied.

Ánh clung to the mane of his prancing horse as he waited for the enemies to pour over him.

From the depth of the ravine, a voice shouted, "Xuan! Xuan!"

The prince was too bewildered to recognize it. But Xuan did.

She screamed, leaning over his shoulder. "Ông Tây!" she shouted back.

Ánh looked down. The water below them churned with foam. Its silver waves curled and splashed against the rocky riverbank. He saw a boat, tossing in the rushing current. A rope tied the vessel's prow to a tree to keep it from being swept away. His stomach gave a painful squeeze, rejecting the vertical distance between him and the boat.

"Yes, it's me, Henri," the boatman called. "Jump! It's your only chance."

Ánh jerked the reins, and his horse reared upward, thrashing its two front legs and neighing. The prince sat erect.

"Hold on," he cried to Xuan.

He felt her arms and legs clutch him. When the horse dropped back to all four hooves, Ánh gave a mighty kick into its sides to make it jump.

Together he and Xuan bounded over the bridge's railing. It broke, and they plunged into the chasm below.

CHAPTER THIRTY

The Mountaineers poured into the citadel. At the entrance, the gates had been shattered. The peasants swarmed down the main road that led to the king's palace, turning south and sloping down to a wide moat. At the water's edge, they were forced to stop. The curving bridge of stone that should have reached to the other side was nothing but a pile of rubble. In its place was a slender wooden plank without a rail.

Destroying the centuries-old bridge was the royal army's final defense against the rebels. The only way for the invaders to enter the Forbidden City was to walk across this narrow board in single file. Beyond it lay the heart of the citadel, the throne room, in ruins. The fire was still smoldering. Billows of black and orange smoke tainted the hot sky.

The Mountaineers spread out along the side of the moat. None of them crossed the bridge. They waited for orders from their leaders.

From behind the throne room, an elephant lumbered forward. On its back were the two remaining members of the Nguyen family, wearing their royal armor. Flanking the animal were a few hundred imperial soldiers who had no choice but to fight their last battle. The beast bellowed its war cry.

An invisible hand parted the peasant troops, creating an open road at the center. Nhạc, the peasant king, mounted high on his elephant and clad in shining iron armor, rode at the head of a caravan of warriors. Their weapons shone like a thousand bursts of the sun.

Among the vanguard, Sister Lucía straddled a gray mare alongside Father François, who rode a spirited bay. For hours she had ridden in a trance, unable to believe the devastation she was seeing, even though she had lived through the war since the raid on Kim Lai. Lady Bui, triumphant atop her beloved Mia, came abreast of the nun and smiled down at her.

"Many of our enemies are dead, Sister," the female warrior said. "I unleashed my wrath on them. Be joyful, because your shame has been avenged."

Lucía looked around and saw a city drenched in blood. Her heart ached for the dead and the dying. She missed the tranquillity of Lepers' Cavern. Revenge was not her motive for traveling here. She came to see Brother João.

King Nhạc turned to face his warriors.

"Welcome to Saygun," he said. "Here lies the city of corruption and sin, where the rats of the Nguyen dynasty sat on the throne. We have killed all but the final two vermin. They will be extinguished —"

A rain of arrows poured on him, whizzing as they flew past. Some struck his armor and bounced off. The royalists had recovered the offensive.

Nhạc ignored them. "I know you are tired from the long battles," he continued. "Many of you have lost either a father, a son, or a brother. I assure you their lives were not wasted. Soon we can all plow the fields, raise the cattle, and live in peace, just as the gods in heaven have proclaimed."

His powerful voice and the bravado of his stance amid the piercing arrows astonished the peasants. They raised their weapons in response to his speech. He barked a command. It echoed through the crowd as his words were passed from one rebel to another.

Lucía watched the men scurry into action. It took her awhile to realize what they were doing. From the rear, mangled cadavers, some missing their heads or limbs, were being passed over the army toward the moat. At the end of the line, the soldiers hurled the corpses into the water. The deep trench became a communal grave filled with arms, legs, and torsos; babies, women, and soldiers. When the mass was level with the earth, the rebels stormed across the bridge of human remains.

Like a flood they spilled through the Forbidden City, mowing down every royal soldier standing in their path. The imperial guards could neither run nor retaliate. Lucía and her warrior companions viewed the macabre performance with divergent emotions — anguish on her part, pride on theirs. She could no longer see the guards protecting the royal elephant. On its back, the two princes were swaying, stranded by the rising tide of men. They did not offer any resistance when the hands reached for them and pulled them from their throne. She watched their bodies disappear into the multitude. Twin jets of blood spurted toward the setting sun.

Two heads, one still contained in a metal helmet, were placed on bamboo trays and brought to King Nhạc. General Zicheng held up the head of Prince Hoàng by his long hair and received shouts of encouragement from his fellow soldiers. The king leaned forward from his seat. He waved a finger to the severed head.

"No more opium for you," he said.

The soldiers burst into laughter.

He turned to the general. "Show me the other."

The warrior fumbled to remove the head from its helmet. The sun was fading fast. The earth was filled with a soft light. After a few unsuccessful tugs, he gave up and lifted the metal flap to reveal the face within. The bloody head inside the helmet stared through the opening with wide blue eyes. In the suffocating hush, Zicheng seemed confused. He looked at the king, muttered something, and shrugged.

With one look at the decapitated head, Sister Lucía fainted.

To François, the death of Brother João was a shock, but not a surprise. It could only have been a plot by Bishop de Béhaine to save the life of his protégé, Prince Ánh. It was a ruthless stratagem, to sacrifice one of his own priests for the sake of his mission. What happened to poor Henri? Did his novice suffer the same fate as Brother João?

The bishop's blind devotion angered François, but it also made him wonder about his own. Would he ever give up his own life or the lives of his followers to ensure Prince Thom's survival? The answer made him realize he did not fully belong in the world of the Mountaineers, nor anywhere else for that matter. He was a twenty-seven-year-old priest, exiled from his homeland, cast adrift in a heathen culture. Fate had made him a perpetual misfit.

Where were the fugitive prince and the bishop? Surely this time they would not be able to escape together. The bishop, a legendary foreigner, would draw attention to the prince. To stay inconspicuous, Ánh would have to travel alone or with a few loyal guards. With the Tonquinese holding the North, and the West Mountaineers holding the land between Hue and Saygun City, Ánh would have no choice but to retreat farther south.

As for the bishop, without the prince, he would never be in any real danger. The rebels would not consider him or any foreigners a threat as long as they didn't take up arms. François expected the bishop had already vacated the citadel. Unless there was a reason for him to linger behind!

Outside the throne room, the peasant soldiers were gathering the imperial concubines, wives, and children, and dividing them into groups according to their family status. Among the court women, he saw the queen of Cochin China, disheveled but full of pride. She moved calmly in spite of the rebels' aggression. Out of each group, the male offspring were taken from their mothers. François heard the children cry and the women scream. Beside a mountain of dead bodies, the children huddled in one another's arms. At their captain's order, the bowmen released their arrows. The crying stopped. Soldiers slashed their sabers into the lifeless bodies.

General Zicheng returned to bow before King Nhạc. With a weary voice, he reported, "Your Majesty, all the blood relatives, wives, and concubines of the Nguyen family have been executed, except for Ánh, his wives, and one concubine. They are nowhere to be found. I was told that one of the women is pregnant. Surely they could not have traveled very far."

"Is there anyone left in the royal quarters or the Forbidden City?" asked the king.

"We searched everywhere, Your Majesty, and found it is all empty."

"Look again, house by house, until you find them."

Zicheng hesitated. "It is getting dark, and our men are exhausted. We cannot keep searching every house in the citadel. What do we do with its citizens, the Buddhist monks, and the foreigners, sire?"

"For now, keep guard over the citadel and spread the message to every door that we mean them no harm. Allow no one to leave. I will establish new order tomorrow."

François listened with relief. He wondered if the bishop and his novice were still somewhere in the fortress. No one noticed him when he dismounted from his horse. Although he had never been to Saygun before, he had an idea where he was going. There had to be a pavilion reserved for the foreign Christians in this complex city. With a bit of luck, he knew he'd be able to find out where it was.

Along a stone-paved road that led him through an orchid garden, François came upon a succession of palace apartments. The sun was sinking fast behind the mountains. Night had already gathered under the tall trees. All the doors and windows were open, their shutters swaying with the breeze.

He could see into the rooms. There was no light in any of the dwellings, no signs of life. The strewn personal belongings, a book left open, and food arranged on a table gave the impression that the occupants had vacated in a hurry. At the end of a street, he came to a communal well. A few feet away, a eunuch huddled behind a wooden vat of fish sauce. François grabbed his collar and pulled him from his hiding place.

"Please spare my life," the eunuch hissed, covering his eyes.

"Cha Cà," François shouted in the frightened man's face. When he saw a hint of acknowledgment, he continued, "Do you know Cha Cà?"

The eunuch nodded, pointing toward a series of pagodas and towers. The tiers of red roofs and gold trim blossomed like lotus petals, adrift on a hilltop.

"Yes, yes, the Christian priest! I know where he lives. Over there! I'll take you."

The compound looked like a Buddhist temple from the outside. The eunuch led him through the galleries that connected the apartments, crossing an open field toward a sandstone tower. It was built in the shape of a Buddha's head, surrounded by smaller buildings to form a mandala, the Buddhist symbol of the universe. He paused in awe. The artist in him was captivated by the splendor of this ancient holy structure.

Then he saw the Buddhist monks — hundreds of them sitting in meditation, so still and silent that at first he mistook them for statues. But their orange robes and brown skin showed they were alive. Each wore the same vague smile, row upon row. He would not dare to disturb even one of them.

The eunuch pulled at his arm and whispered, "This is where he lives." He pointed to an ornate pagoda.

Ignoring him, François climbed the steps to its entrance. The heavy wooden doors were locked. He pulled at the round handle, banging it against the metal frame, then listened to the knocking that reverberated inside.

"Bishop Pierre Pigneau de Béhaine, Novice Henri Monange," he shouted. "Are you in there?"

There was no reply.

He tried again. "It is I, François Gervaise. I've come looking for you. Alone! Open the door."

He placed his ear against the door and could hear movements from the other side. At the squeaking of old hinges, he stiffened. The door slowly opened, and he saw the high forehead of the bishop, furrowed with more creases than he remembered. De Béhaine moved aside, leaving room for François to enter. Once he was inside, the bishop secured the bolt.

"Father François, we meet again. I am impressed that you were able to find me. How did you do it?"

François licked his lips. "Your Excellency, I am glad that you are safe. To find you, I had to think like you. I asked myself, what would Bishop de Béhaine do in this situation? And the answer came to me. It was quite simple."

"What do you mean, *think like me?*"

François ignored the question. He looked around the room, studying the colossal Buddha statues at the end of the hall.

The bishop chuckled. "So you joined the Mountaineers. It is wonderful that we have a spy in the enemy's army."

François glared. For the first time, he wasn't affected by the bishop's intimidation. "I am not a spy, Your Excellency. I joined them because I believe in their cause."

"Impossible! You are not a rebel," the bishop exclaimed.

To François's right was a closed door. A ray of light came from the crack under it. A constant flickering indicated moving shadows inside. The bishop stepped into his range of vision, blocking his view. A baby cried. Its soft sound was quickly muffled.

"Listen to me," pressed the bishop. "You can't be a rebel. I need your help."

François asked with a hint of sarcasm, "The same help you've demanded from Brother João? What have you done with my Henri?"

For once de Béhaine looked abashed. "I didn't do anything to Henri. He disappeared in the confusion. I haven't seen him all day."

"I came from the battle where they killed Brother João," said François. "The Mountaineers mistook him for the prince that got away. Don't you expect me or my novice to give up our lives for your cause!"

"Whether or not you are a rebel, you are still a priest," said the bishop. "My cause is the cause of the Jesuit order. We are here to establish a Christian kingdom on this soil, so we must work together. All my disciples must bolster my authority and support my vision. And my vision is to have Prince Ánh as the next king of Annam. This is also the desire of His Majesty Louis XVI, king of France. I am merely fulfilling his wish, as well as my obligation to His Holiness, the pope."

"I do not serve the king of France," François said. "I serve God. In my quest for the truth, it was His will that brought me to the peasants' army. Their leader, Prince Thom, will soon be the rightful ruler of this country. He is strong, wise, courageous, and compassionate. He will win the civil war and make the kingdom whole. All the bloodshed will end, and the people will be at peace. Their spiritual lives, therefore, will be fulfilled."

The bishop laughed. "I see that you are still as naive, stubborn, and idealistic as you were the first time we met in Avignon. Your youth has blinded you for too long. Peace will never inspire faith in religion and in God. Only war can do that! Chaos and destruction will oppress people and make them despair. That is when they'll fall on their knees and pray."

"Pain and suffering? Are those the goals of your career, Bishop? No wonder you are failing."

De Béhaine chewed his knuckles. His catlike eyes stared in re-proach at François. But even in his agitation, he kept his voice steady. "Priest, you are consumed by your own pride. You are not serving God. I know why you are seeking me out. You are trying to show me your victory, to prove that I am a failure. You have wanted to do that for so long. Well, you have succeeded. You are on the winning side, but only for now! Remember, you are not here to make the heathens happy. You are here to make them Christian. You may offer them a better life today, but I promise them a better life after death."

François turned away. In a low voice, he said, "I didn't come to gloat. My aim was to introduce you to the rebel leader so that our mission could be made easier. But I see clearly how different our beliefs are. Farewell, Bishop. The next time we meet, the two of us will be on opposite sides of a battle. My last warning to you is about those women and that infant you are hiding. The Mountaineers are looking for them. Sooner or later they will find and kill them, includ-ing those who harbor them."

He adjusted his armor and reached for the door.

"Wait!" the bishop called after him.

François looked over his shoulder. In the yellow candlelight, a woman emerged, carrying a newborn baby in swaddling clothes close to her bosom. He was unable to see her face in the dim light. The child sucked at her exposed breast, the reason for its silence.

"You must help me hide them," pleaded de Béhaine.

"Give me one reason why I should."

"Y-you m-must," came the shaking voice of the bishop, "because when it is about deceit, you are the master. I need you, François Ger-vaise. Or should I address you as Vicomte Étienne de Charney?"

His malice cut through François, knocking him off balance.

The bishop continued, "Remember at Hue Citadel when I told you that I knew more about you than you realized? Well, I did."

Suddenly, François felt like a criminal. He choked, repressing his tears. "When did you know?"

"From the first time we met, I have had my doubts about your past. But it wasn't until I discovered the stiletto in your possession that I felt the need to investigate its origin. While you were ill with cholera, I went to see Father Dominique in Villaume. The priest recognized the dagger and was deeply affected by its sight. That particular heirloom, with the coat of arms from a noble family, belonged to the twenty-year-old Vicomte Étienne de Charney." He took a breath and continued.

"You see, Father Dominique was not only the family priest for the de Charneys; he also taught Étienne fine art and music. According to the good father, the vicomte was a promising artist, blessed with nobility, wealth, talent, and handsome looks. However, all that came to an abrupt end when he was challenged to a duel by a Freemason over the daughter of an innkeeper.

"The night before the duel, Étienne vanished, too cowardly to fight his opponent and too ashamed to face his father. Imagine my surprise when I heard your confession. You claimed to have murdered the vicomte and kept his dagger. Did I mention that I also met that Freemason, who has since wedded Helene, the innkeeper's daughter, and still resides in the south of France? His name is François Gervaise."

François shuddered. The mention of his past was shocking, even to him.

The bishop continued, "One thing I didn't understand then — why did you confess to me a crime that you didn't commit? And it occurred to me, it is a matter of pride. You would rather have me judge you as a criminal than as a coward. Cast out from Villaume by your self-inflicted disgrace, you abandoned your identity and came to the charterhouse in Villeneuve lès Avignon. There you heard about my mission to Annam. And you thought that in this faraway land you could start your life over and find your courage."

He chuckled bitterly. "It is ironic, isn't it? You were not only a coward, but also a liar. Still, I accepted you. I saved your life, rescued your soul, and gave you a chance to be the man you wanted to be. For what? To watch you condemn my mission, forsake me, and make a fool of me?"

Lost in his rage, the bishop made a fist and struck a stone statue.

The collision made a hollow sound. He bent and clutched his hand in pain. François hurried over.

"Don't touch me!" he yelled. "Vicomte de Charney, did you find what you have come here for? Remember, I am not the only person who can see you as you really are. I am not your enemy. It is the man you look at in the mirror."

The wall echoed his accusing words. François fell to his knees.

"I am not a coward," he cried. "I didn't fight the duel because I knew I couldn't kill anyone."

For the first time since she entered the hall, the young mother spoke. "Peasant priest, if you truly favor peace, you must help Cha Cả save us." She reached for his hand.

He looked up at her through a wall of tears.

"I am Princess Jade Bình, daughter of King Le of the North. I was betrothed to Prince Ánh when I was ten years old as a peace offering. If the Mountaineers put me and my son to death, my father will declare war on them. Our deaths will only escalate the ancient rivalries between the two kingdoms. If you believe in peace and harmony, then I cast the responsibility for our lives into your hands."

François sank back on the floor. Surely, in the eyes of humanity and of God, to save this kingdom from further destruction he must help Ánh's wives and child to survive. But would he help them to save himself?

Holding his head in both hands, he said, "You know the Mountaineers are looking for you. And they won't rest until they find you. Only extreme measures can help you avoid detection. Are you prepared to do whatever it takes to keep yourself and your child alive?"

She traced her finger across the infant's delicate eyebrows. Her voice was steady. "I will do anything you say," she said, "provided that I am not parted from my child."

"Very well," said François. "Come with me."

CHAPTER THIRTY-ONE

*T*he horse, carrying Xuan and the prince, leaped into the river. Henri flung himself to the edge of his boat to catch the animal's reins. He missed. With a terrible splash, the water opened and swallowed them. The current broke them into three pieces. The prince was the first to emerge, gasping and struggling. Henri grabbed him by the collar. Ánh choked. His eyes blinked with terror.

"Hold on to the side of the boat," said Henri.

"There's water in my eyes," Ánh cried. "I can't see and I can't swim. Help me!"

Henri looked ahead. Twenty feet away, Xuan thrashed against the violent flow. On the cliff above them, as the sky was growing dark, burning arrows spat flames in their direction.

Henri placed Ánh's hand on the boat's rim. "Lift yourself in while I release the boat."

Bolted to the wooden gunwale was an iron prong meant to support an oar. Ánh fumbled and found it. He pulled himself out of the water. As he slid headfirst into the boat, an arrow pierced his upper arm, nailing him to the hull. He screamed, but his voice was drowned out by the shouts of the Mountaineers, who were descending the steep shore. Henri slashed the rope that bound the boat. The river swept them away.

They rode the rapids, passing Xuan. Despite his efforts at the oar, he could not get to her. In the warm dusk, he could see she was becoming exhausted, her arms flailing with diminishing vigor.

"Xuan, Xuan," he screamed, turning the boat against the current.

She saw him and stopped struggling. The swift turbulence tossed her toward him with a dangerous momentum. He let go of the oar to catch her and braced his knees against the rough wood as he pulled her in with all his might. The vessel shuddered and leaned, threatening to turn over. The prince wrenched himself from the floorboard and crawled to the opposite side to balance the boat with his weight.

"Let her go," he bellowed to Henri. "You'll kill us all."

Henri ignored him. She was in his arms, and no force of nature or royal command could part them. He pressed his face against hers, inhaling the aroma of soapberry in her hair. As the boat tumbled downstream, the trees seemed to be flipping like pages of a book. The forest murmured and was filled with a soft, blurry light that erased all his fears. How wonderful it was to be in the mouth of Death and no longer afraid!

"I love you," he whispered in her ear and sank back, embracing her.

She nestled against him. The river curled away behind them as the vessel plunged into the darkness.

The current took them deeper into the jungle. Above, thin shafts of moonlight crept upon them through the foliage. Swarms of mosquitoes came out of their nests and feasted on the runaways' exposed skin. Henri swatted his face and neck. The smell of blood from the squashed insects mixed with the odor of rotting leaves.

They huddled together, cold, wet, and hungry. The rushing of water, the creaking of the boat, and the heavy thud of unseen creatures kept them alert. Henri could find no shelter along the steep, rocky shore.

With Henri's knife, Xuan cut away the arrowhead that broke through Ánh's upper arm. Her movement was skillful, despite the darkness. Ánh rested his head on her shoulder and bit down on a piece of wood. Henri could hear his sniffling and occasionally a breathless hiss. The prince was fortunate that the arrow was not dipped in poison.

"Help me pull the stem out of His Highness," Xuan said to Henri.

The novice intoned a prayer. Then, with a quick tug, the arrow came free in his hand. Xuan tore a strip from her tunic and pressed it against the wound.

Ánh raised his head toward the heavens and howled.

At daybreak, they woke to the distant crowing of a rooster. Thatched huts and thin strands of smoke appeared beyond the thick greenery, signs of a village. The boat was moving slowly as the river divided into many smaller branches. A dozen feet away, the bank was a patchwork of stagnant mires and hyacinth grassland that reached to the edge of the forest. Decay was strong in the air.

Henri rose and rubbed his hands together for warmth. His body was soaked in dew. He yawned and scanned the stream, searching for a place to dock. The water undulated, bubbling with an eerie unease. He craned his neck, then stiffened. What he saw sent a shiver through him.

In the black mud, barely visible in the dead grass, were the scaly backs of crocodiles, dozens of them entwined like tree roots. Xuan, following his gaze, withdrew in dread. The prince, haggard and pale, looked on with indifference. The blood had dried on his wound. He clutched his injured arm to his chest.

Six feet above the stream's surface dangled the branches and secondary roots of a banyan tree. Henri grabbed one and guided his boat to land. The movement of the vessel dispersed the reptiles. Some vanished under the torrid water. Others waddled away.

"I don't want them near me," Xuan whispered.

"Listen to me," said Henri. "We have to find shelter in a village. The prince needs to rest so his wound can heal. I'll go first. You both will follow me. Run as fast as you can."

Without giving her a chance to object, he dipped one foot into the mud. It swallowed him up to his ankle. His movement, although slight, ignited a reaction all across the marshland. The crocodiles lifted their heads in anticipation. The four nearest him scuttled through the mud. Their feet made a slurping noise. Xuan tried to hold Henri back, but he had already gone beyond her reach. The crocodiles, familiar with the terrain, were able to move faster than he. Before they could snap their jaws into his flesh, Henri jumped up and clung to a banyan branch. He hoisted his body upward and swung his legs around the limb. The suddenness of the danger made him scream with nervous excitement.

"I can't watch," whimpered Xuan.

The prince could not help but chuckle. "Fool! If he thinks I am going to do that, he is mad."

Henri came to the end of the marsh, a flat expanse of dry, cracked mud strewn with clumps of grass and rocks. He looked back. The crocodiles were crowding around the boat. One of them raised itself off the ground. Its head was an inch above the vessel, its mouth open. Clear eyes, cone-shaped teeth, and powerful jaws were the weapons it brandished with deadly patience. The prince sat in the hull, holding Xuan in his good arm. She buried her face in her hands. The two of them seemed lost among the creatures, many more than four feet in length.

Ánh stared at Henri, his hand clutching a dagger. Behind him, the water was thick with floating reptiles, brown under an intermittent sun. The boat swayed.

"Do not fear, Your Highness," Henri said, breaking off a tree branch.

With a shout, he thrashed his crude weapon and walked toward the boat. The leaves made a rattling noise, and the crocodiles dispersed. He stopped, realizing in amazement that these swamp creatures could be frightened easily by sudden noises. After a few more thrusts, a path was clear. The prince, with the help of Xuan, got off the boat. Together they ran to dry land.

"Twice you have come back to save us," said Ánh, out of breath. "Why?"

"Hush!" whispered Henri. "I think I hear a voice."

The runaways hid behind a clump of bamboo. The voices seemed to be getting nearer. The strangers spoke to one another in a low and cautious tone. Henri strained to listen.

"I swear I heard someone," said a male voice. "The scream came from this direction."

"Are you sure it was human?" asked a second voice. "It could have been an animal."

The first man replied with conviction, "What I heard was no animal. It was a human voice."

"Very well, let's search for it."

They separated. Footsteps shuffled across the ground. Soon, Henri realized, it would be impossible for them to hide. He looked at Xuan and the prince, asking permission with his eyes. Ánh nodded. Together they jumped into the trail. The prince jabbed his knife at the air.

"Stop," he yelled. "One more step and I will use it."

The men stood still. There were four of them, armed with spears and bows. Their peasant clothing suggested that they were hunters, not soldiers. It occurred to Henri that they could be West Mountaineers.

One of the hunters, dressed only in a loincloth and carrying a quiver of arrows on his back, pointed his bow at the prince. Most of his skin was covered in scars and blue tattoos of ancient symbols. "Look at the middle one and his silk robe," he said. "He must be the dragon prince that we are looking for."

"Prince Ánh?" asked another, scratching his high cheekbone with his spear.

"Be careful, he could be one of the decoys," added the third, the oldest of the four. His whiskers were gray and sparse.

"One thing we know for certain," said the last man, laughing grimly. His authoritative nature gave Henri the impression that he was the leader. "If we find the royal seal on him, he must be the true prince. Seize the seal and capture him alive, and we will bring great fortune to our village. The citizens of Ben Song will be exempted from taxes for at least three years."

The hunters spread, blocking the path. There was no escape, except to return to the river.

Henri whispered to the prince, "We still have the boat, Your Highness. We can get away."

They turned and ran toward the shore. But Henri's hope was quickly dashed. The boat was gone. In their hurry, they had not thought to secure it. The current had carried it away. Henri ran alongside his companions, realizing that they, like him, were in deep despair. The captors were behind them, watching and laughing at their consternation.

On the bed of mud, the crocodiles scattered as they sensed the approaching footsteps. A few bold ones snapped at the intruders, but they, too, withdrew after the initial show of aggression. Xuan plunged into the water, followed by Henri.

He shouted, "The water is shallow. We can make it to the other side, Your Highness."

His words proved false as he stepped into a deeper part of the stream. Henri swam. Xuan paddled beside him. He could feel movement in the water. The reptiles' rough hides lurked beneath the leaf-strewn surface, hidden among the reeds. Despite their passive behavior on land, in the water they became bold at the sight of the runaways.

Luckily, they did not have to swim far. Land was just a few feet away. Xuan stopped abruptly and made a headlong turnaround.

"What are you doing?" Henri shouted. He had to protect her at all costs.

She gathered her strength to reply, "His Highness can't swim. I cannot abandon him."

He grabbed her shirt. "It's too late to turn back. You'll never make it."

She struggled against him. "Let me go!" she shouted. "He is my husband."

Henri refused to release her. "They will not kill him," he said. "We can do more alive than dead."

She wept but stopped resisting. With fading strength, they

reached the opposite bank, only to find that it, too, was infested with crocodiles.

"I am sorry, I am sorry," she kept chanting in a breathless voice. "Your Highness, I never should have left you."

Tears mixed with mud rolled down her cheeks. Henri took her by the hand and ran to a clearing, away from danger.

Across the stream, the prince knelt among the reptiles. Behind him stood the hunters. He raised his hands toward the heavens.

His voice was choked with emotion as he spoke. "Dear ancestors, why must you torment me this way? Am I not the true king? Is my blood not noble? Show me your will. If you want the Nguyens' bloodline to become extinct, let the swamp creatures devour my body. I would rather die in the jaws of these beasts than at the filthy hands of the traitors of Ben Song Village."

The laughter drained from the hunters' faces.

Ánh pressed his hands on the mud and bowed his head three times, giving reverence to his ancestors. Then he rose to his feet. Grabbing the branch that Henri had dropped, he swept a path in front of him. As he reached the water's edge, he stepped on what appeared to be the back of a large crocodile. Xuan screamed. Henri watched in horror. He could not fathom that the prince was about to come to such a bitter end, nor could he bear to witness it. Yet he was unable to look away. The animals made no attempt to snap at Ánh.

The tattooed hunter pulled back his bowstring, aiming. But the chieftain placed his hand on the man's arm. "Stop! We have seen a miracle. Be careful. You must not offend the gods," he said, and fell to his knees.

As the prince walked across the stream, Henri realized that what they all thought to be the crocodile's back underneath Ánh's feet was actually the bottom of the upturned boat. When the vessel floated away, it must have been flipped over by the current or the creatures of the swamp. The hem of Ánh's ornate robe glided on the water's surface, giving the illusion that he was riding a dark-skinned reptile. Henri ran to the bank of the stream to help the prince to land.

The boat slipped deeper into the water.

On the other side, the rebels remained kneeling with bowed heads. "Forgive us," they begged. "We were so blind that we could not recognize the true king."

Ánh turned to the hunters and pointed a finger at them.

"Today you have seen proof that heaven is on my side," he said. "No human can ever take my life. Tell the others, who will tell their children, and their children's children, how the gods protect the rightful king."

He staggered and collapsed into Xuan's outstretched arms. Henri looked away.

PART FOUR

Salvation

CHAPTER THIRTY-TWO

Saygun, 1782

For four years, François's refuge was the Kien Tao Temple, a Buddhist monastery opposite the Christian church. The three women of Prince Ánh's household had shaved their heads and joined the Buddhist nunnery in order to evade the rebels' swords. Because of his ties with the royal family, the bishop had been imprisoned in the same pagoda where he had once held the Christian services — a duty now performed by François.

To fulfill his promise to protect the women, François had remained in the monastery with them. As a way to earn his place in the community, he had undertaken the task of renovating the interior of the great worship hall. By enhancing the beauty of the temple while preaching in his church, he hoped to promote harmony between the Buddhists and the Christians.

His plan was to create one large mural that would be the setting of the main altar. The north and south walls would each have three major paintings, accompanied by smaller side panels — altogether fifteen paintings, each twelve feet high. An enormous undertaking! François never dreamed he would be able to complete the work, but he threw himself into it. The project was a good way to forget himself while being exposed to the native religion.

Peace had settled over the citadel, but in the distance, skirmishes still erupted between Prince Ánh's forces and the Mountaineers. Outnumbered and supported by a handful of loyalists, Ánh's army took on the role of bandits. But on everyone's lips was the miracle of the crocodile, being told and retold, gaining embellishment with each version. By the time the story reached François's ears, it was said that wild beasts of all kinds had been following the prince on his travels, ready to sacrifice their lives to fulfill his destiny.

With each battle that he lost, Ánh always managed to escape unscathed. No bounty the rebel government could offer seemed high enough for anyone to claim the prince's life. Even the Mountaineers believed that the divine forces of heaven were protecting their enemy.

For François, the more news he heard about Ánh, the more he was reminded of his own ties to the prince and the royal cause. He had once helped save Ánh's life on a road outside Hue City. Now, he was guarding his three wives and a child. Though he believed in the peasants' government, he had twice betrayed them. Try as he might, he could not reconcile his conflicting loyalties.

In the temple where he lived, the monks were simple and innocent. Never did they attempt to convert him from Christianity. But since the principles and history of Buddhism were the essential themes of his work, he felt obligated to examine the Eastern doctrines. Their teaching created new dilemmas within his mind. Catholicism, as he knew it, was a strictly traditional dogma that would not accept any deviation, while Buddhism was less like the uncivilized culture he once thought it to be. He floundered, seeking some common ground between the two faiths.

With the help of the monks, François constructed scaffolds out of bamboo poles and easels to hold the wooden panels. Every day for two years they had mixed large vats of foundation paint to seal the wood and keep it from cracking. Ánh's wives, now Buddhist nuns, assumed the duties of the kitchen help. Lady Jade Bình was eighteen and looked twice her age. Her only source of happiness was her son.

The little boy's head was now covered in a thick layer of prickly hair. His mother named him Canh — a word that could either mean *landscape* or *vigilance*. She hoped for the latter. While François worked, the child played nearby. His mother hid behind a partition beside the main altar and spied on them. She was unaware that her silhouette was visible on the screen, nodding like a shadow puppet. Assuming the role of his old teacher, Father Dominique, François taught Canh how to hold the paintbrush.

"No," screamed the boy, tossing the tool away.

The mother laughed. She saw the defiance in her son's eyes, and she was pleased.

At night, François dreamed of Villaume and the impending duel. He hated the image of himself waiting. The old fear returned, transparent and gnawing. Annam seemed an elaborate fantasy.

One night, he woke, gasped, and raised himself on one elbow. In the milky darkness, the mosquito net covering his bed shrouded his vision. Lost and frightened, he listened to the night. Out in the great hall, something or someone moved in a quiet rustle.

François wound up a kerosene lamp to create a burst of light and walked through the doorway leading to the altar. The unmistakable shadow of the Buddhist head monk, Master Chi Tam, with his shaved head and thin neck, stretched upon a wall. An orange robe, faded and tattered at the hem, was draped over one of his shoulders. He was moving from one canvas to another, turning his head this way and that to inspect François's paintings. François was surprised. Master Chi Tam was a devoted truth seeker. He rarely ventured outside his room; his days were mostly spent in meditation.

There was nothing the artist was ready to show. The images were still in their early stage of formation. Only here and there would a face shake itself free of the canvas's constraints, coming to life.

"A true artist must practice his art with effortless strength," remarked the monk without looking at François. His voice was soft yet full of criticism. "Your brushstroke is indecisive. How can you express what you feel?"

François dug the ground with the tip of his sandal. He noticed the old man's ears, thin and wrinkled and engorged with veins, like tree fungus.

"I assure you, thầy, that I possess both endurance and strength. For six years, I have been working without interruption. My technique and education will create a beautiful setting for your temple." His eyes surveyed the dark hall. "Look around you. The pagoda is filthy and badly kept. Nothing has been done for at least a century."

He pointed at the altar, where the sandstone Buddha sat. It was damaged by rainwater from a leaky roof. Half of its face had been washed away. A nest of sparrows sat on the right hollow of the Buddha's shoulder. The monks' crude attempts to mend the flaking paint with a patchwork of new pigments had worsened its condition.

"Still," replied Chi Tam, "a concept may take you four years to formulate. But its execution should never take that long."

The headmaster turned toward the entrance. He motioned with his hand, expecting François to follow. The priest was perplexed, but obliged.

He followed Chi Tam through the great hall and into the kitchen. His footsteps cracked the tranquillity of the room. Ahead, the monk glided gracefully in spite of his age. His saffron-colored cassock absorbed the darkness like an artist's sponge.

In the middle of the kitchen sat a hand-operated rotary quern that the monks used to grind cereals. Two lay brothers were working through the night crushing soybeans to make milk. The mill was composed of two heavy circular stones, one placed flat on top of the other, with a small space in between. A pivot was built in the center. As the handle churned, the upper stone slid on the working surface of the bed stone so the beans could be mashed at a steady rate. A stream of white liquid poured through a groove into a container below, amid the loud popping groans of the soy kernels.

Chi Tam tapped on the novices' shoulders, and they stopped.

"It is late," he said. "You must rest. This can wait 'til tomorrow morning."

The lay brothers bowed their heads and departed the kitchen, leaving the two men alone. François touched the soy milk, examining its velvety texture between his thumb and forefinger.

"Why are we here?" François asked.

"This mechanism produces milk to make tofu," replied Chi Tam. "That is our main diet, the food that preserves a sound mind."

Taking the handle, he planted his right foot forward, assuming a sturdy stance. Then he pulled the handle back and forth, working the machine. His movements produced a loud cracking noise as the stones moved. A deeper sound rose from inside the quern. The massive wheel spun, slowly at first. Soon it gained speed to become a blur. François was amazed to watch the old man maneuvering such a heavy machine. He made it look not only graceful, but effortless. François listened to the drone, entranced. Through a window, the moon shone weakly, and the headmaster, bathed in its light, seemed to levitate. He peered at François, his dark eyes alive with energy. The mill came to a slow halt.

"Now, you do the same," he said. "Show me your endurance. But remember, grinding cereals does not require your muscular strength. It takes spiritual force to make the wheel turn."

Following his instructions, François mimicked the master's stance. He realized right away that it took considerable force to rotate the wheel. The handle he held reached his chest level, and he found he could rest his weight on it to push. But as soon as the mill proceeded to make a half turn, he had to pull it toward him to complete the cycle. Ultimately, he had to push and pull with all his might to keep it rolling. The moonlight was in his eyes. The work caused his arms to tremble after about fifteen minutes, and his breathing became labored. At last, he collapsed against the stone's cold surface, sweating.

"There must be a trick," he gasped. "You are withholding some secret from me."

The monk chuckled, adding fuel to François's frustration.

"Thầy Chi Tam, I am not here to grind soybeans for you," he said indignantly. "I am a painter, and I am restoring your temple with my labor and skills. If you are not happy with my work, just tell me so."

The old man wrinkled his forehead. "Forgive me, foreign man," he said, waving his hands. "You have misunderstood my intention. You speak Annamese well. There is no doubt that you have great respect for our religion and culture. But to renovate the worship hall requires a great deal of work, endurance, patience, and, most important, passion. You seem to lack the control of your energy. Without the heart, it would take you many years just to do mediocre work. Your painting would suffocate before it was even born."

"How do I find my passion?" retorted François. "By grinding beans?"

"This machine is a test," replied the monk.

"Then show me again. I simply cannot pull the handle in the manner that you described."

The monk moved closer to François and once again resumed his position in front of the quern. He fixed his eyes upon the monk's movement. The scent of crushed soybeans rose again, accompanied by his gentle voice.

"You cannot do it," said the master, "because you do not control your breathing correctly. Place your palms on the lever. Press your breath downward after you inhale and stretch your abdominal wall to hold it in. Use that energy to push the handle. When you exhale, keep your breath flowing evenly and slowly while you pull at the lever. Concentrate only on breathing in and out. The force will flow through your limbs more abundantly once you find the right path, and it will churn the machine without your labors. Work will become less work."

François touched the monk's arms as the mill again set into motion. In his hands, the muscles felt loose, just as when they were at rest. The room was silent except for the groan of the stones grinding together. It was a sound he would never forget — the sound of intense but effortless concentration. In that moment, he learned his first lesson in Buddhism.

It took him a year to complete the north wall of the temple. Master Chi Tam had asked him to depict the life of Prince Siddhārtha before he ascended into enlightenment as the Buddha. Images of pain, old age, disease, and death had to be included. They were the reasons for Siddhārtha's quest for salvation to end humanity's suffering.

François, too, was familiar with miseries. His interpretation of Siddhārtha's life was influenced by his own experiences — the part of his life that he had tried to escape. It guided his hands. His paintbrush swept across the wood, only to resurrect his past. The paint pigments stained his hands, and the stench of gum turpentine seeped into his clothing, but his memory was alive and ready to talk. For him, the temple became a sacred place. It stood apart in the city like a separate world, and he lived in its inner sanctum, projecting his memories onto its walls. Alone, scowling under the filtered sunlight, he examined every line, every brushstroke.

The first of the three major panels depicted *The Death of a Prince.* The second was *The Portrait of an Impostor,* who hid behind a mask. And the last one he called *The Mirror of Self,* when Siddhārtha saw his reflection in a river. The four minor panels portrayed ill people dying from incurable diseases, emaciated children enduring the pain of famine, old women hiding in darkness, and the condemned kneeling before an executioner.

When it was time to construct the panels for the south wall, François sketched out a series of illustrations of the Buddha's final trial — the attack of the satanic Lord of Passions, Mara, including his three sons, Flurry, Gaiety, and Sullen Pride, and his three daughters, Discontent, Delight, and Thirst. To ward off the temptations, Siddhārtha engaged in purposeful meditation.

François was familiar with the practice of meditation because he had seen the monks engage in it. But he had no desire to sit with them on the cobblestone for hours under the sun. He discovered that when he painted, calm flowed through his veins. His hand, guiding the brush, executed the commands that floated in his mind. And he was unsure of which part of him — his spirit or his body — was responsible for bringing his art to life.

For the south wall, he created a painting of a jungle setting, with a beautiful pagoda under large trees with hanging tentacles. Siddhārtha, not yet a Buddha, meditated by a quiet pond, dotted with pink water lilies. Fear, self-doubt, and lack of belief stirred the water into a gigantic tidal wave.

The main mural behind the altar was his greatest challenge, for it had to represent the cycle of life, birth, death, and rebirth that the Buddhists perceived as a wheel that never stopped turning. François painted as if he were turning the mill, and in the process, it occurred to him that he forgot everything he had learned, everything he had felt, and everything he had known. No longer tormented by his search for the existence of God, he became free of fear. He wondered if the peace he had discovered was similar to what the monks had described finding in their meditation.

Whatever this feeling was, he knew he must examine it further. Could it be that simple: that the way of the Buddha was to let go?

CHAPTER THIRTY-THREE

Saygun, 1784

*L*ittle Canh peeked from behind his mother. The garden was flooded with bright summer light. Birds were singing, but he couldn't locate them. He spotted a few chicks pecking away near an overgrown hibiscus. But they looked too small and slow to have chirped out such a nice, fast tune.

"*Où êtes-vous?*" he shouted, mimicking Father Phan's voice.

This day, according to Father Phan, was Canh's sixth birthday. But his mother insisted that he was turning seven rather than six. All Annamite children are one year old when they come into the world. His mother, who knew and noticed all things but never seemed to be excited about anything, scolded him whenever he made a mistake about his age.

"Listen to Cha Cả and Father Phan and learn their wisdom, but don't forget who you are," she would say, tapping his chest, and then adding in a whisper, "You are the son of a great Annamite. You cannot forget our ways."

At times, when Canh asked her about his father, his mother would furrow her brow and search Canh's face. Her look of longing always made him sad. "Waiting and solitude are the two curses of being a woman who is married to a great man," she would say.

Canh's father's name had never been uttered, not even in the privacy of the Buddhist cell where they resided. From the portraits of his mother he had found in Father Phan's sketchbook among the other drawings of kings, queens, mandarins, concubines, and elders of the court, he knew she had once been majestic and beautiful in her ceremonial gown. After Canh was born, his mother shaved her head and assumed the gray uniform of the Buddhist nuns, the same as Auntie Lan and Auntie Bao. The three women lived together in a small room behind the kitchen area, isolated from everyone, even the monks. Canh was their only link to the outside world, and that, he believed, was the reason they always reprimanded him.

"Speak to us in our own language," said his mother. "Don't use that foreign tongue. And remember, we don't celebrate birthdays. It's the custom of the West. You are a Christian only with your teachers. When you're with us, we pray to our Lord Buddha. Your father would want it that way."

But the Lord Buddhas he knew best were the wall paintings created by Father Phan. They were either mounted between the red-lacquered columns of the temple, or lay scattered around the main worship room, where the Buddhist monks came to pray each day.

The Buddhas' faces resembled no one in the citadel. Their shellacked surfaces had been polished to a high gloss; incense smoke clouded their pale eyes.

For as long as Canh could remember, he had spent his mornings and afternoons helping Father Phan with his work. To the little boy, the priest's workshop, a small room behind the main altar, was a world filled with playthings and wonders. A door led into a wooden compartment shaped like a ship, and in the center stood a sea monster petrified into a pose, biting in its jaws a wood panel. Father Phan called it an easel.

In the workshop, Canh discovered how much fun it was to make paint out of food. Father Phan allowed him to taste certain things. His favorite color was edible yellow, made from cheese, egg yolks, flour, and milk and mixed into a liquid paste. The rancid stench of cheese would remain on his fingers, like the smell of fermented tofu on his mother when she was cooking.

Captain Petijean, whose copper beard and fuzzy hair were the stolen features of an old woolly lion, brought the paint ingredients to Father Phan from a far-off land he called France. The first time Canh saw the captain, he was frightened. But the crusty seaman's stories of pirates, buried treasures, mermaids, giant sea monsters, and damsels in distress quickly won the boy over. He grew attached to the captain and looked forward to his visits.

Sometimes Captain Petijean came only to see Cha Cả, who could never leave his Christian sanctuary. A long chain, attached to an iron collar, tethered him to a pillar. It rattled each time he moved. When Cha Cả met with his guest, Canh wasn't allowed to disturb them. He was told to sit and guard the entrance until the meeting was over, whereupon the captain would rub his coarse beard across his belly and make him laugh.

Every Sunday, Canh helped Father Phan to hold Mass in the Christian temple. It was the only time the church was open to worshippers. After Mass, two or three mandarins would remain for the catechism. Father Phan complained that he could not understand why so many attended church yet so few would stay for his lectures.

Perhaps the citadel's residents came because they were curious to see the imprisoned bishop, who sat in a chair near the altar throughout the service. At his sides stood two imperial sentries at attention. After receiving Holy Communion, Cha Cả crossed himself and retreated to his room. The chain did not allow his door to shut fully. As soon as he left, so did the public.

In the kitchen, the scent of puffed rice and crushed sugarcane made everything smell delicious. His mother sat on a wooden stool next to a stove. Her naked head, a shade darker than her skin, looked as if it was sprinkled with sand. She stacked the streaming rice cakes on a dish. Specks of rice coated the sugarcane syrup, golden like drops of honey. He licked his lips.

"Má, I thought we don't celebrate birthdays," Canh said, reaching for the treats.

His mother narrowed her eyes and wiggled a finger at him. She dressed him in a new white jacket that had little bronze studs for buttons.

Her voice was guarded. "This shirt contains a secret."

To demonstrate, she pulled back the inside of his left sleeve to reveal an embroidered green dragon, and in his right, the image of Saygun Citadel's gateway. As he paid close attention, she took his left hand and slid it into his right sleeve.

"Watch this! Can you see the dragon entering into the citadel?"

"Why?"

"He is coming home. But you mustn't share this story with anyone, because a jacket like this is only made for a prince."

"Am I a prince, Má?" he asked her.

She pulled the sleeves down to hide the embroidered symbols. "Don't ask silly questions. Eat your rice cakes, and I am going to ask a favor of you." She winked.

His nose wrinkled. He knew immediately what she meant. "No, not that favor, please. Don't make me!"

She handed him a pair of tweezers and unbuttoned her blouse. It was her way of asking him to pluck the hair in her underarms. He threw the tool down.

"No, Má."

She laughed. "Very well, go help Father Phan. He has been looking for you. Remember, he is painting all the Buddhas for the monks in exchange for our refuge. You are a little man. Pay your respect to the good father by lending him a hand."

"Can I show him the dragon in my coat?"

"No," she replied curtly. "Show it to no one."

In the hallway, the singing bird returned, as if calling for him. It fluttered from room to room. His mother returned her attention to the stove. Canh ran to the front courtyard and approached the main temple. His bare toes curled from the coolness of the tiled floor. Above an array of brushes, paints, pots, and dirty rags, he saw a painting near completion. The face of Buddha, very round, adorned with an unfinished halo in charcoal outlines, seemed to be drowsing. His eyes were blue and sunken, hair curled in smooth rolls that were raised from the wooden surface. Behind the main altar, the bird's tweeting seemed to be coming from inside Father Phan's workshop.

He entered, leaving the door ajar. From the opposite wall, just beneath the ceiling, light flowed through several round openings and lit the room in an amber hue. The unfamiliar objects scattered about caught his attention. Breathless with the thrill of intruding, he rummaged through books, papers, and wooden models, until he came to a bookcase. On its lowest shelf, hidden under a stack of manuscripts, was a leather carrying case. Sketches protruded from within its covers. Canh wondered if his mother's portraits were inside.

He pressed his face against the scratchy spines of the books, inhaling the damp, moldy leather. The tips of his fingers caressed the sketchbook, and after a few tugs, he pulled loose some sheets of paper. He fumbled through the drawings, unable to comprehend what he was seeing. Images of a foreign woman stared back at him. In almost every pose, she was naked. Her eyes were a watery blue, and her hair, clouds of chestnut. In one picture, she was holding a loaf of bread. In another, she was staring out a window, wrapped in a white sheet. He studied the figures intently, unable to stop his feet from shifting back and forth. The unseen bird chirped above him, making him jump. Father Phan slowly filled his vision.

Without thinking, he dropped the drawings and ran toward the door.

The priest caught him in his arms. "It's all right," he said. "Don't be scared. You've done nothing wrong." His hand held Canh's jaw, tilting his head. "Look!"

On the easel, something was hidden under a white cloth. Father Phan lifted him up and brought him closer to the covering.

"Go ahead," he said. "Pull it off."

Canh obeyed. As the cotton sheet fell to the floor, he laughed in surprise. Father Phan had painted his face on a tiger's body. He whistled, and Little Canh laughed louder. The child recognized the familiar tune of the mysterious bird. His hand pressed against the priest's lips to touch the music, which blew in between his fingers like the wind.

"Happy birthday, little Canh," said Father Phan, giving him an affectionate squeeze.

CHAPTER THIRTY-FOUR

Pierre unlocked the doors and ventured as far as the chain would allow. Closing his eyes, he greeted the morning sun. His body was bathed in the sparkling warmth that came from above. "Dear God," he whispered, addressing the divine force that governed his life, the reason for all existence.

The doors creaked on their hinges. He heard footsteps and a dog's barking mingled with the incessant, repetitive chant of the Buddhist monks. The usual noise, which hung over Pierre's quarters like a constant droning of rain, was growing louder in recent days. It seemed the Kien Tao monks were preparing their temple for a special occasion.

Annam was still going through its revolution. But his role in the war was now insignificant. His dream of putting Ánh on the throne seemed hopeless. However, he foresaw the future in the prince's son. Little Canh was the last heir — the spark that proved some hope was still burning.

For almost a decade, he had supported the Nguyen family. In doing so, he had severed all ties with other factions. Would the boy provide the fulfillment of his mission? Every day, watching Canh grow, Pierre asked God the same question.

Because of his connections with the Nguyen monarchy, the Mountaineers regarded Pierre as a threat. They would have executed him but were intimidated by his title and influence with the foreign power. Prince Thom of the peasants had issued an edict ordering the bishop to leave Annam and withdraw to India. Fortunately for Pierre, François had persuaded the rebel prince to change his mind. Remaining under house arrest in Saygun was the only way for him to advance his plan without alarming the authorities.

The bishop kicked a dead leaf from the doorstep. Now was the time for action. The little prince was old enough for sea travel. Pierre would take Canh to Versailles, where the boy would help him plead his case to Louis XVI. According to Captain Petijean, Prince Ánh, although weak in forces, seemed to be building support among the Annamites. The fact that the Mountaineers could not kill him had made him a living legend. It was now up to Pierre to bring France into the war against the rebels. Would he be able to persuade the French king to invest in this little kingdom? His biggest obstacle was America, which had been draining France's resources to fight the British. All he had was the innocence of little Canh and his justifiable cause. The rest was in God's hands.

He touched his iron collar, overcome with fatigue. His next step was to escape this prison. But how? Many a time he had asked François to get a pardon from the rebels, but his appeal always met with refusal. He felt that the priest did not try hard enough. He also noticed that after each time he requested help, François's visits became less frequent.

Through the thick foliage, the golden sun glared. A gong resounded from Kien Tao Temple. In the clearing outside the pagoda, where the monks met in meditation, Pierre saw François, sitting in repose. His dark peasant clothing stood out among the sea of orange robes.

Instead of anger, a smile came to his face. The silly priest had just given him an idea about how to get out of his predicament.

François mounted the steps of the church. As usual, Little Canh was by his side. Through the open doors, he saw the bishop reclining in his chair. De Béhaine lifted his head, which had become so bald that it gleamed like shellac on a wooden floor. A red cross was embroidered on the left side of his black robe, and curled in his arms was a calico kitten, white with yellow and black patches. He squinted and watched François.

"You look well rested," de Béhaine commented, stroking his pet.

François beamed. "I just completed all the artwork for the Kien Tao Temple."

"Indeed? I thought you had found a new way to sleep while sitting among those heathen fools."

François ignored the barb. "I finished my last painting just in time for Prince Thom's wedding," he went on.

The bishop's eyebrows arched. "Interesting! What number wife is this? I thought the prince of the poor didn't believe in personal festivities." He turned to Canh, studying him through his half-shut eyes.

"It is His Highness's first marriage," said François. "The bride is Princess Jade Han, youngest daughter of the north king."

De Béhaine reacted to the gossip with a grin of cynicism. "Little Canh's auntie is marrying the rebel leader. The boy's enemy is now his in-law. What irony!"

Canh inched away from François, curiously inspecting the hall. He ran from one Buddha statue to another, looking at them, then at the bishop. "What happened to the Buddhas' faces?" he asked, pointing at the disfigured heads.

"I smashed them, using a mallet," replied the bishop.

Noticing the damage, François sprang to the front doors and slammed them shut. "Why?" he cried out in dismay.

"I was driven mad."

"Your Excellency, when the Annamites see what you did to their statues, they will stone you. Bishop or no bishop."

"Precisely. That is why you must help me get away before they all come to Mass this Sunday."

A fury came over François. He understood that the bishop's act was deliberate and calculated; he had done it to manipulate him. His rage was also the exact reaction the bishop had expected, because in a fit of anger, François would be likely to rid himself of the bishop's bothersome presence.

He shook his head sadly. "If you wanted my help, couldn't you just ask?"

"Father François, I'm aware that I've lost you to the heathens. Many times I've asked you, but you either refused or did nothing."

"But to destroy such beauty. Your Excellency, some of these statues are over a thousand years old."

The bishop roared, "All the more reason to see them gone."

Canh returned to the two men. His eyes rested on the pet in de Béhaine's lap. The kitten and the boy were drawn to each other with obvious mutual fascination.

"Today is your birthday, no?" the bishop asked.

The boy nodded.

"I remember the day you were born. You were as frail and helpless as this little cat. Now look how you have grown. Soon you will be ready to go into the world. Do you want to travel the world on a big ship?"

Again the boy nodded.

He lifted the kitten. "Do you want to hold her?"

The boy approached the animal cautiously with his arms open.

"This cat is my present to you," said the bishop, patting Canh's head.

He turned to François, and his voice shed its enthusiasm. "Will you help me? This will be the last time I'll ask you. It's not my will. It's God's will."

François reached for little Canh's hand. "Let's go," he said to the boy. "Your mother is waiting."

"Please," implored the bishop. "Don't forget you're a priest. And I am still your superior."

François drew a deep breath. "Your Excellency, I have learned to forgo all my burdens. So should you. There is nothing more I can do for you. You'll have to face the consequences of your actions."

As he was leaving, de Béhaine called out, "Vicomte, remember your shame."

His words made François halt.

"Come with me to Villaume," said the bishop. His voice was silken. "All these years in Annam, you have proven yourself with strength, good deeds, and valor. No one can condemn you for your past errors and lack of courage. It is time to confront your foes and reclaim what is rightfully yours — your title, your name, your fortune. With God on your side, and with my efforts as Bishop of Madras on your behalf, Vicomte de Charney, I assure you, your honor will be restored."

François took a step.

The bishop continued, "You are just thirty-three years old. Don't walk in the shadow of shame for the rest of your life."

François turned and stared into the cold amber of the bishop's eyes. "Your Excellency, I thank you for your generosity. The vicomte you've talked about is dead. Any shame he might have had, he took to his grave."

"Liar!" shouted the bishop with full venom. "How can you be so blind? You are the same as the day I met you, a weak-minded coward."

François walked down the steps without looking back. The label "coward" had lost its sting.

The bishop's voice followed him. "With or without your help, I will get myself out of this place."

Two days later, François saw the bright sun outside and decided to make Canh wear a straw hat. Such a funny sight, the boy's body — too small for the wide-rimmed domed cap — scurried about like a mushroom with feet. An elfin pouch, strapped across his chest, held his kitten.

Canh had not let the cat out of his sight since the bishop had given her to him. His mother and Ánh's other two wives were nowhere to be seen. Lady Jade Bình had left Canh in François's care before, but never for more than a day. No one, not even the Buddhist monks, seemed to know their whereabouts. The priest found Lady Bình's behavior unusual and oddly disturbing. He wondered if it had something to do with her sister's celebration with Prince Thom, since today was their big event. To distract Canh from missing his mother, he decided to take the boy along for the experience of a royal wedding.

They walked together. François rolled up his trousers past his knees, a pair of leather sandals protecting his feet from the hot sand. At times, he would carry Canh. But the boy, full of energy and curiosity, wanted to wander off by himself.

Across from the temple and separated by an open field was the West Wing Palace, which once had belonged to Prince Ánh. The new owner and occupant was Prince Thom. Behind the palace lay the orchid garden. To get to the wedding site, they had to cross through this landscaped park, home of many exotic flowers and rare species of birds and insects.

François kept Canh near him for fear the boy might run off into the woods. But Canh was determined to walk. His will was strong, but not his feet, partly because of the rising heat, and partly because of the road, uneven and bursting with roots. Leafless branches reached out and scratched the boy. On either side of the path, orchids of many varieties, thriving on the decaying bark, nestled in the hollows of trees. Billows of yellow pollen swam in shafts of sunlight. The air was heavy with perfume and the buzzing of bees.

They were not alone. The deeper they went in the forest, the more clearly they could hear murmurs of young girls singing. Beyond the orchid garden, past the stands of trees, were green fields laden with peonies, hyacinths, lilies, sunflowers, and deep-colored dahlias. Beyond them were beds of roses, bordering the outer walls of the stables, home of Lady Bui and her mammoth elephants.

The maidens moved from flower to flower, fluttering their rainbow dresses above the greenery as they sang a love song.

I do all the housework;
I weave a bale of silk;
I prepare the inkstand and the writing brushes, leave my heart open
*   to entice the right man.*
A studious husband he has to be;
Pray the gods my hard labors will be repaid.
He shall pass the examination given by the king,
And a mandarin's wife someday I will be.

They paused from their work to wave at Canh and François. Their fingers were dusted with gold specks. François waved back.

He picked a white lily and showed it to Canh. Deep in the funnel of the flower, its pistils were coated with golden powder like the maidens' hands. Dusting gold into the flowers was an ancient method of making candles for the royal household, which he had had an opportunity to see once before.

"Look how the pollen mixes with the gold dust," he explained to the boy. "It is ready for the bees to collect. The wax will then be made into candles to serve the king. When the candles burn, the flames will make the gold sparkle."

Somewhere in the field, a voice sang out:

Heave ho, little brother, where are you going without a mother?
Come here and introduce your handsome father to this nice lady.

The maidens giggled. François blushed. He took Canh's hand and made a dash toward Lake Thien Thu, northeast of the king's palace. The laughter followed them to the end of the road.

Little Canh sniffed the white lily he was holding. The gold dust coated his nose. He hugged his cat, looked up at François, and giggled.

The priest laughed. His worries for the bishop were, for the moment, forgotten.

CHAPTER THIRTY-FIVE

*P*rincess Jade Han's caravan, two and a half months into its journey, approached Saygun City, not by road, but through a network of rivers and streams. When François and little Canh arrived at Lake Thien Thu, a crowd had gathered along the shore, anticipating the bride's entrance. Thick forest covered the opposite shore. They could see trees half submerged in water, their trunks gripping the earth with powerful roots. The sun reflected off the foliage, making it a piercing green.

Far in the distance, a labyrinth of canals emptied into the lake. Murky waves rolled over large blocks and boulders. Horses and water buffalos dotted the landscape. The silhouettes of peasants, small and black, tended their herds, oblivious to the ceremony that was about to take place.

The bridal procession, a flotilla of thirty bright-colored boats, appeared through the haze. Each sported a dozen pairs of bamboo oars, stroking in unison like the long legs of a centipede. The spectators cheered at the sight.

François had not been standing in the crowd long before he noticed Lady Bui. She waved to him. Beneath her straw hat, beads of sweat dappled her tanned skin. A row of freckles was scattered across her cheeks like roasted sesame seeds. Her lips were outlined with the ruby stain of betel sap. She was thin, but her aura of power made her noticeable among those who stood near her. François bowed and withdrew into the multitude. It was his duty to keep Prince Ánh's son out of harm's way.

The woman warrior inched her way through the wall of bodies, her eyes darting as she searched for him. She spotted François, pushed past a group of mandarins, and grasped his shirt, pulling him toward her. François mumbled an embarrassed apology to those nearby.

"Father Phan, it's been a long time since we last met," she said. "How are you? I've heard that you restored Kien Tao Temple, and I wanted to come by and see it. But the elephants keep me busy." Noticing Canh, she added, "Who is this boy? Is he your son?"

The child hid behind his legs.

Ignoring her questions, François said, "How are you, madame? You seem full of vigor, as always."

The woman sighed and stretched until her backbones cracked in a loud sequence. She shrugged. "I trained a group of elephants to per-form for today's event. The beasts were just captured, wild, last year. To break them in took a lot of hard work. Just two weeks ago, one of my men was stomped to death." She tugged at his sleeve. "Come with me. We can see everything from the higher ground."

She pointed to a ledge at the first drop of a waterfall. It was already teeming with guests. Above them were King Nhạc and his family. The stream descended from crag to crag to glide through the dense jungle, screening the rebel leaders from the prying eyes of the spectators.

François shook his head, looking for an excuse to decline her offer. But in her insistence she did not notice. He lifted Canh with one arm. The boy curled up and rested on his shoulder. He climbed an uneven path, keeping a few paces behind the female warrior.

They passed through a cave until they came to an opening where a thin sheet of falling water created a cool, crisp environment. No one paid any heed to François, Canh, or Lady Bui. All attention was riveted on the action on the lake twenty feet below. The lady pushed her way through the guests. François looked for Prince Thom. He could see dark shadows mounted on horseback, waiting for the procession of boats.

On the shore stood a small docking area. A dozen thick bamboo poles were planted into the water and supported a canopy, created to look like a pagoda. Under its roof, large metal rings were lashed to the poles. Thick, linked chains threaded through them, connected by a series of pulleys. The design marked the entrance where the bridal convoy would disembark.

Lady Bui whispered in his ear, "This marriage is a union between the two great kingdoms. Many who have met the bride tell me that she is very beautiful and intelligent, unlike her disgraced sister, the wife of that dog Nguyen Ánh."

"So I hear," replied François.

"Do you want some refreshment?" asked the lady. "I'll tell my son-in-law to bring a coconut for you." She looked down and yelled toward a thatched hut near the water. "Lộc, come here."

Her exuberance wore on François's nerves. He struggled for calm. Lady Bui turned her attention to Canh, studying him through her wary eyes.

Touching the boy's clothes, she wrinkled her nose and asked him, "Who the devil are you to have such nice silk for a jacket?"

The boy pressed closer to François. His hands, wrapped around the priest's neck, slid together inside his sleeves.

"He is my apprentice," said François. "I am teaching him how to paint."

Lady Bui did not seem to listen to him. She peered down at the lake with visible impatience and shouted, "Lộc, where are you?"

A young man, about twenty, emerged, out of breath. In his hand he held a tray of ripe coconuts, open at the top. He broke into a smile when he recognized the priest.

"Father Phan," he cried happily. "Is that really you?"

François nodded.

Lộc's smile widened. The tip of his forefinger tapped his front teeth. "Look, still a perfect fit. I've been so happy ever since you carved these ivory teeth for me."

"You don't come to Mass anymore," said François.

Lộc ran a hand through his short, black hair. "I am married, Father. I have two children to look after. No time."

"Bring your family with you. It only takes an hour on Sunday."

"I'll see to it that he will come to Mass," interrupted the female warrior. She grabbed the drinks and said to Lộc, "Go back to your post. See if Prince Thom needs your help."

The young man disappeared through the cave. Lady Bui handed François and the little boy two coconuts.

"Drink this," she said. "This variety of coconut originated in Thailand. It's smaller but sweeter."

On the shore, a clamor exploded. The boats were entering the lake. The first vessel, also the largest, long and flat like a barge, led the fleet. At its bow glared the carved head of a phoenix. From the bird's crown soared colorful streamers. Twelve oarsmen in red uniforms held their stations on each side of the boat. At the center stood an elaborate cabin, the princess's sanctuary to conceal her from public view. On the deck sat an orchestra of musicians, all dressed in gold and silver. Their instruments ranged from reeds to percussion.

The large eyes on the carved bird batted their lashes. A horn split the air, signaling to the other vessels. The musicians began to play. Their melody leaped across the lake, and the onlookers hushed. As fast as it came, the music dimmed. People watched quietly, not sure what would happen next.

François leaned closer to the ledge. A violin, sweeping like the coo of a nightingale, broke the silence. Its melody was joined by a softer, murmuring flute, and the two sounds lifted each other to dance atop the water's surface. It was the symphony of a young maiden, longing for her consort. Slowly the vessels approached, close enough for everyone to see the detail of feathers painted along both sides.

The caravan on the lake changed its shape. Added to the revelry were the beats of a drum, which grew louder until the sound took precedence over all. Following the hypnotic rhythm, the boats glided closer together and formed a long, continuous chain. The oarsmen hauled in their oars.

To greet his future bride, Prince Thom came down from the higher ground, mounted on his white stallion. His long hair flew in the wind. He was dressed in common peasant garb. It was no surprise to his followers, who referred to him as "the prince of the cloth" to distinguish him from his brothers.

A few feet in front of the leading vessel, large bubbles came to the water's surface. Something was rising from below. Soon François could see what it was. A pair of golden talons with ivory tips flanked either side of the bow. The ship's middle section spouted massive wings, sails that were made out of canvas and held together by a bamboo skeleton, flecked with gold dust. The stern elongated toward the sky, dangling an orb at its tip. With a loud explosion, the orb burst open, and a plumage of streamers completed the phoenix in majestic glory. As the bird's wings flapped, it propelled the vessel toward land.

The only sound from the audience was a collective gasp. No one had ever seen anything so spectacular.

"What an entrance!" remarked the female warrior. "I wonder how Prince Thom will tame such a regal bird."

François glued his eyes to the pier.

The prince slid off his horse. Two servants plastered his feet and legs with lime and areca juice to prevent the leeches in the water from attaching themselves to him. The bridal cabin and the phoenix head were sliding off the main barge and into a sampan. It seemed small in contrast to the princess's wealth.

As the small skiff drew under the canopy, the proud head of the phoenix bowed submissively before the prince.

Prince Thom tore off his shirt and grasped one of the lengthy chains. His muscles rolled in anticipation. At the precise moment when his bride's boat went under the pagoda, he gave a mighty haul. People shouted encouragement to him. From within the shrubs and bushes around the dock, dozens of men appeared. Together they pulled on the heavy chains, and the canopy broke free from the poles. Rising out of the water was a heavy net, made from thick ropes. The boat, entrapped, was lifted out of the water. The pulleys screeched as they were set into motion. With another wrench, Thom's prize was hauled to land amid the roars of his people.

The prince drew a sword and hacked his way through the net. With each slash, the cheers grew more exuberant. Finally, Thom was able to reach inside the cabin. With one hand, he ripped the curtain aside and took a few steps back.

A delicate arm, sprinkled with crushed pearl, reached out from the compartment. The crowd hushed. Thom received her hand as she emerged into the light. She clung to him until her feet touched the ground.

His voice rose through the quiet. "Do any of your sisters possess your grace, your beauty, or your intelligence? Or did I get the best of your family?"

She bent one knee and hid behind the wide sleeve of her tunic. "Compared to my sisters, I am not so refined, for I am the youngest and most foolish. But, dear sir, I am now the most fortunate, for I have been chosen to serve the greatest of all warriors."

Thom lifted his head toward the heavens and belted out a hearty laugh. "Well said, my priceless Jade."

Again, he reached for her hands.

François glanced at Lady Bui and said under his breath, "Madame, I believe your question has been answered: given the right circumstances, even the most regal bird can be tamed."

Slumped on the priest's shoulder, Canh was fast asleep.

At the end of the ceremony, cannons were fired. With the booming explosions, the symbolic conversion of Jade Han from a princess to a wife was complete. The noise jolted little Canh out of his sleep. He looked at the joyous faces around him with dazed recollection. When he saw François, his anxiety subsided. Nearby, Lady Bui was chewing on several helpings of betel and areca nuts — her favorite way to celebrate. The smell of the concoction made François nauseous.

Below them, the remaining boats, which had swept across the entire length of the lake, were entering the makeshift dock one by one. The musicians, the oarsmen, and guests of the bride disembarked, all dressed in their finery. In François's arms, Canh wiggled to break free.

"Má! Má! There is my má," he cried out. His hands reached toward a group of Buddhist monks and nuns who walked in a double row on the pier.

François looked, and he, too, recognized Lady Jade Bình. She shuffled with her head bowed. Her demeanor was like that of her peers, plain and monastic. She was rolling a strand of prayer beads between her fingers. She held her robe with her free hand, but the wind kept trying to unravel the blue garment.

It dawned on him why she had been absent in the past few days. After all, it was her sister's wedding day. Apparently she couldn't resist the chance to watch the event. However, if she had tried to make contact with Lady Jade Han, Canh's mother would have crossed the boundary from having a simple reunion with her sister to creating a political firestorm, since their husbands were mortal enemies.

Without knowing the new princess, François felt sympathy toward her. The sun had not set on her first day of marriage, and already she might have to keep a secret from her husband.

Canh burst into tears. "I want my má," he wailed. His little fists pounded François's shoulder.

Looking down at the crowd, Lady Bui swallowed a wad of betel juice. "Which one is his mother?"

François said, "Please excuse us. We must go."

CHAPTER THIRTY-SIX

At last, Pierre received permission to leave Annam. Lady Jade Bình had brought him the happy news even before Prince Thom's written proclamation arrived.

As he waited for the soldiers to come and set him free, the day grew late. Outside in the courtyard, sunlight faded. Campfires sprinkled their red glow over the citadel. The roads that led to the palaces were lit by thousands of colorful lanterns. The celebration was still going on in the distance. Tired of waiting, Pierre eased himself into a chair with his prayer book.

He was able to read the words as he had done a thousand times before, but doubts assailed his mind.

Why hasn't anybody come? Could the prince have changed his mind? Was the news of his freedom merely a cruel trick?

He wondered if François had something to do with the delay.

In his entire career, Pierre felt his biggest failure had been François Gervaise. At the beginning, he had been optimistic about the artist's potential and sensitivity, in spite of his lies about his scandalous past. But François's radical and stubborn nature had allowed him to be poisoned by the heathen religion. His closeness to the Buddhist community had done irreversible damage to the teaching of Christianity and its commandments.

The artist's intransigence was a personal affront to Pierre. The least François could do was to show him some respect while they were together in this pagan land. He decided to compose a letter to Rome, asking Pope Pius VI to excommunicate François. No one crossed the Bishop of Madras without paying a price. For this errant priest, the cost would be eternal damnation.

Pierre chuckled. As angry as he was, he felt victorious. If it had not been for the artist's gossip, he probably would not have learned in time about the kinship between the Buddhist nun and Prince Thom's bride. Summoning Lady Jade Bình to him, he had little trouble persuading her to go to her sister and plead for his freedom. The nun, meek though she might appear, eagerly embraced any plan that promised to restore her husband to power and place her son on the throne someday. She believed that Pierre was the only avenue to these hopes and dreams.

Under her sister's influence, Lady Jade Han had persuaded her husband to pardon one prisoner for luck on their wedding day. She had chosen him, a holy man.

Could his strategy have failed? He was taking a far greater risk than he normally would, but he had had no choice. Six years of waiting was too long, even for a man whose vision was as farsighted as Pierre's.

He peered into the dimness beyond the entrance. A few dots of lanterns, orange and silver, separated from the sparkling lights that stretched across the terrain to move toward him.

As the lights drew nearer, he could see a group of four porters, carrying a palanquin. Walking before them was François Gervaise.

Pierre stretched his limbs. His liberty was, at last, within grasp.

"I suspect you have something for me?" asked the bishop, clutching his Bible to maintain his composure. He lifted his chin and straightened his posture.

The artist bowed. "I am here at the request of Prince Thom of the West Mountaineers to release you." He handed Pierre a scroll. "This letter will guarantee your safety all the way to Saygun Harbor. The porters will take you there. You will board a ship to France and never return to the kingdom of Annam. If for any reason you set foot on this soil again, your action will be punishable by death. Do you understand?"

Pierre looked up with a glare.

François's eyes searched the room. Inside the church, the Buddha statues had been draped in red veils — the color of marriage and happiness. He remarked, "Your Excellency, you have concealed all the statues' faces. And by tradition, no one is allowed to remove the shrouds until the wedding celebration is over. There will be three more days of festivity. But I guess you knew that. By the time the celebrations are over, and the damage to the Buddhas is discovered, you will be safe, many leagues away from land. As always, you are very shrewd. I must admit you never fail to amaze me."

Pierre exhaled a thin laugh. "You have no idea."

François took an elaborate key from the captain of the guards and removed the bishop's iron collar. Pierre stood with a stagger. The chain had been his umbilical cord for so long that without it he felt out of balance. Still, he pushed aside the hand that François offered for support.

"Farewell, Your Excellency," said François. "We may never meet again."

"I have a plan that is — so splendid." Pierre placed a hand on the artist's shoulder. "We are not yet finished with each other."

He laughed as François withdrew into the darkness.

In time, the artist would discover what he meant. Under the veils, Pierre had left a sealed letter written in French and addressed to Prince Thom. This letter detailed François's guilt in hiding the wives and child of Thom's archenemy while ostensibly serving the rebels. It also exposed the events that led to Pierre's pardon, including the assistance of Thom's bride and her complicity in deceiving her husband.

Because of François's close relationship to the prince, Thom would more than likely ask him to translate the letter. The artist was the only foreigner among the peasants who could read French. If he were as honest and enlightened as he pretended to be, by reading exactly what Pierre had written, François would be digging himself a grave. By the same revelation, Ánh's wives and the rebel's new bride would also be executed or, at the very least, imprisoned. With their demise, the alliance between the Northern Kingdom and the Mountaineers would be shattered. An all-out civil war would break out, weakening both sides.

All this would happen while Pierre was at Versailles with little

Canh, asking for Louis XVI's support to raise an army. By the time he returned to Annam, his protégé, Prince Ánh, would have far fewer obstacles to regaining his sovereignty. And what would Ánh have lost? Not much! Just a few expendable wives.

It seemed more likely to him that François would censor the letter. In doing so, he would prove to Pierre and to himself that he was, all along, a coward. That would not be enough to satisfy the bishop. But the prospect that François Gervaise would live out the rest of his life in disgrace made Pierre beam with delight. He could easily have sent the same letter to Prince Thom in the Annamite writing. But he chose not to. He wanted to allow François the freedom to choose his own fate. It was the bishop's way of challenging the artist to a duel and watching him flee in shame once more.

This would be his last move in the game of chess that they had been playing since the day they met in Avignon. Whatever François decided to do, the bishop knew he had won the game.

On the road that followed Dong Nai River, the porters hauled a palanquin on their shoulders, carrying Pierre through villages with thatched houses and rice fields. They had been moving since the night before, escorting him southward to Saygun Harbor, over a hundred kilometers away from the citadel.

Leading the procession was a team of six imperial soldiers. Their feet stirred up dirt that dulled their uniforms. Some of it seeped up through the wooden floorboard and dusted Pierre's black shoes gray.

It was high noon. The summer heat had just begun its wrath. Here and there hot breezes crept under the quiet trees, swaying a few clumps of leaves, only to evaporate in the featureless sky. Under the tattered eaves of the houses, old villagers squatted on their haunches, weaving bamboo baskets. Others, knee-deep in the muddy fields, plowed the earth with their clumsy animals and primitive tools. Children ran naked with the sun beating on their backs. From the young to the old, all bore the same flat expression.

The bishop shuddered. These images of suffering had once been the reasons why he had decided to pursue his mission. But somehow during his journey he kept wandering on to a different path. Almost half of his life had been spent in Annam, yet he had accomplished little. One thing was clear: his original passion was still burning within him. His dedication had not been altered. There was still time.

Before him, the river laced with other branches into a web of channels. A few gusts of wind, heady with the smell of the ocean, drifted into his conveyance. Far in the distance, a line of the blue sea bordered the horizon. Ships bobbed in the harbor. At his first glimpse of the vessels, his blood sang. Mixed with the joy of returning home was the pain of leaving. Pierre wondered if the converts would be prepared to meet the challenges of their faith without him. One of his main objectives in France would be to recruit new missionaries — many, many more.

"Saygun Harbor!" The guard captain's words lifted Pierre's heart. He was carried across a cement bridge that separated the old citadel from a contemporary downtown section of the city reserved for foreigners and their commerce.

He looked on with wonder, for this was the first time he had ever been in Saygun City proper. Rustic wooden cottages, some with a stucco finish and quaint balconies, flanked the cobblestone streets. Climbing roses, jasmine, and myrtles graced the facades of the homes. The richest merchants had built their mansions around the town's square, which displayed a marble fountain at its center. In other sections, taverns, salons, and fancy hotels bustled with activity. Hiding behind them were the quarters that sheltered sailors and dockworkers, some of whom were natives from Africa and India. The ocean encircled the land, its smooth surface mirroring the sky's vivid blue.

Through the teeming street, the happy tune of a hurdy-gurdy wafted its way from an outside café. Everywhere Pierre looked, he recognized the architectural styles of the French. Even the pungent aroma of fromage reminded him of Paris. Except for the sweltering temperature and an occasional palanquin, there was nothing of Annam in what he saw.

"Welcome to the Paris of the Orient!" said a voice by the window of Pierre's conveyance. "In our last meeting, you promised me two weeks. Your Excellency, it has been over seven months. For a sailor, this is an arduous wait."

Pierre turned and saw the ruddy, grinning face of Captain Petijean. The porters lowered the palanquin. Holding the railing, Pierre emerged from its narrow confines and drew a deep breath.

"I am sorry, Captain. I overestimated my stay."

Both men laughed. Pierre rubbed his neck. It felt eerily bare without the iron collar.

"You are not yet free, Your Excellency," said Captain Petijean. To the leader of the sentries, he said, "That will be all. Cha Cả is now in my care. You are dismissed."

"We cannot leave until the bishop boards the ship and we see him set sail," answered the head guard. The rebel officer then presented the captain with a letter that had been tucked away in his sleeve. "Here is his expulsion permit. Please sign it."

Pierre glanced at the paper and said, "I've been asked to leave this country one time too many. I am beginning to get offended."

Captain Petijean signed the document. "Pray to God this will be your last expulsion. I am too old to keep coming to your rescue."

"When do we leave?"

"Tomorrow morning. Today, you rest in Hotel Claudine, the best in Saygun."

As they walked through the tall iron gates of the stately inn, Pierre clutched all his possessions, which were wrapped inside a cloth. He was dizzy from the heat. Under the stares of the hotel guests, he suddenly felt ill at ease.

Inside Captain Petijean's rooms in the hotel, Pierre sat on a sofa. His body was drenched in sweat. Through the open shutters, the ocean hummed with restless waves.

A twelve-year-old hotel servant in a white uniform waited by a bamboo cabinet. His bare legs and feet seemed black against his pristine shorts. The moment Pierre sat on the sofa, the boy ran to stand behind him. His hands held a large fan, woven from palm leaves. Through his skillful movements, a current of air eased the bishop's discomfort. He felt drowsy in the heavy warmth of the afternoon.

Petijean excused himself and disappeared through the doors that led to his bedroom. He quickly returned, carrying a box wrapped in golden imperial fabric. Pierre raised himself on one elbow. He recognized the red stamp made by the royal jade seal that belonged to Prince Ánh. His exhaustion dissolved.

"Your Excellency," said the captain, "this box was given to me by your protégé, His Highness of Cochin China. He entrusted me to hold it for safekeeping. My instruction was to turn it over to you upon your release from bondage. It must only be opened by King Louis XVI of France. No one else."

He handed the box to Pierre and added, "This has been in my possession ever since my last meeting with the prince, one month after you and I last met."

"How is he? Did he appear well?"

"Oh, yes, sir. Since the fall of Saygun Citadel, he has been running from the rebels. I have failed in my many attempts to meet with him. Each time I was informed of his whereabouts, so were the Mountaineers. He would flee farther south before I had a chance to see him. Eventually, the prince ran out of land and was pushed out to sea. He sought refuge in Bangkok and was granted asylum under the protection of the king of Siam, Phra Buddha Yod Fa Chulalok Rama. That was when I was able to arrange for a private meeting with His Highness. Thank God, my business dealings with the Siamese government have always been on good terms."

Pierre ran his fingers over the wax impression. He was relieved and happy that the prince had managed to hold on to the seal of Cochin China. This small gesture showed him how much his student had matured. "By fleeing to Siam, he demonstrated that he is a lot smarter than I realized."

The captain shrugged. "I agree. But there is a persistent recklessness in his actions. His Highness never seems to plan anything; he just reacts to events around him. That is probably why he loses all the battles."

"It's also probably the reason he is still alive."

Captain Petijean said in a detached manner, "He's been fortunate. With all the stories and legends that surround him, one would think he is a demigod. By many, he has been dubbed 'the slippery dragon' for his numerous escapes."

"The Annamites are like children — simpleminded."

A knock interrupted them. The servant boy put down his fan and ran to open the door. Instinctively, Pierre concealed the box with his robe. A manservant, holding a tray of food and refreshment, entered without speaking. Under a mesh cover, the outline of a roasted fowl made Pierre's mouth water. He had not eaten all day.

The captain resumed his conversation without acknowledging the native. "In a few years he'll behave with more sophistication."

"Or die trying," added Pierre.

The servant set the tray on the table between them, removed the cover, and withdrew. The bishop's first instinct was to reach for the bird's drumstick, but he fought his urge.

Instead, he asked, "When you last saw the prince, did he appear to have a sound mind?"

"He was short of temper, and no wonder. It was a depressing sight. He and I met in a room that would not be fit to house a servant. Imagine meeting with King Zedekiah after he was exiled in Babylon. The prince of Cochin China seems to be in great despair. You are his only hope, Your Excellency."

The aroma of the roasted fowl and spices made Pierre's stomach give a loud growl. The captain heard it.

"My dear Bishop," he cried. His outstretched arms pointed to the food. "You are hungry. Please eat."

Without waiting to be asked again, Pierre grabbed a drumstick. The chicken, cooked to perfection, fell apart at the joints. It tasted as heavenly as it looked. With his free hand, he reached for the other leg.

The captain looked at Pierre, commenting, "You are weary. We have a long journey ahead. Please take my bed and rest after you dine."

"You don't mind?"

"Of course not. It would be my pleasure."

"But wait! What about my special cargo? Was it delivered in good condition?"

Petijean smiled. "You will be pleased with it, I am sure."

Pierre was grateful that he did not have to talk further. The captain was right. He was ravenous and exhausted. "Thank you," he said.

Captain Petijean raised his forefinger. "One last thing, Your Excellency. Your other protégé, Henri, has accompanied the prince to Siam. His devotion to the Nguyen monarchy would make you proud."

Pierre clutched his stomach. Suddenly his appetite was gone.

The next morning arrived with the sparrows chirping on the ledge of the bedroom window. Pierre found the captain out on the hotel balcony, dressed in his uniform, holding a cane. He looked at the bishop with an enthusiasm that had not changed through the years.

"I didn't expect to sleep this much," Pierre said apologetically. "You should have woken me."

"I didn't want to disturb you."

Captain Petijean offered the cane to Pierre. Its handle was crudely carved in the shape of a mallard's head. He said, "I noticed you have trouble walking. In haste, this is the best walking stick the hotel servants could find. When we are in Paris, I will get you a better one."

Pierre held the present between his two fingers, unsure of how to react. "You shouldn't have," he said. "I really don't need it. However, I thank you!" He searched the captain's face. "Shall we leave now?"

"As you wish," was Petijean's reply.

An hour later, they arrived at the harbor. With each minute that flew by, Pierre grew more impatient. The imperial guards who were trailing by his side annoyed him, but he could do nothing but try to ignore them.

Among a flotsam of timbers — long, heavy logs that littered the shore — a sampan was waiting for them. It took him and the captain to a clipper that was, to his surprise, twice as large and stately as the *Wanderer*. At the vessel's stern, hordes of coolies were hauling the timbers across the deck.

The captain shouted over the bustling winds. "This is the *Saint Jacques,* my newest passion."

The first mate tossed a rope ladder over the railing to them. With difficulty, Pierre climbed onboard, declining the captain's offer of assistance. Still, he had to admit that the past six years had taken their toll on him. He must regain his strength to accomplish what lay ahead.

"With this journey, we are shipping a load of teakwood," said the captain. "It is a profitable new commodity in Europe."

Pierre took one last look at Saygun Harbor. The imperial guards on the shore remained unmoving in the sand.

"One day this will be a Christian colony of France," he said.

"No doubt, Your Excellency," replied the captain. "Come with me and I'll show you to your cabin. Someone has been expecting you."

With his cane, Pierre tapped the door of the cabin three times before pushing it open. The room, its floor stained with seawater, was vacant except for a bed. His eyes rested on the figure sitting cross-legged on top of the mattress — a little boy in a princely robe. A calico cat was curled in his lap.

Little Canh looked up. His face brightened in recognition when he saw Pierre. "When is my mother coming?" he asked.

"She is not," Pierre replied. "This journey is just for you and me."

EPILOGUE

Lepers' Cavern, 1785

A round the banks of Lake Tam, the painted storks came early this year.

It was April. The monsoon rains were not expected for another few weeks. The water level in the lake had receded, leaving the soil around it spider-veined. The higher the sun rose toward midday, the greater the furnace it became. Spontaneous fires ignited among the few remaining clumps of grass and were fueled by dry leaves.

The storks were the first birds to return to the Lepers' Cavern. Their wide wings ended in a blush of red on the tips of their white feathers. The fanning of a thousand birds seemed to bring fresh air all the way from the Perfume River, rising to a gale. Soon, masses of dark clouds gathered above with the promise of long-awaited rain.

François stood outside his hut, watching the birds. Their bodies gyrated into an elliptical funnel, spinning off in all directions like bands of streamers. Far away, the mountain seemed to surrender wisps of its moisture to the brown nimbus. As he gazed out into the lake, he thought of the little prince, Canh. His life seemed empty without Canh's voice and laughter. For the sake of the bishop's ambition, the child had been wrenched from him. How calm Lady Jade Bình had been when she told him of the boy's voyage to the other side of the world with de Béhaine.

"Farewell, farewell," he whispered to the wind. "Wherever you are, I hope you are safe."

There was no need for him to bid good-bye to the bishop or the Mountaineers. They had been part of his past for almost a year.

As long as they had known each other, the bishop, with his cunning and devious nature, had coerced François into a contest of wills. Too much time was wasted, too many tragedies had occurred. The artist no longer wanted anything to do with Pierre's politics or his religion. To prevent a civil war, François had burned the bishop's letter. But that was all he could do. François fully expected de Béhaine to return to Annam someday with an army. War was inevitable. The bishop, in his relentless pursuit of his mission, would be more than likely to triumph in the end. As for François, he was at peace in the leper colony.

The sky darkened, and the smell of wet clay permeated the air. He wrapped his arms around his body and rested his head against a tree. The storks had settled down, scattered on land or perched on bare branches in the cajeput trees. Among them were a few black-and-green marsh ducks, salt-and-pepper sandpipers, red-whiskered bulbuls, and other creatures with exotic plumages. All had arrived to partake in the changing weather. When lightning slashed across the pregnant clouds and cracked open the heavens, the rain fell with the force of a waterfall.

He listened to the sound of footsteps, approaching from behind. Lucía came up to him. She raised a yellow parasol over his head.

"Who died?" she asked.

At first, he didn't know what she meant. Then she pointed at a large mound of dirt in front of him. It was a termite nest, but with its raised outline, it resembled a grave.

The answer came to him effortlessly. "Yesterday," he replied.

*I*n 1802, Nguyen Ánh, with the army and navy raised by Bishop Pigneau de Béhaine and financed by the king of France, overcame both the West Mountaineers and the Tonquinese. For the first time in the history of Annam, the North and the South were united into one nation. He was coronated as Emperor Gia Long and renamed his kingdom Viet Nam.

He ruled for eighteen years. His descendants succeeded until the twentieth century, the last imperial dynasty in Viet Nam.

ACKNOWLEDGMENTS

The following people helped me, both emotionally and practically, during the writing of this book:

Frank Andrews

Judy Clain

Christine Cronin

Phuong Khanh Do

Thu Doan

Fiona and Jake Eberts

Michaela Hamilton

Tom John

Brenda Marsh

Peter Miller

Ilona Price

Ninh Quang Vu

Special thanks are due to Dean C. Alfano and Elyse Bloom of the New York University College of Dentistry.

I also want to thank

Corbin and Associates
Little Saigon Radio
Viet Tide Newspaper
Thuy Nga Productions

I could not have written this book without my family — my mother; my brother, Jimmy; my sister, BeTi; and, most important, my father-in-law, the revered writer Nhat Tien, who treats me like his own son.

ABOUT THE AUTHOR

KIEN NGUYEN was born in Nhatrang, South Vietnam, to a Vietnamese mother and an American father. He left Vietnam in 1985 through the United Nations' Orderly Departure Program. After spending time at a refugee camp in the Philippines, Nguyen arrived in the United States. He has written a memoir about his childhood in Vietnam called *The Unwanted,* as well as the novel *The Tapestries,* which was inspired by the life of his grandfather. He lives in California. He can be reached through his Web site, www.kiennguyen.us.